THE BEST OF THE EROTIC READER

THE BEST OF THE EROTIC READER

Anonymous

Carroll & Graf Publishers, Inc.
New York

First Carroll & Graf Edition April 1996
Third Printing March 1997

Carroll & Graf Publishers, Inc.
260 Fifth Avenue
New York, NY 10001

ISBN 0-7867-0343-1

Manufactured in the United States of America

Contents

Pauline the Prima Donna

You must have found me very serious as you read the end of my last letter, but that is just another trait of my character. I always seem to be able to foresee the way a chain of events will unroll, and take into account the various impressions, feelings and experiences that go to make it up. Even the most violent intoxication of the senses has never been able to make me lose my critical facilities, and today, in fact, I am beginning a chapter of my confessions which will prove this statement.

My affair with Franz continued. I was always very prudent and so my aunt suspected nothing and our rendezvous were secret from all those around us. In addition, I refused to be alone with Franz more than once a week. The day of my debut was drawing near and Franz was becoming more and more rash. He thought he had obtained some rights over me, and he was becoming too domineering, like all men who believe themselves sure of an undisputed possession, but this was not how I intended it to be, and I immediately conceived a plan. At the beginning of a brilliant career was I to connect myself with a man of no importance, one to whom I was, on all points, superior? To leave him on bad terms, however, would have been dangerous, for I would then be at the mercy of his indiscretion. It was necessary to be very clever, which I was, for I succeeded in ending our liaison so opportunely and so deceptively that Franz still believes today that if chance had not separated us I would certainly have married him.

The 'chance' was my doing. I had informed my professor that my accompanist had pursued me with his declarations and that I was ready to break off the course of my artistic career in exchange for love in a cottage. However, the good man, who was extremely proud of his pupil and who was counting heavily on my debut, grew very angry. I begged him not to make Franz miserable, and so I reached my goal while Franz reached the Budapest Theatre Orchestra by special engagement. We bade each other a tender farewell; I had broken off my relations without anything to fear.

Shortly after our separation I gave my first performance at the Theatre of the Kärntnertor, and you know how successful it was. I was more than happy. I was surrounded and besieged. Applause, money and celebrity poured my way and I had plenty of suitors, admirers and enthusiasts. Some thought to reach their aim with poems and some with valuable presents, but I had already observed that an artist cannot give in to his vanity or his feeling without risking everything in the game. This is why I pretended to be indifferent. I discouraged all those who came near me and soon acquired the reputation of a woman of unassailable virtue. Nobody had any idea that after Franz's departure I turned again to my solitary joys on Sunday evenings and to the delights of the hot bath. However, I never yielded more than once a week to the call of my senses, although they demanded much more. A thousand eyes were upon me and so I was extremely prudent in my relationships. My aunt had to go everywhere with me and nobody could accuse me of a single indiscretion.

This lasted all winter long. I had a steady income, and I installed myself in a very comfortable and well-furnished apartment. I was accepted in the best society and found myself very happy with my new life. I only regretted rarely Franz's departure, and fortunate circumstances compensated me for it the following summer.

I had been introduced into the house of one of the richest bankers in Vienna, and I received from his wife all of the marks of the truest friendship. Her husband had paid court to me, hoping with his huge fortune to easily conquer a popular actress. When he had been driven away like all the others, he introduced me to his household, thinking to win me that way. Thus it came about that I could come and go there as I pleased. I consistently repulsed his advances and, perhaps because of that, his wife soon became my most intimate friend. Roudolphine, for that was her name, was about twenty-seven years old, a piquant brunette, very vivacious, lively, tender and very much a woman. She had no children and was quite indifferent to her husband, of whose misdemeanours she was painfully aware. The relationship between them was friendly, and they did not refuse themselves from time to time the joys of marriage. Yet, in spite of all, it was not a happy union. Her husband probably did not realise that she was a very warm-blooded woman, a fact she most likely concealed very skilfully.

At the approach of the fine weather, Roudolphine went to live in a charming villa at Baden where her husband used to visit her regularly every Sunday, bringing a few friends with him. She invited me to spend the summer there with her at the end of the theatre season. This stay in the country was to do me a lot of good. Until then we had only talked about clothes, music and art, but now our conversations began to assume a different character. The court that her husband paid to me provided her the opportunity for this. I noticed that she measured her husband's misbehaviour according to the privations which he imposed upon her. Her complaints were so sincere, and she hid so little the object of her regret, that I immediately concluded that I had been chosen as her confidant and decided to act like a simple and inexperienced friend. I had played my cards right and touched upon her weakness; she at once began to explain things to me, and the more innocent I pretended to be and the more I seemed astounded by what she told me, the more she insisted on fully informing me of what filled her heart.

In addition, she took great pleasure in revealing certain physical matters to me. She was utterly astounded at the surprise I showed at discovering these things. She could not believe that a young artist who was always playing with fire could be so unaware of everything. It was only the fourth day after my arrival when we took a bath together—practical instruction could hardly be left out after so many fine speeches—and the more I appeared clumsy and self-conscious, the more amusement she derived from exercising a novice. The more difficulties I made, the more passionate she grew. However, in the bath and during the day she did not dare go beyond certain familiarities, and I realised that she was going to employ all of her cunning to persuade me to spend the night with her. The memory of the first night spent in Marguerite's bed obsessed me in such a way that I was quite ready to yield to her wish. I did this with such a show of ingenuousness that she was more and more convinced of my innocence. She thought she was seducing me, but it was I who was getting my way.

She had the most charming bedroom, furnished with all the luxuries that only a wealthy banker can afford, and with all the taste of a room arranged for a wedding night. It was there that Roudolphine had become a woman. She recounted in detail her experience and what had been her feelings when the flower of her innocence had been taken. She made no secret of the fact that she was very sensual. She also told me that until her second confinement she had never found any pleasure in her husband's embraces, which were then very frequent. Her pleasures, which developed only gradually, had suddenly become very intense. For a long time I could not believe that, having been very ardent myself ever since my youth, but I believe it now. In most cases this situation is the husband's fault; he is in too much of a hurry to finish as soon as he enters, and does not know how to excit his wife's sensuality first, or else he gives up half way.

Roudolphine had compensations; she was charming and avid and only bore her husband's negligence with all the more bad humour. I shall not bother to tell you all the sports in which we engaged in her big English bed. Our revels were delightful, lascivious, and Roudolphine was insatiable in the pleasure she took in kisses and the contact

16

of our two naked bodies. She enjoyed herself for two hours and hardly suspected that these hours were still too short for me, so much did I desire and so much did I pretend to yield only with difficulty and shame.

Our relationship soon became much more interesting, for Roudolphine consoled herself in secret for her husband's pranks. In the neighbouring town lived an Italian prince who usually stayed in Vienna where Roudolphine's husband looked after his financial affairs. The banker was the humble servant of the prince's huge fortune. The latter, about thirty years old, was outwardly a very severe and a very proud man with a scientific education and turn of mind; inwardly, however, he was dominated by the most intense sensuality. Nature had gifted him with exceptional physical strength. In addition, he was the most complete egotist I have ever met. He had but one aim in life, pleasure at all costs, and but one law, to preserve himself by dint of subterfuge from all the troublesome consequences of his affairs. When the banker was there, the prince often came to dine or to tea.

I had never noticed, however, that there was any affair between him and Roudolphine. I learned about it entirely by chance, for she was very careful never to breathe a word of it to me. The gardens of their two villas were adjacent, and one day when I was picking flowers behind a hedge I saw Roudolphine pluck a note from underneath a stone, conceal it quickly in her blouse and hurry away to her room. Suspecting some little intrigue, I peeped through her window and saw her hastily read and burn it. Then she sat down at her desk, I supposed, to compose the answer. So that she would suspect nothing, I hastened to my room and began to sing at the top of my voice, at the same time carefully watching the place in the garden where the note had been left. Soon Roudolphine appeared, walked along the hedge toying with the branches, then so swiftly and adroitly did she hide her reply that I did not catch it. However, I had noticed the spot where she had paused longest, and as soon as she had returned to the house, and when I was certain that she was busy, I dashed into the garden. I easily found the message hidden under a stone. Back in my room with the door locked I read, 'Not today, Pauline is sleeping with me. I will tell her tomorrow that I am indisposed. For you, of course, I am not. Come tomorrow, then, as usual, at eleven o'clock.'

The note was in Italian and in disguised handwriting. You can well imagine that everything was at once clear to me. I had already made up my mind what to do. I did not return the note to where I had found it, for I wanted the prince to come that night and surprise us both in bed. I, the *ingènue*, was in possession of Roudolphine's secret and I felt sure I would not come out of the situation empty handed. Of course, I still did not know how the prince would manage to get to Roudolphine's bedroom.

At lunch we had agreed to spend the night together, which is why she had refused the prince's visit. Over tea she explained to me that we could not sleep together for about a week, for she felt that her period was approaching. She thought this would delude me, but I had already woven my net around her. Above all, I had to get her to bed before eleven o'clock, so that she could find no means of avoiding, at the last minute, the surprise I had prepared for her.

We went to bed very early, and I was so frolicsome, so caressing, and so insatiable that she soon went to sleep out of sheer fatigue. Bosom against bosom, her thighs between mine, our hands reciprocally at the sources of our pleasure we lay there, she fast asleep and I more and more wide awake and impatient. Suddenly I heard the floor of the alcove creak, the sound of muffled footsteps, and the door opened. I heard someone breathing, getting undressed, and at last approaching the bed on Roudolphine's side.

Now I was sure of myself, and I pretended to be very deeply asleep. The prince, for it was he, lifted up the bedclothes and lay down beside Roudolphine, who woke up terrified. I felt her trembling all over. Now came the catastrophe. He wanted to ascend immediately to the throne he had so many times possessed. She stopped him, asking hastily whether or not he had received her reply.

Meanwhile, trying to get where he wanted, he had touched my hand and my arm. I cried out, I was beside myself, shuddering and pressing myself against Roudolphine. I was highly diverted by her fright and the prince's amazement. He had shouted an Italian oath, so that it was no use for Roudolphine to explain that it was her husband coming unexpectedly to surprise her. I overwhelmed her with reproaches and upbraided her with having exposed my youth and honour to such a dreadful scene, because I had recognised the prince's voice. The prince, a gallant and knowing man, soon realised, however, that he had nothing to lose. On the contrary, he was gaining an interesting partner. That was just what I expected him to think. After a few tender and amusing words he went to close the bedroom door, took out the keys, and returned to bed.

Roudolphine was between us. Now came the excuses, the explanations and the recriminations. But there was nothing to be done, nothing could be changed; we would have to keep quiet, all three of us, in order not to expose ourselves to the unpleasant consequences of so hazardous a meeting, a thing it would be hard to explain. Roudolphine calmed down little by little and the prince's words grew sweeter and sweeter. I, of course, was in floods of tears. By my reproaches I forced Roudolphine to make me her confidant and thus her accomplice in this illegal liaison. You can see that Marguerite's lessons and her adventures in Geneva were useful to me. In fact, it was exactly the same story except that the prince and Roudolphine did not realise that they were merely puppets in my hands.

Roudolphine, then, no longer tried to hide from me the facts of her long-standing liaison with the prince, but she also revealed to him what she had been doing with me, the innocent young girl, and she told him how I burned with desire to learn more of these matters. That excited the prince and when I tried to make Roudolphine be quiet she only talked with all the more ardour of my sensuality! I noticed that he was pressing his thighs between those of Roudolphine and was trying in this way to reach the desired goal from the side. From time to time his legs brushed against mine, and I wept, I burned with curiosity. Roudolphone tried to console me, but with every movement the prince made she became more and more distraught. Soon she too squirmed about, trembled passionately, and finally moved her hand to my body to try to make me share her pleasure. Suddenly I noticed another hand straying where hers was already so busy. I could not allow that to continue, for I wanted to remain faithful to the rôle which I had given myself, so I turned over angrily towards the wall and, as Roudolphine had immediately taken away her own hand when she encountered that of her lover on this forbidden path, I was abandoned to my sulking and I myself had to finish secretly what my bed companion had begun.

Hardly had I turned my back on them when they forgot all restraint and all shame. The prince threw himself upon Roudolphine, who opened her legs as wide as possible to receive the beloved guest easily and quickly, and the bed shook at every movement. I was so consumed with desire and envy; I could not see anything, but my imagination was aflame. Then at the moment when the two lovers were fused most closely and overflowed, sighing and shuddering, I myself let loose so abundant a burning flood that I lost consciousness.

After the practical exercise came the theory. The prince was now between Roudolphine and myself, although I do not know whether this was by design or accident. He did not make the slightest movement, and I seemed to have nothing to fear, but I was perfectly aware that I had to keep quiet in order to maintain my superiority, and I waited to see what they would do next. Roudolphine explained to me first that, since her husband neglected her and ran after other women, she had every right to give herself freely to a cavalier so pleasant, so courtly, and above all, so discreet. She was in the best years of her life and did not want, indeed she was not able, to miss all the sweetest of earthly joys, especially since her doctors had advised her not to attempt to repress her natural sensuality. In any case, I knew that she was a very warm-natured woman, and she was sure that I was not indifferent to love, but only afraid of the consequences. She said that she simply wanted to remind me of what we had been doing together that evening before the unexpected arrival of the prince. I wanted to put my hand over her mouth to shut her up, but I could not do this without making a motion towards my neighbour, who seized my hand immediately and covered it with tender little kisses.

Now it was his turn to talk. His was not an easy rôle as he had to weigh every word so as not to hurt Roudolphine's feelings, but I realised by the intonation of his voice that he was more anxious to win me as quickly as possible than he was concerned about upsetting Roudolphine. However, by this time she was obliged to put up with anything in order to keep her secret.

I no longer remember what the prince said to soothe me, to excuse himself, and to prove that I had nothing to fear. I only remember that the warmth of his body was driving me crazy, that his hand was stroking first my breasts, then the rest of my body, and finally the very centre of his desires and mine. The state I was in defies description. The prince advanced slowly but surely; however, I could not allow him to kiss me, for he would then have noticed how I burned with desire to return his caresses. I was struggling with myself; I wanted to have done with this comedy, to put an end to my affected modesty, and to surrender entirely to the situation, but if I did that I would lose my advantage over the two sinners, and I would have been exposed to the dangers of love making with this violent and passionate man; for the prince would not have known how to limit his triumph once he was the victor.

I had noticed how feverishly he had finished with Roudolphine. All my entreaties would have been in vain, and perhaps even a backward movement would not have helped me. Besides, how could I tell whether, at the last moment, I would have been able to restrain myself? My whole artistic career was at stake, but I held my ground and let him do almost anything to me without responding to it, only defending myself desperately when the prince tried to obtain more. Roudolphine was at a loss as to what to say to me, or what she should do herself. She realised that my resistance had to be broken that night if she were going to be able to look me in the eyes the following day. To excite me even more, which was really quite unnecessary, she lay her head upon my bosom, embraced me, licked my breasts, and finally hurled herself between my legs where she pressed her lips to the still-inviolate entry of the temple, and began a play so pleasant that I allowed her complete freedom. The prince had yielded his place to her, and he was now kissing me on the mouth.

Thus I was covered from head to foot with kisses. I was no longer making any attempt to resist, so he placed my hand upon his sceptre, and I permitted this familiarity unenthusiastically. My arm pressed between the thighs of Roudolphine, who was kneeling, and I noticed that the prince's other hand was now in the place where his sceptre had been revelling so short a time before. He taught me to caress it, to rub and squeeze it. The group we formed was complicated but extremely pleasant; it was dark and I was sorry not to be able to see, for one must enjoy these things with the eyes as well. Roudolphine was trembling, excited to the extreme by the kisses she was showering upon me and the caresses she was receiving from the prince. She was half senseless with delight and opened wide her legs, whereupon the prince suddenly straightened himself and took up a position which was thus far unknown to me, bending over and penetrating her from behind. I had pulled my hand away, but he seized it and brought it to the point where he was most intimately united with Roudolphine. He then taught me an occupation which I should never have dreamed of, and which enhanced the rapture of the two pleasure-seekers. I was now to squeeze the root of his dagger and now to caress the sheath which enclosed it. Although I pretended to be ashamed, I was in fact extremely zealous in doing this. Roudolphine kissed and licked passionately and, all three together, we soared quickly to the very summit of pleasure. It was so intoxicating that it took us a good quarter of an hour to recover ourselves. We felt much too hot, and on this summer night we could stand neither the contact of each other's bodies nor that of the bedclothes and we lay naked as far apart as we could.

After this passionate and sweltering action the discussion was resumed anew. The prince talked as calmly about this strange chance rendezvous as if he had organised a party in the country. Basing his assumptions on what Roudolphine had told him, he no longer took the trouble to win me, contenting himself simply with combating my fear of unhappy consequences. He was well aware that he would have no difficulty in convincing me. The virtuosity of my hand, the pleasure which I had tasted and which had been betrayed by my beating heart and the trembling of my thighs had revealed to him how sensual I was. He only had to prove to me that there was no danger and that is what he was trying to do with all the art of a man of the world.

For these reasons he imagined that it would only be a question of time. He therefore did not insist upon the repetition of such a night and soon left us, for dawn was in the offing. He was perfectly willing to sacrifice the length of time spent in pleasure in order to safeguard his secret and his safety. He had to go through the dressing room and a corridor, climb a ladder, go out through a window, crawl back in through a skylight before finding himself in his house again, from where he would have to creep stealthily back to his apartments. The leave-taking was a strange mixture of intimacy, tenderness, timidity, teasing and deference, and when he had left, neither Roudolphine nor I felt like talking things over any more. We were so tired that we fell asleep at once. Later, upon awakening, I pretended to be inconsolable at having fallen into the hands of a man, but I was really furious that she had told him about our pleasures. She did not even notice how much delight I found in her efforts to console me.

Naturally, I refused to sleep with her the next night, telling her that my senses were never to lead me astray from my good resolutions another time, for I never wanted such a thing to happen again; I wanted to sleep by myself, and she was not to believe that I would ever permit the prince to do what she allowed him to do so easily. She was married and it would do no harm if she became pregnant, but I was an artist. A thousand eyes were upon me, and I did not dare do anything like that, which would bring me to disaster.

As I had expected, she then spoke to me about safety measures. She told me she had met the prince at a time when she was not sleeping with her husband because of a quarrel, and that consequently, she did not dare to become pregnant. The prince had calmed all her fears by using condoms, and she told me that I could try them too. She also told me she was quite sure that the prince was very level-headed and had perfect control of his feelings. In any case, he knew another way of preserving a lady's honour and, if I were very nice to him, I would soon learn about it. In short, she tried by every means to persuade me to surrender to the prince, so that I might enjoy the gayest and happiest of hours. I gave her to understand that her explanations and her promises did not leave me entirely cold, but that I was still rather fearful.

Towards noon the prince came to visit Roudolphine, a polite visit which also included me. But I feigned illness and did not appear. This gave them the chance to agree freely upon the measures to take to overcome my resistance and to initiate me into their secret games. As I did not want to sleep with Roudolphine any more, they would probably arrange to surprise me in my bedroom as quickly as possible, so as not to leave me time to repent, and perhaps to go back to town. My surmise proved correct.

All that afternoon and evening, Roudolphine did not mention previous nights to me. She came up to my bedroom that night, however, and sent away the chambermaid. When I was in bed, she went to lock up the anteroom herself so that nobody would disturb us. Then she sat down on my bed and tried to convince me anew.

She described everything to me in the most beautiful and seductive manner and assured me there was nothing to fear. Of course, I pretended that I did not know the prince was in her room and that he might even be listening from behind the door, so I had to be prudent and give in to her arguments little by little.

'But who is to guarantee to me that the prince will use the mask which you described?'

'I will. Do you think that I would let me do anything more with you than what I let him do with me at first? I promise you that he will not appear without a mask at this ball.'

'But it must hurt terribly. You know he guided my hand and made me feel his strength.'

'At the very beginning it may really hurt you, but there are remedies for that, too. You have some oil of almonds and some cold cream. We will smear his lance with them so that he can penetrate more easily.'

'Are you quite sure that no drop of that dangerous liquid can get through to bring about my misfortune?'

'Come now, do you think that I would have given in without that assurance? Everything was at stake then, as I had no contacts at all with my husband at that time. When I had made up with him I permitted the prince everything. But now I arrange things so that he visits me at least once every time the prince has been here. And so I have nothing to fear any longer.'

'The thought of that misfortune horrifies me. Besides, there is still the shame of giving oneself to a man. I do not know what to do. Everything you say charms me, and my senses are urging me to take your advice, but for nothing in the world would I put up with another night like the last, for I know that I should never be able to resist again. You are quite right. The prince is as gallant as he is handsome, and you will never know what feelings were aroused in me when I heard the sounds of your surrender there beside me.'

'I too had a double pleasure in letting you share, although very imperfectly, in what I was feeling myself. I

25

should never have thought that pleasure among three could be as violent as that which I tasted myself last night. I had read about it in books, but I always thought that it was exaggerated. The thought of a woman sharing herself between two men is odious to me, but I think that the accord between two women and a sensible, discreet man is delightful; but of course the two women must be true friends. One of them must not be more timid and more fearful than the other, and that is still your trouble, Pauline, dear.'

'It is just as well that your prince is not here, my dear, to hear your conversation. I really shouldn't know how to resist him, for I am totally consumed by what you have been telling me. Just look how I am burning, here, and how I am trembling all over.'

As I spoke, I uncovered myself—part of my thighs—and placed myself in such a position that if anyone were looking through the keyhole he would not miss a thing. If the prince were really there this was the moment for him to come in—and he did.

As you might have expected of an experienced and perfect man of the world, he understood at once that no talking was necessary, that he should conquer first and talk about it later. By the way Roudolphine had behaved I could see that everything had been arranged in advance. I tried to hide under the bedclothes, but she pulled them off me; I started to weep and she laughingly smothered me with kisses. Although at last I expected the ultimate fulfilment of the desire which had been mine for so long, I still had to be patient, for I had reckoned without Roudolphine's jealousy. In spite of the necessity of making me her accomplice, in spite of the fear of seeing her plans come to naught at the last minute, she was not going to sacrifice to me the first fruits of this day's pleasure. With an expression on her face that I envied, but which I dared not unmask if I were to stay within my own rôle, she told the prince that I had consented and that I was ready to do anything, but that I wanted to be certain of the efficiency of the means used, and that she would like to submit to a demonstration in front of me.

It was obvious that the prince was not expecting such an offer, and that he would have preferred to have carried out this trial directly with me rather than with Roudolphine. She took several of the small bladders from her pocket, breathed into one to show that it was impermeable, then moistened it and put it on with many caresses and giggles. After that she quickly undressed and lay down on the bed beside me, pulling the prince down on top of her, and exhorting me to watch closely so that I would lose all fear.

And so I really did see everything. I saw the delight of this handsome couple. I saw his strength and his power; I saw him penetrate her, and I saw her rise to meet him, and I saw them forget everything around them as the ectasy grew until finally the flow took place amid sighs and shudders of delight.

Roudolphine did not relax the hold of her thighs before she had recovered her senses. Then with a beaming face she removed the condom and showed me triumphantly that not a single drop had overflowed. She took all the trouble imaginable to make me understand that which Marguerite had already explained to me so well, but which I had never been able to procure for myself. For in that case Franz could have used it, too.

Roudolphine overflowed with joy. She had demonstrated to me her supremacy and had gathered the first fruits of the prince, who had certainly been expecting another dish that evening. I decided that later I would take my revenge. The prince, however, was very kind. Instead of making the most of his advantage, he treated us both very tenderly. He took nothing, contenting himself with what we were ready to give him, and spoke with passion of the pleasure which divine chance had brought him in the persons of so charming a pair of women. Describing our relationship in the most glowing colours, he filled in the time that he needed to gather up his strength once more. He was no longer very young, but he was still valiant as a lover, and at last the moment arrived. He entreated me to trust myself to him absolutely. Roudolphine very prettily made the victor's toilet, while I watched, peeping through my fingers. The cold cream was lavishly applied, and at last the longed-for instant arrived: I was going to receive a man. For a long time I had been wondering how I was going to deceive the prince about my virginity, because the first time I had used Marguerite's instrument I had lost that which men prize so highly.

As I wanted to surrender myself and since I had consented to be the third person in their games, I felt that I should behave myself without false modesty, and I let my two companions do all that they desired to me. Roudolphine laid me down on the bed in such a position that my head was leaning against the wall and my two thighs were hanging over the side of the bed, parted as much as possible. With eyes of fire, the prince gazed upon the delights spread before his view. Searing my mouth with burning kisses, he moved my hand away and placed his lance in, sliding it up and down very gently in the font. Roudolphine followed his slightest movement with eyes full of desire. Then he thrust his lance in as gently as possible. Up till then a very sweet sensation had penetrated me, but I had not felt any real delight. As he pressed, however, I was really being hurt and I began to moan.

Roudolphine encouraged me by sucking the tips of my breasts and fondling the place where the prince was trying to get in; she counselled me to arch my thighs upwards as much as possible. I obeyed automatically and the prince suddenly entered with such force that he penetrated half-way. I uttered a cry of pain and began to weep in earnest. I was lying there like a lamb at the sacrifice; however, I had made up my mind to go through with it. The prince moved slowly, this way and that, trying to penetrate further. I felt that all was not well; a muscle, a little skin, something anyway, had stopped him. Roudolphine had stuffed a handkerchief into my mouth to stifle my cries and I was now biting it in pain. I bore everything, however, to attain at last what I had desired so ardently.

Something wet was trickling down my thighs. Roudolphine cried out triumphantly. 'Blood! It's blood!

Congratulations, prince, on obtaining this beautiful virginity.' The prince, who so far had proceeded as gently as possible, quite forgot himself and penetrated so vigorously that I felt his hairs entangled in mine. That did not hurt me too much, though, for the most painful part of the proceedings was over, but my expectations were not satisfied in the slightest. My conqueror became more passionate. Suddenly, I felt something hot flowing inside me, then the vigour relaxed and the member escaped. Really, I should be telling lies if I talked about pleasure. According to what Marguerite had told me, and according to my own experiments, I had been expecting something much greater than that. And I well remembered the enthusiasm my parents had shown too. At any rate, I was glad to see that my trick had succeeded and that I had not been wrong in my calculations.

As I lay there pretending to be unconscious I heard the prince talking enthusiastically about the visible signs of my virginity. My blood had, in fact, bespattered the bed and his dressing gown. This was far more than I had dared to hope for, especially after my wretched attempt with Marguerite's instrument; there was such a tremendous difference between that thing and the prince's mature virility! In any case, it was through no merit of mine that I had still been a virgin, but only through chance.

Virginity is actually a mythical thing anyway. I have often talked to other women about it and have heard the most contradictory statements. Some girls have so wide a membrane that there can be no obstacle to the first entry, while others have one so narrow that even after having several times participated in love bouts a man entering will still think that he is the first. In addition, it is very easy to deceive a man, especially if he believes that the girl is well behaved. This can be done by waiting until her period is about due before she surrenders, when she must moan a bit and twist around as if in pain, and the happy possessor swears that he has been the first, for a few drops of blood from a different source will easily mislead him.

But it was high time for me to awaken from my fainting

fit. I had had my own way, and now I wanted to take pleasure without leaving my rôle of the seduced girl. The most important part had been acted. The prince and Roudolphine found particular delight in consoling me, for they were sure that they had initiated a novice. They both undressed and got into bed with me, the prince in the middle. The bed curtains were drawn and a delightful and indescribable game began. The prince was nice enough not to talk about love, langour or nostalgia. He was merely sensual, but with delicacy; for he knew that this quality is a spice to love play. I was still pretending that I had been violated, but that I was learning all the more quickly.

His two hands were busy with us, and ours with him. The more complicated our kisses became, the more animated our hands were and the more restless our bodies. Our nerves trembled with pleasure. It is a very great delight to kiss such a man, and he would have had to be made of stone not to warm up again. Even so, the second ejaculation had tired him. Sometimes he played with Roudolphine, sometimes with me, but I never let him approach without first having made his toilet, although he was very sure of himself. He gave me his word that I could try without a mask, that I risked nothing, that he was completely in control of himself. But I was not to be so easily tempted from the path I had chosen. So he began with Roudolphine, who lost consciousness two or three times without his strength being diminished. Then he washed and came to me. It still hurt a bit at first, but soon pleasure began to prevail, and for the first time I experienced complete fulfilment.

To prove to me once and for all that he was entirely master of his body, he did not finish inside me, but pulled out without ejaculating while I was half fainting with delight. He tore the condom wildly away and threw himself upon Roudolphine. She told me to come and sit upon her face and that she would calm with her tongue what the prince had brought to fever pitch. I was very reluctant, but a damp cloth refreshed the object of my desires and a charming group was soon composed. While the prince mounted Roudolphine, I knelt with my thighs wide apart over her face. Her tongue had plenty of room for its revels, for her head was thrown back over the pillows. Completely naked, because the prince had pulled off my nightdress in his passionate impatience, I was face to face with this magnificent man who now crushed my breasts against his chest and kissed me unceasingly.

Two tongues revived the fire which had hardly been extinguished. My pleasure increased and my kisses grew more and more passionate as I abandoned myself completely to this double excitement. The prince was enthralled, assuring us that he had never before experienced such happiness. At the moment of the spasm I grew jealous thinking of that warm wave of rapture spreading through Roudolphine and so, pretending to faint, I let myself fall heavily to one side. As I had calculated, I threw Roudolphine's cavalier right out of the saddle, and as I fell I saw their organs disunited where they had been so closely linked before. How fiery red and excited his was, how wide and violently open hers was. It was quite different from anything I had previously seen, though not more pleasant. I frightened them by falling, and they had no thought of pursuing their pleasures further, but came to help me.

I had reached my goal and was not long in coming to my senses. I made no secret of being very happy that I had been initiated with such art into the mysteries of love, but I refused to begin again as I could not stand any more. The prince wished to show us that he could give up the greatest of pleasures if we could not all share it together. He said that he left it to us to content him. I did not know what he was expecting, but Roudolphine, more lascivious than ever, accepted at once. The prince lay back naked on the bed and I had to imitate Roudolphine, who provoked with her fingers the marvellous fountain. As I kissed him and played with the oval containers of his sweet balm, Roudolphine took the shaft in her mouth. Finally, the foamy jet sprang forth and fell upon us all. I would have liked to have taken the place of Roudolphine, who absorbed most of this burning fluid, but I still had to pretend to be inexperienced and just learning everything. You can understand why I cannot forget that incomparable night. The prince left us well before daybreak, and both Roudolphine and I, closely entwined, slept until after midday.

The Amatory Experiences of a Surgeon

It is one of the requirements of society that the feminine portion of it should wear, at least to outward gaze, the semblance of virtue; yet there is nothing in female human nature which is more difficult to adhere to.

Among the males, society tolerates vice of all kinds, which does not actually bring the perpetrator within the pale of the law; but with woman, one false step—nay, the very breath of slander—is sufficient to cast her, a degraded being, without the pale of its magic circle.

Can we picture a more pitiable position than that of a young woman, in the prime of her youth and beauty, condemned to await in silence the adventure of the opposite sex, with the knowledge that the person whom she is prevailed upon at last to accept may, after all, turn out to be an impostor, totally disqualified for performing those functions that are necessary to the happiness of married life.

We medical men are not ignorant of the secret pangs and unruly desires that consume the bashful virgin, and that society with its ordinances prevents her from finding a safe vent for. We have often the means of tracing all the passionate thoughts, and sometimes the secret wanton doings, of those whom kind society has condemned to disease, rather than to allow nature to take its own proper course and allay those symptoms so detrimental to young girls.

Who shall say how many victims have been sacrificed on the altar of mock modesty for fear that the disgrace of the only natural cure for their complaint should blast their characters?

I have alluded to the circumstances which have come to

my knowledge from time to time, with reference to the expedients made use of to allay those raging fires which in too many cases prematurely exhaust the constitutions of our young women; and one of these cases will suffice to prove how ingenious are the designs to cheat society of its whimsical requirements.

A young lady, not yet eighteen years of age, was under my care for a complaint of the bladder, in which the symptoms denoted the presence of calculus, or stone. An operation became necessary, which the patient underwent with unexampled fortitude.

I could not conceal a suspicion from the first that the young girl could, if she choose, enlighten us to the nature of the case; but strange to say, she absolutely preferred to submit to a painful and dangerous operation, with the knowledge that death might possibly ensue, rather than render us any information which might lead to a correct conclusion.

The operation was performed successfully. A mass of calculus was removed, and as these formations never take place without something to build up a 'nucleus,' we began to search.

We recommended the usual examination, only to discover that the formation had for its nucleus a hairpin, which must have been introduced by the fair hands of the young patient herself, doubtless not without a sufficient covering to render the insertion tolerably agreeable.

The result was that the inexperienced girl had allowed the hairpin to become disengaged, and instead of getting into the entrance she had intended, it had slipped into the urethra, and thence into the bladder, from whence the very nature of its shape had prevented its returning.

This instance is only one of a number I could give my readers, illustrative of the shifts young ladies are frequently driven to in order to satisfy, in secret and by illicit means those desires which they are prevented from openly exhibiting and which they dare not appease by nature's only fit and proper remedy, connection with the other sex.

I have promised in these pages a faithful recital of events that, having befallen me, have left a sufficiently warm interest in their remembrance to entitle them to a place here; and true to this promise I am about to relate my adventure in the case of the sisters before alluded to.

As I have already stated, they were daughters of an opulent resident in the town. They both inherited the pretty face and elegant form of their mother, who, when they were quite children, had committed them in her last hours to their father's paternal regard.

I was the medical attendant of the family, and as such it fell to me to be depository of such little complaints as there two young beauties had to make.

At the time I write, the elder was just sixteen.

I had of late observed in her those usual indications of approaching puberty that disturb the imagination of young girls, and I knew from her symptoms that nature was working powerfully within her to establish her claim to be treated as a woman.

One day on calling, I found that Mr H—— had gone out hunting, and would not return until late in the evening. It was then four o'clock in the afternoon of a hot and close summer day. The two young creatures were alone, and received me with the modest grace so captivating to a young man.

I stood and chatted until the time for paying my other visits had passed, and as none of them were pressing and could as well be paid the following day, I remained to tea.

After tea the younger of the two girls complained of headache, and after a little while she went upstairs to lie down, leaving her sister to sustain the conversation.

I played the agreeable with all my powers of attraction. I gazed on her with longing eyes. My looks followed every movement of her body, and my wandering fancy drew an exquisite picture of all her concealed beauties.

Gradually love grew into ardent desire—a desire so strong that I had some difficulty to keep my seat, while my rampant member stood beneath my trousers with the strength of a bar of iron.

37

Each moment only served to increase my fever, while I fancied I observed an embarrassment on her part, which seemed to hint that she was not ignorant of the storm that raged within me. Innocent as she was, and all inexperienced in the ways of the world, nature stirred within her powerfully and doubtless whispered that there was some hidden fascination in my gaze, something wanting to content her.

At length, tea things were sent away, and I could find no reasonable excuse to linger longer by the beautiful being who had so fiercely tempted me.

I rose to go. She rose also. As she did so, a certain uneasiness in her manner assured me that she had something to communicate. I asked her if she felt unwell, pretending that I observed an unusual paleness on her lovely face.

She said she had something to tell me, and proceeded to detail the usual symptoms of a first perception of the menses, which had occurred a few days previously and which had at first much alarmed her.

I assured her on this subject, explained the cause, and promised relief. And on taking my departure I requested her to come to my house on the following day, and said I would then investigate her case.

With what impatience I passed the interval may be easily imagined by any of my readers who have been similarly situated. But as the longest night must have at length an end, so did this, and morning broke to dispel the restless dreams of unruly passion that had held me enthralled.

I anxiously awaited the time of my young patient's arrival, and my heart danced with joy as I heard her timid knock at my street door.

She entered—heavens! how my prick stood—how beautiful she looked.

I stand even now when I think of that sweet vision.

Over a plain skirt of black silk she wore a mantle, such as becomes young ladies, with a neat little bonnet. Pale kid gloves set off her exquisite little hands, and I noticed that her feet were encased in boots any lady might have envied.

I hastened to make her take a seat in my study. I entered fully into the particulars of her case. I found, as expected, that she was experiencing the full force of those sensations which were never intended to be borne without relief, a relief I was panting to administer.

I told her of the cause of her own symptoms. I gradually explained their effects and, without shocking her modesty, I contrived to hint at the remedy:

I saw she trembled as I did so, and fearful of overreaching my purpose, I broke off into a warm condemnation of that state of society that allowed such complaints to blast in secret the youth and beauty of young girls like herself.

I went on to hint at the evident necessity there was for the medical man to supply those deficiencies that society left in the education of young ladies.

I spoke of the honourable faith they maintained in such cases, and of the impossibility of anything entrusted to them ever becoming known.

I saw that she was so innocent as to be ignorant of my purpose, and burning with lust, I determined to take advantage of her inexperience, and to be the first to teach her that intoxicating lesson of pleasure which, like all roses, is not plucked without a thorn.

I gradually drew near her. I touched her—she trembled. I passed an arm around her slender waist; the contact literally maddened me. I proceeded to liberties that to a more experienced girl could have left no doubt of my intention.

Upon her my touches had only the effect of exciting more strongly within her breast those sensations of which she already complained.

I was now fairly borne away by my passions, and throwing my arms round the innocent beauty, I covered her face and neck with fierce and humid kisses.

She appeared to be overcome by her feelings, and seizing the moment, I lifted her like a child from her chair and placed her on a couch. I removed her bonnet and without meeting with any resistance from my victim, for contending emotion had rendered her all but senseless.

I carefully raised up her clothes. As I proceeded, I unveiled beauties enough to bring the dead to life, and losing all regard for delicacy, I threw them over the bosom of the sweet girl. Oh, heavens! what a sight met my gaze as, slightly struggling to escape from my grasp, she disclosed fresh secrets.

Everything now lay bare before me—her mossy recess, shaded by only the slightest silky down, presented to my view two full pouting lips of coral hue, while the rich swell of her lovely thighs served still further to inflame me.

I could gaze no longer. Hiding her face with the upturned clothes, I hastily unbuttoned my trousers. Out flew my glowing prick, standing like a Carmelite's. I sank upon her body; she heaved and panted with vague terror. I brought my member close to the lips. I pushed forward, and as I did so, I opened with my trembling fingers the soft folds of her cunt.

I repeated my thrusts. Oh, heavens! how shall I describe what followed? I gained a penetration. I was completely within the body of the dear girl.

I sank upon her, almost fainting with delight, my prick panting and throbbing in her belly. Oh, the ineffable bliss of that encounter. My pen trembles as I revert to the scene.

What followed, I scarcely know. I pushed again and again, until I felt myself getting dangerously near the crisis.

I observed her soft and still gloved hand beside the couch; I seized it, and covered it with kisses.

Heavens! what fire ran through me. I burned; I was on the point of spending.

Not unmindful of her reputation, even at that intoxicating moment when I felt the approach of the blissful moment of emission, with fear I thrust once more. My prick seemed to traverse the full extent of her belly.

Then, groaning in the agony of rapture, I drew out my bursting member, and falling prone upon her, I drenched her little stomach and thighs with an almost supernatural flood of sperm.

I lay for some time so utterly overcome with the intensity of my feelings that I could only close my eyes and press the dear girl to my breast.

At length I rose; carefully removing the reeking trace of victory, I adjusted the tumbled clothes of my companion, and taking her tenderly in my arms, I placed her in an easy chair.

I shall not attempt to describe all the degrees she went through before she came finally to herself and to a full knowledge of her complete womanhood. That she never blamed me for the part I had acted was the best guarantee that she had not regretted the accomplishment of my pleasing conquest.

On recovering from the confusion and dismay consequent upon the event I have just narrated, my fair patient lost none of her volubility, but talked away on the subject of our recent encounter, and asked so many questions that I had hardly time to reply to them ere she puzzled me with fresh ones.

Before she left me, I had initiated her into the exact proportions and nature of that potent invader whose attack she had so lately sustained.

The handling to which my prick was now subjected in no way reduced its desire for a second engagement, but a consideration for the delicate state of my new-made disciple, and the tender condition which I knew her very little privates must be in, induced me reluctantly to postpone any further attempt, and she departed from my house, if not a maid, yet a perfect woman.

Nothing could exceed the caution with which we concealed our secret enjoyments from every jealous eye, and yet I trembled lest my indiscretion should become known.

There was only one thing for which we both panted, and that seemed too dangerous to be put into execution. Julia had often received the entire length of my large member in her little cunt, but that was the sum total of our bliss; to emit there was more than I dared.

Several weeks had elapsed since the commencement of

our intercourse, and during that period I had been unremitting in my attentions to the youthful charms of my new acquisition.

She pined for the enjoyment, but I knew the risk of indulging her in her desires.

Fear of getting her with child was with me always paramount, for although as a medical man I might have enabled her to get rid of the burden before maturity, yet I was alive to the dangers attendant on so serious an undertaking.

One day, as with many sighs and much regret on both sides we proposed to omit the most usual way of finishing the performance of the Cyprian rites, Julia gave vent.

Julia, worked up almost to frenzy by the sweet friction, refused to permit my withdrawal, and throwing her arms round my loins, she finally detained me, while with wanton heaves and every exertion in her power, she endeavoured to bring me to the spending point.

I was alarmed for safety, and vainly struggling to free my rampant prick from the warm, sticking folds that environed it.

The more I struggled, the closer she held me, and the closer I drew to the dreaded moment, the more she exerted herself to produce the feared emission.

'Stop, stop,' I cried. 'Julia, my darling girl, I shall do it, I know I shall. Oh!'

I could say no more, but with a violent drive forward I sank, spending on her belly; my prick fairly buried in her up to the hair, the semen spouting from me in torrents.

As for my wanton companion, she threw back her head, and received the dangerous fluid with as much enjoyment as if it were herself who was trembling in the rapturous agony of its emission.

Trembling in every limb, as much from the fear of the result as from the excitement of the act, I rose and helped the tender Julia to her feet.

As she got up, a heavy pattering sound announced the return of the fluid, which ran in large drops upon the carpet and ran in rills down her beautiful thighs.

A few days after this affair we were diverting ourselves with sundry little freedoms one toward the other, when Julia, seizing my prick in her soft, white, little hand, threw herself upon the sofa and, drawing me to her, commenced to kiss and toy with my member. This, as may be supposed, afforded me considerable pleasure, and I let her do what she pleased, wondering all the time what her next gambol would be.

From kissing she took to sucking, and this delicious touch of drawing lips soon inflamed me beyond all restraint.

Again she took it between her lips, and holding the loose skin tightly in her grasp, she made her hand pass rapidly up and down the huge white shaft until, heated to the utmost and almost spending, I jerked it out of her grasp.

'Ah, my lad, you were afraid it would come out, were you?'

I replied that I was only just in time to prevent it, upon which with a laugh and a smack on the ticklish part in question, she exclaimed: 'Well, then, my fine fellow, we shall see what we can make come out of that large head of yours.'

Then, suiting the action to the word, she again commenced the agreeable titillation, until with nerves strained to the utmost pitch of luxurious excitement. Jutting out my member before me, I heaved my buttocks up and down, and with a few motions of her hand Julia fairly brought me to the emitting point.

With a sigh of heavenly enjoyment I let fly the hot gushes of sperm on her bosom, while her fair hand, retaining hold of my throbbing prick, received a copious flood upon its dainty surface.

After this we would frequently lie down together on the soft hearthrug and, each with a caressing hand on prick and cunt, produce in one another those delightful effects which, say what people will, give a spur to the passions no man or woman can resist.

We would operate on each other in this way until prudence compelled us to stop for fear of the concluding overflow, and then, waiting for a few minutes, would once more bring our senses to the verge of the impending flood.

These hours were wiled away until a serious cause of anxiety arose to put an end to our security.

As I had feared, Julia proved with child; how could she be otherwise, with such an opportunity?

As soon as she made me acquainted with the fact, I prescribed for her, but without effect. The prolific juice had taken firm hold, and nature was progressing in the formation of the little squalling consequence of our amour.

My anxiety was now intense lest the discovery I saw impending should, in spite of our endeavours, overwhelm us.

Under the circumstances I determined to take a resolute course. I operated on my little Julia. I succeeded. I brought away the foetus, and removed with it all danger of discovery.

The result was not so favourable with regard to the health of my patient. Our overheated passions had put an end to youth's dream of uninterrupted enjoyment in a continual round of sensual pleasure, and Julia had now to reap the harvest of her indiscretion. She soon fell into a weak state of health, and I recommended immediate change of air.

Her father, alarmed at her indisposition, took her to Baden, and after a residence of some months there, the roses again revisited her cheeks.

At Baden she was greatly admired, and soon received an offer for her hand, which her prudent father did not feel justified in refusing; she became the wife of a Russian prince, who, if he did not get with her that unsatisfactory jewel, her maidenhead, at least became possessed of a cunt well practiced in all the arts of love and lechery.

Thus terminated my amour with one of the the most agreeable and most salacious girls I have ever known, and my prick still stands at the recollection of the various luscious scenes in which we were mutually carried away by the violence of lust in its most enticing form.

The Loins of Amon

Withdrawing into the gloom of his dungeon, Ineni slowly walked the few steps around the walls. His mind was lost in bitter thoughts, which, for the moment even clouded thoughts of survival and escape. If only . . . But what sort of commander thought after the event 'if only'? He clenched his fists in fury.

Looking again through the aperture, he felt the immediate hopelessness of his position. All weapons had been taken from him. He had nothing but his tunic and his two hands. The prison was impregnable. The guards were incorruptible in face of the might of the High Priest.

There had, of course, been talk of his harem. He returned to the bed and waited.

Some time later, the slight drone of the guards' voices stopped and there was the sound of soft footsteps beyond the oak door.

Ineni stood up and stepped swiftly to the aperture. Down the stairway, led by an officer of the guard, came his harem, anxious and afraid.

In the chamber they were halted and the guards were ordered to search them. Ineni watched the heavy hands of the guards moving over the soft bodies of the women outside their thin robes. Hands violated even between their legs and buttocks over the slight protection of the robes. The officer stood by to see that no impropriety beyond the embarrassment of the search, took place. These women were the harem of a nobleman—most of them of high rank themselves.

The officer called out in the gloom to the blank door.

'The women are here for your pleasure, my lord. Is it your desire that all should enter?'

47

Ineni surveyed them from his eye-hole. They were all there; the Palestinian, a dozen others and, looking unhappy and forlorn amongst them, his recent acquisition from Kadesh.

'The dimensions of my chamber would not permit of such lavish hospitality,' he called back. 'Have enter but one: the young Syrian girl on the end of the line.'

The guards immediately seized the girl, whose eyes darted, quick and frightened from one to the other as once more rough hands mauled her. This time, the officer, too, approached after the examination by the men, had the girl remove her robe and looked at her more thoroughly. His eyes were dull, inscrutable as he surveyed her pronounced charms, but the eyes of the guards, forgetful of the proximity of the girl's master, lit up with lust at the sight of such beautiful flesh, so thinly covered, it seemed, with a taut, filmy skin. As the officer's hand searched in turn between the girl's legs, one of the rough men licked his lips involuntarily.

'Right, she may enter,' the officer declared after a moment. 'Should she leave before the morning you will keep her here with you. On no account must she be allowed to gossip before the sacrifices are completed.'

The eyes of the guards were riveted on the girl while he spoke. They saw in her an image of sweet, innocent beauty so much intensified from her noble standing and her uncovering before them.

One of them moved with the girl to the door, eyes still fixed on the profile of her face so near to him as, re-clad in her robe, she waited for the door to be opened. The iron bar was withdrawn with an effort and with a grunting tug, the door was swung outwards and the girl slipped into the cell.

She stood just inside in the gloom, staring uncertainly towards the dim shape of Ineni, while the door was re-barred and the sound of the officer's footsteps dwindled. For a moment the guard stood outside the door, staring in through the aperture. But then he decided discretion was necessary from one of his lowly station, even in face of a a condemned man. There was the creaking of the rushes on the divan and a low resumption of conversation.

Ineni moved towards the girl who meekly waited. As he reached her and caught her in his arms, she suddenly clasped him with a furious pressure.

He drew her to the bed, pulling her down alongside him in the gloom. Only their vague outline could be seen from the door.

The girl's hands moved tenderly over his face, her eyes looked bewildered; lovely and bewildered in the twilight.

'What has happened?' she breathed at last and there was disbelief in her voice. 'Why are you here?'

With his lips close to the smooth warmth of her forehead, Ineni spoke quickly and quietly. The girl listened, her fingers digging in continual little pressures into his shoulder.

'The high priests are corrupt,' he explained quietly, intensely. 'They are afraid of my power with the people. They know that I hate their corruption. When I met you in Kadesh, I had been sent on a war mission which it was thought could end only in my destruction. But I returned and they were afraid. So I am here. Nobody knows I am here. But tomorrow I shall be sacrificed to the god Amon and corruption will continue unopposed in Egypt.'

'But—but what of the Pharoah?' the girl asked. 'His name flies throughout Syria. Is he not the lord of Egypt?'

'In name only,' Ineni whispered in reply. 'He is the tool of the priests. Their word is law and they could overthrow him with ease if he tried to shake off their yoke.'

The girl was silent for some time. Tears welled in her eyes and she tried to force them back, but failed, so that they suddenly flowed in profusion over her slim cheeks.

'I—I just don't understand?' she said. 'You were all-powerful in Kadesh. Everyone spoke in awe of your power. And here you are thrown, like a common thief into a cell.'

'The ways of corruption,' breathed Ineni. 'But keep your voice down or the guards will hear.'

'But what can we do—what can we do?' She clung to

him with a desperate longing.

'Whatever is to be done,' Ineni whispered, 'it will be very risky with only a small chance of success.'

'But we must do something?' the girl breathed intensely. 'I should die if you were killed. My life would be worth nothing.'

'A plan occurred to me as I watched the guards searching you,' Ineni went on quickly. 'It involves you and will mean death if it fails. It will also be unpleasant for you—but it is the only chance.'

'I will do anything,' the girl said firmly. 'If you die I shall not want to live anyway.'

Ineni kissed her gently and wiped away her tears with a corner of the hides.

'In a few moments we must pretend to make love,' he whispered. 'But it would be better if we didn't make love in fact so that we shall preserve all our energy.

'After this pretence, I shall send you away. The guards have orders to keep you with them if you leave.'

He hesitated for a moment, searching for the best words to explain his plan. The girl's body was pressed against him, her face pressed against his as she listened.

'Normally they wouldn't dream of touching you, no matter how acute their desire. You are a noblewoman and the wrath of the nobles and the priests would have them slain. But if, while you sit with them on the divan, you make advances towards them they will, if I am not mistaken, have great difficulty in controlling their desires.'

He paused again. The girl's breath was sounding slightly, close to his ear. She said nothing.

'This plan,' Ineni continued tersely, 'is our only chance and you must forgive me the indignity I suggest. You must try to force them to make love to you—and not much force should be necessary.

'One of them has a dagger in his belt. He must be made to see the necessity of keeping his tunic on in case somebody comes. In his passion you must withdraw the dagger from the belt and kill him.'

The girl's grip on his shoulder tightened to a long slow

squeeze and Ineni was afraid she would be unable to carry out his plan—unable through her unwillingness. But when she spoke, her words made him grip her with a burst of love and continue.

'What shall I do with the other man—there are two?' she asked softly.

'That is the difficulty,' Ineni said quietly. 'I can think of only one solution. In order to stab them both you must have them both very close to you, both off their guard. They must both make love to you at the same time.'

There was silence and then the girl said: 'Yes, I see.'

'It will be unpleasant for you,' Ineni added, brushing his lips along her brow, 'and I cannot force you to do it. But it is my only chance of escape.'

'And what after they are dead?' the girl asked.

Ineni felt a surge of hope pass through him at the certainty in the girl's voice.

'Then you will have to pull back the bar and we can escape together through the temple,' he whispered. 'There will be more guards in the temple, but I shall be free and armed. Once out of this cell we shall escape.'

'Where shall we go?' the girl continued her relentless questioning. 'How can we hide?'

'That we shall have to decide in due course,' Ineni replied. 'We will have most of the night before discovery and I know where we can get horses. Can you ride?'

'I was taught by my father.'

'Right. Enough talk. Now we must pretend.'

Outside the door, shadowing through the hole, was a flickering of light. Ineni got up and crept over. A brazier had been lighted in the outer chamber and the guards were sitting quietly on the divan. They appeared to be listening. They are hoping to bear aural witness to the passion of a prince, Ineni thought with grim humour. They shall not be disappointed.

He tiptoed back to the girl and removed her robe. He in turn took off his tunic and lay alongside her. Their bodies were fused together and his penis rose in spite of him, pressing with rigid pain against her thighs. The girl breathed heavily.

'Could we not make love?' she pleaded in a whisper. 'The plan might fail.'

'It will not fail,' Ineni said, quietly. 'It must not fail. We shall need all our wits and strength and one becomes listless after passion is spent. It is better that we deny ourselves until we are safe.'

'I shall long for our safety with all my heart,' the girl said.

'So be it,' Ineni echoed.

For the next half-hour they pantomimed the act of love. Lying in the gloom where their movements would be now undiscernable from the door. The rustlings of the hides, the heavy breathing, the muttered exclamations, the moanings, the whinings, the groan after groan of growing passion, the convulsive explosion of fulfilment. All were there for the benefit of the guards, quietly listening outside, picturing afresh the lush curves of the girl they had seen searched in her nudity.

After the final gasping of the act, they lay silent for some time. Then both dressed quietly.

'Tell them I am asleep,' Ineni whispered. 'And you must act as if you really desire them, as if you mean every movement of your body, every word of encouragement. My life—and yours if you fail—depends upon it.'

'I will do all I can,' the girl whispered back. 'And I shall be thinking of you with every act I make.'

'Amon be with you,' Ineni said.

The girl breathed a prayer and then walked to the door. She banged on the inside and a guard came over.

'My lord has bid me leave him. He is asleep,' she said.

The guard tried to peer past her into the cell but could see nothing. He called out to his companion.

'Our lady wishes to leave. Be ready with your spear.'

The other covered the door from a slight distance, spear raised. His companion eased back the bar and the girl slipped out into the chamber, the light from the brazier shadowing over her, outlining the creases around the fleshy parts of her body, where the robe clasped and offered them. The bolt slid back into place.

'You had better sit on the divan, my lady. It is more comfortable and we have been ordered to keep you here for the night,' one of the guards said, gruffly, embarrassed in the presence of a noblewoman.

The girl thanked them and sat on the divan, while the two soldiers drew away and squatted on the floor at the foot of it.

Very quietly Ineni rose from the hides and crept to the door. He stood back a few inches from the aperture so that he had a good view of the outside, but could not in turn be seen. No light came down the steps from above. It was full night.

Ineni's heart kept up a continued, abnormal thumping as he prepared himself for the events which would end in life or death for him.

The girl had surreptitiously eased up the hem of her robe and she leaned back against the wall, legs apart so the material stretched tightly across her thighs, revealing their bareness under the skirt of her covering up to the gloom of her crutch.

The guards sat with their eyes on the ground, afraid, perhaps, to look at the lightly protected beauty of the girl.

'How boring it must be for you to have to sit in this chamber all night.'

The men looked round. She had succeeded in attracting their attention to herself.

'It gives us no great pleasure, my lady,' one of them replied—and his eyes fell on the open, revealed gulf of her legs under the robe. His companion, too had seen the uncovered intimacy. Their eyes became glued on the dark, firm, muscled flesh of her thighs—and were stuck there. Neither, it seemed to Ineni, had the physical power to remove his eyes from the tempting view.

The girl pretended to be unaware of their lustful eyes, the colour which had flamed to their faces.

'Are no women ever brought to give you a little distraction?' she asked.

She moved her position slightly as if she were

uncomfortable—and succeeded in presenting the men with an even fuller view of the secrets under her skirt. Her thighs, wide under the robe were now all visible and to the furtively searching eyes of the guards, the soft lips of her vagina were there in sight. Their heads, on the level of the divan, were directly in line with her legs and their eyes feasted ravenously—and now almost openly—on the object they would have given their lives to possess.

'Never such luck,' one of them answered. And his voice came out gruffly and uncertainly in his passion so that he had to cough to hide his feelings.

'How inconsiderate of your commanders,' the girl continued.

She rose as if to stretch her legs and strolled around the chamber, clasping her robe about her, outlining her buttocks as she walked away from them. Her bottom seemed contained like a firm pudding in a thin cloth and at its extremeties it rippled out against the cloth.

The men exchanged glances and stared with fixed eyes at the buttocks which rounded and creased like live things before their eyes. The fire threw shadow and light on the ripples of flesh so that they seemed even accentuated.

The girl turned back towards them and in walking appeared to find something wrong with a sandal. A few paces from them she paused and bent in front of them, jostling her sandal with her hand. At her bosom, the loose robe opened out and fell forward so that the guards found themselves looking down a long ravine of cleavage, their hungry eyes roaming over almost completely revealed mounds of round, firm breast-flesh.

Ineni, watching them closely, was aware how hard put to it they were not to leap to their feet and start the rape of the girl, in spite of the penalties which would follow. So far she was playing her rôle well.

'I always feel a great sympathy for guards,' the girl continued. 'They have no fun, while frequently their prisoner has everything he could desire. It seems so unfair.'

'We are not the privileged, my lady,' replied one, tongue

slithering over dry lips.

'But nonetheless you have probably more power and capacity than those in higher places.'

The girl, churned up with nervousness inside, as Ineni well knew, was giving no indication of anything but complete self-possession far beyond her years.

For a moment the guards stared at her, racking their brains for meaning to put to her words, unable to believe the obvious.

'My lord within there, for instance,' the girl continued relentlessly, nodding towards the door behind which Ineni watched. 'He has no more power than to satisfy himself and leave me unsatisfied—and now he sleeps while I can only regret.'

Slow grins appeared on the faces of the guards, grins they were prepared to wipe off at the slightest sign. Now they were sure—but one could not be completely sure with a noblewoman.

The bulges at the loins of their tunics were unmistakable. The girl sat once more on the divan, robe drawn up to reveal several inches of smooth, silky thigh, and motioned to the men to sit with her.

'Is it not ridiculous?' she asked with a smile. 'Two fine men like you, unable to have a woman and a woman like me left unsatisfied because of my lord's weakness. And here we are able to do nothing but sit and dream and wish.'

Her slim fingers played with her thigh, as if absently and her big, doe-eyes swept the two men.

'It is a great pity, my lady,' one of the men replied. 'And anyone who could not spend a whole night with you but must needs send you off at its beginning is no man in my view.'

He had risked all on his remark. The other guard looked at the floor.

The girl eyed the man.

'You would not have done so?' she asked. 'You would have kept me the whole night?'

'And several more besides if it were my choice.'

The other guard had not yet looked up from the floor.

They were playing with dynamite.

'Then you would seem to be the man for me,' the girl replied.

The other guard looked up at last. He grinned. They both grinned. This was a noblewoman with a difference. One could laugh and joke and talk intimately with her. But yet neither consciously dared suggest—not even hope—for more.

'You are so beautiful that I should probably have kept you for life,' the guard added, warming to his compliments.

'Am I so beautiful?' the girl asked, raising an eyebrow and smiling provocatively.

'More beautiful than the lotus blossom,' declared the guard who had not spoken up to this point.

'Ah. You, too, are a man of taste.' The girl encompassed him in her smile.

'But surely you have seen more beautiful women?' She addressed them both.

'I have seen some as beautiful of face and a very few as beautiful as body, but never one of such virtue in both,' the first guard said, boldly.

'And how can you be sure that my body is so beautiful?' the girl asked with a smile.

'My lady, you cannot hide your beauty—and was it not revealed to us when you were searched?'

Both men were now getting obvious pleasure out of simply making suggestive remarks to such a beautiful and noble woman. The bulges in their tunics were enormous and they made no fruitless attempt to hide these gauges of passion from the girl.

'But that was for only a moment. You had no time to judge,' the girl laughed.

'It was enough, but indeed we could have wished for more,' the first guard said, with a ring of passion in his voice.

'Then you shall have it,' the girl declared.

And before the lustful eyes of the men—hardly able to believe what was happening—the girl slithered off the divan and slowly divested herself of her robe. It peeled from off her breasts, which soared into view like great balls of ivory, strongly pointed at their uttermost protrusion by the expanse of nipple. Down from her slim ribs and slimmer waist the garment slipped, clasped her tightly around the broader flesh of her hips a moment and then with an extra tug and wriggle, had flowed off her hips so that her delicately rounded abdomen shot into view, the little muff of dark hair at her pelvis and then the broad, tapering-to-slimness thighs.

The robe slumped to the stone floor in a soft swoosh.

Bending before them so that her breasts hung vertically like the suspended, heavy fruit of a tree, the girl drew the robe from off her sandals and stepped out of it altogether.

'Now you can judge', she said, with a deep lustful look at the men.

She came closer to them, as they sat, mouths open, breath escaping in painful jerks, bodies heaving irregularly with their efforts to control their breath.

Close in front of them she spun around. The firelight flickered on her flesh, shadowing the rounds and hollows of her buttocks, her breasts, her belly as she turned, throwing into relief the lightly moving muscles as they tensed sinuously in her arms and thighs.

So close were the two men that they were aware of the flesh as if the skin was throwing off a light, radiant heat which reached them. They could see the light down on her body, feel in their minds, the texture of the taut, soft-looking skin.

Still they did not move.

'Tell me now am I not beautiful?' the girl asked, gazing down at them.

'My lady, you are so beautiful that you come near to tempting us to sin against our duty, which bids us quietly guard the prisoner, and our class which bids us not to touch a lady of noble birth—save in the spoils of war.'

'Would you like to touch me?' the girl asked, flaunting her hips.

There was a moment's hesitation.

'I should like to stuff my rod into the very depths of you.' The words came out quickly in the coarse expression which was all the soldier knew. The girl smiled at him invitingly.

'And I told you how unsatisfied my lord left me—I give you that right. Stuff me, stuff me with all your might until you are exhausted.'

Both men squirmed with passion at her words—but neither moved.

'We would be killed if we were discovered,' one whispered after a while.

From his hiding place Ineni held his breath. Would their fear overcome their lust and ruin everything?

But the girl had moved up to the men where they sat, open-legged on the divan, great branches thrusting out from between their legs, lifting their tunics in a great undulation.

With a swift movement she knelt in front of them and grasped each great penis in a hand through the cloth, squeezing it, fondling it.

'I need to be satisfied,' she said passionately, 'and now you need to be. I offer you my body—a body such as you have never had. I offer you the nectar between my legs. I offer you anything you want of me. It is past midnight. Nobody will come now until the morning. You will never have this chance again.'

At the feel of her hands both men had writhed their hips uncontrollably and now the first guard, helpless against himself, leaned forward and pulled her roughly onto him, hands running voraciously, fiercely, over her body.

The girl pursued her bridgehead. Her hand slid under the guards' tunics, up their hairy thighs and then clasped, gently, the thick stiff organs she found there, clasped them and then drew soft, cool fingers up their hot lengths.

The other guard, too, not wishing to be left out, had moved in and was feeling the girl all over from a side position.

Her hands slid, relentless, down from their rods to the hot, soft expanses of their testicles. Both men groaned and

58

wriggled in delirium.

'Come on, come on,' the girl entreated.

'Just a moment.'

The first guard tore himself away with an effort, snatched a blazing torch from the brazier and moved towards the cell door. Ineni moved swiftly and quietly back to the bed, lay down and feigned sleep. The torch flickered for a moment or two at the aperture, while the guard endeavoured to peer through the inner gloom. After a moment, satisfied, he moved away and the light receded from the door with him. Ineni rose quietly again and moved once more to the aperture.

The first guard had returned to the divan and was pawing the girl. He pulled her at him and crushed his lips on hers. From his grunt, Ineni could tell that she had slipped her little, lean tongue into his mouth. The man's hands caressed her breasts, clutching them so tightly that they bulged out around his fingers and red marks appeared on the skin as he slid over the smooth expanse.

The other man had, now, boldly slipped his hand between her open legs from behind and was fingering the slim folds of flesh, searching between them for the spot. His other hand stroked and pressed the firm, bamboo-texture of her buttocks.

For some minutes they continued thus, all three breathing fiercely.

And then the girl cried out in passion:

'Oh, put it in me. Quick, put it in me.'

She rolled off the man and flung herself down on the divan, legs wide apart. Both men moved, tunics rolled up above their loins, to get on her as she lay with eyes closed, moaning through open mouth.

Each tried to elbow the other away. Neither succeeded.

'Oh, don't fight over it,' the girl begged, voice broken with passion. 'If one of you can't wait, you can have me together.'

The men looked at her in surprise.

Quickly she rolled onto her side, reached behind her and spread the cheeks of her bottom with her hands.

'One of you must have my behind,' she said.

The two men were in no mood to argue about details. Each simply wanted to embed himself in this beautiful woman without delay.

'All right, I'll have her ass,' the second guard said through his thick breathing.

Falling over each other in their hot desire, each with an enormous penis sawing the air, they fell onto the divan on either side of the girl.

As the first guard, taking the more normal passage, pulled her legs on either side of his hips, Ineni, watching with a turbulent pang of upset in his stomach, thought: shades of the Queen of Arad—but what different circumstances and how much more depends on it.

Both men were coarse and brutal. There was no waiting, no question of finesse. Behind her, while his comrade arranged the girl's legs, the other—all reserve of class gone now—pulled apart her buttocks, spreading them with a great pull on either hand, pressing the anus open with his thumbs. An aiming. And then his fleshy organ barraged against the hole, rebounded on the first attempt, stuck on the second and with a third thrust had seared into her soft back channel to her cry of pain. He showed no gentleness, but, face screwed up in passion and fury, shagged with wild, rapid movements straight into her rectum, bursting in, with a few strokes, to the full length of his organ regardless of the girl's cries.

Meanwhile his companion, slower to get started, had succeeded in drawing up the girl's thighs on either side of him, so that one was crushed under him in the crook of his waist, the other strung limply over his hip.

Without more ado he caught her cool hand and placed it on his penis for her to place it in her vagina for him.

The girl seized it bravely and directed it into the opening of the aperture. Feeling the moist warmth around its tip, the guard heaved upwards with a flexing of his hips and his penis in turn burst into the girl in one great, gluttonous movement, forcing up and up, determined to feel the tight, painful pressure on his organ in one movement before the channel had adapted itself to his intrusion.

Another cry was drawn from the girl, but she held her own and was soon forcing her hips back at the spearing of her behind, forward at the penetration of her vagina with alternate squirms.

Her hands moved around the broad back of the first guard as he buried his organ of pulsing pleasure into her. Her arms encircled him, pulling him into her, thighs clasped him, cradling him warmly against her soft secret. Her hands roamed over his back, down to the belt until they rested on the leather sheath in which the dagger was enclosed.

For a moment, while Ineni started in a sort of hypnotised horror, she fumbled with the sheath, but was unable to unfasten it for fear of attracting attention.

Behind her, the second guard was well taken care of. Forcing his way in and in and in her tight back-passage which clasped his penis in a soft vise, he had no thought in his head but the sensual, almost unendurable pain down there at the protrusion of his loins.

The girl concentrated on the first guard, while her hand rested lightly on the dagger sheath.

'Come on, come on,' she pleaded. 'Stuff me as you said you would. Kill me, shove it in further, further.'

Goaded on, loins alight with the thrill of her coarse words, the guard stuffed and stuffed. His movements grew faster and faster until his body seemed out of control and his face was furrowed all over, his neck stretched and taut with veins standing out on it as if he were about to burst at any moment.

'Oh how wonderful! You're so thick and filling me! I can't stand it! Go on thrust your knob home.'

The girl's wild, coarse words assailed his ear, sharpening his passion, pointing it to a razor edge until it seemed that razor edges were flicking the tender extremity of his penis and then his mouth had opened in a great rough bellow as his loins opened and his juices flooded out through the phallic canal into the soft receptacle of her body.

Ineni muttered to himself, spurring the girl on. What

was she doing? In a moment it would be too late. Sweat stood on his brow and his jaw was taut as he watched.

But the girl had chosen the only moment in which success was inevitable. As the hot discharge shot in bullets into her opening and the guard's head and thoughts were filled with nothing but a furious, all-pervading thunder of release, she undid the clasp with deft fingers, drew out the knife and plunged it deep into his back all in one movement.

He gave an extra jerk which could easily have been one of passion, and let out a sharp cry of pain, which mingled with his roars of fulfilment.

The girl, her face set, eyes filled with horror, but determined in her horror, pulled out the dagger and thrust it into his back again.

Watching, his heart pounding, biting his lips, Ineni saw the little drama enacted fully. Saw the incongruity of a beautiful girl being buggered furiously, while the recent possessor of her vagina, penis still in her, clasped in her legs, gave his last twitches all unknown to his comrade. The blood flowed down from his back onto the divan while the girl wriggle uneasily free of the body. The great penis, wet and slippery with the dregs of sperm, dangled limply to the rush surface on which the body lay.

The girl held the dagger, dripping blood, in front of her. The body had swayed over onto its back. It might have been exhausted from the violent intercourse.

The girl held the dagger tightly, waiting. She didn't want to risk a false blow at the man behind her. In the meantime Ineni could see his great shaft appearing and disappearing with startling rapidity. His hands moved around to the soft belly of the girl, grasping fiercely the soft flesh, clasping and unclasping the slim folds of her abdomen.

His thighs moved up and under her, clasped her hips as his hips smashed at her in quick undulation, his penis skewering into her bottom from all angles, splitting her buttocks apart, still bringing little shrieks of sensual pain from her lips.

His mouth was open. He bit her neck so that she cried

out. His hands moved up, almost in a paroxysm to her breasts, pinching them, twisting them, digging into the nipples. His thighs twined and untwined, his hips undulated and moved in an almost rotary motion. Trying to hurry him, the girl extended her bottom at him, spreading her buttocks, straining her aperture as if she were emptying her bowels so that it met his upthrust in the middle of emptying, aiding his organ on its inward rush into her backside depths.

'Shag!' she whispered. 'Harder. You're making me sore. Make me sore. Go on, lose it in me. Push, push harder!'

Her words reached Ineni as a gentle echo in the chamber and, in passing, he thought he had taught her well, that she had played the rôle tonight well, that she had probably half-enjoyed it after the initial moments.

And then he heard the guard uttering a long drawn-out moan which grew in pitch until with a sudden convulsive thrust which almost hurled the girl onto the corpse in front of her, his penis had shattered its contents into her bottom. It continued thrusting into her in long forceful strokes and a sharp gasp at each painful release, until the reserve had dwindled and drained and the man rolled away from her, his penis sucking out with him, onto his back.

The girl turned over without a moment's hesitation and plunged the dagger into the man's heart.

Leaving it buried there she rushed to the cell door, struggled with the bar a moment and then grated it back from its staples.

Ineni pushed from inside and the door swung open and he stepped out into the chamber.

The girl flung herself, sobbing into his arms, overcome with the macabre horror of the rôle she had played. Her nerves, stretched to breaking point, had momentarily snapped.

Memoirs of a Young Don Juan

Berthe and I heard voices close by, outside the garden. We soon realised that they belonged to some servant girls who had been working in the field just beyond. Since it was now their lunch hour we stayed to watch them.

It had been raining the night before and the newly ploughed earth stuck to the girls' bare feet. Their skirts—they wore just one layer of clothing it seemed—just reached their knees. None of them were great beauties but, all the same, they were well-built sun-bronzed peasant girls, aged between twenty and thirty.

When these women had reached the stream they sat on the grassy bank and paddled their feet in the water.

While bathing their feet they jabbered away, their voices rising in competition with each other.

They sat facing us, no more than ten paces off, so that we could easily distinguish the difference in colour between their brown calves and their much whiter knees which were now completely on view. With some of them we could even make out a hint of thigh.

Berthe did not seem particularly enamoured of this exhibition and she pulled my arm for us to go.

Then we heard footsteps near by and we saw three workmen approaching along the path close to the spot where we had hidden.

At the sight of these men, some of the girls began to fuss with their clothes. One girl in particular drew attention to herself, there was something of the Spaniard in her coal black hair and clear grey eyes sparkling with mischief.

The first of the men, a dull-looking clod, took no notice of the women's presence and, standing directly in front of our hiding place, unbuttoned his trousers to pee.

He took out his member, which looked much the same as mine, except that his glans was completely hidden. He uncovered it to piss. He had lifted his shirt-tail so high that the hair surrounding his genitals was visible. He had also pulled his balls out of his trousers and was scratching them with his left hand while holding his member in his right.

I was as bored by all this as Berthe had apparently been when I had pointed out the peasant girl's calves to her, but now she was all eyes. The girls pretended not to notice him. The second man likewise unbuttoned his trousers and brought forth a prick which was smaller than his companion's, but brown and half-uncovered. He began to piss. At that the girls all burst out laughing, and their shrieks grew even more hilarious when the third also assumed the position.

By this time the first fellow had finished. He uncovered his prick completely and, shaking off the last drops, bent his knees slightly to replace the package in his pants. In so doing he let fly a clear, emphatic fart and gave an 'Aaah!' of satisfaction. Amongst the girls this gave rise to much derisive laughter.

The hilarity increased when they noticed the third fellow's joy-stick. He had placed himself on a slope, so that we could see both his member and the peasant girls seated beyond.

He raised it skyward and sent his stream arching high which set the girls laughing like lunatics. Then the men approached the maids, and one of the latter began to splash water playfully on the stupid-looking work-man. The third man remarked to the brunette who, upon seeing the men arrive, had settled her skirts:

'A lot of good it does you to hide it, Ursula. I've already seen that article you hold so dear.'

'There's plenty of things you haven't seen yet, Valentin! And a lot you'll never see,' Ursula replied coquettishly.

'You think so, do you?' said Valentin, who was now standing directly behind her.

Seizing her shoulders he forced her backward to the ground. She tried to remove her feet from the water, but neglected to keep her light skirt and blouse from billowing upward, so that she was completely exposed from the waist downward. Unfortunately, this enjoyable spectacle lasted only a few seconds.

Nevertheless it had lasted long enough for me to see that Ursula, who had already shown herself to be the proud owner of a pair of splendid calves, also possessed a pair of thighs which in themselves were worthy of the highest honours, and a bottom whose cheeks left absolutely nothing to be desired.

Between her thighs, at the bottom of her belly, lay a bush of dark hair which extended far enough to envelop both pretty lips of her cunt. But there the hair was more sparsely scattered than above, where it covered an area I could not have concealed beneath my hand.

'You see, Ursula,' said Valentin, by now quite excited, 'now I've seen your black pussy.' And without flinching he took the series of blows and insults which the girl, now really angry, rained upon him.

The second man wanted to pull the same trick with another of the girls as Valentin had tried with Ursula.

This second peasant girl was fairly pretty. Her face, neck and arms were so covered with freckles that it was almost impossible to distinguish the real colour of her skin. Her legs were also freckled, but the freckles there were larger and more dispersed. She had an intelligent look about her; her eyes were a deep brown, her hair red and crinkly. She wasn't really pretty, but nevertheless a tempting enough morsel to give a man ideas. And the workman Michel seemed to have a few. 'Helen,' he said, 'you should have a red mound. If it's black it means it must be stolen!'

'Dirty pig!' spat the lovely peasant girl.

He grabbed her as Valentin had done.

But she had had time to get to her feet, and instead of getting a glimpse of her pretty mound, Michel received such a hail of blows full in the face that he must have seen stars.

The other two girls joined in and began to pummel him.

At last he broke away and, pursued by the girls'

69

mocking laughter, ran to catch up with his companions.

The girls had finished bathing their feet and had left. Only Ursula and Helen remained, and they were getting ready to go.

They were whispering together. Ursula burst out laughing and, wrinkling her forehead, made a funny face. Helen was looking at her and nodding her head in assent.

The former seemed to be thinking over what the other had told her. Helen shot a glance around her to make sure that everyone had left, then quickly lifted her skirts in front and, holding them high with her left hand, slipped her right hand between her thighs at the spot where one could see a forest of red hair. By the movement of the hair, which was much thicker than Ursula's, one could see that she was squeezing herself between her fingers, though the thickness of her fleece prevented me from actually seeing the lips of her cunt. Ursula was watching her intently. Suddenly a stream shot forth from the bush of pubic hair but instead of falling straight to the ground, it arched and described a half circle in the air. Both Berthe and I were astonished to see it, for neither of us had ever imagined that women could piss like that. The operation lasted as long as it had with Valentin.

Ursula likewise seemed surprised, and apparently wanted to try it herself, but she gave up the idea, for just then the second and last bell for lunch rang, and the two girls set off rapidly.

Several days passed without anything of further note taking place.

Since the weather had turned bad, I spent most of my time in the library, where I had been pleasantly surprised to come across an anatomical atlas in which I found an illustrated description of the intimate parts of both sexes. The book also contained an explanation of pregnancy and of all the phases of maternity, none of which I had known before.

This interested me especially because the bailiff's wife

70

was then pregnant, and the sight of her enormous belly had greatly aroused my curiosity.

I once had heard her discussing the matter with her husband. Their quarters were on the ground floor right next to mine, near the garden.

Obviously, the events of that memorable day, when I had seen my sister naked, and afterwards the sport of the peasant girls and men, had been constantly with me. I thought of them ceaselessly and my member was constantly erect. I looked at it and played with it often. The pleasure I felt when handling it incited me to continue.

In bed I amused myself by lying on my belly and rubbing myself against the sheets. My feelings grew more and more sentitive every day. A week passed in this way.

One day when I was sitting in the old leather chair in the library, the altas open in front of me to the page describing the female genital organs, I had such an erection that I unbuttoned my trousers and took out my prick. From constant rubbing it now uncovered easily. I was as a matter of fact sixteen by now, and considered myself a man. My hair had grown thicker and resembled a handsome moustache. That particular day I felt such a profound and unaccustomed voluptousness as I rubbed it that my breathing grew short. I tightened the grip on my member, loosened it, stroking back and forth. I uncovered the tip completely, tickled my balls and my arsehole, then examined my glans, which was deep red in colour and as shiny as lacquer.

The pleasure I felt was beyond words. I ended up by discovering the rules for the fine art of masturbation, and stroked my dick regularly and rhythmically, until something happened to me that I had never experienced before.

The feeling was so voluptuous that I was forced to stretch my legs out in front of me and push against the legs of the table. My body slipped down and was pressing against the back of the chair.

I felt the blood surging into my face. My breathing was becoming difficult. I closed my eyes; my mouth dropped slightly open. A thousand thoughts raced through my mind in the space of a minute.

My aunt, in front of whom I had stood naked, my sister, whose pretty little pussy I had explored, the powerful thighs of the two maids—all these images flew across my mind. My hand stroked my prick faster and faster. An electric shock coursed through my body.

My aunt! Berthe! Ursula! Helen! . . . I felt my member swell, and from the dark red glans sprayed forth a whitish liquid, first with a powerful jet, followed by others less forceful. I had just discharged for the first time.

My engine softened rapidly. I now looked with interest and curiosity at the sperm which had spilled into my right palm. It both looked and smelled like the white of an egg, it was thick like glue. I licked it and found it to taste like a raw egg. I shook off the last few drops clinging to the tip of my member, which was now completely subdued, and wiped it on my shirt.

I knew, from what I had previously read, that I had just given myself up to the pleasures of onanism. I looked the word up in the dictionary, and found a long article on the subject, in such detail that anyone who had not previously been aware of the practice would inevitably have been fully enlightened.

The article had once again excited me. The fatigue resulting from my first ejaculation was past. The only tangible evidence of my act was a devouring appetite. At table my aunt and mother remarked upon my appetite, but dismissed it as merely due to growth.

I soon came to realize that onanism is like drink: the more you have, the more you want . . .

My prick was constantly hard, and my thoughts increasingly voluptuous, but the pleasures of Onan could not satisfy me forever. I thought of women and is seemed a shame for me to waste my sperm masturbating.

My tool became darker, and pubic hair a handsome beard, my voice deepened, and a few microscopic hairs appeared on my upper lip. I realized that I lacked only one experience of manhood: *coitus*—that was the term used in books for the activity that was still unknown to me.

All the women of the household noticed the changes that had taken place in me, and I was no longer treated as a child.

The next day, after my morning coffee, the bailiff's wife came in to clean up my room.

I've alrady mentioned that she was pregnant, and I carefully studied the enormous contour of her belly, and the unusual size of her breasts which swung to and fro beneath her light blouse.

She was a pleasant looking woman with pretty features. Until the bailiff had put her in the family way she had been one of the château's maids.

I had already seen women's breasts in pictures and on statues, but never in the flesh.

The bailiff's wife was in a great hurry. She had buttoned only one of her blouse buttons. When she leaned over to straighten my bed, this solitary button came undone, and I saw her entire bosom, for the vest she was wearing was very low-cut.

I sprang to my feet: 'Madam, you'll catch cold!' And pretending to help her rebutton her dress, I untied the ribbon holding it on her shoulders. As I did so her two breasts seemed to leap out of their hiding place, and I felt their bulk and firmness.

The buttons on each breast stood out, they were red and surrounded by a large brownish halo.

Her teats were as firm as a pair of buttocks, and as I fondled them with both hands I could have sworn they were a pretty girl's behind.

The woman was so astonished that I had time, before she recovered her wits, to kiss her nipples at leisure.

She smelled of sweat, but in a way that excited me. It was that *odor di femina* which, as I was later to learn, emanates from a woman's body and, according to the individual, provokes either desire or disgust.

'Oh, ooh! What are you thinking of?—No . . . that's

not right . . . I'm a married woman . . . not anything in the world.'

These were her words as I steered her towards the bed. I had opened my dressing gown and lifted my nightshirt, revealing my member in a dreadful state of excitement.

'Let me alone. I'm pregnant. Oh, Lord God, if anyone should see us!'

She was still resisting, but less forcefully.

As a matter of fact her gaze had not left my sexual parts. She was supporting herself against the bed on to which I was trying to push her.

'You're hurting me!'

'My dear lady, no one can see or hear you.'

Now she was sitting on the bed. I was still pushing. She lay back and closed her eyes.

My state of excitement was beyond all bounds. I lifted her dress, her petticoat, and saw a pair of thighs which fired my enthusiasm even more than had the peasant girls'. Between the closed thighs I caught sight of a small tangle of chestnut-coloured hairs, among which the crack was concealed.

I dropped to my knees, seized her thighs, felt them all over, caressed them, laid my cheeks upon them and covered them with kisses. My lips advanced from the thighs to her mound of Venus, her smell excited me still further.

I lifted her skirt even higher and looked with astonishment at the enormous bulk of her belly, upon which the naval was raised instead of hidden in a hollow like my sister's.

I licked her belly button. She lay motionless, her breasts hanging down on either side. I lifted one of her legs and placed it on the bed. Her cunt came into view. At first I was frightened by the big thick puffy lips coloured a reddish brown.

Her pregnancy gave me a chance to revel in that sight. Her lips were spread and when I darted a glance inside I discovered a real butcher's stall of moist red meat.

Near the top of the lips was the pee hole, crowned by a

small bean of flesh which I knew from my study of the anatomical atlas must be the clitoris.

The upper part of her slit was lost in the hair covering her overly fleshy mound of Venus. The lips were almost hairless, and the skin between the thighs was damp and red from sweat.

All in all it was not a very appetizing picture, but I appreciated it nevertheless because the woman was very clean. I could not help inserting my tongue into her crevice and licking it hastily before moving to the clitoris, which hardened under my passionate tonguing.

I soon tired of this sport, and since the crevice was by now well moistened, I replaced my tongue with my finger. Then I laid hold of her breasts, taking the tips in my mouth and sucking them by turns. I kept my finger on the clitoris, which grew harder and larger until it was as thick as a pencil.

At that point the woman came to her senses and began to whimper but without leaving the position into which I had forced her. I felt slightly sorry for her, but I was too worked up to really care. I talked to her cajolingly, trying to comfort her, and ended up by promising to stand as godfather for the child she was expecting.

I went over and, taking some money from the drawer, handed it to her. She had by then got herself decent again. So I lifted my nightshirt, but felt somewhat ashamed to find myself naked again in front of a woman, especially one who was married and pregnant.

I took her moist hand and placed it on my member. The touch was exquisite.

She squeezed, gently at first, then more firmly. I had grasped her breasts, which held a strange fascination for me.

I kissed her on the mouth, and she readily gave me her lips.

My whole being was attuned to pleasure. I placed myself between her thighs, but she exclaimed:

'Not on top of me. It hurts too much. I can't do it the front way any more.'

75

She got off the bed, turned round and bent over with her face on the bed. She said nothing else, but my instinct supplied me with the solution of the enigma. I remembered once having seen two dogs doing it that way. Following Médor's example, I lifted Diana's skirt—that was her name.

Her bottom appeared before me, a bottom such as I had never even dreamed of. Berthe's may have been pleasing, but it was really nothing next to this. My two cheeks put together wouldn't have made a half of one of these miraculous firm-fleshed buttocks. Like all beautiful breasts and thighs, her bottom was a dazzling white.

In the slit were some blond hairs, and the crack itself was like a chasm dividing her superb cheeks.

Below the colossal buttocks, between the thighs, lay the fat juicy cunt, in which my probing finger burrowed.

I placed my chest against the woman's bare backside and with my arms tried to encircle her elusive belly, which hung down like some stately globe.

I caressed her cheeks, then rubbed my member against them. But my curiosity was not yet satisfied. I spread her cheeks and inspected her arse-hole. Like her navel, it was elevated and though brown, was very clean.

I started to insert my finger, but she gave such a start that I was afraid I had hurt her, so I didn't press the point. I placed my burning prick in her cunt; it was like a knife cutting into a mound of butter. Then I went at it like a madman, slamming my belly against her elastic behind.

I was like one possessed. I was no longer conscious of what I was doing, but I reached the voluptuous climax, and for the first time in my life shot my sperm into a woman's cunt.

After the discharge I wanted to stay for a while in that agreeable position, but the bailiff's wife turned round and chastely arranged her clothes. While she was rebuttoning her blouse, I heard the sound of something dripping: it was my sperm running from her cunt on to the floor. She smeared it underfoot, and dried her thighs on her skirt.

When she saw me standing in front of her, with my red,

moist prick partly erect, she smiled, took out her handkerchief and meticulously dried it.

'Get dressed, now, Monsieur Roger,' she said. 'I've got to go now. And for the love of God,' she added, blushing, 'don't let anyone hear about what happened just now or I'll never forgive you.'

We embraced, exchanged kisses, and she departed, leaving me lost in a flood of new sensations.

Sarah

On the day in question I had no knowledge of my true self. I knew I loved Nature—flowers, animals, scents, textures; the spidery crawl of Grandmother's fine lace shawl on the back of my hand, the soft fur of Olive's old tomcat when he allowed himself to be stroked, indeed the feel of my own smooth flesh on the insides of my upper arms and thighs gave me pleasure. I handled my body with care and confidence but up till now I had let it live its own life and it seemed to get on pretty well without my worrying about it. My breasts were full and firm, my hips rounded and womanly and my belly swelled gently down to a tidy thicket of springy curls, a shade of brownish blonde just darker than the hair on my head. Of the uses to which my attributes might be put, and of the power and pleasure my body could afford me, I had as yet no knowledge.

This night there was no family dinner to arrange as the family was dining out. To my surprise the atmosphere in the servants' hall was far removed from that I had come to expect. On the table stood a collection of bottles which Jarvis was fussing over with a proprietory air.

'Sarah, my dear,' he called as I entered the room, 'come and join our little celebration.'

I approached the table with some trepidation. I had so far received little in the way of friendship from my companions below stairs. Although they had not been cruel to me, until now I had thought of myself as an outsider and tolerated out of necessity. Of the three, Jarvis had been by far the most kindly though our respective duties had thrown us very little into one another's company.

Now he pulled up a chair for me and poured me a

generous draught of liquor.

'Mr Jarvis,' announced Winifred for my benefit, 'has had a little fortune with the gee-gees.'

'A *little* fortune,' said Milly in an ironic tone which implied a weighty addition to the Jarvis coffers.

'A considerable stroke of luck,' cried Jarvis, 'for which I claim no credit beyond the happy accident of running into the only honest Irishman ever to have quit the Emerald Isle.'

'Be careful, Mr Jarvis,' I said, the taste of courage, in the form of gin, burning the back of my throat, 'my father was an Irishman and he was as honest as he was poor.'

'Then let us drink to the memory of your father,' cried Jarvis, holding his glass aloft, 'and bless him for bestowing on the world a lass with such a delightful pair of blue eyes.'

By this I took it that he meant myself and was thus totally disarmed. The other two hooted and made such noises as are the aural equivalent of a dig in the ribs. I had, of course, observed that all parties were ahead of me in terms of liquid refreshment and as a consequence were somewhat drunk. Winifred gazed on me with a motherly benevolence I had not thought possible from one usually so stern; and Milly was as friendly and solicitous of my comfort as she was habitually reserved. I downed my gin and observed that the glass was smartly refilled.

I must make it clear that, though innocent at this time, I was not totally ignorant of the ways of men with women. I was not unduly modest by nature. I knew that my face and my figure rarely went unremarked by the male sex. It would have been extraordinary had I achieved my present age without having to encounter advances. And encountered them I had, though mostly of a fumbling, immature sort and, once or twice, of a more direct but fortunately also drunkenly ineffectual nature. Thus far my swift feet and sober wits had preserved me from nothing more dangerous than a few beery kisses and some heavy-handed fumbling at my bosom.

I could see, of course, that Jarvis was giving me the glad eye and, though surprised by the sudden turn of events, I was not displeased.

He was a compact man, upright and well-formed, only recently past his fortieth year—or so I guessed—with a kindly face and, at the moment, an unmistakably lecherous grin.

'I propose a toast,' he said, 'to the sweetest pair . . .' and here he looked at me ' . . . of lips . . .' here he turned to Winifred ' . . in the kingdom.' At this he seized her and planted a smacking kiss full on her mouth—which did not appear to displease her in the least. In truth, in the half light, with her hair and bodice loose, Winifred looked fully worthy of any affection he might care to bestow on her.

'And now,' cried Jarvis, 'a toast to the finest pair of . . . thighs.' And he launched himself at Milly. There was a squealing and giggling and the scrape of chairs on the floor as Milly sprang up to avoid this sudden assault—thus facilitating Jarvis's attempt to lift her skirts and display her legs.

'Oh, you filthy beast,' she muttered as he hauled her clothing up to her waist. However it seemed to me that she did not protest overmuch and she could surely have done more to prevent the display of her trim and shapely limbs. Jarvis had now successfully laid bare an expanse of creamy white thigh, prettily framed by the close cut legs of her blue drawers and the tops of her stockings.

Still holding her firmly around the waist, with her skirts cleverly pinned out of the way behind her, Jarvis allowed his free hand to stroke and play across her exquisitely exposed legs.

'Look at these pretties,' he urged us, 'did I tell you a lie? Hasn't she got the prettiest, smoothest, whitest pair of thighs? . . .' and so on, all the while running his hand up and over and down the girl's naked flesh. I watched in fascination as his hand crossed over from one leg to the other, fingers running down under her stocking tops, then up underneath the hem of her knickers; then pressing gently with his third finger on the junction of her thighs as his hand fluttered over her most secret triangle. Then two fingers lingered, searching for her very groove beneath the material of her drawers.

'Oh my,' said Milly to no one and laid her head on Jarvis's shoulder.

His hand was strong, stubby, coarse, with filed down nails, blunt fingers and black hairs sprouting between the knuckles. A plain gold band twinkled on the little finger—which now insinuated itself beneath the edging of Milly's underthings. Tantalisingly Jarvis opened the leg of the garment and lifted it up to expose a thatch of black nether-hair. He teased the curls, twined and toyed with the strands to reveal the pouting lips of Milly's most intimate portion. So slowly that I could almost feel its agonising progress upon my own skin, Jarvis's little finger slipped between those tender pink lips and into the very quick of her.

'Oh,' murmured Milly as Jarvis eased in up to the joint and then out and then in again. I watched without breathing as the finger withdrew and, moistened with Milly's evident excitement, slid up to that sensitive spot at the apex of her love-lips. Milly bucked and squealed and rolled her buttocks back against Jarvis's legs but he held her firm, determined, it seemed, to spur her agitation to fever pitch. The gold ring on his finger winked in and out of view, glistening with her juices. A heady smell hung in the air. As I leant forward to drink in the mesmerising sight, I crossed and uncrossed my legs.

Now Jarvis was running the slippery metal of his ring over the pink nub of flesh evermore protuberant at the top of Milly's slit. Faster and faster he rubbed as the girl's breath came in short gasps, now interspersed with an uninhibited string of words that I'm sure she was unaware of uttering:

'Oh, yes, ooh yes, faster, faster, please, frig, yes, frig, do me nicely please, oh Jackie, you beast, stop, don't let me come, poke me, poke me please, oooh, aaah, I want your cock Jackie, oh they're watching, God don't stop, oh so nice, in my cunt, cock, cunt, fuck me after—OH, OH . . .'

In a flurry of wriggling hips and quivering thighs Milly jerked and shuddered and, for a few seconds, seemed to quite lose control of her limbs—if Jarvis had not been holding her I'm sure she would have collapsed in a heap on the floor.

'And now,' said Mr Jarvis, fixing me with the eyes of a starving man, 'who's next?'

To my surprise Winifred said, 'I think it's time we saw exactly what our new girl is made of,' and she pulled me up from my chair.

Truth to tell, such was my state of agitation by this time that I would have happily thrown myself into the arms of Jackie Jarvis had we been by ourselves. But to display such intimate emotions as I had just witnessed before Winifred and the shameless Milly was too much to ask.

However the other participants in this scene of unbridled lechery had different intentions. At Winifred's suggestion Milly had roused herself from her swoon and now latched a firm hand round my wrist.

'Come on, Sarah,' she said, 'be a sport, let's see what's beneath that Goody Two Shoes pinafore.'

And before I knew it Winifred had my other hand and the two held me fast.

'Now Jack,' said Winifred in a voice of sobriety, 'I imagine you'd like to examine Sarah in detail to see if she measures up to the high expectations Lord Coddrington entertains of her.'

'Indeed I would,' said he, 'I know for a fact his Lordship is looking forward to a full report.'

Winifred had contrived to stand behind me and, using her advantage of height and weight, she had forced me up on to my toes with my chest thrust forward and my hands imprisoned behind my back. Milly now began to unbutton and loosen and untuck my clothing so rapidly that, held in the housekeeper's firm grip, there was little I could do to prevent her.

In seconds Milly had unbuttoned my pinafore and laid open the bodice to reveal just the simple undershift that lay between my bare bosom and the burning gaze of three pairs of eyes.

'Well, well,' said Milly, insolently running her hands

over my breasts and feeling them through the material, 'ain't you a well-built girl.'

It was not possible to remove my shift without releasing my hands but, to my dismay, Milly proceeded to slide the straps of the garments off my shoulders. Thus she insinuated the article down my body then, delicately sliding her hands beneath the material onto the naked flesh of my bosom, she lifted my breasts free of their flannel covering.

I knew myself to be rudely displayed, my flesh thrust out into bold relief by Winnie's pressure on my back; my big breasts white and trembling, my shameless nipples pinkly engorged.

They then proceeded to have their fun with me. First Milly stroked and handled my titties, making their delicate tips tingle in a disturbing way.

'Your skin is so smooth,' she said.

'Have you no shame, Milly?' I asked.

'No,' she said simply and kissed me on the lips.

Winnie was less gentle with me in her turn but her rough handling only seemed to fan the spark that Milly's softer ministrations had ignited. Though I was now allowed freedom of movement somehow I made no attempt to break away.

'Take off her clothes,' commanded Jarvis, 'I need to take a closer look at her for his Lordship's sake.'

They lifted me on to a chair in the full glare of the gas light. Eager hands pulled at the fastenings that remained intact. I made no protest and lifted my limbs as required to enable them to disrobe me. Very shortly they had reduced me to just my stockings.

They lifted me onto a chair in the full glare of the light. I tried to cover myself with my hands but Winifred commanded me to hold them behind my back—or else she would make me.

I felt so exposed! I was mortified to exhibit my body this way—yet it had the hypnotic quality of a dream: a dream I often had in which I was displayed naked to faceless strangers and made to adopt poses for their amusement. It seemed that there was a part of my nature that understood what was happening to me better than I did myself.

My audience was delighted with the spectacle I made and generous in their compliments. These remarks were nectar to my vanity. Though I knew that I was fairly made, I had never before been so brutally exposed nor so carefully scrutinised.

'Isn't she a tasty morsel?' asked the housekeeper of Jarvis.

'My eye,' said he in tones of approval. 'A right cracker, I'd say.'

They made me turn back and forth, hold my arms above my head, then turn round so they could feast their eyes full on the flesh of my backside. The nip of my waist, the curve of my hips, the jut of my breasts, the swell of my bottom—all seemed to please them greatly.

Jarvis told me to face him and place my feet apart.

'Open up, my dear,' he said, taking a seat next to the chair on which I stood. 'I have Lord Coddrington's business to attend to.'

'Oh sir,' I cried, 'his Lordship must never know of this! You wouldn't tell him surely!'

'I might and I might not,' came the reply. 'But I can assure you that his Lordship would be most interested in that extraordinary treasure you are attempting to conceal from me just at this moment!'

'Feet apart,' cried Winnie and, seizing my ankles, she forced me into a position of some indelicacy. With Jarvis seated as he was, my most intimate portion was but a few inches from his prurient gaze.

My shame was now nearly complete, for the air was thick with a scent which I knew must be my own and they could clearly see the dew that moistened my sexual parts.

'And now the most important question,' announced Jarvis, '. . . is she still a virgin?'

'I am indeed,' I cried, for it was true.

'I hope so, my dear, for I paid out a lot of his Lordship's money.'

I was hardly in a position to ask him to elucidate on

these mysterious remarks. Indeed I hardly heard them as he delicately ran a finger up the inside of my thigh, from my stocking top to the alert and tender skin adjacent to the triangle of blonde curls that covered my mount. There he delved his inquisitive digit into my moist and hidden groove.

'Oh,' I cried, my loins twitching as a dart of sensation shot through me. 'Oh sir, please don't. This is most indecent.'

But Jarvis had no mercy on my shame and, had he shown any, I dare say his accomplices in debauchery would have been cruelly disappointed. In truth the sensations in my private parts were such that I would have been a little disappointed myself.

Now his fingers were playing with me at will; nibbling and stroking and paddling in my sodden thicket, finding my most secret nub of pleasure and agitating it so sweetly and so knowingly that my knees gave way and I collapsed into the arms of his two lecherous handmaidens.

They laid me on the table, on my back, and spread my legs on either side of the seated Jarvis. It was a grotesque and yet most titillating arrangement—in which the man sat at table to feast on the most succulent part of my anatomy. On either side of me were Winifred and Milly who fondled my neck and shoulders and breasts.

Jarvis now had total possession of my trecherous sexual portion and proceeded to insinuate a finger right into me.

'She's tight enough,' he muttered as his insistent digit eased into my virgin orifice. Then its passage ceased, its progress inhibited by the natural barrier of my uncorrupted state. A broad smile broke across the manservant's features.

'Your mother's an honest woman,' he said to me, 'and so are you it seems.'

'So, she's a virgin, is she—are you sure?' With this Winnie plunged her hand between my legs in Jarvis's place.

Though I recoiled from her fumbling there was little I could do. Indeed I was past the point of any resistance at all. I was totally bewildered—by my humiliation, by this talk of Lord Coddrington and my mother, by the praise heaped upon my person and, above all, by the overwhelming sensations in my most secret parts. It was dawning on me then that my body was not the uncomplicated mechanism I had always believed it to be. At the moment it seemed to have a will and an appetite of its own. Even the coarse manipulations of a matron old enough to be my mother were as the exquisite fingering of a musician on the strings of a harp. And when she took her hand away I could have wept for another player to have taken up the tune. In such a state I was hardly aware of what they were saying.

'She's pure all right,' agreed Winnie.

'And she's a hot little filly, too,' came the reply, 'look at her jib her cunt up, she wants it that bad. For two pins I'd give it to her and his Lordship could go hang.'

But that was not to be my fate.

There was a sound of giggling and a slithering and flapping of clothes. I opened my eyes to see Jarvis, his garments at his feet, stark naked in the dappled light of the fire. His chest was matted with thick black hair, his simian arms hung by his sides and from the forest of hair in his loins sprung a thick staff, its head angry and glistening.

Milly now stood in front of me, her dark hair loose about her shoulders, the points of her breasts clearly outlined through the material of her shift. To my surprise she pulled my thighs apart and bent down to support her elbows on the table between my legs. Suddenly, it seemed, my thighs were captured in the crooks of her arms and her face was buried right between my legs.

'Oh, what are you doing?' I shrieked as Milly's thin warm lips sought out my agitated slit as eagerly as a pig after a truffle.

'She's going to gamahuche you, my darling,' whispered Winnie in my ear. 'You just lie back and enjoy yourself. Mr Jarvis is going to take her from behind so he can enjoy the adorable spectacle you will make. Now you see how much we love you!'

I knew enough not to trust the old bawd, but in one particular she was not lying for Jarvis had upped Milly's shift from behind and was dandling the buttocks now thrust saucily towards him.

With a shameless gesture he ran his fingers in the juice of her crack and anointed the tip of his bobbing organ. Then he positioned himself rudely behind her and slid his shaft smoothly home. I felt the tremor of his entry transmit itself through the gasp and tremble of her lips on my nether-mouth. It was as if the three of us were worms skewered on one pin, wiggling and thrashing in an indistinguishable erotic agony.

Winnie too was transfixed by the same passion. At Jarvis's direction she had unfastened the pinning of her dress so that her huge white dugs now billowed out of her bodice and her skirts were up to her waist exposing the creamy flesh of her belly.

'Frig yourself, Winnie,' commanded Jarvis and the matron needed no second urging. She plunged her hand between her legs and began to manipulate her capacious hole with practised dexterity, spreading her legs as wide as she could and pulling open the flaps of her cunt at Jarvis's instruction.

He now surveyed us all in a libidinous frenzy. To excite his lust still further he told me to place my hand on Winnie's love-hole and to frig her as I would myself. I was willing to indulge this lechery but I did not know how, never having even done it to myself. Winnie herself showed me by placing her hand over mine and directing the play of my fingers over her bewitching motte.

Thus did the four of us take our pleasures. Jarvis pumping into Milly's delectable rear end, she milking and nuzzling my aching nether spot and Winnie writhing and twisting under the eager ministrations of my novice touch.

Though until now I had been a stranger to these delicious pleasures, I knew instinctively that there must be a coming crisis of the flesh. I could feel an emotion building within me that must soon have physical release.

'Oh Lord,' I heard myself say, 'oh heavens, oh dear,'

and it seemed a chorus of cries burst from us all at the same time. Even Milly, with her mouth glued fast to the hungry well between my thighs, seemed to sing a song of ecstacy into my very vitals as a white wave surged through my entire frame and threw me up into a blaze of sunlight and onto a warm, soft bed of bliss.

I opened my eyes to find my head pillowed on the bountiful still-heaving bosom of Winnie the housekeeper. I knew now that the world would never be the same.

Debauched yet still virgin, I awoke the next morning to the knowledge that the world itself contained a world that I knew nothing of. It was strange to think that I had always carried with me the key to this mysterious and intoxicating land and yet only now did I realise how to unlock its secrets.

Lying on my narrow bed with the day not yet begun, I took stock of the events of the previous evening. It was now plain to me why Olive, my step-mother, had been only too happy to see me go. I wondered how much money had found its way into her purse to compensate her for my absence and my usefulness about her house. Yet the realisation that I had been sold for my virginity did not strike me with horror as it might other girls in my situation. The shame, the fear, the praise, the pleasure—this new knowledge had changed me irrevocably from the girl who had come to this house just a few days before.

So this was what men and women did! It explained a great deal to me, made sense of the way my step-mother with her heavy figure and slatternly habits had besotted my father. I had seen them lying together, on top of the bed one hot summer's day and he palping and patting the big moon cheeks of her arse. It made sense too of the way Lord Coddrington's eyes followed me, dwelling on every curve of my uniformed figure—and maybe also of how his children had regarded me in the drawing-room the previous day.

Here lay the crux of my present dilemma. It was obvious that I was shortly to be whisked into his Lordship's bed for his enjoyment of the charms which Jarvis had so reluctantly refrained from sampling. When, I wondered, was my defloration to take place? Now that I had been subjected to the intimate scrutiny of Jarvis and company I could only presume it would be soon.

I confess to an immodest confusion. Most chaste girls in my situation would have plotted their escape from this licentious house—or fainted dead away from terror. But I knew already that I was one of nature's libertines albeit, as I now think, a foolish one. My concern was not to preserve my virginity—or to sell it to the highest bidder—but to bestow it for love. I knew I did not want to yield my maidenhead to an old lecher, no matter how noble or wealthy. I wanted to give it up to William, he of the elegant bearing and warm smile.

I wondered what he would look like in the place of Jarvis in my reminiscence of the orgy in the servant's hall. Would his organ thrust, club-like, from his belly like that stiff, threatening sword of flesh that Jarvis bore? I could not picture it precisely yet the thought excited me. I recalled the way William had regarded me the day before and his words—'a remarkably pretty child'—surely he would accept from me the gift of my virginity?

As I teased at this prospect in my imagination, my fingers naturally strayed to that now mysterious spot between my thighs and made an exploration in the light of my new knowledge. I rubbed the coarse short hairs on my mound and gently pulled open the wings of my cunt to probe within. I traced the outline of a bearded mouth and rolled the tender lips between my fingers, feeling the tingle of remembered new pleasures as I did so.

With both hands now, my legs asplay, I felt inside my hot passage and tried to imagine the entry of such an instrument as Jarvis's. In my mind's eye the bright red plum of his staff took on enormous proportions. Surely such a big thing could not be inserted into the confines of such a narrow corridor? Yet was Milly made so differently to me? She had engulfed that monstrous organ to the hilt, to his hairy balls which had battered her buttocks as he thrust into her! It was such a mystery. A delicious, exciting mystery that held me in a spell I had no wish to break.

Thus, my fingers now stroking, fondling, encircling the nub of flesh at the stop of my split, I frigged myself into a frenzy. Yet I was clumsy. It seemed I was chasing something not quite within my grasp and though I was flooded with a sudden warmth I was not able to scratch at my real itch.

It was time to get up, to clear and lay fires and embark on my daily chores. If I failed to perform my tasks I was certain to be upbraided by Winnie but, after last night, when I had witnessed her puffing and wheezing in the heat of her passion, and when it was I myself who had dictated the ebb and flow of her lusts, I no longer felt fearful of her authority. Besides, evidently I had not been added to the household for my abilities as a drudge. The fires could wait, I had another scheme.

I upped and dressed as quietly as I could. Yet in my impatience I could not help blundering into the end of Milly's bed which lay between my own and the door. She called to me in a voice heavy with sleep, asking if it was time for her to rise. I bent and spoke to the mass of dark hair that fanned over her pillow.

'Go back to sleep,' I whispered. Her face was barely visible but it seemed her eyes were still shut. 'I'll take the teas up.'

I tapped gently on Miss Hilda's door. From behind the door came a muffled sound which I took to be a summons to enter. I did so, bearing the tea tray and with my excuses for Milly already half out of my mouth.

And there they remained, frozen on my tongue, as I regarded the tableau before me. Miss Hilda's bed faced the door so, on the threshold of the room, I looked directly at its foot. As beds go it was a large and sturdy article, as indeed it needed to be to support the vigorous activity that

93

was taking place upon it. I gazed, it seemed, upon a human octopus at whose centre clenched and writhed and thrust a pair of naked male buttocks. The pale skin of this gyrating seat was downed in dark fuzz, growing thick and black in the rude seam which bisected it. Above this mesmerising sight waved, inexplicably, a female foot whose toes wriggled and flexed in dainty abandon.

As my eyes grew accustomed to the dim light I struggled to make sense of the strange shape. Amid the wreckage of the bed linen, the bedraggled sheets half on the floor, I made out the columns of a man's strong thighs as he knelt forwards, a sturdy brown back and a dangling pouch of skin which waggled coarsely beneath the muscular cheeks of that dancing arse. Now I could see that the man had Hilda's legs slung high about his neck and that he was supporting them both in this position, thrusting deep within her body with fiercely energetic strokes. I could hear their breathing, he with slow deep pants, she on a quicker note that indicated laughter—or tears.

My mind was in a turmoil. In my ignorance it seemed incredible that two people could accomplish such things. And Miss Hilda, so well-mannered and proper—and here so abandoned! Or was I witnessing the violent sack of her virtue? Was her bedfellow some crude ruffian who had broken into the house and was now raping my mistress before my eyes? Yet I knew this could not be the case, if only by the way her fingers were toying feverishly with the short black curls that grew at the back of his neck.

Convinced by now that the lovers were too transported to have noticed my ill-timed entrance, I began to edge backwards out of the doorway when Hilda spoke. Her voice was low and breathless but it addressed itself unmistakably to me.

'Put the tray down Milly, you little trollop, and run along. You've seen enough.'

Now did not seem the right moment to explain that Milly was indisposed. Indeed, I imagined that it would cause a degree of consternation were I to do so. Accordingly, my mind buzzing with the implications of Hilda's remarkable peech, I placed the tea tray on the dressing table by the door and turned to go.

As I did so I cast one last inquisitive glance backwards. o my surprise the man on the bed turned to look at me. Then he deliberately shifted position to show me his thick rown staff plunging hungrily into the pink-lipped nest ow revealed between Miss Hilda's suspended thighs. For moment he held it still, in full view, at the entrance to her vet and hungry passage and grinned at me in shameless nasculine pride. Then, as her cries mounted to a higher itch, he stuffed it home deep inside her.

I left the room with my heart hammering against my ibs. What I had seen was coarse, vulgar, obscene. Yet it ad affected me profoundly and what disturbed me most vas that I wanted this rude spectacle for myself. I wanted nuscular arms round *my* body, a mouth fast like a leech to *ny* mouth and a big engine like that one bolting between *ny* thighs. I leant against the wall in the corridor outside he bedroom and closed my eyes as the blood raced crazily hrough my veins.

The swirl of passion had scarcely abated by the time I ntered Mr William's bedroom, bearing yet another tray in ny trembling hands. His room stood on the second floor f the house, facing east, and already early morning spring unshine had pierced the gaps in the drawn curtains of the igh windows. A broad hand of pale sunlight fell squarely cross the bed and the still form that lay between its crisp vhite sheets.

Mr William was deep in slumber, his mouth half-open nd a sleepy gurgle in his breath, whose regular respiration oth reassured me and aggravated my fear of discovery. I ad no conscious plan but it seemed my body had more nowledge of my purpose than my lust drunk brain.

I took hold of the hem of the top sheet and slowly ulled. With surprising facility the bed coverings yielded to ny naughty purpose and fell away from the unconscious orm that lay beneath. Already uncaring of the onsequences, I drew the sheet back to reveal the object of ny desires.

He lay on his back, his limbs spread wide, one arm tucked up underneath the pillow. He wore just a simple night-shirt, unbuttoned at the neck to reveal an expanse of tender, boyish chest and which, in the manner of such garments had ridden up during his night's repose and was now rucked high around his waist. Thus I could gaze with sinful fascination on his almost naked form. He was slender, pale, almost girlish in his making—so different from the brutish Jarvis and the coarse ruffian I had seen but recently lewdly frolicking in Miss Hilda's boudoir. This was no vulgar ape who would leer obscenely at a woman as he roughly violated her femininity. Here lay a beautiful angel who would—surely—divest me of my maidenhead with tenderness and consideration.

But let me not be coy. Of course my eyes were drawn, above all, to the junction of the man's thighs; drawn there first and last to scrutinise every fold of flesh, every mole, every downy hair—every aspect of the instrument which I hoped would disencumber me of my virgin state. And here, indeed, was cause for fascination. If there was a marked contrast between William and the other men I had observed in their natural state, then here lay its epitome. Though the other two manly organs I had seen had been engaged, so to speak, and this one was in repose, here surely was a different order of masculinity.

The article in question lay curled like a tiny sleeping mouse on a cushion of two blue pigeon's eggs. There was no hair there to speak of, just a transparent fuzz of down which I could only observe by sinking to my knees at the side of the bed and bending my head close to the root of my curiosity.

What interested me above all was the mysterious hood of skin which covered the head of this exquisite article and ended in a curl of pretty pink flesh. Where was the great red plum, the focus of Jarvis's battering ram, that had so inflamed my imagination? Could it be wrapped within that dainty fold of flesh, hidden and asleep just like its owner?

My inquisitive nature was in no state to be denied. I cautiously raised my hand and, as gently as I could, ran my forefinger down the length of the tiny organ. The skin was as soft and smooth as a new born baby's. I glanced anxiously at William's face. There was no change in his features or in his regular breathing. He slept on. I touched him with my finger again. And again.

It seemed to me now that the mouse was stirring in its sleep. Now, when I gently stroked the tender crest of flesh I could see that the animal was waking up, was growing miraculously before my eyes. Emboldened, I began to tickle beneath its chin and the head began to twitch. Then—oh my—the whole organ gave a leap and jerked upwards out of my hand. Mouse no more, it had metamorphosed into a stiff snake which pointed upwards against William's belly and danced with a life of its own.

And now I could see the answer to the conundrum that had puzzled me as a pink bulb of flesh stretched the tender rose of skin on the hood of the serpent and emerged into view. Here was the vision that had haunted me since the night before. To be sure, the article was smaller and slimmer than the weapon that had inspired and inflamed me but it was, nonetheless, a worthy recipient of my virtue.

With thumb and forefinger I encircled the neck of this pretty wand and worked the roll of skin beneath the head up and down. I wanted to make the pink nut disappear and reappear, to see again the trick that had so delighted me, but the skin was dry and would not slide freely at my touch. Unthinkingly—instinctively, I suppose—I wetted my fingers with my tongue and applied the lubrication. To my delight the skin rolled up completely to conceal the head, then down again to reveal it once more. It now glowed a deep red in startling contrast to the pearly white shaft on which it so proudly sat.

I leaned closer to drink in this male mystery, to savour the aroma of sleep and sex that rose from William's body. The fat red nut wagged just inches from my lips as I jiggled and fiddled with it, transported in my idiot lust.

What happened next, happened all at once and it seemed that I was powerless to prevent it.

'For God's sake,' said a voice, as a hand grasped the

97

back of my head, 'suck the bloody thing properly.'

And before I could protest, my gentle plaything was propelled between my lips, full into my mouth. There it leapt and jumped as I fought against the insistent pressure on my head which held me fast against his loins.

I could hear William's voice talking in fast, urgent breaths as I stared into his stomach and he thrust and bored and stuffed his truncheon into my mouth.

'I've been watching you, you little minx. I've been awake for a while, observing your tricks. By golly, now you'll have to take what's coming to you—'

And with a flurry of twitches and jerks his staff exploded in my mouth, flooding me with a salty, choking deluge.

Confessions of an English Maid

The days slipped into weeks, the weeks imperceptibly, into months, and almost before I realized it, a year had gone by.

Miraculously, I had escaped all three of the afflictions whose menacing shadows are ever close at the heels of those who traffic with their sexual favours: syphilis, gonorrhea and pregnancy, the Three Horsemen of the Prostitute's Apocalypse.

My health was good, and I had gained in weight, having added several pounds of flesh which improved my figure even though at the cost of some of the juvenile slimness which in the beginning had been such a valuable asset. Nevertheless, I had for some time been observing a gradual change in my physical orgasm which was becoming more and more pronounced, and the condition was one which is not common in the walk of life I frequented.

I will speak plainly. Sexual sensibility, which is that capacity to respond easily and actively to erotic excitation, diminishes rapidly in the majority of professional prostitutes who are obliged to exercise their sexual functions with a frequency far in excess of the provisions of Nature. The sexual act becomes a mere routine in which pleasure or orgasm is only simulated to satisfy the customer's ego.

They moan and sigh and murmur passionate endearments, but if their minds could be read, the hollow mockery would be apparent, for one thought only occupies them: a wish to be finished and rid of the man as quickly as possible.

This is the rule which should have applied to me, but didn't.

Desires which should have been appeased by all too frequent gratification were quieted but for a moment, and almost at once flamed anew with increased insistence. And the tendency was growing. Strange as it may seem, sometimes after having had orgasm effected as many as half a dozen times in a single afternoon and evening, I was obliged to masturbate before being able to sleep. Pathologically and physically, I was oversexed, designed, seemingly, by Mother Nature herself, to be a whore.

Now in this propitious moment there entered into the horizon of my life, for the first time, a really sinister influence. And though in that influence I myself sensed a spirit of perversity, I was drawn toward it like a moth to the candle. Knowing that the destiny it signified was evil, I had not wish to resist it.

Montague Austin—what memories that name evokes. Memories of passion, cruelty, horror, blended with the cloying and intoxicating poison of a transcendental lust which knew no law other than that of gratifying its own frenzy.

I was supposed to have been infatuated with the man, but I never loved him, nor thought I did. No, I did not love him, but I did love the mad transports, the exquisite torment of lust which he, as no other man before or since, had the power to awaken in me. As an addict to the scented dreams of opium, so did I become an addict to Montague Austin. He was to me a fatal drug which held me a willing victim in its embrace.

For the first time, in broaching the subject of a new patron to me, Madame Lafronde manifested a doubt as to the expediency of putting my youth and inexperience to the test which she clearly thought an alliance with Montague Austin would signify.

I had seen the man but once; he was not a regular habituate of Madame Lafronde's house, but her facilities for gathering information were such that within less than twenty-four hours his social position, resources, and such portions of his history as were available on such inquiry were known to her. All the information, excepting that which related to his economic situation, was unfavourable. She summed up her opinion in the one expressive word— rotter. But he had money, and money covers an otherwise inexcusable number of objectionable qualities. Possibly by the exercise of tact and vigilance I could handle him.

As for myself, I was the last person in the world to doubt my own capabilities, so Madame Lafonde finally and with patent misgivings, yielded to my complacent and optimistic self-assurance.

Now let us glance briefly at the man himself.

He was, at the time our paths crossed, thirty-four years of age. The younger son of a titled British aristocrat, he had inherited both money and social position. The social position had been forfeited by dissolute escapades, the money dissipated in part, but enough remained to qualify him still as a rich man. He was married, but according to rumour his profligate ways had brought about an irreconcilable estrangement with his consort.

At first glance one would have marked Montague Austin as an extremely good-looking man. But a less cursory observation would not have failed to disclose signs of a cynical and somewhat cruel character in his darkly handsome face and narrow mouth. A little above average height and signally favoured with regard to other physical characteristics, he was in truth a figure to intrigue feminine imagination.

A feeling of lascivious exhilaration was welling within me as I groomed myself for our first rendezvous. I had lately noticed that the craving for more frequently repeated orgasm was growing on me. It seemed that no matter how often I had it, the longing was never completely satisfied. Even the two or three patrons I had who were sexually potent now left me with the irritated feelings of a woman whose passions have been inflamed and then abandoned in a smoldering state.

It was a little after eleven-thirty. I had slipped out of the parlour, abandoning for the night my role of cigarette girl, and was making my toilette, preparatory to Mr Austin's promised call.

'How nice it would be,' I thought, as I fluffed violet talc over my body, 'if this Austin would suck me French style and then fuck me about three times afterwards.' My nerves tingled at the luscious vision thus evoked and a warm feeling crept through my body. The little scarlet tips of my bubbies swelled up and in the upper part of my cunny I could feel something else getting hard, too.

A few moments after twelve there was a discreet knock at my door and the maid appeared, inquiring whether I was ready to receive Mr Austin. At this moment I was standing before the mirror considering the dress I had tentatively chosen for the occasion, having yielded to an impulse to use one of the short black silk frocks which Daddy Heeley had bought me. Just why it had occurred to me to put on this juvenile costume on the present occasion I could not say; some vague intuition probably, but as it turned out, a fortunate one as far as the effect on my new patron was concerned, though until the arrival of the maid I was still debating, undecided whether to wear it or change to something else more in keeping with the circumstances.

'All right, Maggie,' I answered, 'you may bring him up.'

I tied my short curls back in a cluster with a band of ribbon, sprayed them lightly with my favourite perfume, and was just adding a final touch of powder to my face when footsteps at the door announced the presence of my caller.

The door opened to admit him, closed again, and the steps of the maid receded down the hallway.

Mr Austin paused as he took in the scene which confronted him, then his face lit up approvingly.

After a brief exchange of pleasantries he proved that he was a man who went promptly and without any unnecessary circumlocutions after whatever he wanted. With just the same directness as that employed to overcome Madame Lafronde's reluctance, he proceeded to take immediate advantage of the opportunity which was now his.

Abruptly he gathered me up in his arms and carried me to the bed. Seating himself on the edge he bent over me and his hand began to rummage under my clothing. With just the proper simulation of embarrassment I offered to undress

'Not yet,' he answered, 'you're too pretty a picture just as you are.' But a moment later his questing hand encountered panties which, if not exactly finger-proof, were at least something of an obstacle to easy exploration. He fumbled with them for a moment, then flipped my dress up and on his own initiative set about to unfasten and remove the panties.

I laughed nervously as he pulled them down over my legs. Already I was on fire. My sensibilities were reacting to the brutally frank sexual influence which the man exerted, and covertly I glanced toward his lap. The cloth down the inside of one of his trouser legs was distended over an elongated swelling. It looked enormous. As though drawn by some inner force I placed my hand upon it. It throbbed to my touch and I squeezed it through the clothing which concealed it.

Whether the thoughts that occupied my mind while I had been preparing for his visit were due to a premonition or mere coincidence I cannot say, but the wish I had expressed in thought was converted into a reality.

My dress was up, my cambric panties had been pulled down over my legs and cast aside.

Monty, on the side of the bed, leaning over my knees and supporting his weight on a hand which rested on the bed between my open legs had caught his first glimpse of my naked cunny. His eyes glistened and a faint flush crept over his cheeks. With one sudden movement his face was between my thighs and his mouth nuzzling my cunny. A warm, soft tongue penetrated it, tapping, touching, caressing, and then moved upward. The hot glow of the caress thrilled my senses and I relaxed in languorous abandon to the delicious ravishment.

His lips clenched my clitoris; it pulsed in response to the tugging incitation so vigorously that I was obliged to draw away to avoid orgasm then and there. I was torn between two impulses; I wanted to let it 'come' and at the same time I wanted the delightful ecstasy to last as long as possible.

The problem was not resolved by me, however, but by Monty, who raised up, ripped his trousers open and sprang upon the bed between my trembling legs.

Hard, rigid and hot I could feel it in there, distending my flesh to the limit of endurance, inspiring me with a wild desire to work on it rapidly, violently, until it poured out the balm which the fever within me craved. For an interval he remained poised above me, motionless, looking down into my face. His body did not move but within me I could feel the muscular contractions of the turgid thing which penetrated me. They followed each other with regular precision and each time I perceived that tantalizing twitch my ovaries threatened to release their own flood of pleasure tears.

'Oh!' I moaned finally and, unable to resist the urge, moved my hips in pleading incitation. 'You've got me in such a state! Please do something!'

'All right! Come on!'

And in a second that rigid shaft was plunging in and out in a mad dance of lust.

'Oh! Oh! Oh!' I gasped, and as though incited by my fervour, the turgid arm drove home in shorter, harder strokes.

Higher and higher mounted the swirling tides, lifting me upon their crest, no longer resisting, but an eager, willing sacrifice, panting to yield up the store of passion with which I was surcharged.

I perceived the approach of the crisis, that delicious prelude in which one trembles on the brink of ecstasy, in which the senses seem to hesitate for one sweet moment before the breathless plunge.

And in that critical moment the throbbing weapon which was working such havoc within my body suddenly ceased its movement and was held in rigid inactivity.

Above me I saw a face which smiled sardonically down into mine and vaguely I comprehended that he had stopped his movements with the deliberate intention of forestalling my orgasm in the last moment. But he had stopped too late, the tide had risen too high to recede and with but a

106

momentary hesitation, it swept onward and carried me, gasping, writhing and swooning in its embrace.

When the languid spell which always overcomes me after a hard orgasm had passed, I found him still crouched above me and his cock, as stiff and rigid as it had been at first, still inside me.

'Why did you stop just as I was coming?' I complained weakly. 'You nearly made it go back on me!'

'That's what I was trying to do,' he replied cynically, 'but you put it over anyway. You know the old saying, baby, you can't eat your cake and have it, too. I like to enjoy the cake awhile before eating it.'

'That's all very well,' I rejoined, 'but when there's plenty more cake in the pantry, there's no use being stingy with it.'

'So!' he said, smiling, 'there's plenty more in the pantry, is there? I'm glad to hear it. But tell me this, does the second piece ever taste as good as the first?'

'And how!' I exclaimed fervently. 'The second piece tastes better than the first, and the third better than the second. The more I eat, the better I like it!'

He burst into laughter.

'You sound like you really mean it. I'd imagine that after a few months in a place like this you'd be so fed up on cake it would almost choke you. You're a cute youngster. You're wasting your talents here. What's the story? Innocence and inexperience taken advantage of by some bounder, I suppose?' he added quizically.

'I'm here for two reasons,' I answered calmly. 'The first one is to earn money and the second one is because I like to do what I have to do to earn it.'

'Well, bless my soul!' he gasped. 'What refreshing frankness! And you really weren't seduced by a villain?'

'Seduced, nothing! I was the one that did the seducing.'

'Good for you! You're a girl after my own heart! You and I are going to get along famously, Tessie!'

'Not Tessie . . . Jessie!'

'Ah, yes; Jessie. Pardon me. Well, since you really like cake, how about another piece?'

'I'm ready whenever you are!'

'What do you say we get undressed, and really make a night of it? I didn't expect to stay all night, but I've changed my mind.'

'That suits me, Mr Austin. I'm yours . . . till tomorrow do us part!'

'Not Mr Austin . . . Monty, if you please.'

'All right . . . Monty!' I repeated, giggling.

Whereupon we untangled our respective anatomies, scrambled off the bed, and proceeded to disrobe.

That is, Monty stripped, but when I had got down to my hose and slippers he suggested that I retain these last articles of apparel for the moment. Odd, I thought, how so many men who get pleasure from the sight of a girl's otherwise naked body were so alike in preferring that she keep on the hose and slippers, and I murmured something to this effect to my new playmate.

'Very easily explained, my dear little girl,' he replied. 'Complete nudity may be as suggestive of cold chastity as obscenity, whereas, nudity supplemented by a pretty pair of silkclad legs and neat slippers is the perfectly balanced picture of aesthetic lewdness.'

'But suppose one's legs and feet are pretty enough to look good without stockings? Everybody says I have pretty legs!'

'It's not a question of beauty, but of eroticism. I'll make a clearer illustration. Suppose we take two girls, each equally pretty. One of them stands before us entirely naked. The other is dressed, but she raises her dress and holds it up so we can see her pussy. Which of the two is the most exciting sexually?'

'The one holding up her dress,' I answered without hesitation.

'Right. And that's the answer to your question. You look naughtier with your hose and slippers than you would completely nude.'

My attention was now distracted from the matter of my own nudity to that of my companion. His body was well formed and in admirable athletic trim. Smooth, round muscles rippled under the clear white skin, a pleasing contrast indeed to some of my other paunchy, flabby patrons. But most impressive of all was the rigid weapon which, during the conversation and undressing, continued to maintain its virile integrity, standing out straight and proud from his middle. I glanced at it admiringly.

'How did you ever get that big thing into me without hurting me?' I commented, as I considered its formidable proportions.

'It carries its own anaesthetic, baby.'

'It looks strong enough to hold me up without bending.'

'Baby, it's invincible. I could put you on it and whirl you around like a pinwheel.'

'I'll take the starch out of it and make it melt down fast enough.'

'That's a big order. You may lose a lot of starch yourself trying.'

'Ha!' I scoffed. 'I wager it will be curled up fast asleep in an hour's time.'

A prediction which, as things transpired, turned out to be about one hundred percent wrong.

I returned to the bed and Monty, followed me, placed himself on his knees between my outstretched legs. Gripping the cheeks of my bottom in his strong hands as he sank down upon me, he pushed home the lethal shaft.

Our previous encounter had hardly more than whetted my appetite, so, as soon as I felt his cock well inside, I raised my legs, hooked them over his back, and without loss of time began to work against him. Apparently satisfied with my initiative, he remained still and let me proceed unhindered.

Grinding my loins against him I could feel his pubic hair compressed against my cunny. Moving my bottom from side to side, then shifting into undulating, circular movements, I sought to capture a second instalment of the cloying sweetness with which Mother Nature rewards the efforts of those who labour diligently in her garden.

The first warning of the approaching crisis was manifested by the muscular quivering of my thighs, and Monty, still squeezing the cheeks of my bottom, commenced to raise and lower himself upon me with slow, deliberate thrusts. Now the length of the hot thing was entirely buried within me, distending my flesh to the utmost; I could feel it pressing my womb. Now, it was coming out, slowly, slowly, out until naught but the tip lay cuddled against the quivering lips of my cunny.

A pause, a teasing agony of expectation, and it was going in again, in, in, until the crisp hair at the base was again pressed against my clitoris. Orgasm was creeping upon me, I could feel it coming, and in a frenzy of impatience, I launched my hips upward to meet the thrusts, but, instead of continuing its trajectory, it remained poised midway in its course. My orgasm was trembling in the balance. In desperation I brought it to its fulfillment with a supreme effort and fell back, half fainting.

'What is that, Mister, a system?' I panted when I could speak. 'You played that same trick on me the other time!'

An hour later the suspicion was beginning to dawn on me that, in the realms of erotic prowess, I had met my master. Two hours later, I knew it for a certainty. I had experienced nearly a dozen orgasms while my partner's cock was still stiff and rigid as it had been at the start. On each occasion he had succeeded in making me have an ejaculation without himself rendering any accounting to Nature. It lacked but a few minutes to three.

'You look a bit fagged, baby,' he said smiling quizzically. 'Think you can stand one more piece of cake?'

'Yes!' I replied valiantly, although in truth I was beginning to feel like a squeezed-out sponge. For once in my life I had about had my fill.

This time he rolled me over on my side and with his stomach against my back and his legs pressed against mine, he put it into me from behind, spoon fashion.

I thought to turn the tables on him and, by lying perfectly still, oblige him to work himself into spending heat. But it was unnecessary. He was done playing with me and went right to work on his own accord. Before long the pressure of his arms tightened about me and tensed my body against the harder plunges as a hot flood was loosed inside me with such force that I could distinguish each separate gush as it flung itself against my womb.

I held rigid for a moment in my determination not to let myself go, but the feel of that hot stuff spurting inside me worked havoc with my intentions and about the time the fourth or fifth jet hit me, the brake slipped and I was off again!

The aftermath of this last orgasm was a feeling of extreme lassitude and I was entirely agreeable when my companion, having apparently no further immediate designs upon my person, suggested that we turn out the light and sleep. I dragged myself from the bed, attended to the customary hygienic requirements, divested myself of my slippers, and hose, put on a silk shift, slipped back into bed beside him, and in probably less than ten minutes was deep in sleep.

I slept profoundly, dreamlessly, but not for long.

Something was pressing against my face, brushing my lips, with an irritating persistence which defied my mechanical, sleep-drugged efforts to shake away. I endeavoured to turn my face on the pillow away from it, and the knowledge that it was imprisoned so I could not turn it gradually crystalized in my mind.

As one coming out of a bad dream tries to dispel the lingering shadows, so did I try to free myself of something which seemed to be oppressing me, weighing me down, hindering my movements. I could not do it, and awoke to complete consciousness with a frightened start.

In the dim light which filtered through the curtains from the street illumination was revealed the fact that my erstwhile sleeping companion was now straddled over me, a knee on either side of my body. His hands were under my head, which he had raised slightly, and against my lips, punching, prodding, trying to effect an entrance, was that invincible cock.

I struggled to raise my arms to push him away, and at the same time tried to twist my head sidewise. I could do neither. My arms were pinioned down by his knees, and his hands prevented me from moving my head. At my movements their pressure tightened, a sinister reminder of my helplessness.

Of course I realized what he was doing. He was trying to fuck me in the mouth, something I had never permitted any man to do.

In prostitution, just as in other circles of life, there are social distinctions. The cocksucker is at the low end of the scale and is looked down upon with considerable scorn by those of her sisters who have not yet descended to this level. If among the entertainers in a high-class bordello one is discovered to be guilty of accommodating patrons with her mouth she not only loses caste but stands convicted of 'unfair' practice which makes it difficult for other girls to compete with her without also resorting to the same procedure.

This does not, of course, apply to those places known as French houses where cocksucking is the accepted practice, or to other places of a low and degenerate character wherein nothing is too debasing to be frowned upon.

These, together with the fact that I was both sleepy and exhausted sexually, were the considerations which inspired my efforts to escape the inverted caress which now threatened me rather than those of a strictly moral nature. The man appealed to me greatly in a physical way; I had reacted to his sexual advances with more passion and enjoyment than I had done before with any other patron. Had he endeavoured earlier in the night to seduce me, with a little gallantry and coaxing, into sucking his cock, I might, under the influence of my exhalted passions, have yielded. But I have always been quick to resent anything smacking of impudence or effrontery and, as I have mentioned, I wanted at that moment but to be permitted to sleep undisturbed.

'I won't do that!' I hissed angrily, as I struggled to free myself from his embraces.

'Oh yes you will, baby!' was the confident and surprising rejoinder.

His legs pressed tighter against my sides, constricting my arms so that I could not move them. He lifted my head higher. The end of his cock, with the foreskin drawn back, was right against my mouth.

'You . . . you . . .' I gasped, inarticulate with rage, as I was forced to clench my teeth to keep out the invader.

'Open your mouth, baby!' he ordered coolly, and gave my head a shake to emphasize his words.

When I comprehended that my wishes were to be ignored and that my efforts to dislodge him were useless, full rage took possession of me. For a moment I was on the point of screaming, but sudden recollection of the penalty exacted of girls who permitted scandals or disturbances to arise in their rooms at night stifled the cry in its inception.

We were expected, and presumed to be qualified, to meet unusual situations and resolve them with tact and discretion. Nocturnal disorders were unpardonable calamities and justified by nothing short of attempted murder.

'Open your mouth, baby!' he repeated, and shook my head again, this time with more force.

'All right!' I hissed, 'you asked for it!'

I opened my mouth. His cock pushed in immediately, and as it did so I sank my teeth into it. The intent was vicious enough, but the tough, resilient flesh resisted any actual laceration. Nevertheless, the pain inflicted by my small, sharp teeth must have been considerable.

He jerked it out of my mouth and simultaneously, withdrawing one of his hands from under my head, he dealt me a stinging blow on the side of the face with his open palm.

'Open your mouth, baby!' he repeated, undaunted, 'and if you bite me again I'll knock you unconscious!'

The tears started to my eyes.

'Damn you . . . !' I choked. 'I'll . . . I'll . . .'

The hands subjecting my head were again holding it in a viselike grip. His thumbs were pressing into my cheeks, against the corners of my mouth, forcing it open.

There was nothing to do but yield or scream such an alarm as would arouse the entire household.

I chose the more discreet course and, though almost suffocated with rage, opened my mouth in surrender to the assault which was being launched upon it. The big, plum-shaped head slipped in, filling the cavity with its throbbing bulk.

For a moment I tried to keep my tongue away from it, but there was no space in which to hide. His cock was so big I had to open my jaws to their widest, and my lips were stretched in a round, tight ring.

Further resistance was futile and anymore biting would bring a swift retaliation. So, still boiling inwardly, I relaxed, and let him go ahead.

A faintly pungent taste filled my mouth; the head of his cock, from which I could not keep my tongue, was wet and slippery. Every few seconds it jerked convulsively, forcing my jaws further apart. Pretty soon he began to move it, a short in and out movement. The foreskin closed over it as it receded, leaving only the tip inside my mouth, allowing me to relax my distended jaws momentarily. As it went in, the foreskin slipped back and the naked head filled my mouth again, forcing my jaws apart.

This went on for several minutes, and all the time he held my head with his hands. His cock seemed to be getting wetter but whether from its own dew or the saliva of my mouth I did not know. I wanted to spit, but he would not release me and I was obliged to swallow the excess moisture.

Finally, with the head just inside my lips, he paused, and after holding it still for a few moments, shook my face and whispered:

'Come on, baby! What's the matter with you? Are you going to suck it, or do I have to get rough again?'

I knew nothing of the exact technique of this business, though of course the very title by which the art was known indicated that sucking was in order. Choking, gulping, I tried to suck as it advanced into my mouth. Taking cognizance of my awkward efforts he paused again, and as though for the first time taking into account the possibility that I was in truth a rank novice, queried:

'What's the matter with you? Haven't you really done this before?'

Mutely, I managed to convey a negative by shaking my head.

'Lord love me!' he ejaculated, and then in slightly apologetic tones, 'I shouldn't have been so rough. I thought you were just stalling, my dear! However, it's something every young girl should know, and I'm glad to have the opportunity to be your teacher. Now listen: don't try to strangle yourself! You can't suck while the whole thing is inside! Wait . . .'

He withdrew it until just the head was encircled by my lips.

'Now suck while it's like that, and run your tongue over it!'

'Well,' I thought in disgusted resignation 'the sooner finished the better,' and submissively I followed his indications. Vigorously, if not enthusiastically, I sucked the big round knob and rolled my tongue over its slippery surface.

'That's the way, baby!' he whispered tensely after a few moments. 'That's great! Now . . . hold everything!'

And while I remained passive, he worked in and out in short, quick thrusts. Thus, alternating from one to the other, sucking one moment, submitting to having it rammed down my throat the next, my first lesson in cock-sucking continued.

I was still filled with resentment, but the first fury of anger had spent itself, and my thoughts were now concentrated on bringing the ordeal to a conclusion as quickly as possible. To this end I now tried to make the caress as exciting and fulminating as I could. I sucked the throbbing glans, curled my tongue around it, licking, sucking, coaxing . . . and the effect upon my companion was soon apparent. He groaned with ecstasy and from time to time jerked away from me so that the sensitive glans receded within the shelter of its elastic covering of flesh.

Perceiving that this manoeuvre was designed to delay an orgasm, I redoubled my efforts and when he again tried to withdraw I followed him by raising my head and with my lips firmly compressed around the neck of the palpitating knob, I sucked and licked without pausing.

The muscles of his thighs and legs, pressing against my sides, were quivering. Suddenly he withdrew his right hand from under my head and twisting sidewise reached behind him, groping with his fingers for my cunny. This was insult added to injury in my estimation and I tried to clench my legs against the invading hand. The effort was useless; he forced it between my legs and with the tips of his fore and index fingers he found my clitoris and began to titillate it.

Now began a new conflict. With every atom of mental influence I could bring to bear I tried to force that little nerve to ignore the incitation, to remain impassive to the friction which was being applied to it, to stay inert and lifeless.

I may as well have tried to stay the tides of the sea in their course. The traitorous, disloyal little thing cared not a whit for my humiliation and refused to heed the mental commands I was hurling at it. Despite the fact that it should have been as sleepy as I had been, it came almost instantly awake, hardened, and stood up stiffly.

He rubbed it in a peculiarly maddening way, a soft, twirling movement with the erected button lightly compressed between the tips of his two fingers. The little thrills began to generate, and communicated themselves to the surrounding area, up into my ovaries, down, seemingly into the very marrow of the bones in my thighs and legs.

Why say more? There was only one possible ending.

When the ultimate capacity of resistance was reached and passed, and in the very moment in which my organism was yielding to the diabolical incitation, my tormentor, waiting apparently for this precise moment, loosened within my mouth a flood of hot sperm. I choked, gurgling and gasping, as part of it gushed down my throat and the rest, escaping my lips, ran in hot, sticky rivulets down the sides of my cheeks, over my chin . . .

No sooner had the torrent subsided than he flung himself from me and lay panting on the bed by my side.

With the viscid stuff still dripping from my lips and its peculiar starchy flavour filling my mouth, I sprang from the bed and fled precipitately to the bathroom. First with water, then with tooth powder and brush and finally with repeated rinsings I endeavoured to purify my mouth.

When this was accomplished I went back into the room, turned on the light, and flung myself into a chair where, for a few moments I sat silently glaring at my tormentor who, with drowzy indifference, contemplated me through half-closed eyes.

'Well,' I said frigidly, breaking the silence. 'Aren't you going to congratulate me on my graduation into the cocksucking class!'

He smiled dryly.

'Forgive me, baby. Word of honour, I'll behave quite properly in the future. Anyway, it wasn't so terrible, was it? Listen, I'll tell you a funny story. There was a young French girl just married and her mother was giving her some confidential advice. "Daughter," she said, "the ultimate object of marriage is to have babies. Without the little dears no home is complete. However, the bearing and rearing of children is a confining task which imposes arduous and continuous obligations. It is my advice to you, daughter, that you do not have any babies during the first two or three years. You will then, in after life, not be deprived of the memories of a few years of happiness and freedom from care to which youth is justly entitled." "Ah, mother dear," answered the blushing maiden, "you need preoccupy yourself no further on that score, I shall never have any babies!" "Never?" gasped the mother, "why do you say that you will never have any babies, darling?" "Oh, mother," answered the girl, hiding her blushing face in the maternal bosom, "I shall never have babies because I simply can't force myself to swallow the horrid stuff! I always have to spit it out!" '

'And, so what?' I asked caustically, refusing to unbend at the ridiculous story.

'Don't you see, ha, ha, ha, don't you get the point? She didn't even know there was any other way of doing it. She thought she had to swallow the stuff to get a baby!'

Despite my efforts to remain haughty, my better humour was returning. I have always been like that, quick to anger, quick to forget. There was something about this man which was irresistible. Even his impudence had a saving grace, an ingenuous, disarming quality. Only the memory of the slap he had given me remained to irritate me. He sat there in bed, smiling, a sheet draped carelessly about him, half-concealing, half-revealing the smooth white muscles of his torso. His hair in its ruffled disorder gave him a boyish aspect, throwing a well-formed white forehead into relief against the background of bluish-black curls.

After all, what harm had really been done? And, I suddenly recalled, had he not earlier in the night given me a most delightful ten minutes by putting his tongue in my cunny? The service he had required of me was no less intimate. I shivered involuntarily at the recollection of the short but delicious episode. The last remnants of my resentment faded away. I began to feel slightly ashamed of myself for having made such a commotion.

'Still peeved at me, baby?' he inquired quizzically.

'No,' I answered, my lips twitching into a smile, 'only it was kind of . . . well, startling to be waked up that way from a sound sleep. I suppose you don't believe me, but I never did that before.'

'Of course I believe you, baby,' he interrupted, 'it was easy to see you hadn't any experience. Honestly, I don't know what came over me. You gave me such a stand tonight it came right back on me after I'd been asleep a short time. I woke up, and lay there looking at your pretty little mouth in the dim light, and the first thing I knew I got into a fierce argument with myself about it.'

'What on earth do you mean, an argument with yourself about my mouth?'

'Well, it was like this. At first I said to myself, it's too small, and then I said, no, it might be a tight fit, but it could be done. And the argument went on, until finally it got so hot it had to be decided definitely one way or the other, and so . . . and so . . .'

'And so I got fucked in the mouth to settle it. Very well, Your Highness, shall we retire now, or is there any other way I can serve you?'

'Well, if it's not putting too much of a strain on your hospitality, I'd greatly appreciate a shot of brandy!'

I rang for the maid. After a long wait, she shuffled to the door half-asleep, took the order, and was back again in five minutes with the liquor. When this was consumed, we turned out the light and again composed ourselves for sleep.

When I finally awoke it was late noon and the echoes of some of these lurid dreams were still reverberating through my brain. I felt wet and sticky between the legs and my clitoris was in erection. When I had got my confused thoughts in order and separated the real from the unreal, I sat up in bed and glanced at my companion.

He was sleeping soundly and quietly on his back, his curly head high on the pillow, lips slightly parted over white even teeth. He had thrown the blankets aside and was covered only by a sheet. I glanced downward over the recumbent form. Halfway down its length the sheet rose sharply, projected upward in the form of a little tent. As I fixed my eyes on this significant pinnaclelike projection, I saw that it was jerking sharply at short intervals.

I lifted the sheet without disturbing him. That indefatigable, tireless cock was standing upright, as firm and rigid as a bar of iron. White and graceful the stout column rose from the profusion of dark and tangled curls at its base, its plum-coloured head half-hidden, half-revealed under its natural envelope of satiny skin.

Still holding the sheet up, I looked at his face. It was in the peaceful repose of sound sleep. I thought of my curious dreams and wondered if he too was experiencing rare delights with some nebulous shadowland houri; maybe, even he was dreaming of me!

The thought set me aquiver. Softly I drew the sheet aside. I extended my hand, my fingers closed cautiously around the pulsing column. For a moment I was content to hold it thus, then, watching his face carefully for signs of

119

awakening, I moved my hand up and down, slowly, gently, so that the silken foreskin closed over the scarlet head and then, receding downward, revealed it in its stark-nakedness.

Twice, thrice, I moved it so, pausing after each movement to see whether it was going to awaken him. At the fourth and fifth movement he stirred uneasily, murmuring some incoherent word. I waited, motionless, until his even breathing assured me that he was still deep in slumber, and began again.

'When he wakes up,' I thought, 'I'll make him tell me what he was dreaming about that made his thing hard this way.'

My wrist slid downward, the white elastic skin descended, and again the scarlet head protruded nakedly. As I paused, holding it in this position, I saw a round, glistening drop of limpid transparency emerged slowly from the orifice at the tip.

As I observed this natural reaction to my manipulations a wave of lewdness swept over me, and in an instant I was in a state of passion bordering on nymphomania, dominated by but one thought, one driving desire, and that was to feel the rigid, pulsating thing plunging in my mouth, to suck it and lick it until the spurting essence brought relief to the frenzy which now possessed me.

I literally flung myself upon it, indifferent now as to whether he was awake or asleep, and engulfed the ruby head within the circle of my lips. In a regular fury of lust I sucked and licked and bobbed my head up and down to approximate the motions of ordinary fucking.

Of course, this violent disturbance aroused my companion instantly, but I was too engrossed in my own passion to be hardly more than aware that he was sitting up in bed, and that his hands were clasping my face as though to guide the movements of my bobbing head.

Indifferent to all else I sought to force the living fountain between my lips to pour out its elixir as quickly as possible. Instinctively I knew that when it spurted forth, my own organism would yield in harmony. It was trembling now in that delicious borderland of anticipation, and needed but the final inspiration to precipitate its own shower of lust.

Between my thrusting, encircled lips the muscular flesh seemed suddenly to grow more taut. It held so for a second, and then with mighty convulsions poured out its tribute, wave on wave of hot, pungent ambrosia. Gasping, choking with the deluge which threatened to strangle me, I writhed in the ecstasies of orgasm which came upon me in the same moment.

The reaction to this furious excess was a spell of enervating lassitude. As I came out of it and my chaotic thought took on a semblance of order, I was filled with amazement at the demoniacal frenzy which had taken possession of me. Next came the thought of what had become of the spurting jets that indomitable geyser had poured out. The odd, pungent taste was still in my mouth, but I recalled that I had almost choked with the quantity that had flooded it. When he had assaulted me the night before I had spat most of it out, though I had been forced to swallow some. I glanced at the bed to see if, unconsciously, I had ejected it. The bed was dry and clean. Seemingly, it had all gone down my throat.

I remembered the absurd story he had told me about the French girl.

'Well,' I observed, 'if it's true a girl can get a baby by swallowing that stuff, I guess I'm going to have one.'

The English Governess

With the month of June the full heat of summer descended on London. The dusty streets, now almost empty, baked in the glare of sunlight, and the air was parched and quivering; in Great Portland Street the few trees supplied only the scantiest shade.

The interior of Mr Lovel's sombre house had become metamorphosed by the clear, searching light which penetrated into corners and recesses; the shadows of winter, which had seemed so native to these large dark rooms, were entirely dispelled; the house, indeed, seemed to have a rather uncomfortable air, as if light and sunshine had really no business in it. Even the schoolroom had taken on a new aspect: the furniture of walnut and old oak had lost its grim and surly character, and the funeral black leather armchair, on which Richard had had so often to kneel, his loins bared to receive the cane or ruler at the hands of his strict governess, had an air of dullness and respectability.

The boy had just passed his sixteenth birthday. During the winter he had grown taller and gained some weight; but it was noticeable that the effeminacy of his appearance had increased also. Moreover, if his figure was still slim, his thighs and loins had taken on a further breadth, an amplitude which was emphasised by the close fit of the Eton jacket and trousers he still wore.

Since Harriet Marwood had definitively adopted the method of corporal punishment to bring him to her idea of perfection,—the end to which she was entirely devoted—scarcely a day had gone by without her having had recourse to the whip. His education in the matter of discipline had indeed progressed remarkably: by now, like any other English boy under the authority of a governess, he had learned to resign all judgment on his conduct to his instructress; and he had learned to suffer the most vigorous flogging without protest. Nor was this all. At least one evening every fortnight, strapped to his bed, he was made to endure the protracted torment of a triple correction with strap, birch and cane. These important occasions, however, were no longer announced to him beforehand by the sagacious Miss Marwood: so that for three or four nights a week the boy could not be sure what her nightly visit portended, the rapture of an evening kiss or the ordeal of a special punishment—and uncertainty which was only resolved, at the last moment, by her appearing either fully clothed and with an affectionate smile on her lips, or in her long hooded cape, bare-armed and with the terrible strap in her hand. Thus, his anticipations and even his emotions of pleasure and pain were confounded in a single framework of exquisite tension.

By such treatment he had been brought to an extraordinary height of sensitivity,— and also, it must be admitted, of sensuality. Living in a state of constant nervous trepidation, at the mercy of all the whims of his instructress, he had come to entertain a highly ambiguous attitude towards her. He feared her and he loved her,—but his love was as yet almost entirely sensual. Her hold on him was through the flesh; and it was maintained and increased by the bestowal of the exact contrary of caresses.

As for Harriet herself, her temperament seemed to find full satisfaction in the imposition of such a regime. Why, or how, we do not know. To bring a beaten and degraded look into a boy's face, to rend self-respect out of him in fear, is a sight not especially relished by the ordinary woman. But Harriet Marwood, whatever she was, was not an ordinary woman.

She had said to him one day, 'Richard, I wish you to be in my hands *perinde ac cadaver*,—"like a dead body." That is the motto of the Jesuit Fathers, and it will be yours, too. And to bring you to that condition, I shall not cease chastising and shaming you in every way. In time, you will

126

be grateful to me . . . for it is only in subjection that a boy such as you are can ever know true happiness.'

He did not understand her words; but he was as if hypnotised by her, and accepted all she did without question. As for even dreaming of complaining to his father, that idea was farther than ever from his intention. Harriet herself had entire confidence in her pupil on this latter point,—but nevertheless she was sometimes uneasy concerning Mr Lovel's own possible perception of what was being done to his son. The man of business rarely set foot in the schoolroom; he saw little of Richard,—but nonetheless he noticed him, and it happened that he found the boy's appearance marked by fatigue and melancholy.

'Upon my word, it's simply extraordinary!' he said to Harriet one day. 'What do you make of it, Miss Marwood? Here is a boy who, from what he tells me, simply adores you. He has you constantly with him, he lacks for nothing, you tell me he sleeps and eats well, and I can see for myself his schoolwork is tremendously improved,—and yet, and yet,—what's the matter with him? Why has he that wretched, moon-struck air? And why is he so sensitive that when I press him about it—as I did only yesterday—he is almost ready to turn on the water-works?'

Harriet remained perfectly calm. 'Richard is a boy of a very delicate nature, sir,' she replied. 'In fact, he is so exquisitely sensitive that even yet the slightest reprimand leaves its mark on him for days. As it happened, you were questioning him just a few minutes after I myself had given him a light rebuke. That is the explanation for his nervousness, which is ready to find its outlet in tears.'

Mr Lovel looked at her in admiration. 'How well you understand him!' exclaimed the worthy man.

And one day, soon after this conversation, Harriet saw fit to further improve her position with her employer.

'It is now midsummer, sir,' she said. 'Living in town, in this heat, is not good for a boy of Richard's age and delicacy of temperament. We ought really to go to the country for a month or two. Did you not tell me, sir, that you had a small property somewhere in the country?'

'In Hampshire? Of course!' exclaimed Mr Lovel. 'In fact, why don't you go down to Christchurch with Richard? That will do him a world of good, upon my word! Exactly, Christchurch. An excellent idea, don't you think?'

Harriet cloaked a smile of triumph. When she broke the news to Richard, he too seemed deeply moved.

'We will go to Christchurch together,' she said. 'Down there, I shall have you under my authority even more firmly than here. I will make you a well trained boy indeed, Richard!' She looked at him affectionately. 'Well, are you glad to be going down to the country with me? To live there with me, just the two of us alone?'

'Yes! Oh yes, Miss!' he breathed.

She took him in her arms and kissed him with such warmth that his head reeled.

Mr Lovel wrote to the old couple whom he employed as caretakers of his house at Christchurch; and in a few days Harriet and her pupil were ready to set out.

She packed the boy's trunk with him; and she also made him carry a parcel containing the ruler and a new rattan: the first cane had long since been worn out, and already at least a half-dozen had succeeded it in turn.

'I think,' said Harriet with a kind of bantering gaiety, 'that we shall be able to find in Christchurch everything necessary to whip you with, but it is better to be on the safe side. I have packed my strap, and I may need the cane as soon as we arrive. On the way down, my voice and hand should be enough to keep you in order . . .'

The trip passed without incident, except that Richard leaned out of the train window and caught a cinder in his eye, and the governess declared, in the presence of two very elegant women in the same compartment, that he was a foolish boy and would be soundly thrashed for his imprudence as soon as they arrived at their destination. This announcement had the immediate effect of gaining the favourable notice of the two ladies who, extremely distant heretofore, at once entered into conversation with Miss Marwood without deigning to acknowledge any further the existence of her companion.

They arrived at Christchurch in the evening. Mr Lovel's house was situated a little beyond the outskirts of the town, in the middle of the country and not far from the Stour, the pretty river which flows into the Avon a short distance further on. The old caretaker was waiting for them at the station; Harriet left him to see to their luggage, and set out at once with her pupil in a hired fly.

As soon as they arrived she summoned Molly, the caretaker's wife, and gave her instructions in her duties. The governess had already planned their life in the country, and she now organised matters accordingly. Molly was to do the housework in the early morning and prepare the breakfast, and neither she nor her husband were to set foot in the house at any other time of the day. The old couple occupied the small lodge at the entrance to the grounds, and thus had no further business in the house itself. A caterer in the town was engaged to bring the meals twice a day; Harriet would simply plan the menu and leave her instructions. In this way she and Richard would be always alone and undisturbed.

While waiting for their luggage to arrive, the governess and pupil went on a tour of inspection of their new home, as pleased with it as if they were a newly wedded couple.

The house, standing in the midst of heavily wooded grounds encircled by a high brick wall, enjoyed the greatest seclusion and privacy. At the end of the garden the wall was pierced by a small door which led to the park itself, a pretty stretch of woods made up mainly of oak, ash and birch. From the lawn behind the house, where she was standing with Richard looking at the trees, Harriet observed the white satiny trunks of the birch-trees, and pointed them out to her pupil.

'See,' she said, with a little laugh in her throat, putting her arm around him, 'at least we shall not lack for rods!'

He sighed: it might have been a sigh of trepidation or of pleasure. He was still suffering from the cinder which had lodged in his eye, and he had not forgotten the promise which Harriet had given him in the train.

After the trunks had arrived, and under Harriet's superintendence, the clothes had been unfolded, shaken out and hung up; and the linen unpacked and laid out in the drawers, there was still a good half-hour before dinner.

'Now let us look at that eye of yours,' said Harriet, drawing Richard to the window of her own room.

She explored the under side of the eyelid, and after patient effort succeeded in removing the unlucky cinder; when this was accomplished, she bathed the eye carefully, and then, having dried his cheek with her own handkerchief, she murmured with a smile, 'But after all, I might have saved myself the trouble of bathing your eyes, since you will be shedding tears in a few minutes . . .'

He raised to her a glance full of anguish and appeal.

'Have you forgotten what I promised you in the train?' she said pleasantly. 'Your imprudence deserves a sound whipping, and naturally you are going to get one.' She looked around her thoughtfully. The cane and ruler were already unpacked and lying on the massive mahogany table placed in the middle of the comfortable old-fashioned room. 'Unless you are fastened to my bed,' she resumed, 'I can hardly see how to place you so I can whip you properly . . . No, wait: you will lean over this table and hold on to the far edge with your hands. That is the best way.'

He obeyed, whimpering; but when he was standing in front of the table, stripped to his shirt, he looked at Harriet pleadingly. 'Miss, please! I've never travelled on a train before . . . I didn't know—'

'That is doubtless an extenuating circumstance,' she replied. 'But simple common sense should have told you one does not lean out of railway coaches . . . Bend over at once, sir.—Very good. Now reach out and hold on to this edge. Excellent!' She stepped back and surveyed him with satisfaction. 'Suppose, Richard, that at the moment you put your head out, the train was entering a tunnel! You would have been decapitated, my boy,—just like that. The correction I am going to give you may serve to put a little sense in your head for the future. It seems indeed, Richard, that the whip is the only language you understand . . .'

During this brief lecture she had raised his shirt above his shoulders, and emphasised her remarks with a few ringing slaps which made his flesh shake and quiver. Then, picking up the cane, she proceeded to flog him vigorously for almost five minutes. He wept and writhed, but took good care not to release his hold on the table.

'Very well Richard,' she said at last, laying down the cane. 'You may get up now. And now come here and kiss me, and promise to be more sensible in future.'

His face still bathed in tears, he kissed her smiling mouth as she had ordered, feeling the same disturbance he always felt in bestowing this salute,—this kiss which was, in fact, designed at once as a stimulus to his adolescent sensuality and as a last refinement of humiliation.

His rooms adjoined hers, and Harriet took care that the door between them should remain open at night.

One evening, a few days after their arrival, she said to him, 'I hear you stirring in your bed a good deal, Richard. You toss and turn and fidget. Are you sure you are behaving yourself?'

He was taken aback, feeling a sensation of uneasiness and a certain shameful alarm. 'Oh yes, Miss,' he stammered at last.

'But you are a long time getting to sleep, are you not?'

He mumbled an inaudible reply.

'This evening you will come and read to me in bed. That will leave you tired and able to fall asleep sooner.

That night, after they had said prayers in her room, she put a novel of Mrs Sherwood's into his hands. 'I am going to bed now,' she said. 'You will remain here while I get ready, and then you will read to me.'

'Yes, Miss,' he murmured. He was obviously carried to the height of excitement by the prospect.

Harriet looked at him impassively, hiding the pleasure she took in his nervous disturbance. 'Leave your book on the table for the present,' she said, 'while you help me undress. Come here and unlace my shoes, please.' She sat down on the edge of her bed, drew her skirt up and crossed her legs.

Richard watched her in a kind of stupour.

'Well?' she said. 'Have you turned to stone? Down on your knees with you, and undo my shoes.'

He obeyed, and began to unfasten the laces from the highly arched foot which, encased in its high-heeled shoe of supple fawn-coloured leather, was swinging under his nose. He noticed the slenderness of her ankle; he saw her leg also, in its fine, transparent silk stocking, the lace of her drawers, the hem of a white petticoat. His hands trembled as he untied the shoelaces. When he drew off the shoe itself, his excitement was such that he let it fall on her other foot.

'Clumsy!' said Harriet, leaning over and slapping his face smartly. 'Pay attention how you take off the other, if you please.'

The warm, intimate odour of her unshod feet put his senses in a fever. He rose from his knees, trembling slightly.

'You would make a poor lady's maid,' smiled Harriet, standing up. 'Go and sit down over there, and wait until I am in bed.'

Calmly she began to undress, letting fall first her skirt, then her petticoat; she removed her bodice, and then, standing in corset and drawers, she let down her beautiful hair, shaking it out to its full length so that it fell in a thick wavy mass covering her croup whose firm outline appeared through the fine linen of her drawers; then she divided her tresses and swiftly plaited them in two long braids. When this was done she removed her corset, drawers and stockings, and stood in front of Richard in her shift. His eyes did not leave her for an instant.

'Bring me my slippers,' she said. 'You will find them over there by the window.'

He brought them from their place and laid them in front of her; but she stretched out her naked foot.

'Put them on,' she ordered.

He would gladly have kissed these exquisite white feet with their pink nails, but he did not dare. He fitted the slippers onto them, and then stood up.

Harriet stepped to the closet from which she took a long silk nightdress, and then deliberately let her shift, which was held only by two straps passing over her beautiful bare shoulders, fall to the carpet.

She had taken no precaution to shield herself from the boy's gaze. But he, despite the desire he had to see her, had not dared keep his eyes on her until the very end . . . It was only when she turned back towards the bed, clad from neck to heels in the long ribboned gown and holding her shift in her hand, that he realised that for a few moments she had been entirely nude in his presence. At the thought, his face suddenly glowed a deep red,—as if the display, far from having been accomplished by slow gradations, had been made all at once.

She laid the filmy garment, still warm and impregnated with the odour of her magnificent body, on the back of the armchair where he was sitting, and went into the bathroom.

No sooner had she left than he turned round, seized the shift whose light folds were brushing his nape, and plunged his face into it, breathing in with eager and trembling nostrils the subtle and disturbing perfume which clung in the soft linen creases, intoxicating himself almost to madness. All at once he heard a step behind him.

Harriet had re-entered the room quietly. As he saw his governess beside him, erect and severe in her long night-dress, her penetrating gaze bent on him, his heart seemed to skip a beat.—She saw me! he thought; and, mixed with his resignation to the punishment he knew was coming, he was conscious of a certain pride.

'Richard! What were you doing?'

He did not reply. She took his head between her hands and forced him to look in the face. 'What were you doing?' she repeated. Then she fixed him with a gaze that grew harder and harder. 'Yes,' she said. 'I saw you! You sensual, wicked boy! I have already noticed this side of your nature. I have said nothing, but I have been watching you! Come here, Richard.'

'Miss . . .' he mumbled. He was choking with a peculiar excitement.

Now, for some reason, he did not fear the pain of the approaching correction: he was as if drunk with the sense of his own subjection . . .

Gently, with movements slow and deliberate as those which are part of some ritual, she picked up her shift, folded it once to make a gag of it, and then bound it over his mouth and nose: the filminess of the material did not hinder his breathing,—but every breath was as if it were taken from between her breasts or thighs. Then she bent his body beneath her arm, drew him tightly against her, and raised his shirt; between then there was nothing but the thin silk of her nightdress. Her hand rose, and fell.

At last she drew him to the bed, and sitting down made him kneel between her feet; she leaned over . . . With an impression of ecstasy that was boundless, Richard abandoned himself to the touch of her hands. Never before had she acted thus, never before had he experienced such sensations!—With her head close to his, so that he breathed the heady fragrance of her hair and the perfume of her breath, she was speaking softly in his ear: 'This is how I shall correct your wickedness, Richard . . . Do not mistake this for a caress! This is a punishment, a shameful punishment . . . Whenever I see that you are becoming too fond of me, I shall inflict it on you after I have whipped you well . . . Do you understand, you wicked child!—Now back over my knee with you! I am going to beat you again . . .'

Once more, in the warm, dimly-lit room, was heard the slow, regular cadence of a palm striking flesh: it continued a long time . . .

At last she stopped, sighing deeply; she removed the gag from his face, and then, taking him in her arms, pressed her lips to his in a long, shuddering kiss.

'Try to behave yourself, now!' she said, pushing him away abruptly and slipping between the sheets of her bed. 'Hold your book in your left hand, and put your right hand in mine. Just so, my dear. I wish you to have the constant impression of being in my power, of being in my hand . . .'

He was burning with a fever of the senses, he had no more strength than a two-year-old child. He abandoned his hand to Harriet and began to read.

The reading lasted a long time. In order to turn the pages, he placed his book on the edge of the bed and used his left hand . . .

Harriet was falling asleep. From time to time Richard darted a swift glance at her, seeing her resting quietly, the two heavy braids of hair framing the noble head—the head beautiful as that of a goddess. An even breath raised her creamy half-uncovered breast, and he fought down a wild desire to put his lips to it,—or at least to imprint a kiss on the soft hand which still imprisoned his own and which had struck and caressed him so recently. Then the great grey eyes half opened and were turned on him.

'Close your book now,' she murmured. 'Say goodnight to me, and go to bed like a good boy. And think of what happened to you this evening,—will you not? You will think of it?'

'Yes, Miss,' he whispered.

He bent over her and respired her warm, perfumed breath as their mouths clung together in the evening kiss.

His face a little paler, his cheeks a little hollower than usual, Richard stole into Harriet's empty room. His governess had just gone out, leaving her pupil occupied with some schoolwork which she had set him as a holiday task.

'You will not leave your room while I am gone, Richard,' she had told him. 'If you do, you will be well caned.'

He had obeyed the order, at first: then, despite the warning and the wholesome fear it implanted in him, he had dared to leave his work-table, to open the door, and at last, drawn by his overmastering desire, to enter the bedroom filled with the subtle perfume of the young woman.

His heart was pounding with excitement.—What had she just been doing there? he asked himself. He had no idea, could make no conjecture, but he was seized by an intense nervous disturbance at finding himself alone, for the first time, in this room where she lived, where she slept, this room haunted by the intoxicating fragrance of her clothing, her sachets, her body itself.

He approached the bed, and shivered slightly. On the silk coverlet, beside the pillow, the governess had left a cane whose end was split and beginning to fray.—That cane, he knew it only too well. The previous afternoon he had been whipped with it, as a punishment for his slovenliness in not having replaced a broken shoelace. His flesh was still tender from the effects of this punishment; but the remembered sting of the rattan only intensified the ardour of his desire,—that mysterious and uncertain desire which betrayed itself by an irrational wish to be mastered, scolded, shamed and whipped by his governess, and to touch and breathe the odour of every object belonging to her,—above all, those objects consecrated to her most intimate use.

He picked up the cane with a trembling hand, and pressed his lips to the end which had felt her grip, imagining he could still detect the warmth and scent of the strong hand which had held it. Then, replacing the instrument of his torment, he let his gaze rove around the room. He was uneasy, oppressed, almost stifling, but the desire was stronger than everything else. Trembling in an access of precaution, walking on tiptoe as if he feared to awaken someone in the empty house, he made the circuit of the chamber.

All at once he stopped, riveted to the spot. On a low, straw-bottomed, high-backed chair, whose form recalled that of a *prie-dieu*, a tiny handkerchief of fine batiste was lying, crushed almost flat. In front of the chair stood a pair of high-heeled shoes, from which Harriet had apparently changed before going out.

His throat dry, his heart beating wildly, he bent over and knelt down; he took the handkerchief and carried it to his lips. It exhaled a subtle perfume, the same perfume which he had breathed on that unforgettable evening when his governess had undressed in front of him before going to bed. And this handkerchief was at once crushed and flattened! Immediately he understood that in order to change her shoes Harriet had seated herself on this chair, and therefore—on the handkerchief: the little square of batiste was thus doubly precious to him . . . He kissed it once more, long and passionately, and then hid it under his shirt, against his skin, against his heart.—What delicious hours he would pass that night, he thought, when he could bury his face in it! Already, he was shaken with the thrill of anticipation.

But perhaps even more than the handkerchief, the shoes attracted him. He picked them up, smelled them, covered them with such kisses as a lover would bestow on the body of an adored mistress; he stroked them tenderly, drew back the tongues and tried to kiss the inside, gazed at them with love and reverence and pressed them passionately to his breast. He felt in a confused manner the pointlessness, the madness of these endearments bestowed on inanimate objects,—but then he began to ask himself if they were really so inanimate: he was dimly aware that there resided in this supple leather something more than the idea of the charming foot it had clasped, more than the sweet and intoxicating perfume it gave off, some immaterial essence which he was unable to explain and which, though he did not conceive or clothe the idea in comprehensible terms, was for him the symbol of an exquisite feminine domination . . .

He was about to rise, when a sound behind him chilled him to the marrow. He turned around and saw Harriet.

She was smiling, her thin lips parted in that terrible curve which he knew so well.

As if stricken by paralysis, all the strength fleeing from his body as the blood gushes from an open wound, he could not move for an instant. He tried to rise, but she halted him with a gesture.

'Stay as you are!' she said.

Deliberately, she took off her hat and gloves and laid them on the dressing-table. Then she approached the kneeling boy who, his eyes wide with terror and entreaty, watched her coming towards him without a cry, without a word or a movement.

'You were kissing my shoes, sir!' she said in a low voice. 'Yes, I saw you. You were kissing them . . .' She picked up one of the shoes and, seizing his long hair in her other hand, she rubbed the shoe vigorously against his face, which from being livid swiftly became as red as fire. 'So, you were kissing them!' she cried, her wrath bursting forth. 'So that is what you like, is it? Put your hands behind you! Behind you, I said. There now, kiss it,—kiss it again—you wretched boy! Again—again! Have you had enough of such vileness now?' Her anger suddenly mastered her, and dropping the shoe she slapped his cheek with all the strength of her arm: so hard was the blow that he would have fallen if she had not still held him upright by the hair. Deliberately, she slapped him again.

Her anger was perfectly genuine, evoked by the evidences of a perverted taste which was entirely at variance with her plans.

Released from her grip, Richard crumpled to the thick carpet and lay there prone, his face in his hands, sobbing and gasping weakly.

She regarded him calmly for a few moments; then, with her foot, she turned him over. Little by little, the sensuality of the punished boy was affirming itself now that his fright was receding. Harriet knitted her brows with determination.—I shall have to take further measures, she thought.

'Go to your room, undress yourself, and wait for me there,' she said coldly. 'I am not through with you yet, Richard.'

He obeyed. No sooner had he divested himself of his clothes than Harriet entered his room; she was bearing the leather belt and sleeves she had ordered from the saddler, and her face was stern. 'I did not know we should have occasion for the whipping-harness quite so soon, Richard,' she said quietly. 'Indeed, I had hoped it would not be needed for a long time. But your conduct has shown me that I must take the most extreme measures. You have disappointed me more than I can say . . .'

The note of reproach in her voice affected him even more painfully than the prospect of further chastisement. A great sob of anguish rose in his breast, and falling on his knees before her he burst into tears. 'Oh Miss, Miss,—I'm sorry,' he stammered. 'I—I couldn't help it . . . I'll never do it again! Only please, please don't be angry with me . . .'

'I am no longer angry with you, Richard. I am merely saddened to find such inclinations in you,—and I am, more than ever, resolved to root them out. The whipping you are going to receive will be as much a corrective as a punishment of your wickedness. When it is all over you will be forgiven.—Come, get up and put on your harness!'

Under Harriet's direction he buckled the sleeves on his arms, fastened the belt and attached the strap. 'Very good,' she said. 'Now that you know how to put it on, I shall expect you to do so yourself whenever there is occasion for your wearing it in future.—Turn around now, please . . .'

He obeyed; she drew his arms behind his back, folded them tightly, and snapped the catches into place.

Richard, feeling himself rendered absolutely helpless, experienced a sudden emotion of panic; breaking away sharply, he began to twist and strain against the straps, bending and writhing ineffectually, his face pale, a hunted look in his eyes.

Harriet stood watching his struggles with a detached and impassive air; she well knew the effects of such restraint, and congratulated herself on their success in further breaking her pupil's spirit. For a while she followed his disordered movements without speaking; when they ceased and the boy stood crouched in front of her, panting and tembling, she began to smile.

'Come now, Richard,' she said, 'you see you must resign yourself. There is no use your struggling any longer, you will only tire yourself to no purpose.' She stepped forward and took him by the upper arm, supporting his body which suddenly became weak. 'Lie down on your bed now . . . Very good. I shall leave you now, and I shall not come back until the evening. It is then that we will settle our accounts . . .'

She pulled the coverlet over his trembling body, and drew the heavy curtains; then she turned away without another word and left the room, locking the door behind her.

For Richard, lying helpless in his bed, the hours until evening passed slowly. Outside, the world drowsed through the afternoon of a beautiful English summer day, the sunshine growing ever mellower and more golden as the sun moved lazily across a pure and cloudless heaven, lingering and prolonging itself as if unwilling to leave the quiet country landscape; the hours rang out faintly from the priory church in the town, and they too seemed to be deliberately spacing themselves more and more widely apart, in obedience to some timeless element of the day.

In the darkened bedroom of the house where the pinioned boy lay waiting, time seemed to have stopped altogether. Still tormented by a burning desire for something of which he had no conception, his imagination was tossed between thoughts of punishment and voluptuousness, prospects confused yet complementary, ideas inextricably entangled in a quivering, ambiguous sensibility whose only focus was in the image of the woman whom he loved. Indeed, he was a prey to such closely mingled trepidation and desire that he seemed to be awaiting, in the arrival of his beloved, at once the signal of a martyrdom and an appeasement.—Ah, how many of us, looking back on our own childhood, might not say that we too have been consumed at some time by such a curious amalgam of emotion? And how many would not admit that in such hours of anguished expectation was forged, more strongly than ever, the sensual link which so mysteriously unites the ideas of pleasure and pain?

Harriet herself, perhaps, had known such an experience. Of such a possibility we cannot yet speak with certainty;

but her understanding of the conditions under which the mind is at its most impressionable entitles us to say, at least, that she was a psychologist both profound and practical . . .

Let us look at our heroine for a moment, as she sits alone in the peaceful English garden, awaiting the hour of ordeal.—The far-darting light of the evening sun is touching the dark masses of her hair; a faint breeze stirs the folds of her light, clinging summer dress. Her hands are clasped in her lap, the dark eyelids, fringed with long upsweeping lashes, have half fallen over the lovely grey-violet eyes, her bosom rises and falls tranquilly as she gazes unseeingly towards the rich green woods whose leaves have just begun to curl themselves up at the approach of the summer night . . . A picture, you would say, of all that is sweetest and most ethereal in English womanhood. Ah, but what is it that causes the short, delicate upper lip to curl so charmingly? What thoughts are passing behind that pure brow? *Lector, nec scire fas est omnia!*

She had entered the room so quietly that he had not even heard the rustle of her cape. The cool, pleasant voice startled him.

'Get up, Richard.'

He struggled off the bed and stood before her; he saw the leather martinet doubled in her hand.

'No,' she said, as if reading his thoughts, 'you will not have the strap tonight. But do not congratulate yourself too soon, my dear. I am sparing you a strapping only so that you may make a long and thorough acquaintance with this new martinet.' She smiled, and shook out the heavy leather lashes in her hand. 'I think you will find that it is an instrument quite able to command your respect . . .'

Richard gazed at her and shivered. More even than her anger, he had learned to dread this pleasant, almost quizzical air; she was never, he knew, more merciless than when in such a mood. As the beautiful bare arm swung the lashes through the air again with a soft, hissing sound, the

141

muscles of his loins and thighs contracted spasmodically.

'Bend over, Richard.'

He obeyed, hardly able to control the shaking of his knees as she stepped behind him.

The first blow drew a scream from him. The rounded, tapering thongs had seemed to cut into his flesh like hot blades.

'Oh . . . Miss! Please—I can't—I can't bear it!'

Harriet laughed indulgently. 'Ah, you will have to bear it, Richard . . . You have brought this punishment on yourself, you know.' The martinet lashed him again, drawing another wild scream. 'It stings, does it not?' she said quietly. 'It has a different sting, I dare say, than the sting of your wretched desires. Keep telling yourself that this good whip is driving out those evil inclinations, and be thankful for its virtue . . . Straighten your knees, please! We have just begun.'

Very slowly, very methodically, the correction proceeded.—He is really going to suffer tonight, she told herself, thrilling to the idea of his helplessness and her own power: ah, he will remember this evening for a long time.

Richard was indeed in such an agony as he had never known before. Accustomed heretofore to the keen but superfical smart of strap and cane, he was receiving with a terrified amazement the strokes of an instrument whose bite seemed to penetrate his entire loins, as if the thongs were literally tearing him to pieces. He tried with all his will power to retain his bent position, to keep his knees stiff, to present his loins to his tormentress in the way to which she had so carefully trained him . . . But as the minutes went slowly by he found himself weakening. It was not, he realised desperately, that his resolve was giving away, it was his limbs themselves that were refusing to obey him. He found himself swaying on his feet, his legs bending, his body involuntarily swinging from side to side.

'Richard!' said Harriet in a warning tone. 'You are forgetting your lessons. Do not make me angry with you, or you will regret it.'

'I—I can't help it,' he gasped, straightening up and

142

turning to her piteously. 'I'm trying, Miss . . .'

'You must try a little harder then,' she said. 'Bend over properly now, keep your knees straight, and let us have no more of this foolishness.—Your knees, sir, I said! Your knees!' She lashed him smartly in the tender hollows of his knees,—and with a sharp scream he straightened his legs convulsively. 'That is better,' she said. 'You will find it wiser to do as you are told. Have you not yet learned that?'

She resumed the task of discipline with an appearance of calm. But by now she was deeply stirred: the blood had mounted to her head, her mouth was dry, her breath was coming faster. With her left hand she drew the folds of her cape tightly around her hips, feeling the contact of the material against her bare flesh, stiffening her spine as if she were offering her own magnificent loins to some imaginary flagellant. She began to wield the lashes more swiftly.

But Richard had now reached the limit of his endurance. Absolutely motionless for the past five minutes, his knees locked, gritting his teeth, he had managed to maintain the required attitude. When his strength deserted him, it did so suddenly: almost before he was aware of if he found himself falling limply to the floor.

Harriet, as if balked at the last moment of some wished-for goal, gave an exclamation of rage. 'Get up!' she cried.

He struggled to his knees; but with his arms strapped behind him he found he could get no further. And then, suddenly invaded by an immense and overpowering weakness, he crumpled to the floor once again, sobbing with pain and exhaustion.

'So, you will not obey me?' said Harriet, her voice almost stifled with suppressed fury. 'So much the worse for you!'

She pulled the hood over her head; Richard, seeing the ominous gesture, gave a shriek of terror and closed his eyes. The next moment he felt the leather lashes cutting into him where he lay . . .

For the next minute the governess seemed possessed by a demon. Stooped over her pupil's writhing body, she plied the martinet with all her strength, bringing it down on

143

whatever portion of his flesh presented itself; secure in the knowledge that the harness protected her victim from any injury, she was able to forget everything but her own crescendo of emotion. Under the savage blows the boy rolled and twisted helplessly on the carpet, his whole body doubling and straightening, his legs beating the floor, his pain and terror released in sounds like the insensate howling of an animal . . . Then all at once the tall caped figure drew away from him; the martinet dropped from a nerveless hand; the whole superb body, swaying and supporting itself against a heavy armchair, began to tremble, as long shudders passed through it from head to foot. A great breath, half sob, half groan, burst from her breast,—and prolonged itself slowly into a profound and quivering sigh. She dropped into the chair, her hands pressed to her bosom, and remained there for a full half-minute, breathing deeply.

Through the half darkness of the room, as if from far away, Richard's voice sounded, faint and almost strangled with sobs. 'Miss . . . Oh Miss—is it all over—now?'

'Yes,' said Harriet softly. 'It is all over, Richard.'

She rose and bent over him, unfastening his arms. 'Get up now and come over here,' she said.

With the release of his limbs, and hearing Harriet's tone of tenderness, he felt his fear passing away like a black cloud before a fresh and healing breeze. But more than this, added to his relief like some priceless pendant, he had heard a new note in his governess' voice, something carrying a different message than any ever before conveyed to him, a vibration in which he sensed the expression of a love deeper than any she had hitherto avowed, and with which was mingled the suggestion of some mysterious acknowledgement, of some gratitude . . . As she drew him gently onto her lap, he laid his head against her shoulder, and then, raising his lips to her ear, whispered through the folds of the little hood which still confined her hair, 'Oh Miss, Miss. I love you, I love you . . .'

Harriet tightened the embrace of her arm around the naked boy; in the darkness, her own lips, so recently curled and drawn back in all the ferocity of her ardour, trembled slightly. 'Yes,' she said, in a voice which she strove to render calm.

'I am afraid you care for me only too much, and in a way which I must condemn . . .' She felt the sudden throb which answered the pressure of her hand. 'Richard,' she said in a tone of warning.

He was seized by an uncontrollable trembling, filled once more with that mingled emotion of terror and desire; but it was the latter, now, that dwarfed the former into nothingness. 'Oh Miss,' he whispered, 'I can't help it . . . Please, please don't be angry with me!'

Harriet drew a deep breath; but when she spoke her tone was calm and even. 'Get up now, take off your harness and go to bed,' she said.

She remained seated while she obeyed. The room was now almost dark; outside, the moon had risen above the treetops and was penetrating faintly through the curtains.

Lying on his back, the coverlet pulled up to his chin, Richard watched the tall, silent figure in the chair. Then he saw her rise, and standing erect, draw the hood from her head; he saw the bare arm raised to her throat,—and the next moment, with a splendid movement of the beautiful shoulders, the long cape was slipped off and fell on the chair behind her. Harriet was absolutely nude.

She stood for a moment in the centre of the room, presenting to the boy on the bed a vision of such beauty that he was breathless with ecstasy; then she advanced slowly. He could see her face now in the semi-darkness, grave and intent; but he had no eyes for anything but this magnificent body which swam before him like that of some antique deity.

With a deliberate gesture she drew the coverlet aside, and sat down beside him on the bed. Once again, he felt the intoxicating pressure of her hand.

The two nude figures, shadowy and indistinct in the dark bedroom, remained thus for a few instants; a shaft of moonlight, peering through the narrow opening in the curtains, fell on the motionless white bodies, illuminating them like marble, turning them to a statuary group at once tender and pagan, a piece of sculpture in which was symbolised but one more variant of the ineffable aspiration of mankind, but one more aspect of that divine and multiform Eros who can do no wrong . . .

Her hands began to move slowly, slowly, etching on the boy's affections a message never to be forgotten, a sensual memory, a type and pattern of voluptuousness to which he might turn back with longing for the rest of his life, as if it were the indelible imprint of herself . . . She leaned over and joined her parted lips to his, receiving like a viaticum the breath of his young rapture.

Flossie

My intercourse with the tenants of the flat became daily more intimate and more frequent. My love for Flossie grew intensely deep and strong as opportunities increased for observing the rare sweetness and amiability of her character, and the charm which breathed like a spell over everything she said and did. At one moment, so great was her tact and so keen her judgment, I would find myself consulting her on a knotty point with a certainty of getting sound advice; at another the child in her would suddenly break out and she would romp and would play about like the veriest kitten. Then there would be yet another reaction, and without a word of warning, she would become amorous and caressing and seizing upon her favourite plaything, would push it into her mouth and such it in a perfect frenzy of erotic passion. It is hardly necessary to say that these contrasts of mood lent an infinite zest to our liaison and I had almost ceased to long for its more perfect consummation. But one warm June evening, allusion was again made to the subject by Flossie, who repeated her sorrow for the deprivation she declared I must be feeling so greatly.

I assured her that it was not so.

'Well, Jack, if you aren't, *I* am,' she cried. 'And what is more there is someone else who is "considerably likewise" as our old gardener used to say.'

'What *do* you mean, child?'

She darted into the next room and came back almost directly.

'Sit down there and listen to me. In that room, lying asleep on her bed, is the person whom, after you, I love best in the world. There is nothing I wouldn't do for her,

149

and I'm sure you'll believe this when I tell you that I am going to beg you on my knees, to go in there and do to Eva what my promise to her prevents me from letting you do to me. Now, Jack, I know you love me and you know *dearly* I love you. Nothing can alter *that*. Well, Jack, if you will go into Eva, gamahuche her well and let her gamahuche you (she *adores* it), and then have her thoroughly and in all positions—I shall simply love you a thousand times better than ever.'

'But Flossie, my darling, Eva doesn't—'

'Oh, doesn't she! Wait till you get between her legs, and see! Come along: I'll just put you inside the room and then leave you. She is lying outside her bed for coolness—on her side. Lie down quietly *behind* her. She will be almost sure to think it's me, and perhaps you will hear—something interesting. Quick's the word! Come!'

The sight which met my eyes on entering Eva's bedroom was enough to take one's breath away. She lay on her side, with her face towards the door, stark naked, and fast asleep. I crept noiselessly towards her and gazed upon her glorious nudity in speechless delight. Her dark hair fell in a cloud about her white shoulders. Her fine face was slightly flushed, the full red lips a little parted. Below, the gleaming breasts caught the light from the shaded lamp at her bedside, the pink nipples rising and falling to the time of her quiet breathing. One fair round arm was behind her head, the other lay along the exquisitely turned thigh. The good St Anthony might have been pardoned for owning himself defeated by such a picture!

As is usual with a sleeping person who is being looked at, Eva stirred a little, and her lips opened as if to speak. I moved on tiptoe to the other side of the bed, and stripping myself naked, lay down beside her.

Then, without turning round, a sleepy voice said, 'Ah, Flossie, are you there? What have you done with Jack? (*a pause*). When are you going to lend him to me for a night, Flossie? I wish I'd got him here now, between my legs—betwe-e-e-n m-y-y-y le-egs! Oh dear! how randy I do feel tonight. When I *do* have Jack for a night, Flossie, may

150

I take his prick in my mouth before we do the other thing? Flossie—Floss*ee*—why don't you answer? Little darling! I expect she's tired out, and no wonder! Well, I suppose I'd better put something on me and go to sleep too!'

As she raised herself from the pillow, her hand came in contact with my person.

'Angels and Ministers of Grace defend us! What's this? *You*, Jack! *And you've heard what I've been saying*?'

'I'm afraid I have, Eva.'

'Well, it doesn't matter: I meant it all, and more besides! Now before I do anything else I simply must run in and kiss that darling Floss for sending you to me. It is just like her, and I can't say anything stronger than *that*!'

'Jack,' she said on coming back to the room. 'I warn you that you are going to have a stormy night. In the matter of love, I've gone starving for many months. Tonight I'm fairly roused, and when in that state, I believe I am about the most erotic bed-fellow to be found anywhere. Flossie has given me leave to *say* and do anything and everything to you, and I mean to use the permission for all its worth. Flossie tells me that you are an absolutely perfect gamahucher. Now I adore being gamahuched. Will you do that for me, Jack?'

'My dear girl, I should rather think so!'

'Good! But it is not to be all on one side. I shall gamahuche you, too, and you will have to own that I know something of the art. Another thing you may perhaps like to try is what the French call "*fouterie aux seins*".'

'I know all about it, and if I may insert monsieur Jacques between those magnificent breasts of yours, I shall die of the pleasure.'

'Good again. Now we come to the legitimate drama, from which you and Floss have so nobly abstained. I desire to be thoroughly and comprehensively fucked tonight—sorry to have the use the word, Jack, but it is the only one that expresses my meaning.'

'Don't apologise, dear. Under present circumstances all words are allowable.'

'Glad to hear you say that, because it makes conversation so much easier. Now let me take hold of your prick, and frig it a little, so that I may judge what size it attains in full erection. So! he's a fine boy, and I think he will fit my cunt to a turn. I must kiss his pretty head, it looks so tempting. Ah! delicious! See here Jack, I will lie back with my head on the pillow, and you shall just come and kneel over me and have me in the mouth. Push away gaily, just as if you were fucking me, and when you are going to spend, slip one hand under my neck and drive your prick down my throat, and do not *dare* to withdraw it until I have received all you have to give me. Sit upon my chest first for a minute and let me tickle your prick with the nipples of my breasts. Is that nice? Ah! I knew you would like it! *Now* kneel up to my face, and I will suck you.'

With eagerly pouting lips and clutching fingers, she seized upon my straining yard, and pressed it into her soft mouth. Arrived there, it was saluted by the velvet tongue which twined itself about the nut in a thousand lascivious motions.

Mindful of Eva's instructions, I began to work the instrument as if it was in another place. At once she laid her hands upon my buttocks and regulated the time of my movements, assisting them by a corresponding action of her head. Once, owing to carelessness on my part, her lips lost their hold altogether; with a little cry, she caught my prick in her fingers and in an instant, it was again between her lips and revelling in the adorable pleasure of their sucking.

A moment later and my hands were under her neck, for the signal, and my very soul seemed to be exhaled from me in response to the clinging of her mouth as she felt my prick throb with the passage of love's torment.

After a minute's rest, and a word of gratitude for the transcendent pleasure she had given me, I began a tour of kisses over the enchanting regions which lay between her neck and her knees, ending with a protracted sojourn in the most charming spot of all. As I approached this last, she said:

'Please to begin by passing your tongue slowly round the edges of the lips, then thrust it into the lower part at full length and keep it there working it in and out for a little. Then move it gradually up to the top and when there, press your tongue firmly against my clitoris a minute or so. Next take the clitoris between your lips and suck it *furiously*, bite it gently, and slip the point of your tongue underneath it. When I have spent twice, which I am sure to do in the first three minutes, get up and lie between my legs, drive the whole of your tongue into my mouth, and the whole of your prick into my cunt, and fuck me with all your might and main!'

I could not resist a smile at the naîveté of these circumstantial directions. My amusement was not lost upon Eva, who hastened to explain, by reminding me again that it was 'ages' since she had been touched by a man. 'In gamahuching,' she said 'the *details* are everything. In copulation they are not so important, since the principal things that increase one's enjoyment—such as the quickening of the stroke towards the end by the man, and the knowing exactly how and when to apply the *nipping* action of the cunt by the women—come more or less naturally, especially with practice. But now, Jack, I want to be gamahuched, please.'

'And I'm longing to be at you, dear. Come and kneel astride of me, and let me kiss your cunt without any more delay.'

Eva was pleased to approve of this position and in another moment, I was slipping my tongue into the delicious cavity which opened wider and wider to receive its caresses, and to enable it to plunge further and further into the perfumed depths. My attentions were next turned to the finely developed clitoris which I found to be extraordinarily sensitive. In fact, Eva's own time limit of three minutes had not been reached, when the second effusion escaped her, and a third was easily obtained by a very few more strokes of the tongue. After this, she laid herself upon her back, drew me towards her and, taking hold of my prick, placed it tenderly between her breasts, and pressing them together with her hands, urged me to enjoy myself in this enchanting position. The length and stiffness imparted to my member by the warmth and softness of her breasts delighted her beyond measure, and she implored me to fuck her without any further delay. I was never more ready or better furnished than at that moment, and after she had once more taken my prick into her mouth for a moment, I slipped down to the desired position between her thighs which she had already parted to their uttermost to receive me. In an instant, she had guided the staff of love to the exact spot, and with a heave of her bottom, aided by an answering thrust from me, had buried it to the root within the soft folds of its natural covering.

Eva's description of herself as an erotic bed-fellow had hardly prepared me for the joys I was to experience in her arms. From the moment the nut of my yard touched her womb, she became as one possessed. Her eyes were turned heavenwards, her tongue twined round my own in rapture, her hands played about my body, now clasping my neck, now working feverishly up and down my back, and ever and again, creeping down to her lower parts where her first and second finger would rest compass-shaped upon the two edges of her cunt, pressing themselves upon my prick as it glided in and out and adding still further to the maddening pleasure I was undergoing. Her breath came in short quick gasps, the calves of her legs sometimes lay upon my own but more often were locked over my loins or buttocks, thus enabling her to time to a nicety the strokes of my body, and to respond with accurately judged thrusts from her own splendid bottom. At last a low musical cry came from her parted lips, she strained me to her naked body with redoubled fury and driving the whole length of her tongue into my mouth, she spent long and deliciously, whilst I flooded her clinging cunt with a torrent of unparalleled volume and duration.

'Jack,' she whispered, 'I have never enjoyed anything half so much in my life before. I hope you liked it too?'

'I don't think you can expect anyone to say that he

"liked" fucking *you*, Eva! One might "like" kissing your hand, or helping you on with an opera cloak or some minor pleasure of that sort. But to lie between a pair of legs like yours, cushioned on a pair of breasts like yours, with a tongue like yours down one's throat, and one's prick held in the soft grip of a cunt like yours, is to undergo a series of sensations such as don't come twice in a lifetime.'

Eva's eyes flashed as she gathered me closer in her naked arms and said:

'*Don't* they, though! In this particular instance I am going to see that they come twice *within half an hour!*'

'Well, I've come twice in less than half an hour and—'

'Oh! I know what you are going to say, but we'll soon put that all right.'

A careful examination of the state of affairs was then made by Eva who bent her pretty head for the purpose, kneeling on the bed in a position which enabled me to gaze at my leisure upon all her secret charms.

Her operations meanwhile were causing me exquisite delight. With an indescribable tenderness of action, soft and caressing as that of a young mother tending her sick child, she slipped the fingers of her left hand under my balls while the other hand wandered luxuriously over the surrounding country and finally came to an anchor upon my prick, which not unnaturally began to show signs of returning vigour. Pleased at the patient's improved state of health, she passed her delicious velvet tongue up and down and round and into a standing position! This sudden and satisfactory result of her ministrations so excited her that, without letting go of her prisoner, she cleverly passed one leg over me as I lay, and behold us in the traditional attitude of the *gamahuche a deux*! I now, for the first time, looked upon Eva's cunt in its full beauty, and I gladly devoted a moment to the inspection before plunging my tongue between the rich red lips which seemed to kiss my mouth as it clung in ecstasy to their luscious folds. I may say here that in point of colour, proportion and beauty of outline, Eva Letchford's cunt was the most perfect I had ever seen or gamahuched, though in after years my darling little Flossie's displayed equal faultlessness, and, as being the cunt of my beloved little sweetheart, whom I adored, it was entitled to and received from me a degree of homage never accorded to any other before or since.

The particular part of my person to which Eva was paying attention soon attained in her mouth a size and hardness which did the highest credit to her skill. With my tongue revelling in its enchanted resting-place, and my prick occupying what a house-agent might truthfully describe as 'this most desirable site,' I was personally content to remain as we were, whilst Eva, entirely abandoning herself to her charming occupation, had apparently forgotten the object with which she had originally undertaken it. Fearing therefore lest the clinging mouth and delicately twining tongue should bring about the crisis which Eva had designed should take place elsewhere, I reluctantly took my lips from the clitoris they were enclosing at the moment, and called to its owner to stop.

'But Jack, you're just going to spend!' was the plaintive reply.

'Exactly, dear! And how about the "twice in half an hour".'

'Oh! of course. You were going to fuck me again, weren't you! Well, you'll find Massa Johnson in pretty good trim for the fray,' and she laughingly held up my prick, which was really of enormous dimensions, and plunging it downwards let it rebound with a loud report against my belly.

This appeared to delight her, for she repeated it several times. Each time the elasticity seemed to increase and the force of the recoil to become greater.

'The darling!' she cried, as she kissed the coral head. 'He is going to his own chosen abiding place. Come! Come! Come! blessed, *blessed* prick. Bury yourself in this loving cunt which longs for you; frig yourself deliciously against the lips which wait to kiss you; plunge into the womb which yearns to receive your life-giving seed; pause

156

as you go by to press the clitoris that loves you. Come, divine, adorable prick! Fuck me, fuck me, fuck me! Fuck me long and hard: fuck and spare not!—Jack, you are into me, my cunt clings to your prick, do you feel how it nips you? Push, Jack, further; now your balls are kissing my bottom. That's lovely! Crush my breasts with your chest, *cr-r-r-ush* them, Jack. Now go slowly a moment, and let your prick gently rub my clitoris. So . . . o . . . o . . . Now faster and harder . . . faster still—now your tongue in my mouth, and dig your nails into my bottom. I'm going to spend: fuck, Jack, fuck me, fuck me, fu-u-u-uck me! Heavens! what bliss it is! Ah, you're spending too, bo . . . o . . . o . . . oth together, both toge . . . e . . . e . . . ther. Pour it into me, Jack! Flood me, drown me, fill my womb. God! What rapture. Don't stop. Your prick is still hard and long. Drive it into me—touch my navel. Let me get my hand down to frig you as you go in and out. The sweet prick! He's stiffer than ever. How splendid of him! Fuck me again. Jack. Ah! fuck me till tomorrow, fuck me till I die.'

I fear that this language in the cold form of print may seem more than a little crude. Yet those who have experience of a beautiful and refined woman, abandoning herself in moments of passion to similar freedom of speech, will own the stimulus thus given to the sexual powers. In the present instance its effect, joined to the lascivious touches and never ceasing efforts to arouse and increase desire of this deliciously lustful girl, was to impart an unprecedented stiffness to my member which throbbed almost to bursting within the enclosing cunt and pursued its triumphant career to such lengths, that even the resources of the insatiable Eva gave out at last, and she lay panting in my arms, where soon afterwards she passed into a quiet sleep. Drawing a silken coverlet over her, I rose with great caution, slipped on my clothes, and in five minutes was on my way home.

The Diary of Mata Hari

Paris, 19 . .

In the beginning I liked the milieu I found at Madam
Desiree's place very much; her clients consisted mainly of
members of the middle class. She had, as she proudly
assured me, an exceptionally 'fine' class of customer.
'They are all very well brought up; yes, most of them have
had a good education.

'In my establishment you will not find those Apaches
that scare a lady and trick her out of a few pennies, entirely
aside from the fact that they try to use the material for
free, and not only that, they work it too hard. Whenever
such a man sleeps with a girl, the poor thing can't be used
again for at least twenty-four hours . . .'

These prospects did not deter me in the least, on the
contrary I would enjoy being worked over rather well. But
the greatest attraction for me was being able to 'work' in
Madam Desiree's house with my face hidden behind a
mask. Madam Desiree insisted upon it, because she
realised full well that this little 'trick' had its own special
added attraction. Moreover I worked very cheaply.
Anyhow, the set-up was cheaper than a piquant gown or
real silk stockings. However, she did not object when the
ladies used their own fineries when the overall effect would
be enhanced by them. And after all, she was the one who
made the largest profits from them.

Whenever I arrived I would slip through the entrance of
a small café which was connected with a secret door to
Madam Desiree's house. Drinks and other orders were also
delivered through this door and the Madam of this fairly
reputable, well-managed bordello made a good profit from
them also. Once arrived, I would climb the small and very

161

narrow spiral staircase till I reached my own little apartment on the second floor. It was my very own, tiny little bedroom with an even tinier little toilet. Both rooms were very clean and decorated according to the typical taste which one might expect in these small hidden shrines dedicated to the services of lustful Venus.

The moment I reached my room, I must admit that I quickly and happily divested myself of my clothes, especially my expensive lingerie. I draped a huge shawl, an exquisite piece of Turkish handwork, around my body, the long fringes clinging to my nude thighs. This shawl had the added advantage that it could be draped around my body in a thousand different ways, each one of them enticing, without ever hiding too much . . .

On other days I dressed in a tricot which consisted merely of holes; I mean that my flesh showed through a net whose mazes were almost two centimetres in diameter. Obviously I never forgot to wear a pair of black stockings worked with open lace. This particular costume drew the open admiration of Madam Desiree. 'Oh, Madam,' she was always very free giving us the title Madam unless she suddenly preferred to introduce us as her co-workers, 'you really do your best for my house, but believe you me, and I always tell the other ladies exactly the same, my profits are also yours!'

The most exciting moment, at least for me, was that of the 'selection', namely that particular moment when we were put in touch for the first time with the unknown person visiting this home of carnal pleasures to feast, however shortly, his physical senses. Actually 'putting in touch' is slightly exaggerated; this moment, in which we had to stand in line, forming a parade of more or less nude female bodies, was dedicated to feasting the eyes of the visitor. To look at us was supposed to put the guest in the proper mood; to suggest to me that we were there only for his pleasure . . . all he had to do was take his pick. The only thing he had to do really was to make up his mind which one of us would be his temporary true love.

These minutes of waiting always gave me a pleasant

tickling thrill—it was invariably me who was selected. And it was always my pleasure, because I had the right to look through a secret peephole at the unknown visitor and whenever I agreed to stand in line for the 'selection', it meant that his type would please me as a partner.

The more selection, the greater profit. Madam Desiree knew full well that not only did Paris have many women who were ready and willing to increase their small budgets by 'sacrificing' an occasional afternoon, but that there were many others who also had a small budget which they were more than willing to enlarge, namely the joys of the flesh—and some of them were more than willing to pay her for it.

I have spent many fabulous hours; the charm to be in a place which is dedicated to only one goal, exactly the same one for which the male visitors came to it, was in my opinion worth more than the few thousand franc notes I gave her. Even though I insisted firmly that 'my customers' handed over their money (it would have humiliated me not to be considered a good professional), I was never stingy toward my 'colleagues' or the owner of this for me so invaluable institution.

Ah, whenever the doorbell rang, whenever a happy hubbub of naked bodies ran to and fro to pick up something to cover themselves, then rushed toward the narrow staircase, laughing in anticipation—maybe today there would be a real good piece of ass—tumbling into the reception room to line up in sacred tradition . . . faces expressionless, standing erectly, waiting to be selected—oh, how entertaining this was for me!

And then the more or less excitedly inspecting gentlemen would point out one of us, one who conformed to his particular ideal of eroticism, one who in his mind could give him the delights he secretly hoped for, and with an imperceptible nod of his head he would select the person with whom he intended to have a delightful sexual bout.

As I said, I was most often the one who was selected. I am not trying to brag, but I was considered the queen-bee of our little group and frequently they put me in the most advantageous position. Whenever I had my gentleman it was the turn of the others; this was the established procedure. Madam Desiree never failed to congratulate my latest conquest on his good taste and excellent selection—'The lady is a wonderful companion, but I leave the final decision up to yourself!' she used to say.

I remember one visitor in particular as an exceptionally understanding partner. In the beginning I treated him like all the others; upstairs in my little room I threw my arms around his neck and whispered into his ear: 'Well, we are going to have ourselves a good time, aren't we?'

And I would grope into his pants, trying to open his fly as quickly as possible so that I could have a good look at the most important requisite for the following ceremony.

'What's your name, darling?' I'd ask, the moment I had his rapidly growing hard-on in my hands.

Most of the time they'd murmur just about any kind of a name, but this time my opponent said quite clearly, 'Call me Mimile—my real name is Emile . . . And what's yours?' His question was polite but firm.

'My name is Lolotte, my big darling!' I tried to copy the tone of voice of the true inmates to avoid any possible detection and to prevent my partner from getting the wrong picture.

'But come on, he is so beautifully hard and I'd love to have him in me as soon as possible.' With those words I pulled him toward the bed. We almost fell down upon it; in my enthusiasm I had pulled quite hard on the incredibly stiff instrument. The next moment this strange man, whose strong build had attracted me from the first moment I laid my eyes upon him, lay between my widely spread thighs and I felt his entire weight against my bosom. Since he pushed with all his force against my body, I could not do anything but guide his powerfully swollen prick toward my yawning crotch and let him disappear into it.

The moment this fantastically hot prick discovered its entry, Mimile started to jab and hump furiously, pinning me down on the bed. Since I had one hand free, I grabbed his big balls and started to squeeze them with the same rhythm in which his hard pole was pushing up and down. I completely forgot that these organs are to a man his most sensitive possessions. Mimile seemed completely unperturbed by my counterattack and paid no attention as he doubled the force of his jolts while voluptuously groaning and moaning. It is hardly surprising that his behaviour led me into true ecstasy and the hotly desired climax came much quicker than I had expected . . .

'Oh, you screw splendidly . . . fantastic . . . oh, please, fuck me as wild as you can . . . please, don't hold back darling, quick . . . *quicker* . . . no, really, you are not hurting me . . . *aah*, great—more, please, please . . . more . . . I have to . . . please go on . . . yes, yes, that's it . . . oh, you—now . . . *now* . . . aah . . . *aa-aa-aah!*'

I had made my first number. But Mimile was coming, too, and I felt his hot jism spurt into me at the exact moment that I reached my own climax.

'That's a pity,' he murmured rather dully. 'I came much faster than I had hoped—now it's all over and I just started to like you so well.' And with these words, my partner, who believed the game was over, was about to get up and put on his clothes. But he was mistaken. It was far from me to treat him like a professional trollop would have done and I had only one desire. I wanted to enjoy the pleasure he had given me with his well-proportioned pecker at least once more and, if possible, several times . . .

'Please, stay awhile, Mimile. Do you really want to go? Can't I play around a little bit with your big rod?' I smiled coquettishly at him and could see that he was rather bewildered about my request which is sort of unusual in a public house.

I took a towel and started to dry off his sopping wet love arrow. I noticed that it had lost some of its attractive hardness, but it was still pretty big and I was convinced that with the proper treatment I could make it stand up all over again. My experience told me that this was one of those men who had a considerable power of quick recuperation. And that pleased me enormously since it was the sole reason of my being in a place like this; to find a dong capable of performing something extra special . . .

Even while I was still playing around with the half hard rod, it started to get a new erection and when I suddenly decided to take the whole machine into my mouth it only took a few moments before it was as hard and stiff as it had been when Mimile came into my room a short while ago. It was a fantastic experience to feel how the proud man completely filled my mouth. Even though it was difficult, I succeeded to play around with the heavy knob and lick it with my tongue, causing it to throb excitedly and make Mimile cry out: 'You are driving me wild—come on, let's make another round, I've got to come once more . . . let me . . . I have to lay you . . . you've got a . . . I have to . . . you . . . I've got to put it into your cunt quickly . . .'

There was nothing I wanted more. But the moment Mimile wanted to pin me down again, I rolled away from under him. 'No, not this way . . . wait a moment . . . I want to get fucked from behind!'

I loved this particular position. Besides, I knew that my behind a work of art in itself—firm and round—fired every man whom I honoured this way to his greatest performance. The strength and intensity of the pushes I received in this position had convinced me completely of this.

It is fantastic to stick your behind freely up in the air and take in a prick slowly between your legs. So I pushed myself back and felt his hard lance shove into my hole. Almost immediately Mimile started to hump me thoroughly and the speed was, at least for the beginning, quite satisfactory. Slowly he pushed deeper and deeper into my body and I felt the instrument of my partner filling out my entire womb. Mimile worked without stopping. He banged with renewed vigour against my buttocks and grabbed alternately one or the other of my full, dangling breasts, squeezing them as hard as he could. Our bodies welded together in a beautiful curve; the knees of the man nestled themselves into the back of my knees and his hairy muscular chest pressed against my back. The big mirror next to my bed reflected our picture—I looked at it and was thrilled by what I saw. It never tired me to watch the frolicking of the two bodies working together in the act.

Throughout my life I have always had a weakness for mirrors. And especially whenever the mirror shows me a second couple busy with what is most important and most pleasant: a good screwing . . . Is it not far more pleasant to know that there is another couple busy with the same intimate occupation right next to you? Ah, even the mute couple in the mirror caused extra excitement; if it were only possible to see those parts in action which one feels, but it is so difficult to take a good look when the straining bodies start their voluptuous convulsions.

Mimile was not entirely disinterested in these same impressions; he turned around to look in the mirror at my beautifully rounded backside—and I made it even easier for him by turning slightly sideways—to convince himself optically that I returned every one of his jolts with one of my own.

'Are you very horny, Mimile?' I asked him, so that I could enjoy the pleasures of sound as well as those of touch and sight. 'Do you like my backside—yes? . . . I love to be fucked from behind . . . so very, very much . . . just push a little harder . . . I can stand it . . . ah, that feels good—that feels terribly good . . . ! Just go deeper if you can, Mimile—*auaah . . . aaaah*! You've got to come here more often . . . always . . . ask . . . for . . . me . . . I want to feel your prick—every day—deep-inside me . . .'

Mimile banged with all his force against my ass. 'Just you wait, I'll screw you so hard that you won't know whether you're coming or going . . . you horny bitch . . . you would love to have a prick like mine in you all the time wouldn't you . . . It's all right with me . . . I'm gonna give it to you good, baby . . . you can have it any time you want to as long as you behave yourself . . . I'll fuck you all night . . . I—you—you . . .'

With these words, which had not failed to have their desired effect upon me and which made me enjoy the entire situation even more, the unfortunately independent human

167

nature demanded its due—Mimile squirted his second load into my thirsty innards and pulled out without saying another word.

'But Mimile, please, don't do that . . . I haven't come yet . . .' I protested. 'Come on, quickly, put it back again . . .!'

'Aaaaah, that was fantastic my little Lolotte—dammit, I haven't enjoyed myself so much in quite a long time . . . What? You didn't come . . . ?' Mimile was quite surprised, and at the same time very flattered that the inmate of a 'house' was begging him explicitly to be satisfied once more by him. That had never before happened to him!

'You'll have more chances during the remainder of the night, little one . . . I'm sure you'll come at least once more,' he tried to reasssure me condescendingly.

'That's quite possible, but I want you to screw me, Mimile!' I had not yet given up hope.

'Well, you know I would love to—but look at it, you can see for yourself that I couldn't possibly bring it up!' and he looked down upon his rather droopy instrument with which we had made such beautiful music together.

'Bah, there is nothing wrong with it. It just needs a little extra excitement. Just wait, I have something for the gentleman which is guaranteed to put him in the proper mood again—yes, my dear Mimile, I have a weakness for you!' I really had a fantastic idea.

'I like you very much, too, Lolotte, and as far as I am concerned I'd never say "no", but I am afraid that for tonight . . .'

I did not listen to him. I went to the door, opened it slightly and called, 'Madam, could you please send Vivienne up to my room?'

And when I turned back to Mimile and saw his questioning expression, I explained what I had in mind. 'You will like her, little Vivienne is my younger sister, and her type is the absolute opposite of mine—if that does not excite you my darling . . .'

Mimile perked up his ears. 'Your sister? Really? That's

fantastic . . . and you both work in the same cathouse?'

I noticed that my little improvisation had the desired effect. At the same time Vivienne entered. I liked her best of all my colleagues and the two of us were quite intimate together. She was quite often my partner whenever one of the clients desired to cavort with 'two ladies at the same time', or when two couples had to be formed.

'Vivienne, may I introduced to you Mr Mimile—well, what do you say, dear friend, do you like my little sister, isn't she a real doll?' Unquestionably Vivienne's charms were very enticing; she was of medium size, very soft and she was a blonde, the particular silvery blonde hair which one only finds in the northern parts of France and in Belgium. Her eyes were large and blue like forget-me-nots. Her most visible charms were very pointed, not at all small breasts, which formed a piquant contrast to her otherwise frail figure; they bobbed up and down with every step. She forced them a little bit to do so, but the overall effect was so incredibly charming that one could easily forgive her this little mannerism. Even though she was already nineteen years old, she did not look a day over sixteen and, for this age an incredibly oversized bosom added extra spice which the real connoisseurs in our establishment considered a first-class titbit.

'Well, my dear Mister Mimile, so you are a little lecher, one of those people who can't get their fill with only one woman,' and Vivienne leaned against the big man, who put one arm around each of us, and looked with lustfully burning eyes from Vivienne to me and back. Mimile seemed to be content, but I had only one desire, and that was to speed up the proceedings.

'Take off your chemise Vivienne, and show the gentleman what you can do. I am sure that Mimile will show you in return the full impact of his virility—one favour is worth another,' I urged my little girl friend on. Now the three of us were sitting on the wide bed.

'Listen, Mimile, I will take your little brother into my mouth again and meanwhile you and Vivienne can start to get to know each other a little better; but when I have made

169

him ready then you have to promise me to stick him in me again!' Said and done. The dangling thing already showed signs of getting up again. And, when I took it between my lips and at first very softly, almost superficially, then a little bit stronger and finally truly energetically started to suck on it, his erection began much quicker than I had hoped for. It stood up proud and stiff, with a hardness that promised fulfilment of my wildest desires. I would lie if I were to claim that I did not get pleasure out of trying to drive this huge cock into my gullet; however, I was afraid that Mimile would come too soon again, otherwise I would have played around with it much longer. And I was also very excited to notice the quivers that ran through Mimile's athletic body because of the unexpected pleasures and exciting new tricks that Vivienne played on him—aah, I knew them too, too well. My eyes burned passionately when I looked at those two. She pressed one of her pointed breasts into his face, at the same time Mimile was using one hand to fumble around with her firm buttocks and the other to squeeze her free breast. Then she started, because she knew full well what a greatly desired plaything her big bosom was, to put first one and then the other breast into his mouth, enticing him to suck the full, red and very hard nipples.

At the same moment I let the now hard and throbbing snake slide out of my mouth and decided that now my time had come!

I shoved Vivienne aside and straddled Mimile's big body. I took his big heavy prick in both hands and put it in position upon my crotch. As if he had waited for that signal, the sudden bucking of the man under me caused his magnificent arrow to pierce deeply into my waiting hole.

Vivienne knew exactly what I expected her to do. She threw her full weight upon Mimile's chest, pressing him down upon the bed in such a way that only his loins could move. He obliged with full force because the moistened crotch of Vivienne rested upon his lips and his wildly swinging hands had taken firm hold of my pulsating breasts. The combination of these feelings brought in me a complete frenzy. He no longer pushed against my down-pressing belly but raced up and down as if he were whipped by electrical jolts, quickly and regularly, driving his dong deeper and deeper into my sopping, longing cunt. Vivienne was rubbing her behind across his chest and I could clearly hear the smacking of Mimile's lips as he was trying to crawl around with his tongue in Vivienne's moistened hole. I tried to put off my climax as long as I could, but I was no longer master of my nerves and was unable to dam the flood that ran through me—it kept going on and on, releasing the sweetest feelings which pushed me three, no four times into seventh heaven . . . The other two also were reaching their climax. Vivienne's body stretched momentarily like a steel spring, floated away from Mimile's lips, stayed up in the air for just a second and collapsed, a small frail bundle of weakened flesh, resembling the fainted body of a very young girl. Our mutual partner bucked up high for the last time, releasing an enormous load of jism against my diaphragm and also collapsed. Without moving, the powerful body under me lay there like a dead lump.

This was one of those nights in which I got my money's worth at the house of Madam Desiree . . .

Teleny

Are we not born with a leaden cowl—namely, this Mosaic religion of ours, improved upon by Christ's mystic precepts, and rendered impossible, perfect, by Protestant hypocrisy; for if a man commit adultery with a woman every time he looks at her, did I not commit sodomy with Teleny every time I saw him or even thought of him?

There were moments however when, nature being stronger than prejudice, I should right willingly have given up my soul to perdition—nay, yielded my body to suffer in eternal hell-fire—if in the meanwhile I could have fled somewhere on the confines of this earth, on some lonely island, where in perfect nakedness I could have lived for some years in deadly sin with him, feasting upon his fascinating beauty.

Still I resolved to keep aloof from him, to be his motive power, his guiding spirit, to make of him a great, a famous, artist. As for the fire of lewdness burning within me—well, if I could not extinguish it, I could at least subdue it.

I suffered. My thoughts, night and day, were with him. My brain was always aglow; my blood was overheated; my body ever shivering with excitement. I daily read all the newspapers to see what they said about him; and whenever his name met my eyes the paper shook in my trembling hands. If my mother or anybody else mentioned his name I blushed and then grew pale.

I remember what a shock of pleasure, not unmingled with jealousy, I felt, when for the first time I saw his likeness in a window amongst those of other celebrities. I went and bought it at once, not simply to treasure and dote upon it, but also that other people might not look at it.

—What! you were so very jealous?

—Foolishly so. Unseen and at a distance I used to follow him about, after every concert he played.

Usually he was alone. Once, however, I saw him enter a cab waiting at the back door of the theatre. It had seemed to me as if someone else was within the vehicle—a woman, if I had not been mistaken. I hailed another cab, and followed them. Their carriage stopped at Teleny's house. I at once bade my Jehu do the same.

I saw Teleny alight. As he did so, he offered his hand to a lady, thickly veiled, who tripped out of the carriage and darted into the open doorway. The cab then went off.

I bade my driver wait there the whole night. At dawn the carriage of the evening before came and stopped. My driver looked up. A few minutes afterwards the door was again opened. The lady hurried out, was handed into her carriage by her lover. I followed her, and stopped where she alighted.

A few days afterwards I knew whom she was.

—And who was she?

—A lady of an unblemished reputation with whom Teleny had played some duets.

In the cab, that night, my mind was so intently fixed upon Teleny that my inward self seemed to disintegrate itself from my body and to follow like his own shadow the man I loved. I unconsciously threw myself into a kind of trance and I had a most vivid hallucination, which, strange as it might appears, coincided with all that my friend did and felt.

For instance, as soon as the door was shut behind them, the lady caught Teleny in her arms, and gave him a long kiss. Their embrace would have lasted several seconds more, had Teleny not lost his breath.

You smile; yes, I suppose you yourself are aware how easily people lose their breath in kissing, when the lips do not feel that blissful intoxicating lust in all its intensity. She would have given him another kiss, but Teleny whispered to her: 'Let us go up to my room; there we shall be far safer than here.'

Soon they were in his apartment.

She looked timidly around, and seeing herself in that young man's room alone with him, she blushed and seemed thoroughly ashamed of herself.

'Oh! René,' said she, 'what must you think of me?'

'That you love me dearly,' quoth he, 'do you not?'

'Yes, indeed; not wisely, but too well.'

Thereupon, taking off her wrappers, she rushed up and clasped her lover in her arms, showering her warm kisses on his head, his eyes, his cheeks and then upon his mouth. That mouth I so longed to kiss!

With lips pressed together, she remained for some time inhaling his breath, and—almost frightened at her boldness—she touched his lips with the tip of her tongue. Then, taking courage, soon afterwards she slipped it in his mouth, and then after a while, she thrust it in and out, as if she were enticing him to try the act of nature by it; she was so convulsed with lust by this kiss that she had to clasp herself not to fall, for the blood was rushing to her head, and her knees were almost giving way beneath her. At last, taking his right hand, after squeezing it hesitatingly for a moment, she placed it within her breasts, giving him her nipple to pinch, and as he did so, the pleasure she felt was so great that she was swooning away for joy.

'Oh, Teleny!' said she; 'I can't! I can't any more.'

And she rubbed herself as strongly as she could against him, protruding her middle parts against his.

—And Teleny?

—Well, jealous as I was, I could not help feeling how different his manner was now from the rapturous way with which he had clung to me that evening, when he had taken the bunch of heliotrope from his buttonhole and had put it in mine.

He accepted rather than returned her caresses. Anyhow, she seemed pleased, for she thought him shy.

She was now hanging on him. One of her arms was clasped around his waist, the other one around his neck. Her dainty, tapering bejewelled fingers were playing with his curly hair, and paddling his neck.

He was squeezing her breasts, and, as I said before, slightly fingering her nipples.

She gazed deep into his eyes, and then sighed.

'You do not love me,' at last she said. 'I can see it in your eyes. You are not thinking of me, but of somebody else.'

And it was true. At that moment he was thinking of me—fondly, longingly; and then, as he did so, he got more excited, and he caught her in his arms, and hugged and kissed her with far more eagerness than he had hitherto done—nay, he began to suck her tongue as if it had been mine, and then began to thrust his own into her mouth.

After a few moments of rapture she, this time, stopped to take a breath.

'Yes, I am wrong. You love me. I see it now. You do not despise me because I am here, do you?'

'Ah! if you could only read in my heart, and see how madly I love you, darling!'

And she looked at him with longing, passionate eyes.

'Still you think me light, don't you? I am an adulteress!'

And thereupon she shuddered, and hid her face in her hands.

He looked at her for a moment pitifully, then he took down her hands gently, and kissed her.

'You do not know how I have tried to resist you, but I could not. I am on fire. My blood is no longer blood, but some burning love-philtre. I cannot help myself,' said she, lifting up her head defiantly as if she were facing the whole world, 'here I am, do with me what you like, only tell me that you love me, that you love no other woman but me, swear it.'

'I swear,' said he, languidly, 'that I love no other woman.'

She did not understand the meaning of his words.

'But tell it to me again, say it often, it is so sweet to hear it repeated from the lips of those we dote on,' said she, with passionate eagerness.

'I assure you that I have never cared for any woman so much as I do for you.'

'Cared?' said she, disappointed.

'Loved, I mean.'

'And you can swear it?'

'On the cross if you like,' added he, smiling.

'And you do not think badly of me because I am here? Well, you are the only one for whom I have ever been unfaithful to my husband; though God knows if he be faithful—my husband; God knows if he be faithful to me. Still my love does not atone for my sin, does it?'

Teleny did not give her any answer for an instant, he looked at her with dreamy eyes, then shuddered as if awaking from a trance.

'Sin,' he said, 'is the only thing worth living for.'

She looked at him rather astonished, but then she kissed him again and again and answered: 'Well, yes, you are perhaps right; it is so, the fruit of the forbidden tree was pleasant to the sight, to the taste, and to the smell.'

They sat down on a divan. When they were clasped again in each other's arms he slipped his hand somewhat timidly and almost unwillingly under her skirts.

She caught hold of his hand, and arrested it.

'No, René, I beg of you! Could we not love each other with a Platonic love? Is that not enough?'

'Is it enough for you?' said he, almost superciliously.

She pressed her lips again upon his, and almost relinquished her grasp. The hand went stealthily up along the leg, stopped a moment on the knees, caressing them; but the legs closely pressed together prevented it from slipping between them, and thus reaching the higher storey. It crept slowly up, nevertheless, caressing the thighs through the fine linen underclothing, and thus, by stolen marches, it reached its aim. The hand then slipped between the opening of the drawers, and began to feel the soft skin. She tried to stop him.

'No, no!' said she; 'please don't; you are tickling me.'

He then took courage, and plunged his fingers boldly in the fine curly locks of the fleece that covered all her middle parts.

She continued to hold her thighs tightly closed together,

especially when the naughty fingers began to graze the edge of the moist lips. At that touch, however, her strength gave way; the nerves relaxed, and allowed the tip of a finger to worm its way within the slit—nay, the tiny berry protruded out to welcome it.

After a few moments she breathed more strongly. She encircled his breast with her arms, kissed him, and then hid her head on his shoulder.

'Oh, what a rapture I feel!' she cried. 'What a magnetic fluid you possess to make me feel as I do!'

He did not give her any answer; but, unbuttoning his trousers, he took hold of her dainty little hand. He endeavoured to introduce it within the gap. She tried to resist, but weakly, and as if asking but to yield. She soon gave way, and boldly caught hold of his phallus, now stiff and hard, moving lustily by its own inward strength.

After a few moments of pleasant manipulation, their lips pressed together, he lightly, and almost against her knowledge, pressed her down on the couch, lifted up her legs, pulled up her skirts without for a moment taking his tongue out of her mouth or stopping his tickling of her clitoris already wet with its own tears. Then—sustaining his weight on his elbows—he got his legs between her thighs. That her excitement increased could be visibly seen by the shivering of the lips which he had no need to open as he pressed down upon her, for they parted of themselves to give entrance to the little blind God of Love.

With one thrust he introduced himself within the precincts of Love's temple; with another, the rod was halfway in; with the third, he reached the very bottom of the den of pleasure; for, though she was no longer in the first days of earliest youth, still she had hardly reached her prime, and her flesh was not only firm, but she was so tight that he was fairly clasped and sucked by those pulpy lips; so, after moving up and down a few times, thrusting himself always further, he crushed her down with his full weight; for both his hands were either handling her breasts, or else, having slipped them under her, he was opening her buttocks; and then, lifting her firmly upon him, he thrust a finger in her backside hole, thus wedging her on both sides, making her feel a more intense pleasure by thus sodomising her.

After a few seconds of this little game he began to breathe strongly—to pant. The milky fluid that had for days accumulated itself now rushed out in thick jets, coursing up into her very womb. She, thus flooded, showed her hysteric enjoyment by her screams, her tears, her sighs. Finally, all strength gave way; arms and legs stiffened themselves; she fell lifeless on the couch; whilst he remained stretched over at the risk of giving the Count, her husband, an heir of gipsy blood.

He soon recovered his strength, and rose. She was then recalled to her senses, but only to melt into a flood of tears.

A bumper of champagne brought them both, however, to a less gloomy sense of life. A few partridge sandwiches, some lobster patties, a caviar salad, with a few more glasses of champagne, together with many *marrons glacés*, and a punch made of maraschino, pineapple juice and whisky, drunk out of the same goblet soon finished by dispelling their gloominess.

'Why should we not put ourselves at our ease, my dear?' said he. 'I'll set you the example, shall I?'

'By all means.'

Thereupon Teleny took off his white tie, that stiff and uncomfortable useless appendage invented by fashion only to torture mankind, yclept a shirt collar, then his coat and waistcoat, and he remained only in his shirt and trousers.

'Now, my dear, allow me to act as your maid.'

The beautiful woman at first refused, but yielded after some kisses; and, little by little, nothing was left of all her clothing but an almost transparent *crêpe de Chine* chemise, dark steel-blue silk stockings, and satin slippers.

Teleny covered her bare neck and arms with kisses, pressed his cheeks against the thick, black hair of her armpits, and tickled her as he did so. This little titillation was felt all over her body, and the slit between her legs opened again in such a way that the delicate little clitoris, like a red hawthorn berry, peeped out as if to see what was going on. He held her for a moment crushed against his chest, and his 'merle'—as the Italians call it—flying out of his cage, he thrust it into the opening ready to receive it.

She pushed lustily against him, but he had to keep her up, for her legs were almost giving away, so great was the pleasure she felt. He therefore stretched her down on the panther rug at his feet, without unclasping her.

All sense of shyness was now overcome. He pulled off his clothes, and pressed down with all his strength. She—to receive his instrument far deep in her sheath—clasped him with her legs in such a way that he could hardly move. He was, therefore, only able to rub himself against her; but that was more than enough, for after a few violent shakes of their buttocks, legs pressed, and breasts crushed, the burning liquid which he injected within her body gave her a spasmodic pleasure, and she fell senseless on the panther skin whilst he rolled, motionless, by her side.

Till then I felt that my image had always been present before his eyes, although he was enjoying this handsome woman—so beautiful, for she had hardly yet reached the bloom of ripe womanhood; but now the pleasure she had given him had made him quite forget me. I therefore hated him. For a moment I felt that I should like to be a wild beast—to drive my nails into his flesh, to torture him like a cat does a mouse, and to tear him into pieces.

What right had he to love anybody but myself? Did I love a single being in this world as I loved him? Could I feel pleasure with anyone else?

No, my love was not a maudlin sentimentality, it was the maddening passion that overpowers the body and shatters the brain!

If he could love women, why did he then make love to me, obliging me to love him, making me a contemptible being in my own eyes?

In the paroxysm of my excitement I writhed, I bit my lips till they bled. I dug my nails into my flesh; I cried out with jealousy and shame. I wanted but little to have made me jump out of the cab, and go and ring at the door of his house.

This state of things lasted for a few moments, and then I began to wonder what he was doing, and the fit of hallucination came over me again. I saw him awakening from the slumber into which he had fallen when overpowered by enjoyment.

As he awoke he looked at her. Now I could see her plainly, for I believe that she was only visible to me through his medium.

—But you fell asleep, and dreamt all this whilst you were in the cab, did you not?

—There was, as I told you before, a strong transmission of thoughts between us. This is by no means a remarkable coincidence. You smile and look incredulous; well, follow the doings of the Psychical Society, and this vision will certainly not astonish you any more.

—Well, never mind, go on.

—As Teleny awoke, he looked at his mistress lying on the panther-skin at his side.

She was as sound asleep as anyone would be after a banquet, intoxicated by strong drink; or as a baby, that having sucked its fill, stretches itself glutted by the side of its mother's breast. It was the heavy sleep of lusty life, not the placid stillness of cold death. The blood—like the sap of a young tree in spring—mounted to her parted, pouting lips, through which a warm scented breath escaped at cadenced intervals, emitting that slight murmur which the child hears as he listens in a shell—the sound of slumbering life.

The breasts—as if swollen with milk—stood up, and the nipples erect seemed to be asking for those caresses she was so fond of; over all her body there was a shivering of insatiable desire.

Her thighs were bare, and the thick curly hair that covered her middle parts, as black as jet, was sprinkled over with pearly drops of milky dew.

Such a sight would have awakened an eager, irrepressible desire in Joseph himself, the only chaste Israelite of whom he had ever heard; and yet Teleny, leaning on his elbow, was gazing at her with all the

183

loathsomeness we feel when we look at a kitchen table covered with the offal of the meat, the hashed scraps, the dregs of the wines which have supplied the banquet that has just glutted us.

He looked at her with the scorn which a man has for the woman who has just administered to his pleasure, and who had degraded herself and him. Moreover, as he felt unjust towards her, he hated her, and not himself.

I felt again that he did not love her, but me, though she had made him for a few moments forget met.

She seemed to feel his cold glance upon her, for she shivered, and, thinking she was asleep in bed, she tried to cover herself up; and her hand, fumbling for the sheet, pulled up her chemise, only uncovering herself more by that action. She woke as she did so, and caught Teleny's reproachful glances.

She looked around, frightened. She tried to cover herself as much as she could; and then, entwining one of her arms round the young man's neck—

'Do not look at me like that,' she said. 'Am I so loathsome to you? Oh! I see it. You despise me.' And her eyes filled with tears. 'You are right. Why did I yield? Why did I not resist the love that was torturing me? Alas! it was not you, but I who sought you, who made love to you; and now you feel for me nothing but disgust. Tell me, is it so? You love another woman! No!—tell me you don't!'

'I don't,' said Teleny, earnestly.

'Yes, but swear.'

'I have already sworn before, or at least offered to do so. What is the use of swearing, if you don't believe me?'

Though all lust was gone, Teleny felt a heartfelt pity for that handsome young woman, who, maddened by love for him, had put into jeopardy her whole existence to throw herself into his arms.

Who is the man that is not flattered by the love he inspires in a high-born, wealthy, and handsome young woman, who forgets her marriage to enjoy a few moments' bliss in his arms? But, then, why do women generally love men who often care so little for them?

Teleny did his best to comfort her, to tell her over and over again that he cared for no woman, to assure her that he would be eternally faithful to her for her sacrifice; but pity is not love, nor is affection the eagerness of desire.

Nature was more than satisfied; her beauty had lost all its attraction; they kissed again and again; he languidly passed his hands all over her body, from the nape of the neck to the deep dent between those round hills, which seemed covered with fallen snow, giving her a most delightful sensation as he did so; he caressed her breasts, suckled and bit the tiny protruding nipples, whilst his fingers were often thrust far within the warm flesh hidden under that mass of jet-black hair. She glowed, she breathed, she shivered with pleasure; but Teleny, though performing his work with masterly skill, remained cold at her side.

'No, I see that you don't love me; for it is not possible that you—a young man—'

She did not finish. Teleny felt the sting of her reproaches, but remained passive; for the phallus is not stiffened by taunts.

She took the lifeless object in her delicate fingers. She rubbed and manipulated it. She even rolled it between her two soft hands. It remained like a piece of dough. She sighed as piteously as Ovid's mistress must have done on a like occasion. She did like this woman did some hundreds of years before. She bent down; she took the tip of that inert piece of flesh between her lips—the pulpy lips which looked like a tiny apricot—so round, sappy, and luscious. Soon it was all in her mouth. She sucked it with as much evident pleasure as if she were a famished baby taking her nurse's breast. As it went in and out, she tickled the prepuce with her expert tongue, touched the tiny lips on her palate.

The phallus, though somewhat harder, remained always limp and nerveless.

You know our ignorant forefathers believed in the practice called *'nouer les aiguillettes'*—that is, rendering the male incapable of performing the pleasant work for which

185

Nature has destined him. We, the enlightened generation, have discarded such gross superstitions, and still our ignorant forefathers were sometimes right.

—What? you do not mean to say that you believe in such tomfoolery?

—It might be tomfoolery, as you say; but still it is a fact. Hypnotize a person, and then you will see if you can get the mastery over him or not.

—Still, you had not hypnotized Teleny?

—No, but our natures seemed to be bound to one another by a secret affinity.

At that moment I felt a secret shame for Teleny. Not being able to understand the working of his brain, she seemed to regard him in the light of a young cock, who, having crowed lustily once or twice at early dawn, has strained his neck to such a pitch that he can only emit hoarse, feeble, gurgling sounds out of it after that.

Moreover, I almost felt sorry for that woman; and I thought, if I were only in her place, how disappointed I should be. And I sighed, repeating almost audibly,—'Were I but in her stead.'

The image which had formed itself within my mind so vividly was all at once reverberated within René's brain; and he thought, if instead of this lady's mouth those lips were my lips; and his phallus at once stiffened and awoke into life; the glands swelled with blood; not only an erection took place, but it almost ejaculated. The Countess—for she was a Countess—was herself surprised at this sudden change, and stopped, for she had now obtained what she wanted; and she knew that—'*Dépasser le but, c'est manquer la chose.*'

Teleny, however, began to fear that if he had his mistress' face before his eyes, my image might entirely vanish; and that—beautiful as she was—he would never be able to accomplish his work to the end. So he began by covering her with kisses; then deftly turned her on her back. She yielded without understanding what was required of her. He bent her pliant body on her knees, so that she presented a most beautiful sight to his view.

186

This splendid sight ravished him to such an extent that by looking at it his hitherto limp tool acquired its full size and stiffness, and in its lusty vigour leapt in such a way that it knocked against his navel.

He was even tempted for a moment to introduce it within the small dot of a hole, which if not exactly the den of life is surely that of pleasure; but he forebore. He even resisted the temptation of kissing it, or of darting his tongue into it; but bending over her, and placing himself between her legs, he tried to introduce the glans within the aperture of her two lips, now thick and swollen by dint of much rubbing.

Wide apart as her legs were, he first had to open the lips with his fingers on account of the mass of bushy hair that grew all around them; for now the tiny curls had entangled themselves together like tendrils, as if to bar the entrance; therefore, when he had brushed the hair aside, he pressed his tool in it, but the turgid dry flesh arrested him. The clitoris thus pressed danced with delight, so that he took it in his hand, and rubbed and shook it softly and gently on the top part of her lips.

She began to shake, to rub herself with delight; she groaned, she sobbed hysterically; and when he felt himself bathed with delicious tears he thrust his instrument far within her body, clasping her tightly around the neck. So, after a few bold strokes, he managed to get in the whole of the rod down to the very root of the column, crushing his hair against hers, so far in the utmost recesses of the womb that it gave her a pleasurable pain as it touched the neck of the vagina.

For about ten minutes—which to her felt an eternity—she continued panting, throbbing, gasping, groaning, shrieking, roaring, laughing, and crying in the vehemence of her delight.

'Oh! Oh! I am feeling it again! In—in—quick—quicker! There! there!—enough!—stop!'

But he did not listen to her, and he went on plunging and re-plunging with increasing vigour. Having vainly begged for a truce, she began to move again with renewed life.

187

Having her *a retro*, his whole thoughts were thus concentrated upon me; and the tightness of the orifice in which the penis was sheathed, added to the titillation produced by the lips of the womb, gave him such an overpowering sensation that he redoubled his strength, and shoved his muscular instrument with such mighty strokes that the frail woman shook under the repeated thumps. Her knees were almost giving way under the brutal force he displayed. When again, all at once, the flood-gates of the seminal ducts were open, and he squirted a jet of molten liquid down into the innermost recesses of her womb.

A moment of delirium followed; the contraction of all her muscles gripped him and sucked him up eagerly, greedily; and after a short spasmodic convulsion, they both fell senseless side by side, still tightly wedged in one another.

—And so ends the Epistle!

—Not quite so, for nine months afterwards the Countess gave birth to a fine boy—

—Who, of course, looked like his father? Doesn't every child look like its father?

—Still this one happened to look neither like the Count nor like Teleny.

—Who the deuce did it look like then?

—Like myself.

—Bosh!

—Bosh as much as you like. Anyhow, the rickety old Count is very proud of this son of his, having discovered a certain likeness between his only heir and the portrait of one of his ancestors. He is always pointing out this atavism to all his visitors; but whenever he struts about, and begins to expound learnedly over the matter, I am told that the Countess shrugs her shoulders and puckers down her lips contemptuously, as if she was not quite convinced of the fact.

The House of Borgia

After the dissolvement of her marriage, Lucrezia withdrew to the Convent of San Sisto in the Appian Way—partly to escape the various items of scandal which were rocking Rome, partly to appear to act with the decorum her situation demanded.

She was to spend a period of some six months in her own private quarters, taking part with the nuns in daily prayers, joining with them in much of their work.

For some weeks she lived with them, praying, making baskets, carving small figurines in wood, walking in the quiet grounds, feeding their dozen hens. She was happy for a time to be free of the world in which she always felt a little as if she was living on the summit of a volcano that was likely to erupt unexpectedly.

But, at the end of that time, accustomed as she was to fierce and frequent intercourse, she began to feel an aching void in her loins, began to consider how to best soothe it.

During her walks in the grounds she had particularly befriended a young nun who had been in the convent only a short time before her. This young girl, whose name was Carlotta, was designated to show Lucrezia how to make the baskets and the little wooden figurines.

They got on very well and it soon became apparent to Lucrezia that the younger and unworldly Carlotta was quite fascinated by her.

Lucrezia managed, cleverly, to discover that the girl, who had never had a lover, was taking ill to her new and voluntary exile. She felt in her a need which she didn't understand, although listening to her confused explanations, Lucrezia was only too well aware of the trouble—the young girl needed a good fuck.

Carlotta was very attractive in her own way. She was dark, with a long face and slightly Jewish nose dominating long, well-defined lips. Her body was completely concealed under the shrouds of her long robes, but the melancholy attraction of her face was quite enough to excite Lucrezia in her present manless state.

Giving way to the girl's hinted-at curiosity, Lucrezia began, during their walks in the grounds, to tell her a few things about her sexual life. But always she exaggerated the brutality of the male, making him sound an utter, unbearable brute.

'I don't think I could stand to have a man using me in such a way,' Carlotta said one morning as they sat staring at the water lilies in the little stream which ran sluggishly through the lower reaches of the convent grounds. 'I should feel stripped of any sense of dignity I'd ever had.'

Lucrezia took the plunge.

'Yes. If the choice was between man and this convent, I would choose a cloistered existence within these walls,' she said. 'But, fortunately there are other things one can do.'

The girl raised her fine, dark eyebrows.

'What—other things in place of a man?'

'A woman, Carlotta. Women are much gentler and more loving than men. And they understand a woman's needs whereas most men are selfish and oafish in their lovemaking.'

'But . . .'

'I think,' Lucrezia went on quickly, 'much as I respect the Mother Superior and the individual right of choice, that any woman who locks herself away in a prison is betraying her function as a woman and displaying a fear of the world which belief in God should not justify.'

Carlotta stared at her, shocked. She had never dared to voice such sentiments, but they fitted well with her present mood of boredom and rebellion.

'You only have to look at the majority of the women here,' Lucrezia continued, 'and you see immediately that they're women who are too ugly or too witless to succeed in a competitive and natural world.'

She took Carlotta's hand.

'But you don't belong among them, Carlotta. You are lovely and full of life which won't allow itself to be kept in check forever.'

The girl was flattered and moved by the words which were spoken to her in such sincere tones. They sped her own unformed impulses along the channel that Lucrezia intended.

'I feel you are right,' she said. She glanced at the distant figures of the other nuns wandering in the upper part of the grounds among the trees. 'I'm beginning to wish I hadn't taken my vows.'

'You should make the best of things as they are,' Lucrezia said. 'We are both in the same cul-de-sac of frustration. We should help each other.'

'But what can we . . . ?'

'We can take the place of men for each other.'

The girl dropped her eyes and gazed down at the lilies. There was a silence for some seconds.

'I—I wouldn't know how . . . and—and I'm not sure that it's . . . '

'We all have deep centres in our beings which others may never reach,' Lucrezia cut in, 'but unless they do, unless we try to help them to, we all live lonely, unsatisfied lives, lives which wrinkle us up with bitterness, the feeling of having missed what was essential.'

Carlotta raised her eyes from the stream and found herself unable again to withdraw them from Lucrezia's deep, compelling gaze.

'Come to my quarters after evensong tonight,' Lucrezia went on, 'and I will show you what it means to reach that centre.'

The dull peal of a bell calling them in to prayer cut short any reply the young girl might have made. She stared at Lucrezia, dropped her eyes at last and walked away toward the building. Lucrezia smiled after her for a moment and then slowly followed her.

That evening, alone in her quarters—two rooms at the far

end of a wing of the convent—Lucrezia, garbed only in a dressing gown, waited for Carlotta to come. She was almost certain she would come although the girl had given her no answer. She knew how the possibility of sexual adventure could play on one's nerves, stimulating, frightening, exciting all at the same time.

For Lucrezia, too, this would be the first lesbian experience and the idea filled her with the same lustful chill of eagerness that her first fuck had—especially as she had been deprived of her conjugal and fraternal rights for some weeks now.

She found herself unable to keep still as the minutes went by following evensong. She rose time and time again and looked out of the sloping window down to the grounds. At last she sat on her bed and tried to concentrate on the pages of Boccaccio's *Il Decamerone* which she had smuggled into the convent with her.

As time passed she became more and more anxious. If Carlotta didn't come now she would die of frustration. She put down the book and stared out of the window again before walking into the next room where she studied herself in a small, silver-backed hand mirror.

Her heart leapt as there came a light tapping on her door. She ran to open it and almost clasped the young girl to her bosom as she drew her into her room.

Carlotta smiled at her briefly and stood uncertainly just inside the door while Lucrezia closed and bolted it.

'Make yourself at home', Lucrezia urged, turning around to her.

Nervously, the girl went to the window and looked out as if to reassure herself that the outside world was there, solid and unchanged. Lucrezia watched her pretending to interest herself in the exploration of the rooms, pretending to examine the few books, flicking pages over with a pointless speed.

'I was afraid to come,' she said at last. 'Wasn't that ridiculous—we are quite free to visit one another's rooms.'

'We are quite free to act as we please,' Lucrezia added.

'Yes,' the girl said uncertainly.

194

'I have another gown—why don't you make yourself more comfortable and put it on,' Lucrezia suggested.

She handed over the garment and Carlotta took it nervously.

Lucrezia turned away and studied *Il Decamerone*, listening to the rustle of clothes as Carlotta slipped out of them. She kept swallowing with nervous excitement.

At a well-judged moment she glanced around and caught her companion naked. Carlotta gazed at her with wide, embarrassed eyes and Lucrezia glanced back at her book immediately. But not before she'd had a glimpse of the girl's small, firm breasts, high up and dark, with the splodge of dark nipple giving them body, and her slim figure below it with the eye-catching fuzz of dark hair above her thighs. Lucrezia felt almost matronly beside the girl's small proportions.

She did not look up again until the girl came and sat beside her on the bed. Carlotta seemed to have lost some of her uncertainty. It was as if she'd reminded herself that she had, after all, come for a specific purpose and that there was no point in trying to pretend she hadn't.

Lucrezia replaced the book on a shelf over the bed and lay back on it, looking at her companion. Carlotta looked even more attractive out of her nun's sombre garb, and the long V-neck of the gown revealed a smooth stretch of her succulent-looking skin between her breasts. The beginning of their bulge on either side of the valley of flesh was heaving with a nervous emotion.

'You are really very lovely,' Lucrezia told her. 'It was a great mistake for a girl like you to get such a mad idea in her head that she wanted to pass the rest of her days in a tomb.'

The conversation brought a sense of normality with it and Carlotta's voice hid a trace of relief as if a spell had been broken.

'If you hadn't come, I might never have realised it,' she answered.

'Sooner or later you would have—but I'm glad it's through me that your revolution is to be achieved.'

195

Carlotta had again, as in the afternoon, become lost in Lucrezia's eyes. They seemed to hold her hypnotically. She came, as if Lucrezia had commanded her, and lay down on the bed beside her. Lucrezia touched the girl's cheek, lightly.

'Remember that this is the only way to liberate yourself from the horror and monotony of a death in life,' she said softly as her lips followed her hand.

Lucrezia was not very surprised to find that a relationship with a woman gave her as strong an erotic urge as with a man. It was as if it were something she'd always known, even when her conscious thought had included nothing but images of Cesare's, her father's, Giovanni's embraces. Now she felt the soft, smooth skin of the girl's cheek against her lips, a softness and a leafy fragrance which were missing in a man, and she felt her spirit stirred with the upsetting excitement of a new and forbidden experience about to come to fruition.

She slipped her hand into the girl's gown and Carlotta winced. Then her hand was caressing the small, firm breast with the lightest of touches. Her lips moved over the girl's face without losing contact—and found her lips. The lips were still, slightly reluctant and unsure. But as Lucrezia's hand moved from one breast to the other and tweaked the nipple, as her tongue played hide and seek with Carlotta's lips, the mouth opened with a sound which was near to a sigh, the lips relaxed and then kissed back.

Lucrezia's tongue gave up its game and lunged right out to fill the mouth which opened and spread at its assault.

Gently, her hand untied the belt of the gown. The material slipped slowly down to the bed off the glossy flesh of Carlotta's hips and thighs.

Lucrezia's hand rested on the girl's waist for a moment, the index finger playing with her navel. She noticed the girl was trembling faintly, like a leaf in the merest zephyr. She let her hand float away over the glassy expanse of flesh, lingering, unhurried, exploring every part while her tongue continued to caress the moist, heavily-breathing lips.

As her advancing fingers encountered the silky fan of

196

pubic hair, she slowed. She let her fingers course through it as through money. Under it she could feel the flesh swollen in a little mound, like a slight rise in the ground covered with a fine grass.

Carlotta wriggled her hips very slightly. She seemed ashamed of their movement, which was like an effort at escape.

Lucrezia sucked heavily on the lips which were trembling now in unison with the body.

With her free hand, she awkwardly unpulled her own belt and then pushed the plump flesh of her thigh against Carlotta's.

Slowly, as if stroking a timid animal, she allowed her fingers to continue on their downward progress. They moved down the rise and into the hot, little hollow between the oozing flesh of Carlotta's tightly-gripped thighs. Her path was barred for the moment by the instinctive inward pressure of those thighs. She stroked all the flesh she could reach and was rewarded with a sudden seepage of moisture around her fingers.

She moved her lips off Carlotta's and kissed her neck.

'Relax, darling,' she whispered. 'Open your legs.'

'I can't bear it,' Carlotta whispered back after a moment. 'It makes me jump every time you touch me.'

'All right—just let it go naturally. It'll come.'

Lucrezia went on with her gentle fondling. The hollow was very warm now and Carlotta was letting out an odd 'oh' every so often from deep down in her throat.

Moving her lips down the neck, over the slim shoulders, Lucrezia invaded the breasts which were taut and straining with sensation. She closed her mouth over a nipple and sucked hard and strong, bringing forth gasps of torment from the girl.

Carlotta's thighs relaxed and, awaiting her moment, Lucrezia was able suddenly to advance her fingers so that the texture of flesh changed and she knew she was in the beginning of the wet ravine formed by those nether lips. Carlotta clasped her thighs together again, crushing the tormenting hand, but Lucrezia bore the weight and tickled the wet flesh with her fingertips.

She drew on the nipple again with her lips, sucking in as much of the breast behind it as she could.

Carlotta thrust her breast at the lips which seemed to be drawing milk from her shapely udders. She arched her hips and gave way suddenly, opening her thighs, relaxing them so that the raping hand was suddenly right between her legs, the fingers in at their target.

Lucrezia moved a finger in the suddenly conquered vagina. Carlotta groaned in submission.

Slowly Lucrezia titivated and explored the flood-washed well. She pushed in through the tight ring of flesh, to the accompaniment of a little squeal from Carlotta. She thrust up, and then up again, feeling the hips withdraw instinctively, pull up away from the hand and then ooze back as they became used to the exquisite pressure.

Steadily Lucrezia sucked the breast, gnawed it, remembering all the things she liked a man to do and doing them with that greater finesse which was born of her own intimate, subjective knowledge.

Her fingers could move more loosely, more freely now. The ravine had become a great river, like a dried-up wadi suddenly swollen with the seasonal rains, the channel leading from it had become bigger, more accommodating and the hips were moving and bobbing against hers, brushing her flesh with another's exciting, strange flesh.

Breathing hard herself, Lucrezia moved her finger out of the hole and fastened it on the hard little clitoris which had reared up with its first touch from an alien hand.

Carlotta cried out and then spread her thighs in complete, won-over invitation as the finger bit into that little stem of sensitive flesh. She was wriggling incessantly, her mouth wide open, gasping for air.

'Oh God, oh God!' she exclaimed.

Lucrezia worked furiously and delightedly on the clitoris which expanded at her touch, grew harder, longer. She could feel passion growing in it as her finger and thumb pinched it, tweaked it, stroked it, masturbated it. There was only one thing left to make Carlotta's initiating delight into utter rapture.

Lucrezia slid down her body, revelling in the tight, straining pressure of flesh against hers. Her wet lips followed the swells and hollows of the body in their descent. She withdrew down to Carlotta's thighs with them. She ran her lips down the thighs, kissing tantalizingly on their buttery, yielding insides. The thighs twitched, clasped her head, relaxed. She heard the fury of Carlotta's moans washing down upon her ears like the continual flow of waves against a reef.

Her thighs clasped and unclasped, tensed and untensed continually; her hips wriggled like fish on a hook and she was fastened to the bed with her own overwhelming passion which was no longer timid but demanding.

Sliding her lips up the thighs, Lucrezia met first the slippery ooze of fluid glossing the tops of the legs. She lapped it like a dog. It represented the passion of a lovely girl—nothing unpalatable about that.

Over the swamp and to the very brink of the ravine, a plunge of the tongue and she was kissing and licking in that inundated wadi which squirmed and pressed against her and squashed its side flat against her mouth.

She searched, her tongue leading her blindly in the wadi until she found that steep, stiff monument. She grasped it in her lips and Carlotta's hips went mad, writhing and twisting so that Lucrezia had to hang onto her prize as if she were on a wild horse. But she clung to it, sucking it voraciously while a thin whine of passion, broken often by a deep moan, crashed down on her ears from the tortured face high up above her.

Her hands grasped those slim hips. How slim they were compared to her own. They made Carlotta seem that much more girlish, innocent, helpless.

She slid her hands under the hips and ran them all around the firm, tense balls of bottom. What an excellent little bottom.

She squeezed and worked its pliable bulk as she sucked and licked. The buttocks tightened and relaxed in her hands, swinging wildly in torment. The girl had become a raging form of sexuality. There seemed nothing left of her except a moaning, writhing mass of sensual flesh.

Lucrezia pulled the buttocks apart forcibly. They were hot in the crack between them. There were a few young hairs and then a sweating smoothness. Her fingers slipped over it like little snakes.

. The anus nestled there, unprotected now and she rifled it with her fingers the way she'd liked her father to intrude in hers. And Carlotta had no reticence any longer. She didn't even try to press her backside cheeks together. On the contrary she pressed them wide and back so that Lucrezia's finger actually penetrated the anus, the tight little ring of flesh, near to her sucking lips.

She used her tongue on the clitoris which seemed so big as to be unreal. There was a taste of salt and parsley in her mouth; the liquid was running over her face, growing into a torrent.

Above, out of sight, she heard Carlotta's sob.

'Oh, oh, it's here, it's here,' she heard her cry, out of control.

She sucked even more furiously, jabbing her finger deeply into the tight, tearing hole. She was terribly excited herself. She got a vicarious pleasure from the girl's helpless passion.

Following on her gasped out words, Carlotta twisted first one way and then the other in a quick, shivering convulsion. Her mouth opened wide and a long, continuous moan of sound exploded from it as she clasped her thighs around Lucrezia's head and squeezed.

The grip on Lucrezia was strong and suffocating, but she bore it until it slowly relaxed and the thighs fell away.

She straightened up, realising just how hot her loins had become. A little longer and she'd probably have come herself.

She looked at Carlotta. The girl seemed to have collapsed in a coma. She lay with her head thrown back dramatically, her arms wide out beside her head. Her eyes were closed, her breasts heaving in a great swell of emotion.

Lucrezia lay down alongside her and kissed her shoulder. After a while she spoke..

'Wasn't that worth a year in a convent? Isn't it worth anything on earth?'

Carlotta's eyes opened slowly, sleepily. She'd lost all trace of her early embarrassment.

'I feel purged,' she said softly. 'I feel satisfied and purged of all the frustration and not knowing that I've ever felt.'

Lucrezia smiled at her and kissed her bare arm.

'You obviously enjoyed it,' she agreed. 'Your enjoyment was so infectious that I almost had a climax myself.'

Carlotta opened her eyes again and looked at her. Realisation had dawned that there were, of course, two of them, that Lucrezia had given her undreamed-of pleasure, that it was now up to her to reciprocate.

'I'm not at all expert,' she said. 'I shan't know what to do.'

Lucrezia began to quiver with anticipation.

'Just do what I did,' she said with a break in her voice. 'And that will be wonderful.'

'I have got to get my breath back a moment.'

They lay together for a few minutes longer. Lucrezia could hardly wait and she kept pressing her round belly against Carlotta's side and tensing her pelvis against her.

'God, I want it very badly!' she muttered.

At that Carlotta turned over toward her and she fell backwards on the bed. She lay there staring up at the ceiling concentrating on herself, looking inward at the sensation inside her.

She felt the warm face come down on her breasts. To Carlotta her breasts were enormous in comparison with her own. They just asked to be nestled against, to be used as a pillow in which to bury one's face.

The face brushed against the tight, hurting points of her breasts, piquing her with a spearpoint of ecstatic pain that rushed straight to her genitals. And then those cool, well-defined lips closed on her nipple in a soft, fondling grip that made her squirm already.

They began to suck, drawing her pear of breast into the mouth, drawing it in, in, swallowing it, sucking it, pulverizing it with sharp, needed pain.

Lucrezia's legs began to jerk in spasms and the unknown fingers slid down her body, the image of her own, and went straight to the spot which played no timid games with them but waited, wide open like a trap, thighs wide apart and squirming.

Lucrezia held her breath waiting for the contact, expecting it, but still jumping with delight when it came. Cool fingers caressed her long, deep cleft which was stinging as the juices were washed into it from her inner regions.

The fingers explored like timid animals—and everywhere they touched and slid they left a burning, a prickling sense of near-destruction.

Lucrezia groaned. She liked to groan. She let the groans escape from her mouth—not that she could really have controlled them—to show her appreciation of what was being done to her.

Then with a sudden jump she felt the fingertips find her little erection. That was too much. She squirmed her hips in a movement that was almost circular, that was wild, exaggerated.

And the fingers were relentless. They pressed there, loved there, pinched there, gave no quarter although her moans became helpless sobs of passion.

Lucrezia felt her hole growing wide. The love-juice was swamping, too, and her belly was in unbearable torment. There couldn't be much more to go.

'Your mouth, your mouth!' she pleaded.

The fingers came out of her sultry cleft giving her a brief respite. But they were replaced immediately by a pair of cool lips which seized on her clitoris, sending a shock through her whole body.

'Oh, wonderful, wonderful!' she gasped. She could hardly utter the words. They tumbled out in a rush of sound which was mostly escaping breath, wheezing out like steam from a hot spring.

The mouth was working hard, giving her no chance to catch her breath. She was out of breath as if she'd been running hard.

And then the hands, remembering, slid around her hips and dug handfuls from her big buttocks, rummaging between them to find the anal orifice.

'Wonderful, wonderful!' she breathed again, lost and helpless.

She felt the heat like a great wood fire down in her passage. It was as hot as a lump of smouldering charcoal, felt ready to splinter into pieces at any moment.

'It's coming . . . it's . . . coming . . . oh!' she gasped, more as an outlet for her feeling than as a warning. She jerked her legs this way and that as if they were puppets and she held the strings. Speech was now impossible. The sounds from her mouth were animal noises, enlarging in abandon with every lick of that tongue on her erect little organ.

She clamped her legs around Carlotta's head and squeezed her loins up at her face, forcing, straining, arching. She felt the burst, the splintering and she cried out, stifling her cries with her fist as the last suck drew her liquid passion through her channel.

A new and regular activity was begun in the quiet haven of the convent.

My Secret Life

One night soon after this, I met at the Argyle rooms Helen M and was struck with her instantly. My experienced eye and well trained judgment in women, as well as my instincts told me what was beneath her petticoats and I was not deceived. I have had many splendid women in my time, but never a more splendid perfect beauty, in all respects.

Of full but not great height, with the loveliest shade of chestnut hair of great growth, she had eyes in which grey, green and hazel were indescribably blended with an expression of supreme voluptuousness in them, yet without bawdiness or salacity, and capable of any play of expression. A delicate, slightly retroussé nose, the face a pure oval, a skin and complexion of a most perfect tint and transparency, such was Helen M. Nothing was more exquisite than her whole head, tho her teeth were wanting in brilliancy—but they were fairly good and not discoloured.

She had lovely cambered feet, perfect to their toes; thighs meeting from her cunt to knees and exquisite in their columnar beauty; big, dimpled haunches, a small waist, full firm breasts, small hands, arms of perfect shape in their full roundness. Everywhere her flesh was of a very delicate creamy tint, and was smooth to perfection. Alabaster or ivory, were not more delicious to the touch than her flesh was everywhere from her cheeks to her toes.

Short, thick, crisp yet silky brown hair covered the lower part of her motte, at that time only creeping down by the side of the cunt lips, but leaving the lips free, near to at her bumhole, a lovely little clitoris, a mere button, topped her belly rift, the nymphae were thin, small, and delicate. The mouth of the vulva was small, the avenue tight yet

207

exquisitely elastic, and as she laid on her back and opened her thighs, it was an exquisite, youthful, pink cunt, a voluptuous sight which would have stiffened the prick of a dying man.

Her deportment was good, her carriage upright but easy, the undulations of her body in movement voluptuous, and fascinating; every thing, every movement was graceful; even when she sat down to piss it was so—and taking her altogether, she was one of the most exquisite creatures God ever created to give enjoyment to man.—With all this grace, and rich, full, yet delicate of frame, she was a strong, powerful woman, and had the sweetest voice—it was music.

I saw much of this in her at a glance, and more completely as she undressed. Then the sweetest smell as if of new milk, or of almonds escaped from her, and the instant she laid down I rushed lasciviously on her cunt, licked and sucked it with a delight that was maddening. I could have eaten it. Never had I experienced such exquisite delight in gamahuching a woman. Scarcely ever have I gamahuched a gay woman on first acquaintance, and generally never gamahuched them at all.

As I went home with her in a cab I had attempted a few liberties, but she repulsed them.—'Wait till we get home, I won't have them in the cab.'—Directly we arrived I asked what her compliment was to be.—No she had never less than a fiver.—'Why did you not tell me so, and I would not have brought you away.—What I give is two sovereigns, here is the money, I am sorry I have wasted your time'—and was going.—'Stop,' said she—'don't go yet!'—I looked in my purse and gave her what I could—it was a little more than the sum I'd named—and promised to bring her the remainder of a fiver another day. Then I fucked her.—'Don't be in such a hurry,' I said, for she moved her cunt as women either do when very randy, or wishing to get rid of a man. That annoyed me, but oh my God my delight as I shed my sperm into that beautiful cunt, and kissed and smelt that divine body, and looked into those voluptuous eyes. I had at once a love as well as lust for her, as my prick throbbed out its essence against her womb.—But *she* had no pleasure with *me*.—She was annoyed and in a hurry, she had another man waiting in another room in the house to have her—as she has told me since.

What was in this woman—what the specific attractions, I cannot say, but she made me desire to open my heart to her, and I told rapidly of my amatory tricks, my most erotic letches, my most blamable (if any be so) lusts; things I had kept to myself, things never yet disclosed to other women, I told *her* rapidly. I felt as if I must, as if it were my destiny to tell her all, all I had done with women and men, all I wished to do with *her*, it was a vomit of lascivious disclosures. I emptied myself body and soul into her. She listened and seemed annoyed. She did not like me.

Nor did she believe me. Two days afterwards, I took her the promised money, she had not expected it, and then deigned to ask if she should see me again. No. She was far too expensive for me—not that she was not worth it all.—Yea more—but blood could not be got out of a stone.—I had not the money and could see her no more.—'All right,' she replied very composedly and we parted. As I tore myself away, my heart ached for that beautiful form, again to see, smell, to kiss, and suck, and fuck that delicious cunt, to give *her* pleasure if I could. Tho I saw her afterwards at the Argyle rooms—even went to look at her there, I resisted.—What helped me was the belief that I was distasteful to her, why I could not tell, and a year elapsed before I clasped her charms again.

On leaving her that day, I could think of nothing but *her*, went to a woman I knew, and shut my eyes whilst I fucked her, fancying she was Helen M.—'You call me Helen,' said she. 'You know a woman of that name I suppose,'—I told her it was the name of my sister. Not the only time the same thing has happened to me, and in exactly the same manner with other ladies when fucking *them*, but thinking of *another*.

One night at the Argyle rooms, Helen spoke to me. I had several times been there solely to look at her, each time she seemed more beautiful than ever, yet beyond nodding or saying, 'How do you do,' we held no conversation, for she was always surrounded by men. I used to sit thinking of her charms with swollen pego, then either found outside a lady, or once or twice selected one in the room, so that Helen could see, and ostentatiously quitted the salon with her. I felt a savage pleasure in doing so.—A species of senseless revenge.

Sitting by my side, 'You've not been to see me again.'—'No.'—'Why?'—'I'm not rich enough.'— 'Nonsense, you've got some other woman.'—'None.'— 'Come up.'—'No, I'll let no woman ruin me.'—We conversed further, she got close to me, her sweet smell penetrated me, and in spite of myself I promised to see her next day.

She had changed her abode, had a larger house, three servants and a brougham. I had a sleepless night thinking of coming felicity, and on a lovely spring afternoon, hot as if in the midst of summer, she was awaiting me with an open silk wrapper on, beneath it but a laced chemise so diaphanous, that I could see her flesh and the colour of her motte through it. Her exquisite legs were in white silk, and she'd the nattiest kid boots on her pretty little, well cambered feet. She was a delicious spectacle in her rooms, through the windows of which both back and front were green trees and gardens.

'Say I'm not at home to any one,' said she to the maid. Then to me, 'So you have come.'—'Did you doubt me?'—'No, I think you're a man who keeps his word.' Then on the sofa we sat, and too happy for words I kissed her incessantly. She got my rampant cock out and laughing said, 'It's quite stiff enough.'—'Let me feel *you* love,' said I putting my hand between her thighs.—'Why don't you say, cunt?'—again I was silent in my voluptuous amusement, kissing and twiddling the surface of her adorable cleft. 'Oh let us poke.'—'Why do you say poke—say. fuck,' said she moving to the bed and lying down.

'Let me look at your lovely cunt.' She moved her

210

haunches to the bedside and pulled her chemise well up, proud of her beauty. Dropping on my knees I looked at the exquisite temple of pleasure, it was perfection, and in a second my mouth was glued to it. I licked and sucked it, I smelt it and swallowed its juice, I could have bitten and eaten it, had none of dislike to the saline taste which I've had with some women, no desire to wipe the waste saliva from my mouth as it covered the broad surface of the vulva in quantity, but swallowed all, it was nectar to me, and sucked rapturously till, 'That will do, I won't spend so—fuck me'—said she jutting her cunt back from my mouth.

Quickly I arose and was getting on the bed when, 'No—take your things off—all off,—be naked, it's quite hot—I'll shut the window,' which she did, and throwing off her chemise sat herself at the edge of the bed till I was ready.—'Take off your shirt.'—As I removed it, she laid on the bed with thighs apart, the next second my pego was buried in her, and our naked bodies with limbs entwined were in the fascinating movements of fucking. What heaven,—what paradise!—but alas, how evanescent. In a minute with tongues joined, I shed my seed into that lovely avenue, which tightened and spent its juices with me. She enjoyed it, for she was a woman voluptuous to her marrow, my naked form had pleased her I was sure, not that she said that *then*, she was too clever a Paphian for that.

We lay tranquilly in each other's arms till our fleshy union was dissolved. She then—as she washed—'Aren't you going to wash?'—'I'll never wash away anything which has come out of your cunt you beautiful devil, let it dry on, I wish I could lick it off.'—'You should have licked me before I washed my cunt, you baudy beast,'—she rejoined, laughing.

She then came and stook naked by the bedside.—'Aren't you going to get up?'—fearing her reply. 'Let me have you again,'—I said.—She laughed and gave me a towel—'Dry your prick—you can't do it again.'—'Can't I,—look?' My pego was nearly full size. She got on to the bed, laid hold of it, and passed one thigh over my haunch, my fingers titillated her clitoris for a minute, and so we lay lewdly handling each other. Then our bodies were one again, and a fuck longer, more intense in its mental pleasure, more full of idealities, more complete in its physical enjoyment to me, was over within a quarter of an hour after I had had her the first time.—Nor did she hurry me, but we lay naked, with my prick in her lovely body, in the somnolence of pleasure and voluptuous fatigue, a long time, speechless.

Both washed, she piddled (how lovely she looked doing it), put on her chemise and I my shirt. Recollecting my first visit and her hurry, 'Now I suppose you want your fiver and me to clear out'—said I bitterly and taking hold of my drawers, for I felt a love almost for *her* and sad that I was only so much money in her eyes.—'I didn't say so, lie down with me.'—Side by side on the bed we lay again.

She was not inquisitive. Hadn't I really a lady whom I visited, she knew that I'd had Miss * * * * * and Polly * * * * I had had, she'd spoken about me to them.—Why didn't I see *her*. Hadn't I a lady, now tell her—I only repeated what's already told.—Then the vulgar money business cropped up.—No, she never had and never would let a man have her, for less than a fiver. Going to a drawer, she showed me a cheque for thirty pounds and a letter of endearments. 'That's come today, and he only slept with me two nights.'

She'd soon again my soft yet swollen cunt stretcher in her hand, and fingered it deliciously, never a woman more deliciously. I felt her clitoris, and kissed her lovely neck and cheeks almost unceasingly.—'Give me a bottle of phiz,' said she after a minute's silence—I complied.—'It's a guinea mind.'—'Preposterous, I'm not in a bawdy house.'—'It's my price, my own wine, and splendid.'—Of course I yielded, who would not when such a divinity was fingering and soothing his prick? It was excellent, we drank most of it soon, and then she gratified me after much solicitation, by lifting her chemise up to her armpits and standing in front of a cheval glass for my inspection, pleased I fancied by my rapturous eulogiums of her loveliness—and exquisite she was.—'You know a well made woman when you see one,' she remarked.—Then quickly she dropped her chemise,—she'd not held it up a minute,—it seemed but an instant,—and refused in spite of my entreaties to raise it again.—'You have seen quite enough.'—Again on the bed we sat, again our hands crossed and fingers played on prick and cunt,—silent, with voluptuous thoughts and lewd sensations.

Then came the letch—'Let me gamahuche you.'—'I won't you beast.'—'You did the other day.'—'Be content then, I won't now'—and she would not. But I kissed her thighs, buried my nose in the curls of her motte, begging, entreating her, till at length she fell back, saying, 'I don't like it, you beast.'—Her thighs opened and crossed my arms, whilst clasping her ivory buttocks my mouth sought her delicious scented furrow, and licked it with exquisite delight. She at first cried out often, 'Leave off, you beast.' Then suddenly she submitted. I heard a sigh, she clutched the hair of my head—'Beast—Aha—leave off—beast —aherr'—she sobbed out. A gentle tremulous motion of her belly and thighs, then they closed so violently on my head, pinching and almost hurting me,—she tore at my hair, then opened wide her thighs—a deep sigh escaped her, and she had spent with intense pleasure. (That vibratory motion of thighs and belly, increasing in force as her pleasure crisis came, I have never noticed in any other woman, when gamuhuching them, tho most quiver their bellies and thighs a little as their cunt exudes its juices.)

With cock stiff as a rod of iron, with delight at having voluptuously gratified her, wild almost with erotic excitement,—'I've licked your cunt dry—I've swallowed your spending my darling' (it was true), I cried rapturously. 'Let me lick your cunt again.'—'You beast, you shan't.'—But as she denied it, lustful pleasure was still in her eyes.—'Let me.'—'No, fuck me.'—At once I laid by her side, at once she turned to me—grasped my pego, and in soft voice said, 'Fuck me.'—'You've just spent.'—'Yes—

fuck me—go on.'—'You can't want it.'—'Yes, I do, fuck me, fuck me,'—she said imperiously. I didn't then know her sexual force, her voluptuous capabilities, did not believe her. But I wanted *her*, and she was ready. On to her sweet belly I put mine, plunged my pego up her soft, smooth cunt, and we fucked again a long delicious fuck, long yet furious, for though my balls were not so full, I felt mad for her, talked about her beauty whilst I thrust, and thrust, and cried our bawdy words, till I felt her cunt grip and she, 'You beast,—beast,—Oh—fuck me——you beast—aher'—and all was done, I'd spent and she with me.

And as she spent, I noticed for the first time on her face, an expression so exquisite, so soft in its voluptuous delight, that angelic is the only term I can apply to it. It was so serene, so complete in its felicity, and her frame became so tranquil, that I could almost fancy her soul was departing to the mansions of the blest, happy in its escape from the world of troubles amidst the sublime delights of fucking.

Then she wished me to go. But only after a long chat, during which she laid all the time in her chemise, her lovely legs, her exquisite breasts showing, she was curious and I told her more about myself than I'd ever told a Paphian. 'When shall I see you again?'—'Most likely never.'—'Yes I shall.'—I told her it was impossible. 'Yes, come and sleep with me some night.'—Laughing, I said,—'I can't do it more than three times.'—'I'll bet I'll make you.'—Then with sad heart, and almost tears in my eyes, I repeated that I should not see her again.—'Yes—you will—look—I'm going to the races tomorrow'—and she showed me a splendid dress.—'I'm going with * * * of the 40th.' How I envied him, how sad I felt when I thought of the man who would pass a day and night with that glorious beauty, that exquisite cunt at hand for a day and night.

Helen and I now began to understand each other (tho not yet perfectly). She knew I was not easily humbugged, so abandoned largely Paphian devices, treated me as a friend,

214

and her circumstances compelling her to avoid male friends, and not liking females much, and it being a human necessity to tell someone about oneself, I became to some extent her confidante. She then had a charming, well furnished little house, replete with comfort, and her own. I have eaten off her kitchen boards, and the same throughout the house. She was an excellent cook, cooked generally herself and liked it, was a gourmet. It was delightful to see her sitting at table, dressed all but a gown, with naked arms and breasts showing fully over a laced chemise, with her lovely skin and complexion, eating, and drinking my own wine, she passing down at intervals to the kitchen. We ate and drank with joy and bawdy expectation, both of us—for she wanted fuck-ing.—Every now and then I felt her thighs and quim, kissing her, showing my prick, anxious to begin work even during our dinner.

Afterwards adjourning to her bedroom, we passed the evening in voluptuous amusements—we had then but *few* scruples in satisfying our erotic wishes.—Soon after had *none.*—How she used to enjoy my gamahuching, and after a time abandoning herself to her sensations she'd cry out, 'Aha—my—God—aha—fuck spunk'—and whatever else came into her mind, quivering her delicious belly and thighs, squeezing my head with them, clutching my hair, as her sweet cunt heaved against my mouth when spending, till I ceased from tongue weariness. Sometimes this with my thumb gently pressing her bum hole, which after a time she liked much. Then what heavenly pleasure as I put my prick up her, and grasping her ivory buttocks, meeting her tongue with mine, mixing our salivas, I deluged her cunt with sperm.—Never have I had more pleasure with any woman, with few so much.

Resting, we talked of *her* bawdy doings and *mine*—of the tricks of women.—We imagined bawdy possibilities, planned voluptuous attitudes, disclosed letches, suggested combinations of pleasure between men and women, and woman with woman—for Eros claimed us both. In salacity we were fit companions, all pleasures were soon to be to us legitimate, we had no scruples, no prejudices, were philosophers in lust, and gratified it without a dream of modesty.

One day I told her again of the sensitiveness of my pego, that with a dry cunt the friction of fucking sometimes hurt me, that my prick at times looked swollen and very red, unnaturally so.—French harlots—more than others—I found washed their cunts with astringents, which my prick detected in them directly, so when I was expected, I wished H not to wash *hers* after the morning, her natural moisture then being so much pleasanter to my penis.—No saliva put there, is equal to the natural viscosity, mucosity of the surface of a vagina.—But from her scrupulously cleanly habits, I had great difficulty in getting her to attend to this.

That led one day to her asking, if I had ever had a woman who had not washed her quim after a previous fucking. She then knew my adventure with the sailor, that at Lord A's, and at Sarah Frazer's—but not the recent one at Nelly L's.—I told her that I had not with those exceptions.—'I'll bet you have without knowing.' She told me of women where she had lived, merely wiping their cunts after a poke, and having at once another man and of its not being discovered; of she herself once having had a man fuck her, and his friend who came with him, insisting on poking her instantly afterwards.

We talked soon after about the pleasure of fucking in a well buttered cunt, and agreed that the second fuck was nicer if the cunt was unwashed. I racked my memory, and recollected cases where I had had suspicions of having done so. Helen who always then washed her quim, again said it was beastly.—I said that if more agreeable to me and the woman, there was nothing beastly in it; nor cared I if there was, fucking being in its nature a mere animal function, tho in human beings augmented in pleasure, by the human brain. 'So why wash after, if the two like it otherwise?'

About that time I found I had not quite as much sperm as in early middle age, testing that by frigging myself over a sheet of white paper, and wished to see what a young

216

man spent both in quality and quantity. We chatted about this at times, and one day she told me she had a man about thirty-five years old, who visited her on the sly, but very occasionally; a former lover who had spent a fortune on her (I know since his name, his family, and that what she told me was true). She let him have her still, for gratitude. He was very poor but a gentleman, and now he helped her in various ways. It struck me she liked him also, because he had as she told, a large prick. I found she had a taste for large pricks, and described those of her former friends who possessed such, in rapturous terms. This man spent much, I expressed a desire to see it, and after a time it was arranged that I should see this cunt prober, him using it, and her cunt afterwards, but this took some time to bring about. In many conversations, she admitted that she had not more physical pleasure from a great prick, than from an average sized one. 'But it's the idea of it you know, the idea of its being big, and it's so nice to handle it.'

I was in her bedroom as arranged, he was to have her in the adjoining room. She placed the bed there, so that when the door was very slightly opened I could see perfectly thro the hinge side. We were both undressed, she with delight describing his prick, repeating her cautions to be quiet, and so on.—A knock at the street door was heard. 'It's his,' said she, and went downstairs.—Some time passed, during which I stood on the stair landing listening, till I heard a cough,—her signal—then going back and closing my door, I waited till they were upstairs and I heard them in the back room. Opening mine ajar again I waited till a second cough. Then in shirt and without shoes, I crept to their door which was slightly open.

They were sitting on the edge of the bed, she in chemise, he in shirt, feeling each other's privates. His back was half towards me, her hand was holding his large tool not yet quite stiff; but soon it grew to noble size under her handling. Then he wanted to gamahuche her, she complied, being fond of that pleasure as a preliminary. He knelt on the bed to do it, tho he'd wished to kneel on the floor.—She insisted on *her* way, to keep his back to me.

217

So engrossed was he with the exercise, that when her pleasure was coming on, I pushed further open the door (hinges oiled) and peeping round and under, saw his balls, and that his prick was big and stiff—I was within a foot of him.—But he noticed nothing, all was silent but the plap of his tongue on her cunt, and her murmurs. When she had spent once, he laid himself by her side, kissing her and feeling her cunt, his stiff, noble pego standing against her thigh,—she pulling the prepuce up and down, and looking at the door crack. After dalliance prolonged for my gratification, he fucked her. She pulled his shirt up to his waist when he was on her, so that I might contemplate their movements. I heard every sigh and murmur, saw every thrust and heave, a delicious sight; but he was hairy arsed, which I did not like.

Then said she, 'Pull it out, he'll wonder why I have been away so long; you go downstairs quietly, and I'll come soon.' He uncunted, they rose, I went back to my room. He had been told that she was tricking the man then keeping her, and knew that a man was then in the house, and *he* there on the sly was happy to fuck her without pay—for he loved her deeply—and not at all expecting or knowing that his fornicating pleasures, were ministering to the pleasure of another man.

Then on the bedside she displayed her lovely secret charms—a cunt overflowing with his libation.—It delighted me, my pego had been standing long, I seemed to have almost had the pleasure of fucking her as I witnessed him, and now to fuck her, to leave my sperm with his in her, came over me with almost delirious lust. 'I'll fuck you, I'll fuck in it,' I cried trembling with concupiscent desire.—'You beast—you shan't.'—'I will.'—'You shan't.' But she never moved, and kept her thighs wide apart whilst still saying, —'No, no.'—I looked in her face, saw that overpowering voluptuousness, saw that she lusted for it, ashamed to say it. 'Did *you* spend?'—'Yes.'—'I will fuck.'—'You beast.'—Up plunged my prick in her.—'Ahaa'—sighed she voluptuously as my balls closed on her bum. I lifted up her thighs which I clasped, and

218

fucked quickly for my letch was strong. 'Ain't we beasts,' she sighed again.—'I'm in his sperm, dear.'—'Y—hes, we're beasts.' The lubricity was delicious to my prick. 'Can you feel his spunk?'—'Yes dear, my prick's in it.—I'll spend in his spunk.'—'Y—hes—his spunk.—Aha—beasts.'—All I had just seen flashed thro my brain.—His prick, his balls, her lovely thighs, made me delirious with sexual pleasure.—'I'm coming—shall you spend, Helen?' —'Y—hes—push—hard—ahar.'—'Cunt—fuck—spunk,' we cried together in bawdy duet—her cunt gripped—my prick wriggled, shot out its sperm, and I sank on her breast, still holding her thighs and kissing her.

When we came to, we were both pleased.—'Never mind Helen if we are beasts—why say that if you like it?'—'I don't.'—'You fib, you do.'—After a time she admitted that the lasciviousness of the act, had added to the pleasure of coition greatly—to me the smoothness of her vagina seemed heaven.—I was wild to see all again, but circumstances did not admit of it then, yet in time I did, and one day after he and I had had her, 'Go down to him,' said I, 'don't wash, and let him have you again on the sofa.'—The letch pleased her, he fucked her again, and thought he was going into his own leavings. When she came up, I had her again, I was in force that day.—Her taste for his lubricity then set in, and stirred her lust strongly,—she was in full rut—I gamahuched her after she had washed, thinking where two pricks had been, and half an hour after she frigged herself. Whilst frigging, 'Ah! I wish there had been a third man's spunk in it.'—'You beast—ah—so—do I.'—She rejoined as she spent, looking at me with voluptuous eyes.

We often talked of this afterwards, and agreed that the pleasure of coition was increased by poking after another man, and we did so when we could afterwards with her friend and others. Sometimes it is true she shammed that she allowed it only to please *me*, but *her* excitement when fucking told me to the contrary. She liked it as much as I did, and it became an enduring letch with her.

Whether Helen or any other woman—I've known

several who liked it—had increased physical pleasure by being fucked under such pudendal condition, it's not possible to say.—With me owing to the state of my gland, no doubt it did. But imagination is a great factor in human coition, and by its aid, the sexual pleasure is increased to something much higher than mere animalism. It is by the brain that fucking becomes ethereal, divine, it being in the highest state of excitement and activity during this sexual exercise. It is the brain which evokes letches, suggests amatory preliminaries, prolongs and intensifies the pleasure of an act, which mere animals—called 'beasts'—begin and finish in a few minutes. Human beings who copulate without thought and rapidly *are like beasts*, for with them it is a mere animal act.—Not so those who delay, prolong, vary, refine, and intensify their pleasures—*therein is their superiority to the beasts*—the animals. What people do in their privacy is their affair alone. A couple or more together, may have pleasure in that which *others* might call *beastly*—although *beasts* do nothing of the sort—but which to them is the highest enjoyment, physical and mental. It is probable that every man and woman, has some letch which they gratify but don't disclose, yet who would nevertheless call it *beastly*, if told that others did it, and would according to the accepted notions—or rather professions—on such matters, call all sexual performance or amusements *beastly*, except quick, animal fucking. But really it is those who copulate without variety, thought, sentiment or soul, who are the *beasts*—because they procreate exactly as *beasts* do, and nothing more.—With animals, fucking is done *without brains*—among the higher organised human beings, fucking is done *with brains*—yet this exercise of the intellect in coition is called *beastly* by the ignorant, who have invented a series of offensive terms, to express their objections.—Their opinion of the sweet congress of man and woman—which is love—is, that it should be a feel, a look, a sniff at the cunt, and a rapid coupling—*very like beasts that!!!*

H had still two servants, but who were changed often now

for some reason or another, I guessed to facilitate intrigue. More frequently than otherwise her female relative—the scout—in whom she had great confidence, together with some very young girl and a charwoman, did the work of the house, this looked also suspicious, and the arrangement as if made to favour intrigues. Indeed H laughingly admitted almost as much. She now was assumed to have quitted gay life for good, and to have consecrated her temple of love to one sole worshipper. I certainly believe that she was inaccessible to men (myself and a lover excepted), was never seen at the haunts of the frail ones, nor at theatres or other places of amusement, and she had cut nearly every Paphian acquaintance of old days. I enquired of women, and at places when they ought to know, but none had seen her. One thought she was ill, most that she was being kept.

H spoke well of her protector. She was proud of his personal appearance, of his being a gentleman, an Oxford man, well born and so on, all of which he was. She said she loved him. She was fond of her home and even of domestic duties. She was a very active woman, was very clean, and those duties and reading occupied her. She was very clever, and indeed had most of the qualities which go to make a good wife. She was a gourmet, and most extravagant in her food, liked cooking it herself, would give five shillings for a pint of green peas or other choice food, even if she had to borrow the money to pay for them—but she much preferred going into debt. This is an illustration of, I believe, her sole extravagance. She could write well, compose charades, and even write rhymes which were far from contemptible.

But her nature was luxurious, her sexual force so great that it conquered. One man could not satisfy her. Altho when with her protector he fucked her twice daily, and she frigged herself twice or thrice as well—did it even before his eyes she told me—and I who saw her weekly fucked her twice or thrice and between our love exercise often times she frigged herself—no sham, not done to excite me, there was no object in that—such was her strong appetite for voluptuous delight, the craving of her flesh. She delighted in bawdy books and pictures, and generally in all voluptuousness—yet for all this she was not a Messalina quite.

Sometimes now she was left alone for a week or two or longer by her friend, tho he idolized her,—but he couldn't help his absence. Then the strong promptings of her carnality placed her in great temptation. Frigging did not satisfy her, her cunt yearned irresistibly for the male. My talk, she averred, so excited her, that when she thought of that alone it led to her giving way to her passions. That I don't believe, tho it might have added fuel to the flames.—She took a fancy after a time to another man. This came about through going to see a dashing gay woman whom she'd not seen since she'd been in keeping. The man therefore was a mere chance acquaintance. He was known in Paphian circles for his physical perfections, and the desire for his very big prick really was the reason for her wishing once to see him, and then for a time her taking to him. But more of this hereafter.

I afterwards witnessed him using his tool. It added greatly to her pleasure to know that I was a spectator. The deed done, he gone away, she came to me, her eyes humid with recent pleasure—still lustful. We fucked, and talked. The idea of my prick being in the avenue his had quitted increased the pleasures of us both when fucking—hers I think more even than mine. Soon after our eroticism entered on even a higher phase of luxuriousness.

When she had thoroughly made the acquaintance of the man with a bigger prick than that of her lover—the biggest she had ever known, she said—she described it rapturously and the delight she felt when it was up her. The gentleman with whom she lived as already said poked her twice daily when there, her poor lover fucked her frequently, I gave her my doodle then once a week, besides gamahuching her which I never failed to do, and in addition to all this she frigged herself nearly every day.—Yet all this did not give her an excess of sexual pleasure, with all her fucking, frigging, and gamahuching, she looked the very picture of

222

health and strength, and had both.

She had met as said this man by chance, was told about him, and it was the idea of his size which affected her sensuous imagination.—He was, she found in the long run, a mean hound, who enjoyed her lovely body yet was often half fucked out before he had her, and scarcely made her the most trifling presents. The size of his prick had made him notorious among gay women, she discovered at last, and he got more cunt than he wanted for nothing. I often advised her to cut him, for she told me all about her affairs with him; not that I preached morality but saw that it was a pity to risk an evidently good chance of being settled comfortably for life. Yet if she wanted another man—if variety was essential, 'Have him but beware,' I used to say.

I expressed one day a wish to see his pego of which she was always talking. She was proud at that, her eyes glistened voluptuously as she told me of the arrangements for my view. She had long liked telling her letches to me—a willing listener who had no canting objections.—Tho I cautioned her to take care not to be caught by her protector.—She used to reply—'What have I to live for except it.—Philip and I have no society, we can't afford it now—it's a year since I've been to the theatre,—there is nothing but my house, and playing at cards and fucking, to amuse me.'—'My darling, fucking is all in life worth living for, but be prudent.'

The plan of her house then, owing to the way she and her protector occupied the back bedroom, did not favour a secret peep at her with the man, who had become knowing and wary in such matters, by passing most of his time with harlots, and she had a difficult task in humbugging him. It was to come off in the parlour. I at a signal was to go downstairs from her bedroom barefooted, peep thro the parlour door left ajar, was not to make the slightest noise, and retire directly the consummation was effected.

On the day, I was waiting expectantly in her bedroom, heard footsteps enter the parlour, went down cautiously to the half landing—heard:—'Ahem'—went lower—heard

223

bawdy conversation and then, 'It's right up my cunt.' Knowing from that that my opportunity had arrived, I pushed the door slightly more open.—She was on the top of him on a sofa, her face hid his from seeing me.—She was kissing him, her chemise was up to her armpits, her bum moved slowly up and down showing a thick prick up her. 'It's not stiff,' said she angrily. 'You've fucked before today.'—'I've not fucked since yesterday.'—She'd uncunted him as she spoke, and out flopped a huge prick not quite stiff.—There she lay over him thighs wide apart—cunt gaping wide—his prick underneath it.—It was a dodge of hers to gratify my sight, to show me the procreator she was proud of enjoying.

Then she got off, and stood by the side of him, still leaning over and kissing him, to hide his eyes whilst she frigged him. His prick soon stood and a giant it was. She got on to him again, impaled herself, and soon by the short twitching shoves of her buttocks, and the movement of his legs (in trousers) I saw they were spending—In a minute his moist tool flopped out of her cunt, and I crept upstairs leaving them still belly to belly on the sofa. She had told him that her sister was in the bedroom, to which I soon after heard her coming up, and him going down to the kitchen. Oh the voluptuous delight in her lovely face as she laid on the bedside to let me see her cunt, and the delight she had as my prick glided up it softened by his sperm, and her lewd ecstasy as my sperm mixed with his and hers in spasms of maddening pleasure—for now she delighted in this sort of copulation, said it made her feel as if she were being fucked by both of us at once.

This spectacle was repeated afterwards on a bed in the garret—but after a time she sickened of him and saw him no more.—She however still had her large-pricked poor lover. She had at various times with string measured the length and circumferences of both of these pricks. The way to get proper measurements was carefully discussed by us. I have the lengths and circumferences of the two pricks, and of Phil's all measured when stiff, round the stem half way down—and from the centre of the tip to where the prick joins the belly.

This big-pricked man was a coarse looking fellow tho stalwart and handsome. He would stop at the house and feed at her expense, and scarcely give her a present, yet he was not a poor man, but a man of business as she knew, and as I took the trouble to ascertain. H told me soon all about him. I was certainly the only confidante she could have in this letch.—He was reckless enough to let a youth from his place of business bring him letters whilst at H's and she got acquainted with the lad.

H told me one day that she was in bed with big-tool, when the youth brought him a letter. They both lewd, began chaffing the boy, asked if he'd ever seen a woman naked, and pulled the bed clothes down so as to show her naked to her waist. She permitted, nay liked the lark, and admitted to me she hadn't then seen the prick of a lad of that age, stiff or limp.—'Show her your cock and she'll show you her cunt,' said big-tool. The boy, glowing with lust approached the bed. H opened her thighs invitingly, his master got up and pulled the lad's cock out of his trousers as stiff as a horn, she opened her thighs wider, the man gave the lad's prick one or two frigs, and the sperm squirted over H's thighs.—This, as I happened not to be there, was told me the day after it had occurred.

The next time I saw H we talked over this masturbating frolic with the lad. She had been fucked by him twice, and the letch gratified, desired no more of him. But his youth and inexperience started in me a wish to see him fucking, to be in the room and then for us all together to do what we liked erotically. Before I left it had all been planned.

On the evening about a fortnight after, H looked lovely in laced chemise, crimson silk stockings, and pretty slippers.—As she threw up her legs showing her beautifully formed thighs and buttocks, the chestnut curls filling the space between them, relieved by a slight red stripe in the centre, never had I seen a more bewitchingly voluptuous sight. Rapidly my cock stood stiff and nodding, tho I was a little out of condition.—What a lovely odour it had as I gently licked her clitoris for a minute. But we had other

225

fish to fry. 'Harry's here,' said she. I stripped to my shirt, then be came up, a tall slim youth now just turned seventeen. Quickly *he* too stripped, for he knew the treat in store for him. I laid hold of his long thin tool, which was not stiff, and he seemed nervous.

How strange seems the handling of another's prick tho it's so like one's own. 'Show him your cunt.'—Back she went on the bed exhibiting her charms. The delicious red gap opened, his prick stiffened at once, and after a feel or two of his rigid gristle, I made him wash it tho already clean as a whistle.—I'd already washed my own. Then a letch came on suddenly, for I had arranged nothing—and taking his prick in my mouth I palated it. What a pleasant sensation is a nice smooth prick moving about one's mouth. No wonder French Paphians say that until a woman has sucked one whilst she's spending under another man's fucking, frigging, or gamahuche, that she has never tasted the supremest voluptuous pleasure. Some however had told me that they liked licking another woman's cunt, whilst a woman gamahuched them, better than sucking a prick in those exciting moments. But erotic tastes of course vary.

I laid him on the side of the bed alternately sucking or frigging him.—H was lying by his side, and he put his left fingers on her cunt.—I had intended to let him have his full complete pleasure in my mouth, but changed my mind. Then we laid together on the bed—head to tail—making what the French call sixty-nine or *tête-bêche*, and we sucked each other's pricks.—He was pleased with the performance.—H laying by our side said she should frig herself. Whether she did or not I can't say, being too much engrossed with minetting his doodle.—He did not illuminate me with skill, and after a little time we ceased and his prick drooped.

Then I mounted his belly as he lay on his back, and showed H how I used to rub pricks with Miss Frazer's young man, and putting both pricks together made H clutch them as well as she could with one hand.—But two ballocks were too large for her hand.

Helen's fingers had been feeling her own quim, almost the entire time since we had all been together, and her face now looked wild with voluptuousness.—She cried out 'Fuck me, fuck me' and threw herself on the edge of the bed, thighs distended, cunt gaping. But I knew my powers were too small that night to expedite my pleasure crises, and wished to prolong the erotic excitement, so would not fuck her nor let him.—But I gamahuched her. Then he did the same. She lay full length on the bed, he knelt between her legs, and whilst he plied his tongue upon her vulva, I laid on my back between her legs and his, and took his prick in my mouth. I felt her legs trembling and heard her sighs of delight, she was entering into the erotic amusement with heart and soul, cunt and bumhole as well, as I knew by her movements, ejaculations, and then tranquility. She spent just as a rapid ramming of his prick between my tongue and palate, told me he was about to spend also. So I rejected his tool quickly.

With rigid prick and incited by H he continued licking her cunt till she spent again. Then I laid them both side by side on the edge of the bed, he began frigging *her*, and I frigging *him*.—'It's coming,' said he, and at the instant out shot his sperm in four or five quick spurts, the first going nearly up to his breast.—How the young beggar's legs quivered as his juice left him. Helen leant over and looked as he spent.—His sperm was thinner than it should have been, tho he said he had neither fucked for a fortnight, nor frigged himself for a week. I believed he lied.—My sperm would have been at his age thicker after a week's abstinence. The last time he had fucked her before me it was much more and thicker. He reaffirmed that he had not spent for a week, and she declared he had not fucked *her*, so I suppose it was true.

He washed and pissed, again I played with his doodle and questioned him. He had he said buggered a man once, and frigged one.—Now he had a nice young woman, who let him have her for half a crown when he could afford it, but he only earned a pound a week and had to keep himself out of that. His prick was soon stiff again.—He gave her

227

cunt another lick, and then we went to work in the way. I had arranged with her when by ourselves. He did not know our game.

H in our many conversations on erotic whims and fancies, had expressed a great desire to have two pricks up her orifices at the same time. She wanted to know if it were possible, if sexual pleasure was increased by the simultaneous plugging of cunt and bumhole, and wondered if it would increase the pleasure of the man. I had shown her pictures of the positions in which the three placed themselves for the double coupling, and we arranged to try that evening. He was not now to know what we were at, his inexperience coupled with his excitement at being fucked by a most lovely creature, were calculated to leave him in the dark as to the operations at her back door. But we were obliged to be cautious.

He laid on the bedside his legs hanging down, whilst she standing with legs distended and enclosing his, leant over him—I watched the operation from the floor kneeling, and saw his doodle going up and down her cunt. Then when we knew his pleasure was increasing, I lubricated her bumhole with my spittle, and rising pressed my pego between her buttocks and against his prick, touching it from time to time as she moved her cunt on it. I did this as a blind. Soon after. 'Do you feel my prick?' said I. 'Yes.'—He didn't, for I was then putting my finger against it, but he was too engrossed with his pleasure to notice it. Then she backed her rump artfully, and his prick came out, as she pushed her buttocks towards me, and she kept on talking to him whilst making a show of introducing his pego again to her pudenda.

At the first push my prick failed. It was right in direction—for I had tried the orifice with thumb and finger—all inconvenient nails removed—and knew the road was clear. —Push—push—push with still failure, and then came nervous fear. There were the loveliest buttocks that belly ever pressed, or balls dangled against, smooth, sweet-smelling flesh, an anus without taint or hair, a sweet cunt and youthful prick, and a woman wanting the supremest voluptuousness. Every erotic incitement to sight, touch,

228

and imagination was there, but all was useless. My nature rebelled. Tho I wanted to do what she and I had talked of and wished for, my recreant prick would not rise to the needful rigidity—the more I strove the less my success.

I was mad not for myself but for *her* disappointment—it was *her* letch.—We had discussed the subject many times, and I longed for her to have sperm shed in her cunt and fundament at the same time. Further trial was useless, his prick was again worked by her, and I knew by her manner that she was near her crisis, when anxious to give her other orifice, the pleasure, kneeling I licked her bumhole then thrust my thumb into it, took his balls in my other hand and thumbuggered her whilst I squeezed his cods. She cried out. 'Oh—bugger, fuck,'—when madly excited and both spent. Then his prick flopped out wet and glairy from her cunt into my hand which was still beneath his balls—I arose and so did sweet H looking with bright voluptuous eyes at me.—He lay still on his back with eyes closed and prick flopping down, with a pearl of spunk on its tip. Then too late my damned, disgraced prick stood stiff like an iron rod, and could have gone into a virgin's arsehole or slipped into H's with ease. Sheer nervousness stopped it from doing duty, aided I think by a natural dislike—much as I desired the novelty,—novelty *with* her and *for* her.

The strongest fuckstress, with unlimited capability for sexual pleasure, the most voluptuous woman, the woman with the most thirsty cunt I ever knew, guessed my condition and state of mind. —'*You* fuck me, dear,' said she, and falling back on the bed opened her thighs. Her cunt was glistening with what he had left there.—He'd not uncunted two minutes, nor she finished spending four, yet she wanted my prick—either to gratify me or herself.

Randy enough I went near and pulled open the lips, saw the glistening orifice, pushed fingers up and withdrew them covered with the products of *her* quim and *his* doodle, and looked in her voluptuous eyes.—'Fuck—come on—fuck me.'—'You can't want it.'—'Yes—do me—do it.'—Harry then roused himself, I caught hold of his tool still thickish. 'Wash it, piddle, and she'll suck *you* whilst I

229

fuck *her*.'—*He* who only had spoken the whole evening in monosyllables, did that quickly. I laid him on the bed and she leant over him standing and bending, laid her face on his belly, her bum towards me.—'Suck his prick, dear'—'I shan't.'—She wouldn't, entreaty was useless, I could not wait, so opening her lower lips for a final look at the sperm, put my prick up her.—Oh! what a sigh and a wriggle she gave as I drove it hard against her womb. Her liking always was for violent thrusts, she liked her cunt stunned almost.—It gives her the greatest pleasure she often tells me. (When at a future day I dildoed her, she liked it pushed violently up her.)

I husbanded my powers, urged her to gamahuche him, hoping she would.—Her refusals grew less positive, and at last into her mouth went his prick but only for a minute.—'There I've done it,' said she.—His doodle had stood, but drooped directly her lips left it.

She'd do it no more, but laying her face on his prick, wriggling her backside, saying,—'Oh fuck me—fuck harder—go on dear.' What a fetch she has when she tightens her cunt round my prick and wriggles her lovely bum, it is almost impossible to stop thrusting!

But I would not finish, pulled out my prick and felt with pleasure its now spermy surface. I turned her round on to her back at the edge of the bed, and put him standing between her thighs. Then belly on belly, cock to cunt, all sorts of postures suggested themselves to me whilst they posed so, and I varied them till I could vary no longer.

Then I made him kneel on the bed over her head, his belly towards me. His prick hung down still biggish just over her head, whilst into her cunt I drove again my stiff stander and fucked, bending my head towards him to catch in my mouth his prick. She laid hold of it and held it towards me, I took it into my mouth and fucked her, holding her thighs and sucking him.—The young beggar's prick soon stood again—went half down my throat.—'Is his prick stiff again?' said she, spasmodically.—'Yes'—I mumbled.—'Oh, we're beasts—fuck me, fuck.'—But as my pleasure came on her mouth pleased me best, I let go his prick, and sinking over her put my tongue out to meet hers, and with mouths joined we spent.—He had slipped on one side when I relinquished his doodle, and when I raised myself and severed my wet lips from hers—our pleasure over—he was looking at us, and she with closed eyes had found and was clutching his doodle stiff still. What a treat for the young beggar.—Thousands would give a twenty-pound note to have seen and done all this. He had the treat for nothing.—All was her device, her lecherous suggestion.

Then we all washed, drank more champagne, and after a slight rest we both felt Harry's pego. Taking it into my mouth it stiffened.—'Can you fuck again?'—'I'll try,' said he.

Ready as if she had not been tailed for a month, her eyes liquid and beaming with voluptuous desire, she turned at once her bum towards him at the side of the bed, and gave him free access. I guided his pego, and the young chap began fucking hard again.—Then I laid myself on the bed, her face now on *my* belly, but in spite of all I could say she would not suck *me*. Was she frightened that *he* would tell Donkey prick of her? Annoyed I arose, and slipping my hand under his belly, frigged her little clitoris whilst he was fucking her on her back, I could feel his prick going up and down, in and out of her cunt, and felt even his balls—which are small.—From time to time I left my post to view the operators from afar, to see his bum oscillate and her thighs move.—It was a long job for him, but *she* spent soon.—The more she spends, the more violent at times seem her passions.—'Ah—don't stop, Harry—fuck— let your spunk come into my cunt,' she cried as she spent. He didn't spend but worked on like a steam engine.— 'Spunk—Spunk'—she cried again. Flap, flap went his belly up against her fat buttocks, the sound was almost as if her bum was being slapped by hand.—I thought he'd never spend so long was he in her, till I saw his eyes close.—'Are you coming?'—'Yhes.'—'Ahh—fuck, fuck,'—she screamed again, her whole frame quivered then action ceased, she slipped a little forward fatigued, his belly and pego following with her, and there they still were in copulation both silent and exhausted.—Soon after she uncunted him, and without a word turned onto the bed and laid down—I looked at her cunt and squeezed his prick, felt madly lewd but had no cockstand—I dare not excite myself too much now—I was envious, dull at not being able at once to fuck her again.

She lay with eyes brilliant, humid with pleasure and a little blue beneath the lids, and very red in face. She looked at me intently. 'Do it again,' said she.—'I can't.'—'You can, I am sure'—leaning on one elbow she raised her upper knee, her cunt slightly opening, and I felt it. He was washing.—'Put it in for a minute.'—'It's not stiff .'—Reaching out a hand she gave it a grip.—'You *can* fuck,' said she edging herself to the bedside again and opening her thighs. 'Do it this way just as I am lying.'—I could not resist and put my pego where she wished it—would do anything to bring my prick to touch her cunt.—It was not three inches long—but directly the tip was on her vulva and she rubbed it there, it began to swell. Stiff, stiffer it grew as she nudged it into her cunt. 'It's quite stiff,' said she—I feared a relapse and set to work vigorously, sucked her sweet mouth, exhausted it of spittle which I swallowed and then we spent together, *he* now looking on.—It was an exciting but killing fuck to me—my sperm felt like hot lead running from my ballocks, and the knob felt so sore as I spent, that I left off thrusting or wriggling, and finished by her repeating cuntal compressions and grind, in the art of which she is perfect mistress.—When I first knew her and her cunt was smaller, she never exercised that grip even if she had it—now her lovely avenue tho certainly larger to the fingers, is fatter inside, and has a delicious power of compression.

Harry now was silent, and she at last seemed fatigued, yet sitting by his side began again restlessly twiddling his cock. There were evident signs of its swelling—I felt it, but my lust was satisfied and I cared no more about feeling it. We chatted and drank awhile, and then she laid herself along the bed as if going to repose. Not a bit of it—her lust was not sated yet. She put a hand on to his tool and said, 'Fuck me, dear.' He said he could not. 'Try—I'll make you.' H's eyes when she wants fucking have a voluptuous expression beyond description.—It appeals to my senses irresistibly.—It is lewdness itself, and yet without coarseness, and even has softness and innocence so mixed with it, that it gives me the idea of a virgin who is randy and seeking the help of man, without in her innocence quite knowing what she wants, what he will do, and that there is neither shame nor harm in trying to get the article of which she does not know the use. Her voice also is low, soft and melodious—I was sitting when I saw that she was now in furious rut.—I've seen her so before—and she said to the lad 'Get on me—lay on me dear.'—'I can't do it.'—'You shall,' said she impetuously. 'Lay on my thigh.' The slim youth turned at once his belly on to hers. *He* had now no modesty left—we had knocked that out of him quite.

Wildly almost, she pulled his head to hers and kissed him, her eyes closed, her bum jogged, down went one hand between their bellies, a slight movement of *his* buttocks, a hitch of *her* bum, a twist, a jerk, then up go her knees and legs, her backside slips lower down, and by a slight twist she had got his prick into her. Then she gave two sharp heaves, clutched his backside and was quiet—her eyes were closed—I would give much to know what lewd thoughts were passing through her bawdy brain just then, a flood of lascivious images I'm sure, whilst her cunt was quietly, gently clipping his doodle. She opened her eyes when I said,—'Fuck her well.'—'Fuck dear,' said she to him and began gently her share of the exercise. He began also shagging, but quietly. 'Is your prick stiff?' said I—'Yhes.'—A strong smell of sperm, prick, cunt and sweat, the aroma of randy human flesh now pervaded the hot room,—the smell of rutting male and female, which stimulated me in an extraordinary way. I got lewd, my prick swelled, and for a moment I wanted to pull him off and fuck her myself, but restrained myself and put my hand under his balls to please my lust that way.

If he was a minute upon her he was forty.—Never have I had such a sight, never assisted at such a long fucking scene. She was beautiful in enjoying herself like a Messalina all the time—I squeezed his balls and gently encouraged him with lewd words, she with loving words till she went off into delirious obscenity. With her fine, strong, lovely shaped legs, thighs, and haunches she clipped him, he couldn't if he would have moved off her. Every few minutes she kissed him rapturously crying,— 'Put out your tongue, dear, kiss—kiss.—Ahaa-fuck-fuck harder—put your spunk in my cunt.'—Then came pro-longed loud cries.—'Ahrr—harre'—and she violently moved her buttocks, her thighs quivered—and after screeching.—'Aharrr'—beginning loud and ending softly, she was quiet and had spent. But a minute after she was oscillating her bum as violently as ever, and crying, 'Spend Harry, spend—kiss—kiss—put out your tongue—kiss— you've not spent—spend dear, kiss'—and her kisses resounded.

I moved nearer to her, and standing, slid my hand under her raised thighs and gently intruded my middle finger up her bumhole.—Her eyes opened and stared at me bawdily. 'Further up,' sobbed she in a whisper, her bum still moving. Then she outstretched her hand, and grasped my prick, and I bending to her, we kissed wet kisses. His head then was laying over her left shoulder hidden, he was ramming like a steam engine, and neither knew where my finger was, nor thought of aught but her cunt, I guess.

Again he put his mouth to hers, their tongues met, and she still holding my pego, on went the fuck. The ramming indeed had never stopped for an instant. My finger was now well up her bum, his balls knocking against my hand, and each minute her bawdy delirium came on.—'Now— spend Harry—spend.—Oh God—fuck—fuck—bugger.— Aharr—aharr.'—Again a screech, again quietness, and as languidly he thrust again she stimulated him.—'Fuck dear, that's it—your prick's stiff—isn't it?'—'Yhes'—'Your spunk's coming.'—'Y—hess.'—'Ahaa—spunk—fuck.—

Ahharr'—she screeched. The room rang with her deliriously voluptuous cries, and again all was quiet. So now was *he* for he'd spent, and out came my fingers as her sphincter strongly clipped it and *she* spent.

I thought it was all over but it was not, her rutting was unabated. 'Keep it in dear—you'll spend again'—'I can't'—'Yes, lie still.'—Again her thighs clipped his, and her hands clutched his backside. I felt under his balls the genital mucilaginous moisture of their passions oozing. His prick was small and I slid my finger up her cunt beside it.—He never noticed it. 'Don't you beast,'—said she.—'Give me some champagne.' I withdrew my moistened finger, gave her a glass, filled my mouth with some and emptied that into hers. She took it kissing me. She was mad for the male tho she murmured after her habit.—'Ain't we beasts?'—'No love, it's delicious, no beast could do what we do.'—He lay now with eyes closed, almost asleep, insensible, half only upon her, his face half buried in the pillow.—She raised her head partially, not disturbing his body, I held up her head, and a full glass of champagne went down her throat.—Then she fell back again and put her hand between their bellies. 'Is his prick out?' said I.

No reply made she—I put my hand under his buttocks, touched his prick which was still swollen, found she was introducing it to her quim and it touched my hand in doing it.—I saw that heave, jog and wriggle of her backside, her legs cross his, her hands clamp onto his buttocks, the jog, jog gently of her rump, then knew that again his pendant doodle was well in her lubricious cunt, and that she'd keep it there.—'How wet your cunt is, Helen,' said I.—'Beast' she softly murmured and began fucking quicker, tho *he* lay quite still.—Her eyes were again closed, her face scarlet. 'Feel his balls,' said she softly.—'Do you like my doing it?'—'Yes, it will make him stiff—do *that* again.'—Her eyes opened on me with a fierce bawdiness in them as she said that.—The exquisite voluptuous look, the desire of a virgin was no more there—delirious rutting, obscene wants in their plentitude was in them, the fiercest lust.—Up went my finger in her bum,—'Aha.—Aha—God'—sobbed she in quick staccato ejaculations.—'Fuck me dear.'

He roused himself at that, grasped her buttocks, thrust for a little time then relaxed his hold and lay lifeless on her. 'I can't do it, I'm sure.'—'You can, lay still a little.'—Still he laid like a log, but not she.—An almost imperceptible movement of her rump and thighs went on, ever and anon her eyes opened on me with a lustful glare, then closed again, and not a word she spoke whilst still her thighs and buttocks heaved.—I knew her cunt was clipping, was nut-cracking his tool,—often times I've felt that delicious constriction of her cunt, as in bawdy reverie I've laid upon her, half faint with the voluptuous delight of her embrace.—Some minutes ran away like this, whilst I was looking at her nakedness, feeling *his* balls withdrawing my finger from *her*, then gently, soothingly replacing it up her bum, frigging my own prick every now and then—none of us spoke.

Then more quickly came her heaves, he recommenced his thrusts. 'Fuck dear,—there—it's stiff.—Ahaa—yes—you'll spend soon.'—'Yes' murmured he.—'Yes,—shove hard—give me your spunk.' All was so softly murmured and with voices so fatigued, that I could scarcely hear them. Again I took my finger from her bumhole (for the position fatigued my hand), on they went slowly, again he stopped, again went on, each minute quicker, and soon furiously rammed hard whilst she heaved her backside up and down, thumping the bed which creaked and rocked with their boundings, and the champagne glasses on the tray jingled. Up into her bumhole went my finger. 'Aharr,' she shivered out.—'Bugger—fuck—fuck Harry—quicker—aharr—my God—I shall die—y'r spunk's—com—com—aharr—God—I shall go mad.'—'Ohooo' groaned he. Her sphincter tightened and pinched my finger out, another bound up and down, one more scream, then both were squirming, another scream from her, a hard short groan from him, and then she threw her arms back above her head, lay still with eyes closed, mouth wide open, face blood red, and covered with perspiration, her bosom heaving violently.

236

He rolled half off her, his prick lay against her thigh dribbling out thin sperm, his face covered with perspiration and again half buried in the pillow and laying nearly a lifeless mass at once he slept. Her thighs were wide apart, no sperm showing: his spend must have been small. Both were fucked out, exhausted with amorous strain.

My strength had been gradually returning, and my prick stood like a horn as I felt again his prick, and thrust my fingers up her lubricious cunt. No heed took either of my playing with their genitals.—I forgot the pains in my temples—cared not whether I died or not, so long as I could again penetrate that lovely body, could fuck and spend in that exquisite cunt. Pouring out more champagne I roused her and she drank it at a draught. 'Am I not a beast?' said she falling back again.—'No love, and I'll fuck you.'—'No, no. You cannot, I'm done and you'd better not.'—'I will.' Pushing the lad's leg off hers—he fast asleep—and tearing off my shirt, I threw myself upon her naked form and rushed my prick up her. Her cunt seemed large and wet but in a second it tightened on my pego.—Then in short phrases, with bawdy ejaculations, both screaming obscenities, we fucked.—'Is my prick larger than his?'—'Ah, yes'—'Longer?'—'Yes—aha, my God leave off, you'll kill me—I shall go mad.'—'Ah, darling—cunt—fuck.'—'Aha—prick—fuck me you bugger—spunk in me arsehole fuck—bugger—fuck—fuck.'—With screams of mutual pleasure we spent together, then lay embracing, both dozing, prick and cunt joined in the spermy bath.

'Get up love, I want to piddle,' said she. I rolled off her belly.—She rose staggering but smiling, kissed me and looked half ashamed. Her hair was loose, her face blood red and sweaty, her eyes humid with pleasure, and puffy and blue the skin under her eyes. She sat on the pot by the bedside looking at me and I at her, and still with voluptuous thoughts she put up her hand and felt my prick.—'You've fucked me well.'—'My God! aren't we three beasts—I'm done for.'—'So am I.'

I'd fucked her thrice, he thrice.—She spent to each of

237

our sexual spasms and many more times. During their last long belly to belly fucking *she* kept him up to it for *her* whole and sole pleasure, for she was oblivious of *me*.—She must have spent thrice to his once, for her lovely expression of face, her musical cries, her bawdy ejaculations during the orgasm—I know them full well by long experience—were not shammed. That would have been needless and impossible.—The tightening of her bumhole on my finger told the same tale, for the sphincter tightens in both man and woman when they spend.—She'd also frigged herself, been gamahuched by both of us, and spent under all. For two hours and a half, out of the four and a half I was with her that night, either finger, tongue, or prick had been at her cunt and for one hour and a half a prick *up* it.

Impossible as it seems even to me as I write it—absurd, almost incredible—she must have spent or experienced some venereal orgasm—something which gave her sexual pleasure, which elicited her cries, sighs and flesh quiverings, with other evidences of sexual delight, from twelve to twenty times. She may not have spent always, her vaginal juices may have refused to issue, their sources may have been exhausted after a time, yet pleasure she had I am sure. The amusement was planned by us—so far as such a programme can be, jointly for our joint erotic delight.—Harry was but a cypher tho an active one, a pawn to be moved for our mutual delight, and nothing more—tho of course much to his delight—lucky youth.

I thought of the orgy perpetually until I saw her again three days after. I couldn't get to her before.—She looked smiling and fresh as ever, not a trace of fatigue was on her face, but she admitted that she was quite worn out that night, and had spent as nearly as she could tell, twelve or fifteen times, had laid a bed all next day, drank strong beef tea, and that such another night would almost kill her.

The first week of my return from abroad I telegraphed a meeting with H. Getting no reply I went to her house which was empty. I telegraphed the scout, got no response, went there and *she* had flown, but I found that her letters were sent to a neighbouring chandler's shop—I wrote there naming an appointment in the dark and there found H waiting. All was changed, she lived in the country, was not sure if she could meet me, but if so at great risk, didn't know when or where but in a week would let me know. We drove through a park which was on the road to her station and felt each other's carnal agents, I besought her to get out and let us fuck against a tree. She was indignant at the proposal, and it ended in our frigging each other in the cab, face to face, kissing and tonguing, to the great injury of her bonnet, and a little soiling of her silk dress and my trousers. Who would care where sperm fell in such an entrancing ride?

A week after, a place of rendezvous was found, at a convenient snug little house where we met generally.— Before she'd taken anything off but her bonnet and I my hat, we fucked on the bedside with intense mutual delight. Directly I'd uncunted, we both stripped stark naked and got into bed, drank champagne there, and fucked and fucked again till my pego would stiffen no longer; fucked four times, a great effort now for me, but not for her. But frigging and gamahuching always satisfied her as a finish—luckily.

Then our meetings were at longer intervals apart, which only made them more delicious. But I alas, am obliged to husband my strength more than formerly, so the long intervals suit me better.

When next we met, we found that the mistress of the establishment had voluptuous photographs, pictures, and engravings by hundreds, and one or two chests full of the bawdiest books in English and French.—We revelled in them that day for all were placed at our disposal.—We sat feeling each other's genitals between our fuckings, looking and commenting on artistic display of nudities and erotic fancies, and wishing we could participate in such performances ourselves. They awakened ideas which had slumbered in me certainly. She said in her also, but she always declared that I had put desires into her head unknown before. We were well matched.

Living far off now, without a male or female friend with whom to talk about sexualities, more than ever now she looked to our days of meeting, and hours of unrestrained voluptuousness. After hearing all she had done at home even to domestic details—which she was fond of telling as showing her domestic comfort,—lust and love in all its whims and varieties we talked about. 'Did you ever do that?' 'Do you recollect when I showed you * * * prick?'—'When did so and so occur?' So ran our talk. How often he'd fucked her or gamahuched her, how often she'd frigged herself, the sperm *he* spent, and all the domestic bawdy doings were told me with delight, and similar frankness exacted from me.—Then came wishes. 'Let Mrs * * * * * get us another woman, you fuck *her* whilst she gamahuches *me*,' was a request made whilst after fucking, we laid reposing in the bed.—I agreed.—'Let her be stout, I'd like one as stout as Camille.'—These are the very words said funnily enough in a half shamefaced way—for absence and the change in her circumstances, at first seemed to impose some stupid modesty on her.—But both of us liked to call a spade a spade.

All was accomplished. The abbess as I shall call her, we ascertained would procure us every pleasure, tho only cautiously and from time to time she disclosed her powers. A very plump and almost fat, handsome woman of two and twenty was our first companion.—'Don't let *me* ask her, *you* say that *you* want her to lick my cunt—I don't want her to think that *I* wish it,'—said H. So it was done, we had champagne, I stripped the plump one, then asked H to look at her quim—which she was longing to do—and then incited her to the gamahuche. Bawdy talk and wine raising our lust made us friends soon, and Miss R jumped at the idea of gamahuching the other. Then naked all three (warm weather now). Looking-glasses arranged so that H could see all, she laid on the bed-side whilst R gamahuched her. On the bed by H's side I also laid, she frigging me during her pleasure. 'Aha—God—lick quicker.—I'm spending,'—and she spent nearly pulling my prick off during her first ecstasy.

Pausing for a minute, R recommenced, for H likes to continue uninterruptedly at that luscious game, till she has spent at least twice. It was a lovely sight to see H with her beautiful thighs, and the coral little gash set in the lovely chestnut hair, which R held open for a minute to admire. Then her mouth set greedily upon it, her hands under H's buttocks, the dark hair of R's armpits just peeping, her big white buttocks nearly touching her heels. I stooped down this time and peeped along the furrow past the bumhole, and could just see the red end of her cunt with the short crisp hair around it. Then straddling across her waist, my prick laying on her back between her blade bones, I watched the lovely face of H which in her sexual ecstasy is a lovely sight. 'Fuck, fuck her,' she cried to me. But I wouldn't. Next minute saw H's lovely eyes fixed on mine, whilst with soft cries she spent.

A rest, more champagne, a discourse about the pleasures of woman cunt licking woman and of men doing it, and H again was on the bed.—'Oh, I'm so lewd I want a fuck so,' said R—'He'll fuck you, won't you?'—I complied. Further back on the bed now the better to reach her cunt with her tongue, with pillows under her head lay H when R recommenced her lingual exercise on the sweet and fresh-washed quim. I standing up now at R's back.—'Fuck her, and spend when I do,' said H—R's bum towards me was almost too fat a one as she bent, so I made her bend lower, and then between the buttocks went my prick, dividing two well haired, very fat lips of her sanctum of pleasure. She adjusted her height to the exercise when my tip was well lodged, my balls were soon against the buttocks, every inch of my prick up a cunt deliciously lubricated by its owner's randiness.—'It's up her cunt love,' I cried, began fucking and R began gamahuching. All now was silence but the lap now and then of R's tongue on H's cunt. 'She's coming darling—I shall spend,'—I cried at length.—'Oh—God—fuck her, fuck, slap her bum,' cried

H writhing and sighing.—My slaps on the fat arse resounded, as R writhed and shivered with pleasure whilst licking on, and both of us spent as H spent under the tongue titillation. Then with slobbered prick and wet cunts we got up. Soon after standing by the bedside I fucked H whilst she frigged Miss R. Never were there three bawdy ones together who enjoyed the erotic tricks more than we did.

These delightful voluptuous exercises were repeated with variations on other days. R sucked my prick and took its libation whilst I was lying full length on the bed, H kneeling over my head, I licking her clitoris, the looking glasses so arranged that H could see all. Another day I fucked R whilst she frigged H. Then I put my prick into both women and finished in R's cunt, which completed that day's amusement.

Soon afterwards we noticed wales upon R's capacious white buttocks. It was from her last whipping she said. That disclosed what in time was sure to have become known to us. That the abbess was an expert in flagellation, that swells both old and young came under her experienced hand. Questioned, the abbess told us all, was indeed proud of her performances, showed us the varied apparatus with which she either tickled or bled the masculine bums, and women's as well, or superintended men flogging female bums. Such as the fat arsed R's were preferred, tho some she said liked younger and thinner buttocks. Some brought and birched a woman whom they liked and fucked, some a special woman to birch them. They all paid very handsomely for bleeding a fair pair of buttocks.

R told us that flagellation of *her* backside made her lewd an hour after or so. She liked the birch just to hurt slightly the cunt lips. Then if she couldn't get a man, she frigged herself—that some girls said it did not affect them lewdly—others that it did.—We talked quietly with the abbess about this. Both H and I desired to see the operation, and heard that some men liked to be seen by other men when being flogged. If we would come on a certain day, there would be then a gentleman who had a

242

taste for being made a spectacle, and she would arrange for us to see—for pay of course.

We went on the day but the man didn't appear. Two ladies were ready waiting to flog him. The abbess said it didn't matter, something had detained him, that when he disappointed he always paid the money for all concerned. One of them was dressed as a ballet girl, the other only in chemise, such were his orders.—She in chemise, was a sweet faced, dark haired shortish girl of nineteen, with fine teeth. We asked her to our room to take wine, and it ended in H frigging her and my fucking her, then in my fucking H, whilst she looked at the other's quim, and we agreed she would be better for our amorous games than R.—I will call this dark one 'Black.' She had one of the most delicate, refined, cock stiffening, slightly lipped, slightly haired cunts I ever saw: it resembled H's cunt years ago. Black took at once a frantic letch for gamahuching H—and who wouldn't?—When *my* mouth covers it, I can scarcely tear it away from it.

At our next visit the flagellation came off. As H, who'd only had her chemise on, and I my shirt and wearing a mask, entered the room, there was a man kneeling on a large chair at the foot of the bed, over which he was bending. Over the seat and back of the chair was a large towel to receive his spendings. He had a woman's dress on tucked up to his waist, showing his naked rump and thighs, with his feet in male socks and boots. On his head was a woman's cap tied carefully round his face to hide whiskers—if he had any—and he wore a half mask which left his mouth free.—At his back, standing, was one youngish girl holding a birch and dressed as a ballet dancer, with petticoats far up above her knees, and showing naked thighs. Her breasts were naked, hanging over her stays and showing dark haired armpits. Another tall, well formed, tho thinnish female, naked all but boots and stockings, with hair dyed a bright yellow, whilst her cunt and armpits' fringes were dark brown, stood also at his back—a bold, insolent looking bitch whom I one day fucked after she'd gamahuched H—tho I didn't like either

243

her face, cunt, form, or manner—but she was new to me.

What he had done with the women before we entered we were told afterwards by yellow head, was very simple. He'd stripped both women naked, and saw the one dress herself as a ballet girl, nothing more. Neither had touched his prick nor he their cunts. When the door was closed after we entered, he whispered to the abbess that he wanted to see my prick. Determined to go thro the whole performance, I lifted my shirt and showed it big but not stiff. He wanted to feel it but that I refused. 'Be a good boy or Miss Yellow (as I shall call her) will whip you hard,' said the abbess.—'Oh—no—no—pray don't,' he whispered in reply. He spoke always in whispers. Then he said H was lovely and wanted to see her cunt, which she refused. He never turned round during this but remained kneeling. Then after childish talk between him and the abbess (he always in whispers), 'Now she shall whip you, you naughty boy,' said the abbess—and 'swish' the rod descended heavily upon his rump.

'Oho—ho—ho,' he whispered as he felt the twinge. I moved round to the other side of him where I could see his prick more plainly. It was longish, pendant, and the prepuce covered its tip nearly.—Swish—swish—went the birch, and again he cried in whispers.—'Ho, ho.'—H then moved round to my side to see better.—Yellow head from behind him felt his prick.—The abbess winked at me.—Then he laid his head on the bedstead frame and grasped it with both hands, whilst very leisurely the birth fell on him and he cried. 'Ho—ho.'—His rump got red and then he cried *aloud*.—'Oh, I can't'—then sunk his voice to a whisper in finishing his sentence.—Yellow head again felt his prick which was stiffer, and *he* sideways felt *her* cunt, but still not looking round.

Then was a rest and a little talk, he still speaking in whispers. The abbess treated him like a child. I felt Yellow head's motte, she looked at H to see if *she* permitted *me* the license. Yellow head then took up the birch, and H and I moved to the other side of the bed. Both of us were excited, H's face was flushed with lust, I felt her cunt, and she my pego, now stiff. 'Look as those two,' quoth the abbess. We, and both the women laughed.—The patient had turned his head to look, but could see nothing but us standing.—Swish—swish, fell heavily the rod on his arse, now very red indeed.—'Let me lick her cunt,' whispered he, nodding at H.—She refused.—'I'll give her five pounds,' he whispered. H hesitated, but short of money as usual, at length she consented, beside she was lewd to her bumhole—'I shall spend,' she whispered to me as she got on to the bed and saying aloud, 'Five pounds, mind.'—'He'll pay, he's a gentleman,' murmured the abbess.

Then was the spectacle such as I never saw before nor shall again. H settled on the bed, thighs wide apart, quim gaping, legs over the bed frame, cunt close up to the victim, but too low for his tongue to reach the goal. The abbess, Miss Yellow head and I, pushed pillow after pillow under her lovely bum till it was up to the requisite level, and greedily he began licking it. I moved round him again, looking curiously at his prick which was now stiff.—'Let *him* feel it,' he whispered more loudly than usual. I felt and frigged it for a second. Whilst I did so, swish—swish—fell the rod on his rump, which writhed.—'Um—um—hum,'—he murmured, his mouth full of H's cunt. 'Ahrr,' sighed H, whose lovely face expressed her pleasure, for she was lewd. Yellow head laid hold of his prick, gave it two or three gentle frigs, and out spurted a shower of semen. Then he was quiet with his mouth full on H's open quim, whilst still Yellow head continued frigging his shrinking organ.—'Have you spent?'—said I. 'Damn it, I was just coming,' said H, jogging her cunt still up against his mouth, wild for her spend. But he was lifeless, all desire to lick her had gone.

At a hint from the abbess we went to our bedroom.—'Fuck me.'—On the bed she got, her cunt wet with his saliva, my prick nodding its wants and lust, up I plunged it in her wet cunt, thrust my tongue into her sweet mouth, our salivas poured into each other's, and we spent in rapture, almost before we had begun the glorious to and fro of my prick in her lubricious avenue.

Neither of us had seen such a sight before, never had either of us even seen anyone flogged, and we talked about it till the abbess came up. The man had left, but only gave three sovereigns for H's complaisance. 'No doubt she's kept the other two,'—said H afterwards. The young ladies were still below, would we like to have a chat with them? Our passions were well roused, H at once said 'Yes,' and up they came. We had champagne, giving the abbess some, then all talked about flagellation. The younger woman showed marks of the birch on her bum, and when the abbess had gone, we heard more about the rich victim, whom both had seen before and who was between fifty and sixty. He always had two women, but not always they two, they'd never known him allow strangers to be present when he was flogged, and he wanted to know if H would whip him some day. (She never would.) Then we all four stripped, both women gamahuched H and whilst the younger one was doing *that* I fucked Yellow head, whose cunt I couldn't bear. Then *she* gamahuched H and I without any effort fucked up the other girl and found *her* cunt delicious.—In the intervals we laid pell mell on the bed together, topsy-turvy,—arsy-versy, and any how and in all sorts of ways, looked at each other's cunts, the two women both sucked my prick to stiffness but no further and Yellow head put her finger up *my* bum as I fucked the younger girl at the bedside feeling H's lovely sweet cunt whilst I did so, and as *her* rump was towards me I paid the finger compliment to *her* bumhole.—We had champagne till all were tight, and gloried in most unrestrained bawdiness in act and talk. We all pissed, and I felt their amber streams whilst issuing, and pissed myself against Yellow head's cunt, H holding the basin.—Then fatigued with lustful exercises—H excepted—we had strong tea, and went our ways. A veritable orgy, and an extravagantly expensive one.

Now it was very clear and frankly avowed by H, that our meetings were the delight of her life, that tho happy at home they were friendless nearly, and she looked forward to meeting me with the greatest pleasure, not only to tell me all, but to indulge with me in reminiscences, and have bawdy afternoons with other women. 'And it's your fault, you've told me more than all the men and women together whom I've known.'—But there were hindrances. Sometimes two or three weeks intervened between our meetings at the abbess'; tho each meeting brought some bawdy novelty.

When next we met we had little Black and not Miss R for our companion, and Black and I together gave H her complete dose of pleasure. Two fucks, a frig, and three or four gamahuches, some by me, some by Black, seemed the quantum which she called a jolly bawdy afternoon. All were pleased, for B loved gamahuching H, and being gamahuched by *me*, and tho so young, willingly sucked my pego to its liquid culmination.—H still refusing to do that, or to touch B's quim with her tongue.—What with conversation about fucking in general—of the erotic caprices of men, of money gained and spent, sexual incitements, etc. etc.—in which conversations the abbess joined now at times—we passed most voluptuous afternoons or evenings.—But the cost was heavy—for the abbess' house was quiet and expensive, and champagne and a second gay lady added much to the sum total of the expenses of meeting H.

We from time to time gratified our letches in the various ways already described and epitomised. The conversations we had at other times with Misses R and B and occasionally with the abbess, were delightful. Both told us their experiences, and how, when, and where, pricks first penetrated their unscathed virgins' quims. The abbess told us of strange letches of her clients and of flagellation experiences. So there was nothing erotic that we did not know. Indeed there was little that we had to learn. Looking one day at a print of two women and two men fucking altogether, 'I should like you so to fuck a woman, whilst I am also fucked at your side,' said H. I agreed that it would be delicious. At other meetings on recurring to the subject, we resolved to have that amusement and that Black should be the other woman. 'But who the other man?' The abbess consulted said she knew a gentleman who could be one, but would be masked.—I didn't like that, nor did H, but towards the middle of the summer, H met at a town two miles from her residence, a gentleman who years before when she was gay, had tailed her. She'd talked and walked with him, he got passionate for her, *her* quim she admitted got hot, and forgetting all,—and she risked much,—let him strum her. Then her lusts fully roused, she'd gone to him again. When she told me of this I cautioned her, besought her.—'Oh! He has such a fine prick,' said she laughing, as she drank a glass of champagne. Yet this woman really loved her own man, but as in years before let her passions conquer her.—At church every Sunday after this she felt she was not good enough to be there. Lust is omnipotent.

Then he worried her. She'd refused to let him have her again, unless he'd be one of the party of four (she said). He, wild to possess her agreed, a day was named and Black informed. He was to be without a mask, I to wear one if I liked—for I didn't know what manner of man he might be, tho I'd no fear of a trap or trick on her part.—On the day H was there with Black and this temporary sweetheart, I entered the room masked, we began with luncheon which I had taken, and champagne of very good quality which the abbess kept in stock—for none but gentlemen entered her house,—and when we'd finished two bottles we were all ready for any bawdiness, our talk alone would have roused the prick of a dead man. Both the women had been sitting with chemises only on, we men without coats and waistcoats, for it was a hot day, the sun was shining, the sky clear, all was bright as day in that snug room, the scene of so much love making.

H sat on her friend's knee (Fancy I shall name him), and pulled out his pego, which out of lingering modesty, at the unaccustomed exposure to another male I suppose, was not stiff, tho large and pendant. Black did the same to me, and my tool was in similar condition.—'Make his stiff,' said H laughing, which in a minute the girl did, for the sight of H with her chemise now up to her rump, feeling his pego whilst he fingered her crimson gap, would have stiffened me without the aid of Black's fingers. His was now stiff and in handsome state.—'Isn't it a fine one?' said H proudly.—I'd guessed before that her old letch had made her give herself to the man—a big prick was her delight, her ideal of the male.—His was bigger every way than mine, was, indeed, a noble cunt stretcher. I longed to feel it, but *mauvaise honte* restrained me. H, who from many a conversation knew that I should like, said. 'Feel it—here,'—giving it an inviting shake and looking bawdily at me. Relieving mine from Black's fingers I went and felt it.—At once he grasped mine, and in silent delight we for the minute played with each other's ramrods. 'Let *me* feel it too,' said Black who came close to us and completed the group.—I put one hand between her thighs and felt her hot gap—gap now longing for a stretching, thirsting for the male libation—whilst I handled *his* stiff rod and H handled *mine*. Hands across—a salacious quartet.

Then all stripped to our skin, put the looking glasses so as to reflect us, and in varied groupings viewed ourselves. It was, 'Do this.'—'Lay hold of his prick.'—'Let Black hold it as well.'—'Oh! You hurt my cunt.'— 'Feel H's cunt, Black,'—etc. etc. Not a minute were we in the same position, restless letches were in all of us, bums to bellies, prick crossing prick we men placed them, both pricks stiff as horns. The women delighted, Black knelt down and took my prick in her mouth, her bum towards a glass, incited to that by H. Stooping I took *his* noble tool into mine, and so on, till stimulated by these lascivious preliminaries, 'Oh!—my God—fuck me,' said H. Going to the bed and pushing the glasses into position, she mounted it; in a minute Black followed, and we men were by the bedside ready to cover them.

All had washed pricks and cunts at the beginning, and all were ready for the luscious games.—'No, at the side,' said H changing her mind. There she got, and Black laid by her side. Both opened wide their thighs. H lay with her handsome central furrow, of deeper crimson tint now than years ago, wider spread and fuller now are the curls around it, shining like satin was the surface of the pretty gap. Black's pretty youthful black haired slit shone like coral, showing its tiny nymphae as she lay with finger on her clitoris, put there in her impatient randiness to give incipient pleasure, and make we men more lewd.—'I'll fuck *you* dear H.' 'No, Fancy shall fuck me, you fuck B.'—The biggest prick and the novelty fetched her. I threw myself upon my knees, and licked all over the smooth and pulpy surface of her sweet scented cunt, whilst Fancy seeing my initiative, licked the other's little randy split.—'Oh—Fuck-fuck'—cried H impatiently. Rising I clutched her thighs and drove my glowing prick right up her cunt. 'You shan't fuck me with that mask on,' cried she, and ere I could prevent it uncunted me and drew my mask from off my face. 'Let Fancy fuck me first.'—Reckless now, glad to be rid of the mask which heated my face, I let it lie where it fell, and turning round again I felt his noble shaft, just as he approached the eager slit of H. Then I went to B and drove my pego up her. The next second his balls were against H's bum, his shaft engulfed, and mine up B's little cunt.

This with loud and bawdy talk, then all was quiet. Pleasures too great were ours now for utterances, as pricks and cunts were joined, and we fucked close together, side by side, the women's thighs touching, the glass sideways showing us all. Each could see all—the women's legs held up, the men's arses oscillating with the up and down, and in and out movements of their pricks, in the warm moist quims. Putting one hand out I felt his buttocks.—H tried to put her hand on to B's motte.—'Oh! Look at us fucking,'—cried she. She loves the spectacle of naked copulation, and we never fuck in this house without fixing our eye upon the glasses, where we see our every movement.

She sighed 'Ahaa,'—her belly heaved—B's ivory plump buttocks reciprocated my thrusts, she pushed her legs up higher as she felt my prick's friction.—Rapidly both women's arses now jogged and heaved, as our pricks ammed harder, faster, and wriggled in the cuntal depths. Aherr—spunk—fuck,'—cried H.—She loves the bawdy ries. 'Fuck.'—'Are you spending, Black?'—'Aha-yes-punk,'—cried B sympathetically.—'My spunk's spending n your cunt dear.'—'Aher.'—'Yhes—fuck,' and in a Babel of lascivious cries, bodies heaving, arses jogging, hort jogs, cunts wriggling and gripping, bellies and thighs huddering with the luscious pleasure, out shot our spunk. Then bending over our women, with gentlest movements queezing our pricks into the cunts gorged to overflowing with the soft mucus, in soothing baths of our blended pendings lay our pricks weltering, all of us quiet, xhausted, dying away after the delirium of the crisis lissolving in the lingering, blissful, soothing volup-uousness of our sexual pleasure, oblivious of all but the blessed conjunction of prick and cunt.

Such bliss can't last forever.—With senses returning we nen stood erect, pricks still in cunts, but dwindling in the ubricious emulsion of our making. We talked, still holding up the women's legs, who lay with humid eyes, glad to retain the pleasure-giving implements up them. Has he spent much H?'—'Lots, I'm full, it's running out of my cunt,' said H—for I thought of her first.—'Let me ee.'—'You shan't you beast,'—laughing.—'Don't let her egs close Fancy,—keep your thighs apart B.'—Fancy ntered into the fun and withdrew his dripping pego as nine quitted B's glutenous gap. I closed on H, and saw fat perm rolling from her heated quim—opaque and thin ogether.—He'd spent fully, I had deluged B's little tight vulva. H opened wider still her thighs for my inspection. He had left the women, having, it seemed, no taste for the glorious sight, and began washing his tool.

H who knew my letch and had her own, tho saying, Beast,' remained quiescent, expectant.—She knew the ight would stimulate my lust, and I felt her lovely ubricious gap with one hand, and with the other B's nucilaginous vulva. How smooth and large cunts feel after heir spend, and the male libations are in them.—I plunged or a second my fingers up both cunts, I paddled in the

251

sperm and my prick stiffened, pulsated with desire. Old letches came on me, I put my prick up H. But when half entered, shaking her head silently she pushed me off and winked, looking across at him, who with his rump towards us was still washing. I understood, she didn't wish *him* to see that. Soon after he did.

Then all washed. The women squatting, H beginning to piddle after ablution. I put out my hand and caught the amber stream, at which he laughed.—Naked then all sat down, the abbess brought more champagne, and said it was a pretty sight to see us naked. As we drank, H with one hand was feeling his prick as they sat together on the sofa. Black sitting on my thigh was feeling mine.—'Isn't his a fine prick?' said H. It had swollen again. The abbess felt it, chuckled and said. 'Ain't it a beauty?' Then after feeling mine and patting H's haunches.—'Hasn't she a nice bum?—two pricks standing.—Oh! What a pretty sight,' and then she left the room.

We put on chemises and shirts, for hot as it was, in our climate long continued nudity often causes chilliness. Talk of prick and cunt and fucking them went on, and of but little else, every now and then feeling our pricks and cunts quite indiscriminately, he mine, I his, lifting shirts and chemise at times to gratify our eyes, H now feeling his and mine at the same time, H lolling bawdily on a sofa with him, B and I lolling upon the bed.

More champagne and more pissing. I held his tool to see the watery spout. Then we placed the women against the bedside with bums towards us, to compare the beauty of their notches, then slapping their buttocks with our pricks, pulling the hairy lips apart, tickling the stripes with tongues, and other lascivious whims and fancies, our passions were soon roused. H said, 'Let's fuck,'—before we men were ready.—I knew the lot of spending she could give, the fucking she needed when in rut as she was today—the day long anticipated and prepared for.—Again all stripped and went to the soul stirring, delicious, sexual embrace. The embrace when man and woman are angels to each other, tho the power of fucking is the gift of every animal in creation, is the function of a beast. But how Divine the pleasure in body and mind when doing it.

'I won't fuck yet I'll gamahuche,'—said I, wishing to husband my sperm. H ready, opened her thighs, and my tongue tickled her till she went off shrieking in her voluptuous delirium. She was frigging B with one hand, holding Fancy's prick—which now again stood nobly— and with the other.—H and I suggested all, he seemed passive but ready.—'Gamahuche me,' said she to him directly I had given her pleasure. Down he knelt and licked her vulva which she'd only wiped. She didn't disguise her pleasure, gave way to it with all its delirium of movements and words. 'Oh—God go on—ahrr—feel his prick—is it stiff?' I felt his rigid staff with lascivious delight.—'Stiff as a poker.' 'Ahaa,—I can see you—aha—frig it.'—I did.—'Aha, I shall spend—don't make him—spend. —Aha—spunk—fuck,'—and again her cunt gave out its pearlyjuices whilst violently she frigged Black who lay on the bed next to her with head turned towards, and watching her raptures.

Up he got with moistened lips, and without a word plunged his big pego up her, she nothing loath. I watched them for a while, then looked beneath his ballocks which were ample in size, well wrinkled, then took it in my hand and squeezed it gently. A shudder of delight passed through him. 'I'm feeling his balls.—Suck my prick, Black dear.'—'I want to frig her,' said H.—'No, come.'—B came and stooping took the red tip of my pego into her mouth and tongued and licked and played with it, whilst I held his balls, looking at H's face. And he fucked on till her heavenly smile came. Then he groaned lightly and again filled her vulva with his sperm.

Taking my prick from out of B's mouth I pushed it between his buttock furrow, till it touched his ballocks—out came his prick, and at once I went between H's thighs, caught up her drooping legs, and rushed my prick now bursting with desire, up her lubricated cunt, overflowing again with his mucilage. She laughed aloud now, and so did he. Champagne was doing its work, all modesty, if we'd had any, was gone. I thrust and thrust, glorying in its lubricity, in being in the soft avenue his prick had quitted.—B sprang on the bed.—'Show me your bum,' said he.—With her buttocks turned towards him.—'Fuck me so,' said she.—But he'd just spent, and to see *me* fucking was his pleasure. He hadn't washed.—'Let me feel your prick,' said I.—'Let *me* feel it,' cried H with excited eyes. Relinquishing one of her legs I grasped his gummy tool—a fine big handful even now—and pulled him by it close to me. H put the leg I'd dropped up and rested on his haunch. Then feeling him, looking at B's little black haired notch pouting red from between her buttocks, I fucked and spent, and that randy devil H spent again.

'Why didn't you fuck *me*?' said B angrily, as I pulled my prick out of H's cunt. She was a little elevated and quarrelsome.—'Gamahuche her,' said H who sat up looking now fatigued in her eyes—no wonder?—'You didn't spend with me,' said I.—'I'll swear I did.'—I knew her force, her stirring lewdness, but liked to tease her so. I pushed her back and put my fingers up her cunt, whilst watching B, who in a temper pushed Fancy off, who was gamahuching her. 'You don't do it nice.'—We all laughed.—'Fuck me.'—'I can't yet,' said he.—'I'll frig myself, let me feel your prick.' H got off the bed. —B laid herself lengthwise on it, and felt his prick, he standing by her side whilst she frigged herself. Then—'Fuck me, I hate frigging,' and getting off she rushed to the champagne.—There was none.—'You've had enough,' said H.—'I haven't, and you've had all the fucking.'—'What if I have?'—Then was a wrangle, in which H told B she'd come there to help to amuse *us*, and might leave if she liked.

More champagne, Black got quite screwed and outrageously bawdy, mad for prick. We were all getting screwed and Fancy particularly so. An hour ran away, H wouldn't minette me or him.—'Gamahuche me B, and when stiff I'll fuck you,' said I.—'No, you fuck *me* whilst I gamahuche *him*.'—H was then handling F's tool but relinquished it. I laid on the bed and B minetted me to rigidity, then I tongue tickled her quim a little, then on the bedside kneeling over her, she sucking *me*, Fancy fucked *her*, looking at my rump, H looking on and feeling his ballocks from behind.

'Suck on,' I cried. But B who had before half frigged herself spent and let go my prick leaving me unfinished.—'He's a fine prick,' were the first words she uttered.—'He has,' said H eulogistically.

More champagne and sweet cakes sent for. The abbess came up, said we were making a dreadful noise, and some friends of hers were below.

A little quieted, soon after we put both our pricks into both cunts, and talked about that. Then we mounted the bed, he fucked H, I fucked Black, both couples side by side and close together. We had fancies even then, and lying on the top of them felt each other's woman, and showed our pricks.—Then encouraging each other bawdily, we fucked till we spent amidst a chorus of lustful words. Just then in came the abbess again, and smacked my rump as I was lying on B, and giving her the last wriggle with my prick.

Then we had tea—then more wine—and again incited each other to further exercises.—Groggy, weary, fucked out all, yet lewd still, we kissed all round and then left one by one, I first, and never shall see the like again.—It *was* an orgy. All the erotic whims which two men and two women could do together in five hours, I think we did.

The Autobiography of a Flea

In the hundred years since it first gripped the imagination of an eager readership, The Autobiography of a Flea *has achieved a degree of notoriety known to only a handful of erotic novels. Though often banned by the authorities – as recently as the early 1980s an innocuous (and inept) video based on the book was regularly seized by the British police – like many other 'dirty' books this one refuses to die, indeed the novel is as difficult to eradicate as the robust vermin of its title. Yet its appeal is not obvious. Based firmly on anticlerical themes made popular in France in the eighteenth century in books such as Gervaise de Latouche's* Dom Bougre *and Mirabeau's* Libertin de Qualité, *it recounts the loss of innocence of a young girl at the hands of those who should be protecting her, namely her priest and her guardian uncle. Inevitably, in a book of this nature, the young lady takes to sexual excess like a drunk to free beer and a wild time is had by all. What distinguishes the story, and doubtless has earned it a permanent place in the affection of generations of readers, is the personality of the narrator. As indicated by the title of the book, the tale is told by a flea.*

Blessed by a 'mental perception and erudition which placed me for ever upon a pinnacle of insect grandeur' our flea lives on the luscious flesh of young Bella – 'a beauty – just sixteen – a perfect figure, and although so young, her soft bosom was already budding into those proportions which delight the other sex.' Poised upon such an adorable meal ticket, the flea is in the perfect spot to recount every nuance of her exhausting adventures. The following excerpt finds Bella reporting for the first time to the formidable Father Ambrose as a consequence of losing her maidenhead to her sweetheart Charlie. The priest has fortuitously witnessed the adolescent tryst and, on pain of disclosure to her guardian, has commanded Bella to meet him in the sacristy the next day . . .

Curiosity to learn the sequel of an adventure in which I already felt so much interest, as well as a tender solicitude for the gentle and amiable Bella, constrained me to keep in her vicinity, and I, therefore, took care not to annoy her with any very decided attentions on my part, or to raise resistance by an illtimed attack at a moment when it was necessary to the success of my design to remain within range of that young lady's operations.

I shall not attempt to tell of the miserable period passed by my young protegée in the interval which elapsed between the shocking discovery made by the holy Father Confessor, and the hour assigned by him for the interview in the sacristy, which was to decide the fate of the unfortunate Bella.

With trembling steps and downcast eyes the frightened girl presented herself at the porch and knocked.

The door was opened and the Father appeared upon the threshold.

At a sign Bella entered and stood before the stately presence of the holy man.

An embarrassing silence of some seconds followed. Father Ambrose was the first to break the spell.

'You have done right, my daughter, to come to me so punctually; the ready obedience of the penitent is the first sign of the spirit within which obtains the Divine forgiveness.'

At these gracious words Bella took courage, and already a load seemed to fall from her heart.

Father Ambrose continued, seating himself at the same time upon the long-cushioned seat which covered a huge oak chest:

'I have thought much, and prayed much on your account, my daughter. For some time there appeared no way in which I could absolve my conscience otherwise than to go to your natural protector and lay before him the dreadful secret of which I have become the unhappy possessor.'

Here he paused, and Bella, who knew well the severe character of her uncle, on whom she was entirely dependent, trembled at his words.

Taking her hand in his, and gently drawing the girl to the same seat, so that she found herself kneeling before him, while his right hand pressed her rounded shoulder, he went on.

'But I am wounded to think of the dreadful results which would follow such a disclosure, and I have asked for assistance from the Blessed Virgin in my trouble. She has pointed out a way which, while it also serves the ends of our holy church, likely prevents the consequences of your offence from being known to your uncle. The first necessity which this course imposes is, however, implicit obedience.'

Bella, only too rejoiced to hear of a way out of her trouble, readily promised the most blind obedience to the command of her spiritual Father.

The young girl was kneeling at his feet. Father

Ambrose bent his large head over her recumbent figure. A warm tint lit his cheeks, a strange fire danced in his fierce eyes: his hands trembled slightly as they rested upon the shoulders of his penitent, but his composure was otherwise unruffled. Doubtless his spirit was troubled at the conflict going on within him between the duty he had to fulfil and the tortuous path by which he hoped to avoid the awful exposure.

The holy Father then began a long lecture upon the virtue of obedience, and the absolute submissions to the guidance of the minister of holy church.

Bella reiterated her assurance of entire patience and obedience in all things.

Meanwhile it was evident to me that the priest was a victim to some confined, but rebellious spirit which rose within him, and at times almost broke out into complete possession in the flashing eyes and hot passionate lips.

Father Ambrose gently drew the beautiful penitent nearer and nearer, until her fair arms rested upon his knees, and her face bent downwards in holy resignation, sunk almost upon her hands.

'And now, my child,' continued the holy man, 'it is time that I should tell you the means vouchsafed to me by the Blessed Virgin by which alone I am absolved from exposing your offence. There are ministering spirits who have confided to them the relief of those passions and those exigencies which the servants of the church are forbidden openly to avow, but which, who can doubt, they have need to satisfy. These chosen few are mainly selected from among those who have already trodden the path of fleshly indulgence; to them is confined the solemn and holy duty of assuaging the earthly desires of our religious community in the strictest secrecy. To you,' whispered the Father, his voice trembling with emotion, and his large hands passing by an easy transition from the shoulders of his penitent to her slender waist.

'To you, who have once already tasted the supreme pleasure of copulation, it is competent to assume this holy office. Not only will your sin be thus effaced and pardoned, but it will be permitted you to taste legitimately those ecstatic delights, those overpowering sensations of rapturous enjoyment, which in the arms of her faithful servants you are at all times sure to find. You will swim in a sea of sensual pleasure, without incurring the penalties of illicit love. Your absolution will follow each occasion of your yielding your sweet body to the gratification on the church, through her ministers, and you will be rewarded and sustained in the pious work by witnessing – nay, Bella, by sharing fully those intense and fervent emotions, the delicious enjoyment of your beautiful person must provoke.'

Bella listened to this insidious proposal with mingled feelings of surprise and pleasure.

The wild and lewd impulses of her warm nature were at once awakened by the picture now presented to her fervid imagination – how could she hesitate?

The pious priest drew her yielding form towards him, and printed a long hot kiss upon her rosy lips.

'Holy Mother,' murmured Bella, whose sexual instincts were each moment becoming more fully roused. 'This is too much for me to bear – I long – I wonder – I know not what!'

'Sweet innocent, it will be for me to instruct you. In my person you will find your best and fittest preceptor in those exercises you will henceforth have to fulfil.'

Father Ambrose slightly shifted his position. It was then that Bella noticed for the first time the heated look of sensuality which now almost frightened her.

It was now also that she became aware of the enormous protuberance of the front of the holy Father's silk cassock.

The excited priest hardly cared any longer to conceal either his condition or his designs.

Catching the beautiful child to his arms he kissed

her long and passionately. He pressed her sweet body to his burly person, and rudely threw himself forward into closer contact with her graceful form.

At length the consuming lust with which he was burning carried him beyond all bounds, and partly releasing Bella from the constraint of his ardent embrace, he opened the front of his cassock, and exposed, without a blush, to the astonished eyes of his young penitent, a member the gigantic proportions of which, no less than its stiffness and rigidity completely confounded her.

It is impossible to describe the sensations produced upon the gentle Bella by the sudden display of this formidable instrument.

Her eyes were instantly riveted upon it, while the Father, noticing her astonishment, but detecting rightly that there was nothing mingled with it of alarm or apprehension, coolly placed it into her hands. It was then that Bella became wildly excited with the muscular contact of this tremendous thing.

Only having seen the very moderate proportions displayed by Charlie, she found her lewdest sensations quickly awakened by so remarkable a phenomenon, and clasping the huge object as well as she could in her soft little hands, she sank down beside it in an ecstasy of sensual delight.

'Holy Mother, this is already heaven!' murmured Bella. 'Oh! Father, who would have believed I could have been selected for such pleasure!'

This was too much for Father Ambrose. He was delighted at the lubricity of his fair penitent, and the success of his infamous trick (for he had planned the whole, and had been instrumental in bringing the two young lovers together and affording them an opportunity of indulging their warm temperaments, unknown to all save himself, as, hidden close by, with flaming eyes, he watched the amatory combat).

Hastily rising, he caught up the light figure of the

young Bella, and placing her upon the cushioned seat on which he had lately been sitting, he threw up her plump legs and separating to the utmost her willing thighs, he beheld for an instant the delicious pinky slit which appeared at the bottom of her white belly. Then, without a word, he plunged his face towards it, and thrusting his lecherous tongue up the moist sheath as far as he could, he sucked it so deliciously that Bella, in a shuddering ecstasy of passion, her young body writhing in spasmodic contortions of pleasure, gave down a plentiful emission, which the holy man swallowed like a custard.

For a few moments there was calm.

Bella lay on her back, her arms extended on either side, and her head thrown back in an attitude of delicious exhaustion, succeeding the wild emotions so lately occasioned by the lewd proceedings of the reverend Father.

Her bosom yet palpitated with the violence of her transports and her beautiful eyes remained half closed in languid repose.

Father Ambrose was one of the few who, under circumstances such as the present, was able to keep the instincts of passion under command. Long habits of patience in the attainment of his object, a general doggedness of manner and the conventional caution of his order, had not been lost upon his fiery nature, and although by nature unfitted for his holy calling, and a prey to desires as violent as they were irregular, he had taught himself to school his passions even to mortification.

It is time to lift the veil from the real character of this man. I do so with respect, but the truth must be told.

Father Ambrose was the living personification of lust. His mind was in reality devoted to its pursuit, and his grossly animal instincts, his ardent and vigorous constitution, no less than his hard unbending nature made him resemble in body, as in mind, the Satyr of old.

But Bella only knew him as the holy Father who had not only pardoned her offence, but who had opened to her the path by which she might, as she supposed, legitimately enjoy those pleasures which had already wrought so strongly on her young imagination.

The bold priest, singularly charmed, not only at the success of his strategem which had given into his hands so luscious a victim, but also at the extraordinary sensuality of her constitution, and the evident delight with which she lent herself to his desires, now set himself leisurely to reap the fruits of his trickery, and revel to the utmost in the enjoyment which the possession of all the delicate charms of Bella could procure to appease his frightful lust.

She was his at last, and as he rose from her quivering body, his lips yet reeking with the plentiful evidence of her participation in his pleasure, his member became yet more fearfully hard and swollen, and the full red head shone with the bursting strain of blood and muscle beneath.

No sooner did the young Bella find herself released from the attack of her confessor upon the sensitive part of her person already described, and raised her head from the recumbent position into which it had fallen, than her eyes fell for the second time upon the big truncheon which the Father kept impudently exposed.

Bella noted the long and thick white shaft, and the curling mass of black hair out of which it rose, stiffly inclined upwards, and protruding from its end was the egg-shaped head, skinned and ruddy, and seeming to invite the contact of her hand.

Bella beheld this thickened muscular mass of stiffened flesh, and unable to resist the inclination, flew once more to seize it in her grasp.

She squeezed it – she pressed it – she drew back the

folding skin, and watched the broad nut, as it inclined towards her. She saw with wonder the small slit-like hole at its extremity and taking both her hands, she held it throbbing close to her face.

'Oh! Father, what a beautiful thing,' exclaimed Bella, 'what an immense one, too. Oh! Please, dear Father Ambrose, do tell me what I must do to relieve you of those feelings which you say give our holy ministers of religion so much pain and uneasiness.'

Father Ambrose was almost too excited to reply, but taking her hand in his, he showed the innocent girl how to move her white fingers up and down upon the shoulders of his huge affair.

His pleasure was intense, and that of Bella was hardly less.

She continued to rub his limb with her soft palms and, looking up innocently to his face asked softly – 'If that gave him pleasure, and was nice, and whether she might go on, as she was doing.'

Meanwhile the reverend Father felt his big penis grow harder and even stiffer under the exciting titillations of the young girl.

'Stay a moment; if you continue to rub it so I shall spend,' softly said he. 'It will be better to defer it a little.'

'Spend, my Father,' asked Bella, eagerly, 'what is that?'

'Oh, sweet girl, charming alike in your beauty and your innocence; how divinely you fulfil your divine mission,' exclaimed Ambrose, delighted to outrage and debase the evident inexperience of his young penitent.

'To spend is to complete the act whereby the full pleasure of venery is enjoyed, and then a rich quantity of thick white fluid escapes from the thing you now hold in your hand, and rushing forth, gives equal pleasure to him who ejects it and to the person who, in some manner or other, receives it.'

Bella remembered Charlie and his ecstasy, and knew immediately what was meant.

'Would this outpouring give you relief, my Father?'

'Undoubtedly, my daughter, it is that fervent relief I have in view, offering you the opportunity of taking from me the blissful sacrifice of one of the humblest servants of the church.'

'How delicious,' murmured Bella; 'by my means this rich stream is to flow, and all for me the holy man proposed this end of his pleasure – how happy I am to be able to give him so much pleasure.

As she half pondered, half uttered these thoughts she bent her head down; a faint, but exquisitely sensual perfume rose from the object of her adoration. She pressed her moist lips upon its top, she covered the little slitlike hole with her lovely mouth, and imprinted upon the glowing member a fervent kiss.

'What is this fluid called?' asked Bella, once more raising her pretty face.

'It has various names,' replied the holy man, 'according to the status of the person employing them; but between you and me, my daughter, we shall call it spunk.'

'Spunk!' repeated Bella, innocently, making the erotic word fall from her sweet lips with an unction which was natural under the circumstances.

'Yes, my daughter, spunk is the word I wish you to understand it by, and you shall presently have a plentiful bedewal of the precious essence.'

'How must I receive it?' enquired Bella, thinking of Charlie and the tremendous difference relatively between his instrument and the gigantic and swollen penis in her presence now.

'There are various ways, all of which you will have to learn, but at present we have only slight accommodation for the principal act of reverential venery, of that permitted copulation of which I have already spoken. We must, therefore, supply another and easier method, and instead of my discharging the essence called spunk into your body, where the extreme tightness of that little slit of yours would doubtless cause it to flow very abundantly, we will commence by the friction of your obedient fingers, until the time when I feel the approach of those spasms which accompany the emission. You shall then, at a signal from me, place as much as you can of the head of this affair between your lips, and there suffer me to disgorge the trickling spunk, until the last drop being expended I shall retire satisfied, at least for the time.'

Bella, whose jealous instincts led her to enjoy the description which her confessor offered, and who was quite as eager as himself for the completion of this outrageous programme, readily expressed her willingness to comply.

Ambrose once more placed his large penis in Bella's fair hands.

Excited alike by the sight and touch of so remarkable an object, which both her hands now grasped with delight, the girl set herself to work to tickle, rub and press the huge and stiff affair in a way which gave the licentious priest the keenest enjoyment.

Not content with the friction of her delicate fingers, Bella, uttering words of devotion and satisfaction, now placed the foaming head upon her rosy lips and allowed it to slip in as far as it could, hoping by her touches, no less than by the gliding movements of her tongue, to provoke the delicious ejaculation of which she was in want.

This was almost beyond the anticipation of the holy priest, who had hardly supposed he should find so ready a disciple in the irregular attack he proposed; and his feelings being roused to the utmost by the delicious titillation he was now experiencing, prepared himself to flood the young girl's mouth and throat with the full stream of his powerful discharge.

Ambrose began to feel he could not last longer without letting fly his roe, and thereby ending his pleasure.

He was one of those extraordinary men, the abundance of whose seminal ejaculation is far beyond that of ordinary beings. Not only had he the singular gift of repeatedly performing the veneral act with but very short respite, but the quantity with which he ended his pleasure was as tremendous as it was unusual. The superfluity seemed to come from him in proportion as his animal passions were aroused, and as his libidinous desires were intense and large, so also were the outpourings which relieved them.

It was under these circumstances that the gentle Bella undertook to release the pent-up torrents of this man's lust. It was her sweet mouth which was to be the recipient of those thick slippery volumes of which she had had as yet no experience, and, all ignorant as she was of the effect of the relief she was so anxious to administer, the beautiful maid desired the consummation of her labour and the overflow of that spunk of which the good Father had told her.

Harder and hotter grew the rampant member as Bella's exciting lips pressed its large head and her tongue played around the little opening. Her two white hands bore back the soft skin from its shoulders and alternately tickled the lower extremity.

Twice Ambrose, unable to bear without spending the delicious contact, drew back the tip from her rosy lips.

At length Bella, impatient of delay, and apparently bent on perfecting her task, pressed forward with more energy than ever upon the stiff shaft.

Instantly there was a stiffening of the limbs of the good priest. His legs spread wide on either side of his penitent. His hands grasped convulsively at the cushions, his body was thrust forward and straightened out.

'Oh, holy Christ! I am going to spend!' he exclaimed, as with parted lips and glazing eyes he looked his last

269

upon his innocent victim. Then he shivered percep-
tibly, and with low moans and short, hysteric cries,
his penis, in obedience to the provocation of the young
lady, began to jet forth its volumes of thick and glutinous fluid.

Bella, sensible of the gushes which now came slop-
ping, jet after jet into her mouth, and ran in streams
down her throat, hearing the cries of her companion,
and perceiving with ready intuition that he was enjoying to the utmost the effect she had brought about,
continued her rubbings and compression until gorged
with the slimy discharge, and half choked by its abundance, she was compelled to let go of this human syringe, which continued to spout out its gushes in her
face.

'Holy Mother!' exclaimed Bella, whose lips and face
were reeking with the Father's spunk. 'Holy Mother!
What pleasure I have had – and you, my Father, have
I not given the precious relief you coveted?'

Father Ambrose, too agitated to reply, raised the
gentle girl in his arms, and pressing her streaming
mouth to his, sucked humid kisses of gratitude and
pleasure.

A quarter of an hour passed in tranquil repose uninterrupted by any signs of disturbance from without.

The door was fast, and the holy Father had well
chosen his time.

Meanwhile Bella, whose desires had been fearfully
excited by the scene we have attempted to describe,
had conceived an extravagant longing to have the
same operation performed upon her with the rigid
member of Ambrose that she had suffered from the
moderately proportioned weapon of Charlie.

Throwing her arms round the burly neck of her confessor, who whispered low words of invitation, watching as she did so, the effect in the already stiffening
instrument between his legs.

'You told me that the tightness of this little slit,'

and here Bella placed his large hand upon it with a gentle pressure, 'would make you discharge abundantly of the spunk you possess. What would I not give, my Father, to feel it poured into my body from the top of this red thing?'

It was evident how much the beauty of the young Bella, no less than the innocence and *naiveté* of her character, inflamed the sensual nature of the priest. The knowledge of his triumph – of her utter helplessness in his hands – of her delicacy and refinement, all conspired to work to the extreme of lecherous desires of his fierce and wanton instincts. She was his. His to enjoy as he wished – his to break to every caprice of his horrid lust, and to bend to the indulgence of the most outrageous and unbridled sensuality.

'Ay, by heaven! it is too much,' exclaimed Ambrose, whose lust, already rekindling, now rose violently into activity at this solicitation. 'Sweet girl, you don't know what you ask; the disproportion is terrible, and you would suffer much in the attempt.'

'I would suffer all,' replied Bella, 'so that I could feel that fierce thing in my belly, and taste the gushes of its spunk up in me to the quick.'

'Holy Mother of God! It is too much – you shall have it, Bella, you shall know the full measure of this stiffened machine, and, sweet girl, you shall wallow in an ocean of warm spunk.'

'Oh, my Father, what heavenly bliss!'

'Strip, Bella, remove everything that can interfere with our movements, which I promise you will be violent enough.'

Thus ordered, Bella was soon divested of her clothing, and finding her Confessor appeared charmed at the display of her beauty, and that his member swelled and lengthened in proportion as she exhibited her nudity, she parted with the last vestige of drapery, and stood as naked as she was born.

Father Ambrose was astonished at the charms which

271

now faced him. The full hips, the budding breasts, the skin as white as snow and soft as satin, the rounded buttocks and swelling thighs, the flat white belly and lovely mount covered only with the thinnest down; and above all the charming pinky slit which now showed itself at the bottom of the mount, now hid timorously away between the plump thighs. With a snort of rampant lust he fell upon his victim.

Ambrose clasped her in his arms. He pressed her soft glowing form of his burly front. He covered her with his salacious kisses, and giving his lewd tongue full licence, promised the young girl all the joys of Paradise by the introduction of his big machine within her slit and belly.

Bella met him with a little cry of ecstasty, and as the excited ravisher bore her backwards to the couch, already felt the broad and glowing head of his gigantic penis pressing against the warm moist lips of her moist virgin orifice.

And now, the holy man finding delight in the contact of his penis with the warm lips of Bella's slit, began pushing it in between with all his energy until the big nut was covered with the moisture which the sensitive little sheath exuded.

Bella's passions were at fever height. The efforts of Father Ambrose to lodge the head of his member within the moist lips of her little slit, so far from deterring her, spurred her to madness until, with another faint cry, she fell prone and gushed down the slippery tribute of her lascivious temperament.

This was exactly what the bold priest wanted, and as the sweet warm emission bedewed his fiercely distended penis, he drove resolutely in, and at one bound sheathed half its ponderous length in the beautiful child.

No sooner did Bella feel the stiff entry of the terrible member within her tender body, than she lost all the little control of herself she had, and setting aside all thought of the pain she was enduring, she wound her legs about his loins, and entreated her huge assailant not to spare her.

'My sweet and delicious child,' whispered the salacious priest, 'my arms are round you, my weapon is already half way up your tight belly. The joys of Paradise will be yours presently.'

'Oh, I know it; I feel it, do not draw back, give me the delicious thing as far as you can.'

'There, then, I push, I press, but I am far too largely made to enter you easily. I shall burst you, possibly; but it is now too late. I must have you – or die.'

Bella's parts relaxed a little, and Ambrose pushed in another inch. His throbbing member lay skinned and soaking, pushed half way into the girl's belly. His pleasure was most intense, and the head of his instrument was compressed deliciously by Bella's slit.

'Go on, dear Father, I am waiting for the spunk you promised me.'

It little needed this stimulant to induce the confessor to an exercise of his tremendous powers of copulation. He pushed frantically forward; he plunged his hot penis still further and further at each effort, and then with one huge stroke buried himself to the balls in Bella's light little person.

It was then that the furious plunge of the brutal priest became more than his sweet victim, sustained as she had been by her own advanced desires, could endure.

With a faint shriek of physical anguish, Bella felt that her ravisher had burst through all the resistance which her youth had opposed to the entry of his member, and the torture of the forcible insertion of such a mass bore down the prurient sensations with which she had commenced to support the attack.

Ambrose cried aloud in rapture, he looked down upon the fair thing his serpent had stung. He gloated over the victim now impaled with the full rigour of his huge rammer. He felt the maddening contact with inexpressible delight. He saw her quivering with the anguish of his forcible entry. His brutal nature was fully aroused. Come what might he would enjoy to his utmost, so he wound his arms about the beautiful girl and treated her to the full measure of his burly member.

'My beauty! you are indeed exciting, you must also enoy. I will give you the spunk I spoke of, but I must first work up my nature by this lascivious titillation. Kiss me, Bella, then you shall have it, and while the hot spunk leaves me and enters your young parts, you shall be sensible of the throbbing joys I also am experiencing. Press, Bella, let me push, so, my child, now it enters again. Oh! oh!'

Ambrose raised himself a moment, and noted the immense shaft round which the pretty slit of Bella was now intensely stretched.

Firmly embedded in his luscious sheath, and keenly relishing the exceeding tightness of the warm folds of youthful flesh which now encased him, he pushed on, unmindful of the pain his tormenting member was producing, and only anxious to secure as much enjoyment to himself as he could. He was not a man to be deterred by any false notions of pity in such a case, and now pressed himself inwards to his utmost, while his hot lips sucked delicious kisses from the open and quivering lips of the poor Bella.

For some minutes nothing now was heard but the jerking blows with which the lascivious priest continued his enjoyment, and the cluck, cluck of his huge penis, as it alternately entered and retreated in the belly of the beautiful penitent.

It was not to be supposed that such a man as Ambrose was ignorant of the tremendous powers of enjoyment his member could rouse within one of the opposite sex, and that with its size and disgorging capabilities of such a nature as to enlist the most powerful emotions in the young girl in whom he was operating.

But Nature was asserting himself in the person of the young Bella. The agony of the stretching was fast being swallowed up in the intense sensations of pleasure produced by the vigorous weapon of the holy man, and it was not long before the low moans and sobs of the pretty child became mingled with expressions, half choked in the depth of her feelings, expressive in delight.

'Oh, my Father! Oh, my dear, generous Father! Now, now push. Oh! push. I can bear – I wish for it. I am in heaven! The blessed instrument is so hot in its head. Oh! my heart. Oh! my – oh! Holy Mother, what is this I feel?'

Ambrose saw the effect he was producing. His own pleasure advanced apace. He drove steadily in and out, treating Bella to the long hard shaft of his member up to the crisp hair which covered his big balls, at each forward thrust.

At length Bella broke down, and treated the electrified and ravished man with a warm emission which ran all over his stiff affairs.

It is impossible to describe the lustful frenzy which now took possession of the young and charming Bella. She clung with desperate tenacity to the burly figure of the priest, who bestowed upon the heaving and voluptuous body the full force and vigour of his manly thrust. She held him in her tight and slippery sheath to his balls.

But in her ecstasy Bella never lost sight of the promised perfection of the enjoyment. The holy man was to spend his spunk in her as Charlie had done, and the thought added fuel to her lustful fire.

When, therefore, Father Ambrose, throwing his arms close round her taper waist, drove up his stallion penis to the very hairs of Bella's slit, and sobbing, whispering that the 'spunk' was coming at last, the excited girl straightway opening her legs to the utmost, with positive shrieks of pleasure let him send his pent-up fluid in showers into her very vitals.

Thus he lay for full two minutes, while at each hot and forcible injection of the slippery semen, Bella gave plentiful evidence by her writhings and cries of the ecstasy the powerful discharge was producing.

The Wantons

It is London in the mid-50s, the era of the Teddy Boy. Sixteen year old Linda is both appalled and fascinated by these flamboyant young tearaways – she'd like to know them better but she doesn't dare. Her home life, however, provides no safe haven. Her mother hates her – or so she feels – and her new step-father ogles her opulent young body in a funny way. On the night her mother stays at her aunt's house the reason for that funny look becomes all too clear as the step-father forces his way into her bedroom and into her bed. This experience, unwanted and repulsive though it is, awakens a rampant sexual curiosity in Linda and when she tells her friend Betty she is no longer a virgin, Betty can't help feeling a little jealous. Thus the two of them are in a receptive mood when they attend a dance and make friends with two swaggering Teds, Des and Jim. The boys whisk them off to a party in Hampstead and introduce them to a whole new world . . .

The atmosphere was pungent and smoky and the softly-tuned jazz from the record player mingled like an aural incense.

Linda and Desmond lay on the floor listening to the music and he stroked her bottom through her dress.

'Let's have another drag,' she breathed, moving her hand slowly towards the thin cigarette between his lips. They had told her not to expect anything from the first one and she had gone on smoking while they smoked, quietly inhaling, taking in a lot of air with the smoke as they suggested. Now she felt tranquilly wonderful. The room around her seemed a world in which she would live forever. She had no idea of the time and didn't care. All around her were friends, all those couples lounging and lying in the big room, hardly speaking, fondling a little, talking quietly. Betty was over there lying on the floor looking up at the ceiling with a smile on her face and Jim was lying with her, looking at the ceiling too.

She felt a great liking for Des and a great intimacy with him. He was stroking her bottom gently, feeling its round bulge lingeringly and he had a kind look on his face. She felt she was safe and at peace with Desmond. She never wanted to go home. Home! She smiled happily. It didn't bear thinking about.

She drew in on the cigarette and the smoke passed in a dry relief down her throat; the sweet, exotic aroma floated to her nostrils and she breathed deeply, with concentration. Then she relaxed and passed the butt end back to Desmond and the music enveloped her softly in an erotic wave of peace the way his arm and his gently stroking hand enveloped her.

Sam was sitting next to the record player. It was he who made possible this peace, this discovery. She felt tender towards him and to his mistress whose money had provided this Hampstead flat.

The record slid to an end and after a while someone put on another. Most of the girls were young – about eighteen and the men a few years older except for Sam who looked about thirty. His mistress was supposed to have a lot of money.

'Linda.' It was Betty's voice. She moved her head and looked over. Jim had undone the top buttons of her dress and had his hand inside. 'I feel good.'

Betty was going to have it tonight. Linda knew that for sure as she smiled back. This marihuana, "pot" they called it, was great stuff.

She listened again to the record. It was very clear. Everything was very clear, even the sound of Desmond's hand stroking her buttocks and Jim rustling Betty's dress.

'How do you feel?'

She looked up at Des.

'I feel wonderful.'

Her heart overflowed with tenderness for him and she knew that she could tell him anything if she wanted to, that he felt the same for her. She leaned up and kissed him suddenly, tenderly, on the cheek and he moved his hand from the full flower of her buttocks down between them over the dress, sharply aware of the sudden cleavage into separate orbs. His fingers between her legs pressed through the dress and briefs to the fleshy line of her labia. The tenderness she felt flushed in a tender, warm desire to give herself. Desmond felt soft warmth under his hand.

'Any room outside?' he asked Sam softly. It seemed to Linda that his voice rang clearly through the room.

Sam jerked his head absently towards the door and resumed his glazed concentration on the music.

'Let's go,' Des whispered to her, pressing his fingers meaningfully against the hot, giving ridge between her legs.

'All right.'

They rose quietly and she was suddenly aware of a floating unsteadiness in her limbs. Nobody took any notice of them. She was vaguely aware that Jim was kissing Betty and that Betty had one breast bare and protruding from her dress. Around the room everyone seemed to be necking or lying still.

With an arm around her, steadying her, they left the room quietly. Outside, the air was cooler, the thickness of the atmosphere cleared and for the first time she felt slightly dizzy and gave a giggle.

'What's the matter?' Desmond grinned at her.

'Nothing – I felt a bit dizzy that's all.'

He caught hold of her then and kissed her, pressing her hard against a wall so that she felt dizzy again as if she were sinking slowly through turns and turns of a spiral staircase.

His hands cupped her buttocks, pushing her hips out from the wall against his hips. She heard the loudness of his breathing. She put up her hands and caught his face and pushed her tongue into his mouth and rubbed her lips against him, murmuring little sounds all the time.

He released her suddenly and drew her along the passage and through a door into a bedroom. Moonlight came in through a window beyond a glass partition which cut the room in two. It all seemed hardly real. She was vividly aware of a number of objects which seemed to come toward her suddenly and unexpectedly and have no relation with one another.

Des pushed the partition back a little without switching on the light and they passed through into the small room beyond. Thankfully she sank down onto the bed, pulling him down with her. The sensation of lying down and the roaming in her head was a delicious combination and she felt tender and generous and her body seemed like an acutely strung instrument ready for ecstatic sensual use.

'Take your clothes off,' Des whispered, in the moonlight.

'Take them off for me,' she whispered back, settling snugly on the bed.

She felt his hands pulling her dress gently up over her hips, her breasts, felt him move her arms and pull it off over her head. The cool air and the cool counterpane refreshed her skin like a shower. She felt him fumbling with her brassiere and he pulled her half up, holding her against him. Her face came up against his loins and she rubbed her cheek against him. But something kept her at a distance from his body, a great, hot bulge in his trousers. She turned her face towards it, looking at it. She felt a tenderness towards it, a desire to caress and fondle. Slowly she moved her hand on his leg as he held her, still-fumbling. The bulge was farther away than she'd anticipated, but her hand reached it and closed over it, creasing the trousers around it. Far above her she heard him gasp and against her hand she felt the flexing of bulge and hips behind it.

Gently she squeezed it through the cloth, trying to

fell its length. She kissed the bulge tenderly and on an impulse bit it gently through the clothing.

She saw his hand come whitely down between her face and the bulge and, fascinated, watched it pull at buttons which jerked undone one after the other.

She pushed his hand away and, with her movement, felt her bra slip down off her breasts. There was still a wild floating in her head, but she focused on the opening and pushed her hand through it. Her hand was assailed by the heat of his loins. She searched around with her fingers, pulling aside his shirt, eventually finding the slit in his pants while he strained impatiently against her. She felt the hot, hard length against her hand – hard; but with a soft, delightful surface. She pulled and it shot out through the opening. Des grunted above her.

It felt beautiful in her hand; a long, white, hot, soft-textured length of stiff Plasticine to play with and mould.

She could see it white, almost luminous in the moonlight. He let her feel it, breathing heavily, pressing against her as he held her up on the bed.

The length of white substance was almost the whole range of her vision. Beyond that was only the vague floating and the clear sound of his breathing.

She stroked it and slowly pulled back the skin from the end-knob which glowed redly at her in contrast with the soft folds of the drawn-back whiteness. Gently she moved her fingers on it and held it in her hand, squeezing slightly and then harder to see how hard he could stand it. The object was hot and slightly pliable under her hand – a beautiful thing.

His hand came down over hers at last and he moved her hand up and down with his over his penis. She began the gentle massage and continued when he let go and pushed his hips out at her with a gasp.

He began to squirm and rock on his feet. She could feel the rocking movement against her and it seemed to make her float farther away with her white penis in her hand.

The sound of his passion was like a rushing sea above her and again his hand came down and pulled her hand away. She released him reluctantly and then he had caught hold of her face and was jabbing his penis gently against her soft lips. For a moment she didn't understand what was going on, but the pressure was there, heavily, on her mouth and automatically her lips opened and the white flesh plunged into her mouth. For a moment she fought against it, afraid she would choke, but he held it there and reached down to stroke her breasts. Floating, hardly aware of what she was doing she began to move her mouth against the soft velvet which filled it.

She was aware of a trembling behind her breasts, almost as if it had nothing to do with her directly and she sucked at the heat between her lips, trying to cool it.

Above her was the moaning, rushing from his lips; his hand pressed hard against her hair, forcing her against his loins. She licked the knob with her tongue, enjoying its smoothness. It was like a big, velvety lollipop which she would eventually swallow. She caught it in her hand, holding it against her mouth while she sucked the end; nothing seemed strange in her activity; she sucked as if she did it every day of her life in a normal routine.

In her floating, spiralling mind it seemed that the great thing was expanding, that it would fill her mouth and plunge down her throat, perhaps to emerge through her vagina. She felt a giggle deep inside her and sucked harder.

Above her, his moaning had reached a frenzied pitch and he was no longer rocking, but had locked his thighs together and was rigidly flexing his hips at her while he leaned slightly backwards with the top part of his body.

She heard the moaning break into little barks, coughing barks of sound and he pushed into her mouth, grazing the velvet organ along her teeth, choking her. And she felt her mouth flooded suddenly with a hot, sticky wetness which encircled her tongue and lodged on her palate and oozed down her gullet.

He sank against her and she realized vaguely that it was finished, found the knob, slight and limp now, still in her lips and gave it a few little sucks and licks before letting it flop out against his trousers.

She lay back on the bed, aware of its whiteness, like the whiteness of him. Through the window there was only the silver space of the sky washed in the moonlight. It seemed to envelop her; she felt a great delight in it.

After a little while she felt him against her, naked, warm and soft-skinned and his hands ran fluidly over her bare breasts and pulled her briefs down over her thighs and off her feet. He was sitting up looking at her. He kissed her belly, her breasts, moved his lips moistly over her soft body. He kissed her knees, her thighs and she was tenderly excited.

His lips moved up her thighs. He turned her over and kissed her buttocks, her back, running his lips down her spine. She shivered delightedly and he turned her on her back again and opened her legs. She felt his face there, slightly rough between her thighs. She was floating happily, sensually, and all she had to do was lie there and he would give her joy.

And suddenly his mouth had moved up between her warm thighs to the long lips between her legs, his tongue had darted out and into her vagina. She pulled up her legs, gasping and then reached down to grasp his head as she actively began to move into a rhythm with him, unable just to lie, wanting to float and writhe and twist, unearthly and above the world in a torment of strange passion.

Desmond buried his face in her crotch and sucked

her clitoris. He was fairly high, but nowhere near the way she was. What a find! he was thinking. What a hot little bitch! And now he was going to fuck the daylights out of her. God, how she was writhing and wriggling and clutching at him and moaning! It was going to be a real kick hearing her moan all the time as if she were in agony.

Against his lips he felt the soft, ragged moistness of her nether lips, the hard slipperiness of the clitoris and then he withdrew and slithered up onto her, wriggling up between her legs, crawling onto the slim strength of her body.

He lay along her and she lay under him with her eyes closed and her lips moving like prayers in the moonlight. She was pretty, damned pretty. God, what a kick! And her pretty face and excellent body were tormented now in a marihuana maelstrom which was making sex seem like the end of the world.

He was sent by the pot he'd had and the sight of her puckered face and the feel of her body underneath him and he covered her mouth passionately with his, sucking at her moist, lost lips and tongue the way he'd sucked at her clitoris.

Her breasts were like soft, pointed cushions beneath him and her hips like a pillow. He strained against her, crushing his prick against the little lawn of hair down there at the point. She wriggled against him and moaned.

Slipping down on her a little, he guided his prick at her cranny with his hand. It was throbbing with a certain feeling of frustration.

He moved a hand against her thighs and she pulled them higher – and then he had crushed slowly, agonisingly through the labia up into the vagina, high up towards the cervix and was beginning to undulate his behind between her legs. His frustration disappeared on the first entry and all his high excitement zipped down through his body to that one penetrating rod of sensation lost in her fleshy passage.

Up and down, up and down, gently, gently and growing stronger his hips played, while his penis drove in and out, in and out and an explosion of sound escaped his lips on every stroke.

The girl grasped his shoulders and then put her arms tightly around him as if she were hanging onto some whirling machine at a fair; her mouth hung open letting out a stream of low sound. His penis, cleaving into her, had a permanent acute sensation as if he wanted to pee and couldn't. Her tight little passage sucked pains of joy out of his lost flesh with each thrust.

God, oh, what a kick, oh, oh; the words danced in a vague *pas de deux* with a plethora of feeling in his head. Her skin caught and brushed and battled with his as she wriggled against him. Her thighs squeezed and released and as he explored farther and farther, letting the knob lead on into the welcoming tunnel, she swung her legs up and wrapped them around his waist, crushing him in a vise as she gasped out.

She was gone, really gone, with eyes closed, just a body abandoning itself. What a sexy little bitch! And he was half gone and it was wonderful, out of this world, that great sucking pool of joy down there where they met and mingled and he dominated and she gave and begged for more.

He put his hand around her buttocks. What delightful mounds they were – a little too big for his hands, they overflowed and he could lose his fingers in them as they relaxed. When they tautened he pushed his fingers between them and felt the little anus. It was a tiny little slit, like an unopened vagina in a small child. She squirmed, squirming with squirms as he touched it. She contrived to press it against his fingers as with her arms she pulled his hips at her loins. He dug his finger at its resistant surface and felt the little, glossy crack give and his finger worm in a little.

'Oh Des, oh, Des,' she moaned as his finger moved into the soft hole. He moved it around within the tight cavity to bring more passion from her limbs as he shagged her.

As his hips writhed and squirmed, impelling his rigid member up between her hot, flailing thighs he rubbed his chest across her breasts, feeling the hard nipples brush his firm flesh, feeling the full, solid flesh of the breasts resist and give and suck against him.

She brought down her slim thighs from around him and spread them out on either side, horizontally so that tendons showed between thighs and crotch. He rammed into the greater depth that that gave him and she jerked with the sudden excruciating expanse of his filling.

She reached around him with her arms and pulled his head onto hers, biting his lips, thrusting out her tongue, licking him, biting and licking and sucking his neck. When he bit her neck, she cried out and hugged him closer, swinging back her thighs to press him into her.

His rhythm which had grown farther and almost brutal began to slow as he felt the end drawing ecstatically near.

She too began to wriggle all the time, clamping her buttocks together on his hands, pushing her hips flat into his and then relaxing, moaning and gasping and waving her tongue in his mouth.

God, this time he would die! It was too excruciating to bear! He soared slowly, crushingly into her, up and up, never ending, a feast of sensation all the way.

He was vaguely aware that she was almost delirious, rocking and moaning against him and flexing her loins with every stroke. He heard her gasp in a long drone of excitement and pain, felt her wriggle in a sharp, furious movement as he pulled her behind at him and then she was pressing her hips at his off the bed for several seconds as she cried out her fulfillment.

She continued to hold him tightly, with her lips moving in a prolonged ecstasy while he forced his staff up and up in great, grand, final movements, feeling the tissues of her passage clutching at him, drawing the lifeblood from his penis which would surely shatter into total destruction.

'Oh God, God, you lovely bitch, ooh, oh!' His knob seemed to be growing and growing, heavy with its imminent discharge. His whole length of penis seemed to expand, to hurt, to have a needle running sharply down its centre. He dug his nails into her, felt her hands around him, digging, urging, asking for his sperm. His penis had grown to an enormity and she was groaning again. It was going to suddenly turn inside out, it would burst. He gasped, caught his breath and then lost it in a great surging of his lungs as needle after red-hot needle of ecstatic pain shot hotly and wetly from him to her in a culminating blaze.

He wriggled his prick into her even when it was growing limp and empty. He didn't want it to be over, that delight which was better than he'd had before.

At last he lay still on her hot, rounded body, which was still as death, but with a heart he could feel pumping at a declining fury of speed.

She opened her eyes at last and smiled at him, kissing his cheek.

'God, that was wonderful,' she whispered.

'You said it.'

He felt a great contentment and satisfaction; a temporary euphoria in which he wanted to lie for as long as possible.

'You're heavy,' she said after a while, and he rolled off and lay beside her with one arm across the peaks of her breasts.

He felt now the full effects of the pot. He wanted to lie absolutely still and take delight in the fact of being warm and still and able to watch the moonlight and have his arm across her warm, smooth breasts.

They lay for a long time without speaking, perfectly still.

The opening of the outer door and a shaft of light flooding the outer room and cutting across the wall beyond the foot of their bed disturbed them slightly, but not even enough to make them turn their heads. They remained still, looking at the long yellow shaft lighting up the yellow wallpaper and the top of a chest of drawers. They heard the door close.

'Nobody here,' came Jim's voice, hazy and strange, from the other room.

There was the sound of footsteps across the outer room followed by that of someone falling on the bed.

'Oh, I feel as if I'm not really here.' It was Betty's voice, slow and careful as if she was having difficulty in speaking.

Linda stirred, attempting to sit up, but Desmond held her down, putting a finger to his lips.

'Perhaps we'll see something amusing,' he whispered with a wink.

Linda stifled a giggle. What a joke. Betty was about to be fucked for the first time and she and Des would probably be witnesses. How funny!

'Get down on the other side of the bed,' Des whispered. They slid nakedly off the bed and crouched down on the side away from the partition. Des reached up and pulled their clothes down with them.

There was a murmur of voices from the other room. Linda was trying to stifle her growing desire to laugh.

The light flashed on in the other room and filtered dimly through the partition. They heard Jim moving and then his voice saying: 'Looks as if someone was in the other room, but it's empty now. You want to go in there?'

Linda held her breath.

'No, I can't move off this bed. Let's stay here.'

290

There was silence with a few muffled noises for a time and then Betty's voice.

'Why don't you turn the light off?'

'No, I want to see you. God, you're beautiful.'

Gently Des and Linda eased themselves up. The light came through very dimly. They climbed softly onto the bed and lay out flat facing the partition, watching.

Betty was lying on her side, her back towards them, unclothed and Jim, in a similar state of nudity, was leaning over her on the bed.

'Jees, she's almost as good as you,' Des whispered.

She looked pretty good, Linda admitted to herself. Slim shoulders which curved down in a long line to her hip, exaggerated by her reclining position. Her bottom was bigger than Linda's, each separate buttock seeming to belong to the other, cast in an embracing, oval mould. Her thighs were shorter, more muscular – that was what gave her the dumpier, slightly more sexy appearance; her calves were slim and strong.

She saw Jim's body, too, with its hair. It seemed to be almost covered with hair: on his chest, his shoulders, his thighs, his belly and in a great fuzz around his fat, white erection. Linda felt a thrill of excitement to think that a few days ago she'd been a virgin and now she'd seen three pricks and been fucked by two men.

They watched Betty, saw her put out her hand and touch the giant rod. All her nervousness, her inhibitations had disappeared, Linda noticed. That was the pot.

Jim slid down beside her and they saw him kiss her, watched Betty roll back so that she was flat on the bed and her breasts pointed to the ceiling. They were whoppers, Linda thought. She remembered how they had developed before hers and how embarrassed Betty had been about them at first.

Their faces were fused and Linda saw Jim's hand

stray away and flow over first the right breast and then the left. She could hear Betty's breathing quite clearly.

'She's a virgin,' she whispered to Desmond.

'No kidding!'

Desmond looked through the partition into the clearly-lit room with an interest that approached envy. What a feeling of power that was to be initiating someone into the ways of sex. He wondered how long it would take Jim to find out.

They saw Jim's hand stray away over her ribs down over the belly and the film of hair that was just visible. Betty kept her legs together for the moment, but as he fingered her around the sweating vault of her crotch, she opened them for him.

'He's lucky,' Linda whispered. 'If it hadn't been for the pot she'd have been terribly embarrassed – she might not even have wanted it at all.'

'She'll be a damn good fuck once she knows how,' Des murmured. 'D'you see the flesh on those hips.'

'How about me?' Linda pouted.

'Oh, you're tops already.' He risked the rustle to rub his hand over her rump and she hid her face because she wanted to giggle again.

Jim, meanwhile, had pushed his fingers into Betty's vagina. She had cried out at first, but now she was wriggling around with her thighs half open and her head moving from side to side as he kissed her neck.

Jim took her hand at last and placed it around his prick, squeezing it round him. They saw his organ shooting out over Betty's hips as he lay alongside her.

'She's learning,' Des whispered, as Betty began to squeeze and caress the rigid flesh and Jim began to breathe heavily and push his hips and thighs against her side.

Jim moved his mouth down and they saw the outermost angle of her breast with its cherried nipple disappear into his mouth. Betty gave another shriek and clutched his head after having moved as if to push him away.

'I wonder what they'd say if we burst in on them now,' Linda whispered with a grin. 'I don't think I can stand much more of this.'

'Nuts,' Des whispered back. 'Nothing more exciting than being a Peeping Tom. I want to see how she looks when she's having it for the first time.'

By now Jim's penis was flaming red, turning almost purple. He moved as if to climb onto Betty, and they heard the words falter from her lips: 'No, not yet, not for a bit.'

Jim sank down again and they could see his wrist jerking about between her thighs.

'I – I didn't tell you – but I'm a virgin,' Betty said softly.

At first they could see that Jim hardly believed her.

'God almighty,' he said at last. 'Where you been all this time – and with a body like that?'

Linda hid her face in the counterpane again and Des followed suit. Jim had looked comically surprised – almost hurt that she'd never known a man before.

He recovered eventually, while she lay with eyes closed, wriggling quietly against the wrist between her muscular, white thighs, and he began his digital penetration with greater care and relish. He actually looked down towards her slit as if he wanted to see what a virgin's hole looked like. Des, watching, felt a fresh pang of desire.

Kissing her breasts, mauling her, Jim was gradually getting her more and more excited. She'd spread her legs wide, now, and was squeezing his penis so hard that he had to tell her to ease off.

'Do you think we can try it now?' he panted.

There was a moment of hesitation. Linda knew just what fear, excitement and desire for complete abandon were battling in Betty's head.

'Yes, all right.'

Jim knelt up and climbed between Betty's legs. Her knees came up chest high on either side of him. Linda, seeing his fat thing stabbing out like a spar at an angle of 75 degrees with his belly felt a sudden desire to be filled again, but she couldn't take her eyes from the drama of devirgination. Des, too, lay transfixed.

Gently Jim stretched out on Betty, who gave a little whimper of anticipation as she felt his thighs move out under hers, his knees against her upturned buttocks.

They almost lost sight of his prick, as he guided it with his hand, but they heard Betty's sudden shrill gasp and saw her jerk as if she'd been stung.

'Ooooh, oh!' she gasped. 'Oh, please.' Her head was flung back and in spite of her gasps she made no effort to push him off. She was taking it very well after the preliminary fingering.

When Jim's hand came away they could see where his prick had made a bridgehead. Just the knob and a bit more inside her; the rest they could see, white and somehow tense-looking. Betty had a look of strain about her for the moment. They could see the delightfully voluptuous line of her buttocks, tensed, slightly lifted in the strain, waiting for further shock. It hollowed in like a piece of moulded clay.

'What I wouldn't do to have those buttocks in my hands,' Des was thinking. 'I'd give her something she'd remember for her first time.'

'Stop moving, they'll hear you,' Linda squeaked.

He realised he'd been moving his hips on the bed. He grinned and put his hand between her legs. In answer she pushed her hand under him, searching for his prick. He turned over towards her, still watching the others through the partition. She saw his prick had fattened again into its burden of desire. She caught it and began to move the skin softly up and down. Trying to stifle his breathing, Des let her start to toss him off. The pulsation in his penis was the more acute from his watching the spectacle.

Linda, too, turned her eyes back to the partition while continuing to massage the stiff mast of flesh at her side. It gave her a vicarious thrill to be filling Des with sensation, to be able to feel his great, hot doughy thing in her hand, between her deft fingers.

Betty was giving a series of little shrieks back in the other room, while Jim gently edged into her. His face was an open key to his passion. His mouth hung open, panting and his face was screwed up, tense. He won't hold himself back much longer, Des thought, watching and feeling his own passion rise as he followed their movements and felt the relentless hand on his penis.

Jim had placed his hand under Betty's bottom and pulled her hips up towards him a little, ranging his organ. Betty, with her eyes closed, the corners screwed up in a pain which was still half anticipation, was trembling and gasping.

Suddenly, with a firm thrust of his hips, Jim surged into her. They saw his white prick tear right in, disappearing, inch by inch, smoothly and quickly, from their view.

His head went back as he thrust. The tight, resisting passage gave him a sensual joy which was almost unbearable. Betty's head strained back into the pillow and her body arched up in shock as she gave another little scream.

'Oh, oh, oh, you're hurting me!'

But there was no quarter now. Jim had lost his prick in her and there was no going back. He couldn't even if she really wanted him to.

After several slow strokes which brought his penis almost right out into their vision and then plunged it right back again so that they could see where his black bush of hair met the raw flesh of her love lips, Betty's cries of pain calmed and settled into groans which could be a mixture of pain and passion.

Jim lowered his head and they saw her lips move

round toward his, as she felt his breath on her cheek. Her face was screwed up with a torture which was exquisite. They were making so much noise now, that they couldn't hear the laboured breathing from the next room.

In, in, in. Betty's virgin body was rifled, her channel scourged by a great, foreign body which marihuana had made her want more than ever. And now she knew the pain and ecstasy of it, the completion of herself, the end of those nights of wondering, fearfully desiring, unknowing.

Linda and Des watched gluttonously, following every movement as the two crushed bodies became one and sank into a single rhythm, sometimes faster, sometimes slower, according to the lead which Jim gave.

They watched the muscles on her thighs contract as they pressed him, saw her buttocks tense and relax, her breasts flattened slightly under his weight. Above all they watched that source and centre of the joy, that strangely naked section where his piece of protrusion fitted into her hollow and their hair mingled and moisture began to run and slide around her crotch and over his prick as it withdrew. Linda watched, fascinated as Jim's balls swung slightly, skinnily with their movement. Her hand moved, still on Desmond's penis, and in her mind it was moving on Jim's.

Desmond was straining. In *his* mind his prick was plunging into Betty, giving her the first experience she'd ever had of sex; his hands held those buttocks, his teats weighed on hers, his mouth on hers, his face hotly against her moist, helpless lips in her hot face.

Jim was gasping for breath as he buried himself in the soft suction of Betty's virginal tautness. He wanted to be brutal now and he pushed her thighs back towards her breasts leaning up from her, pushing with his hips, giving them a last flick into her so that some of his hairs were also sucked in with his flesh and reappeared moistly dripping. Betty writhed slightly, gasping, helpless, lost in herself, hardly aware that it was he, Jim, doing this to her, aware only that her body, that aching channel in her belly, was filled with a strange object which seemed to split it and rub it with an exciting, titillating rhythm which seemed to be growing to a white heat in the wandering haze of her mind.

Desmond, gasping quietly, one hand over his mouth, stared fixedly at the wet, raw area into which Jim's prick was slipping and then fixedly at Betty's tormented face, the face which that raw area was producing, which Jim's raging organ was producing. He watched, stared, fixed his eyes, concentrating until they bulged from his head because he could feel himself coming, and he wanted to be almost feeling that flesh when he came. Beside him Linda was breathing heavily, too, excited by his excitement and by the furious winding up of her friend and his friend in the other room. The air seemed to be filled with gasps and vague, sensual movement.

'I'm coming, I'm coming!' Desmond moaned softly.

Linda wriggled quickly in towards him, surprised that she should think of the counterpane. She turned over onto her back so that she could get her hip under his soaring flesh without changing her grip. He stared and stared through the partition until suddenly he tensed, seized her and bit her neck in a long roar of breath, and she felt a stream of hot liquid make a wet, punctuated path all the way across her belly.

In the other room the locked couple were coming to their climax. That was obvious from the animal noises they were making. Taking advantage of the noise, Linda slipped off the bed for her handkerchief. She wiped the sperm from her belly and wiped Desmond's penis before getting back onto the bed to watch the final throes.

Betty was wriggling like a worm suddenly come into

the light. Her face was contorted with a sort of pain. While they watched they saw her lips move very quickly and then her mouth open very wide as she suddenly convulsed against the body above her and inside her.

The pot's pretty good to get a climax for a virgin, Desmond thought.

Now it was only Jim and he was very near the end. He'd moved his hands to her shoulders as if pinning her to the bed against her will and was leaning up, putting the whole of his weight on her drawn-up thighs. His face, too, was wracked with passion, and his teeth seemed to be gritting together. They saw him slow suddenly, thrust, thrust, thrust and then push hard against her as he choked and then again, choking again and so several times until he'd emptied all into her.

When they'd been lying quietly for a while Desmond and Linda went laughing in to them. The pot made it all very funny and Jim and Betty weren't at all offended that they'd been watched.

The Romance of Lust

The Romance of Lust, or Early Experiences *is one of the world's most notorious erotic texts. Here is a veritable cornucopia of lubricity from the Victorian era featuring possibly the most precocious and prodigious of sexual heroes, young Charlie Roberts. His remorseless pursuit of a thorough sexual education is spread over the course of four volumes, leaving the reader panting with exhaustion and our hero – incredibly – panting for more. It is the youthful Charlie's greatest delight to lure his elders and supposed betters into compromising positions and scarcely a member of his family can resist his phallic charm. However, in this excerpt from the opening of Volume Four, we see the indefatigable Charlie spreads his net beyond his own relations and undertakes the wholesale seduction of his landlady's family . . .*

I had taken lodgings in Norfolk Street, Strand, for the convenience of being near King's College. It was at the house of a Mrs. Nichols, tall, powerfully built, masculine, but a kind and motherly looking widow of fifty-two – an attentive and bustling landlady, looking herself to the better cooking, and having a plain cook, who was also a general servant, to help her downstairs, and two nieces to do the waiting and attendance on her lodgers upstairs. The younger was there alone when I entered the lodgings; her elder sister had had what they called a 'misfortune,' and was then in the country until she could be unburthened of it. She was expected back in about six weeks. Meanwhile, as the winter was not the season, I was the only lodger, and the younger had only me to attend to; her name was Jane; she was but a little thing, but very well made, good bubbies and bottom, which I soon discovered were firm and hard, projecting fully on both sides. She was fairly good looking, but with a singular innocent manner of freedom about her that made me imagine she had as yet had no chance of a 'misfortune.' In a week we became intimate, and after often praising her pretty face and figure, I snatched a kiss now and then, which at first she resented with an attractive yet innocent sort of sauciness. It was in her struggles on these occasions that I became aware of the firm hard bosom and bottom.

Up to this time my flirtations were without ulterior object, but the reality of the attractions of these hidden charms raised my lustful passions. I gradually increased my flatteries and caresses, squeezed her bubbies, when I sometimes drew her on my knee and was kissing her, and as at first she resisted my drawing her to my knee, I took occasion to lay hold of her buttocks, which I found more developed than I could have supposed. Gradually her resistance to these little liberties ceased and she would quietly sit on my knee and return the kiss I gave. Her dress was a little open in front, so from feeling her bubbies outside, I gradually got to feeling their naked beauties inside. I now thought I could attempt greater familiarities, so one day when seated on my knee with one arm round her waist, I pressed her to my lips, and while so engaged, whipped my free arm up her petticoats, and before she had become aware of the movement, had got my hand upon her mount, a very nicely haired one, She started up to a standing position, but as I held her close clasped round the waist she could not get away, and her new position enabled me the easier to get my hand between her thighs and thus to feel her charming pouting little cunt. I began attempting to frig her clitoris, but stooping she drew her cunt away, and looking at me with a droll innocent expression of alarm, and with a perfect unconsciousness of the import of her words, cried, – 'Oh! take care what you are at. You don't know how a lodger this last summer suffered for seizing me in that way and hurting me very much. I screamed out, aunt came up, and, do you know, he had £50 to pay for his impudence.'

I could not but smile at the extraordinary innocence of the girl.

'But I do not hurt you, dear Jane,' said I, 'and don't mean to do so.'

'That was what he said, but he went on in a most horrible way, and not only hurt me very much, but made me bleed.'

'It would not be with his hand, you see I only gently press this soft hairy little thing. I am sure that don't hurt you.'

'Oh no! if that was all I should not mind it, it was when he pushed me on the sofa, and pressed upon me, that he hurt me terribly, and you must take care what you are about, or you too will have to pay £50.'

There was a curious air of innocence in all this; it was evident to me the fellow had got into her, and broken her hymen with violence, and then her screams had prevented his finishing his work. Her manner convinced me that she was really not aware of the consequences, or rather had not as yet really had her sexual passions aroused.

'Well, my dear Jane, I neither intend to hurt you or make myself liable to pay £50, but you will not refuse me the pleasure of feeling this nice little hairy nest, you see how gentle I am.'

'Well, if you will do me no more hurt than that I shan't refuse you, because you are a nice kind young gentleman, and very different from the other rough fellow, who never chattered with me and made me laugh as you do – but you must not push your fingers up there, it was something he pushed up there that hurt me so.'

I withdrew my finger, and as, at my request, she had opened her thighs a little, I felt and caressed her very nice little cunt, and with a finger pressed externally above her clitoris, I could see that she flushed and shivered on feeling me there. However, I did no more than gently press and feel all her hairy mount and fat pouting cunt; she said I must let her go, or her aunt would be coming up.

The first step was now gained. Gradually I progressed further and further; felt her charming bare arse as she stood before me, got her to let me see the beautiful curls she had got on her cunt, then came to kissing it, until at last she opened her thighs and let me tongue it, to her most exquisite delight. I made her spend for the first time in her life, and soon she came to me for it. I had gradually introduced a finger up her cunt while licking her clitoris and exciting her so much that she was unconscious of my doing it; then two fingers, and after she had spent deliciously, I made them perform an imitation of a throb, which made her jump and ask what I was doing. I asked if she did not feel that my fingers were inside of her sweet Fanny.

'You don't say so. It was there I was so hurt.'

'But I do not hurt you, dear Jane?'

'Oh, dear no, it makes me feel queer, but it is very nice.'

'Well, now you know that I have two fingers inside, I will use my tongue again against your charming little clitoris, and work the fingers in and out.'

I did so, and she soon spent in an agony of delight, pressing my head down hard on her cunt, and crying – 'Oh! oh! it is too great a pleasure!' and then died off, half insensible. Another time I repeated this she told me not to forget to use my fingers. Having made her spend twice I took her on my knee, and told her that I possessed an instrument that would give her far more pleasure than tongue or finger.

'Indeed?' said she, 'where is it? I should so like to see it.'

'You won't tell.'

'Oh, no!'

So pulling out my stiff-standing prick, she stared in

amazement. She had really never seen a prick, although it was evidently a prick that had deflowered her, for with my fingers I had explored her cunt, and found no hymen there. I put her hand upon it; she involuntarily grasped it firmly.

'This enormous thing could never get into my body, look, it is thicker than all your fingers put together, and only two fingers feel so tight.'

'Yes, darling, but this dear little thing stretches, and was made to receive this big thing.'

I was exciting her clitoris with my finger, she grew evidently lasciviously inclined, so saying, 'Just let me try, and if it hurts you I will stop; you know I am always gentle with you.'

'So you are, my dear fellow, but take care not to hurt me.'

She lay down on the bed, as I desired, with feet up and knees laid open. I spat on my prick, and wetted the knob and upper shaft well, then bringing it to her cunt, well moistened by my saliva in gamahuching her, I held open the lips with the fingers of my left hand, and half buried its knob before getting to the real entrance.

'Don't flinch, dearest, I shall not hurt,' And I got it well over the knob, and buried it one inch further.

'Stop!' she cried, 'it seems as it would burst me open, it so stretches me.'

'But it does not hurt you, dearest?' I had immediately stopped before asking the question.

'No not exactly, but I feel as if something was in my throat.'

'Rest a little, and that will go off.' I slipped a finger down on her clitoris, and as I frigged it she grew more and more excited, giving delicious cunt pressures on my prick, it gradually made its way by the gently pushing I continued to make without other movements. It was more than half in when she spent, this not only lubricated the interior, but the inner muscles relaxing, a gentle shove forward housed it to the hilt, and then I lay quiet until she recovered from the half fainting state her last discharge had produced; soon the increased pressures of the inner folds showed that her passions were awakening afresh. She opened her eyes and, looking lovingly, said I have given her great pleasure, but she felt as if something enormous was stretching her inside to the utmost. Had I got it all in?

'Yes, dearest, and now it will be able to give you greater pleasure than before.' I began a slow withdrawal and return, frigging her clitoris at the same time, for I was standing between her legs. She soon grew wild with excitement, nature prompting her, her arse rose and fell almost as well as if she was mistress of the art. The novel combination of prick and finger quickly brought on the ecstatic crisis. I, too, was wild with lust, and we spent together, ending in an annihilation of all our senses by the extreme ecstasy of the final overpowering crisis. We lay panting for some time in all the after-joys. Dear Jane begged me to give her some water, as she felt quite faint. I withdrew, still almost in a standing state, got her some water, helped her up, seated her on the sofa and kissed her lovingly as I thanked her for the exquisite joy she had given me. She threw her arms round my neck, and with tears in her eyes told me I had taught her the joys of heaven, and she should always love me, and I must always love her, for now she could not live without me. I kissed and dried her eyes, and told her we should in future enjoy it even more when she got accustomed to it.

'Let me see the dear thing that gave me such pleasure.'

I pulled it out, but it was no longer at the stand; and this surprised her. I explained the necessity of its being so, but said she would quickly see it rise and swell to the former size if she continued to handle it so nicely. It rose almost before I could say as much. She fondled it, and even stooped and kissed its ruby head. We should quickly have got to another bout of fucking if the ringing of the call bell had not brought us to a sense of its imprudence; so after arranging her hair and dress, she hastily descended with some of the breakfast things.

Of course, so good a beginning led to constant renewals and Jane quickly became extremely amorous, and under my instruction a first-rate fucker.

As all my dear friends were not in London, I was fortunate in having such a *bonne bouche* to comfort me. My sisters passed every Sunday with me, and both got some good fucking out of me in every way, without raising any suspicions in the house.

A month after I had taken up my residence at Mrs. Nichols's, Jane's sister arrived. She was a much finer woman than Jane, broad shouldered, wide-spread bosom, which, in after-days, I found had not suffered by her 'misfortune,' but then she had not suckled it. Her hips were widely projected, and she was grand and magnificent in her arse. Naturally of a very hot temperament, when once she had tasted the magnificent weapon I was possessed of, she grew most lasciviously lustful, and was one of the best fuckers I ever met with. Her power of nip almost equalled my beloved aunt's. Jane was fair, Ann was dark, with black locks and black hairy cunt – a very long cunt, with a small tight hole in it, and above it a wide-spread projecting mount, splendidly furnished with hair. Her clitoris was hard and thick, but with little projection. She also became madly fond of arse-fucking, and particularly liked me to spend therein. This was partly to prevent any consequences leading to a second 'misfortune.'

On her first arrival Jane was much afraid she would discover our connection and we took every precaution, although I, in my heart, wished this might occur, for as she occasionally waited on me, I grew lecherous upon one whose charms, even covered, excited me greatly. I always flattered and praised her magnificence of figure whenever she came alone to me, but as Jane generally was running in and out, I did not attempt further action. One morning I overheard Mrs. Nichols tell Jane to put on her bonnet and go to Oxford Street on some errand; I knew thus that Ann would attend on me, and there would be no chance of interruption from Jane, so I determined to come at once to the point. We had become on friendly, chatty terms, and when she had laid breakfast I asked her to help me me on with my coat, which done, I thanked her and with one arm round her waist drew her to me and kissed her. 'Hallo!' said she, 'that is something new,' but did not attempt to withdraw, so giving her another kiss, I told her what a glorious woman she was, and how she excited me – just see. I held one of her hands, and before she was aware, placed it on my huge prick, that bulged out of my trousers as if it would burst its way through.

She could not help squeezing it, while she cried -

'Goodness, gracious! what an enormous thing you have got!'

Her face flushed, her eyes sparkled with the fire of lust that stirred her whole soul. She tried to grasp it.

'Stop,' said I, 'and I will put it in its natural state into your hand.'

So pulling it out, she seized it at once, and most lasciviously gazed upon it, pressing it gently. She evidently was growing lewder and lewder, so I at once proposed to fuck her, and thinking it best to be frank, and put her at her ease, I told her that I knew she had had a 'misfortune,' but if she would let me fuck her I should be on honour to withdraw before spending, and thus avoid all chance of putting her belly up.

She had become so randy that she felt, as she afterwards told me, she could not refuse so splendid a prick of a size she had often dreamt of, and longed for.

'Can I trust you?' said she.

'Safely, my dear.'

'Then you may have me – let me embrace that dear object.'

Stooping, she kissed it most voluptuously, shivering at the same time in the ecstasy of a spend produced by the mere sight and touch. She gave one or two 'ohs,' and drawing me to the bed by my prick, threw herself back, pulling her petticoats up at the same time. Then I beheld her splendid cunt in all its magnificence of size and hairiness. I sank on my knees and glued my lips to the oozing entrance, for she was one who spent most profusely, her cunt had the true delicious odour, and her spunk was thick and glutinous for a woman. I tongued her clitoris, driving her voluptuously wild. So she cried -

'Oh! do put that glorious prick into me, but remember your promise.'

I brought it up to that wide-spread, large-lipped, and immense cunt. I fully expected that big as I was I should slip in over head and shoulders with the greatest ease. So you may imagine my surprise to find the tightest and smallest of entrances to the inner vagina I almost ever met with, it was really with greater difficulty I effected an entrance than I had with her little sister, whose cunt presented no such voluptuous grandeur. It was as tight a fit as Ellen's was to me on our first coition. Tight as it was, it gave her nothing but the most exquisite pleasure, she was thoroughly up to her work, and was really one of the most voluptuous and lascivious fuckers I have ever met with, excellent as my experience has been. I made her, with fucking and frigging, spend six times before I suddenly withdrew my prick, and pressing its shaft against her wet lips, and my own belly, spent deliciously outside. Shortly after it rose again, and this time after making her spend as often as before, for she was most voluptuously lustful, when I withdrew, she suddenly got from under me, and seizing its shaft with one hand, stooped and took its knob between her lips, and quickly made me pour a flood of sperm into her mouth, which she eagerly swallowed and sucked on to my great delight.

We should have had a third bout but for the necessity of her going down to her aunt.

I breakfasted, then rang to take away. Again we had a delicious fuck, and a third when she came to make the bed and empty the slops. This third time I begged her to kneel on the sofa, and let me see her gloriously grand arse, and when I had to retire I would show her a way that would continue both our pleasure. So after fucking her from behind, and making her spend far oftener than me, I withdrew, and pushing it up between the lips over the clitoris, with my hand round her waist. I pressed it tightly against her cunt and clitoris, and continued to wriggle my arse, made her spend again as I poured a flood all over her belly. She declared it was almost as good as if inside.

After this very shortly I proposed to push its nose into her bottom-hole, and just spend within.

With reluctance at first, it ended in her not only liking the point there, but deliciously enjoying my whole prick within, and eventually it was always the receptacle of a first discharge induced by fucking, and a second fuck completely carried on in that more secret altar of lust. She became a first-rate *enculeuse*.

It soon happened that both sisters knew of the other enjoying me, and it ended in their slipping down from their attic, where both slept in the same bed, to my room, and we had most delicious fucking and double gamahuching.

Ann was by far the finest and the most lascivious fuck, but little Jane had a certain charm of youth and also of freshness, which got her a fair share of my favours.

We carried this on for several weeks until use made us careless and noisy.

The aunt, when no lodgers occupied the room, slept

overhead, and, probably being sleepless one morning, when it was early daylight, heard our voices, came down and surprised me in the very act of fucking Ann and gamahuching Jane, who stood above her and presented her cunt to my lecherous tongue. A loud exclamation from their aunt roused us up at once.

'Get to bed, you dreadful hussies.'

They fled without a moment's hesitation.

Mrs. Nichols then began to remonstrate with me on the infamy of my conduct. I approached the door apparently to get my shirt, for I was stark naked, but in fact to shut and lock my door, and then to turn on Mrs. Nichols, who apparently had quite forgotten she had only her short shift on, which not only allowed the full display of very fine, firm and ample bubbies, but not falling below the middle of her thighs, showed remarkably well made legs and small knees, with the swelling of immense thighs just indicated.

My stiff-standing prick in full vigour, and if anything still more stimulated by the unexpected beauties shown by Mrs. Nichols, I turned upon her and seizing her round the waist from behind, pushed her forward, and before she could recover herself I had hauled up her 'cutty sark,' seen a most magnificent arse, and into her cunt – not without somewhat painful violence, before she could recover from the surprise of the attack.

She screamed out murder, but there was no one who could hear but the girls, and they knew better than to interrupt me. I kept fucking away in spite of cries, and passing an arm round her body, with my finger I got to her clitoris, which sprang out into considerable proportions. My big prick and the frigging of her clitoris produced their natural result. In spite of herself she grew full of lust. I felt her cunt pressures, and knew how her passions were rising. Speedily, in place of resisting, she began to cry, 'Oh, oh,' and breathe hard, and then most gloriously wriggled her splendid arse, and as I spent she too was taken in the delicious ecstasy of the final crisis. She lay throbbing on my delighted prick until it stood as stiff as before. I began a slow movement, she made no resistance, except crying out, 'Oh! dear, oh! dear,' as if in spite of regrets, she could not help enjoying it; indeed, at last she said -

'Oh! what a man you are, Mr. Roberts; it is very wrong of you to do this, but I cannot resist enjoying it myself. It is years since I did such a thing, but as you have done it, it makes me wish you should do it again. Let us change position.'

'Very well, but you must throw off this tiresome chemise, or I won't withdraw.'

As her lust was so excited, she made no objection, so withdrawing we stood up; she drew her shift over her head, and displayed a far more splendid form, with an exquisitely fair and dimpled skin, than I could have thought possible.

'My dear Mrs. Nichols, what a fine perfect form you have got, let me embrace you in my arms.'

She was nothing loath, flattered by my praise. She laid hold of my cock with one hand, and closely clasped me with the other arm, while I threw an arm and hand round on her truly magnificent arse, and with my other hand pressed on a wonderful pair of bubbies as hard and firm as any maid of eighteen. Our mouths met in a loving kiss, our tongues exchanged endearments. She said -

'You have made me very wicked, let me have this enormous and dear fellow again.'

I said I must first gaze on all her beauties, especially on her gorgeous and enormous bottom. She turned herself round in every way, delighted to find that I so ardently admired her.

She then lay down on her back, and spread wide her legs, and called to me to mount and put it in.

'First I must kiss this beautiful cunt, and suck this superb clitoris.'

312

Her mount was covered with closely curled brown silky locks; her cunt was large with grand thick lips and well-haired sides. Her clitoris stood out quite three inches, red and stiff. I took it in my mouth, sucked it, and frigged her cunt with two fingers, which went in with the greatest ease, but were nipped tightly the moment the entrance was gained, and I frigged and sucked until she spent madly with absolute screams of delight. I continued to suck and excite her, which quickly made her cry out -

'Oh, darling boy, come and shove your glorious prick into my longing cunt.'

I sprang up and buried him until our two hairs were crushed between us. She held me tight for a minute without moving, then went off like a wild *Bacchante*, and uttered voluptuous bawdy expressions.

'Shove your delicious prick further and harder. Oh, you are killing me with delight.'

She was a perfect mistress of the art, gave me exquisite pleasure, and, I may add, proved afterwards a woman of infinite variety, and became one of my most devoted admirers. Our intrigue continued for years, while her age, as is the case with good wine, only appeared to improve her. Her husband was not a bad fucker, but having only a small prick, had never stimulated her lust as my big splitter had done.

We had on this first occasion three other good fucks, which she seemed to enjoy more and more.

As I had previously fucked the girls pretty well, my prick at last refused to perform. We had to stop fucking, but I gamahuched her once more after again posing her, and admiring her really wonderfully well made and well-preserved body. She had a good suck at my cock, without bringing him up again.

At last we separated, but not before she made a promise that she would sleep with me that night, and a glorious night we had. I had the more difficult task

313

of reconciling her to my having her nieces. I used to have them one night, and sleep with her the next.

Ann, as I have said, was one of the lewdest and most lascivious women I had ever known. I had told them of the beauty of their aunt's whole person, and of her wonderful clitoris, and how she liked me to gamahuche it. This awakened the tribadic passions of Ann to gamahuche her aunt.

I, at last, persuaded her to let Ann join us, and both were afterwards extremely glad I had done so, for both were thorough tribades, and lasciviously enjoyed each other, while being fucked by me in turns. Mrs. Nichols too, once she got used to arse-fucking, delighted in it, and we had the wildest orgies together.

Therese

Caught in the pursuit of certain solitary pleasures and in consequence confined to a convent, young Therese embraces religion with a great fervour. Such is her piety that her health begins to suffer – Therese is not a girl to do things by halves – and on medical advice she is sent home to her mother. It is then that she meets the two people who are to become the most important influences in her life – the venerable Father Dirrag and his devoted disciple Eradice. This lady is blessed with the same passionate temperament as Therese and the two become confidants, drawn to one another by their religious devotions. However there is one blemish on their friendship – the jealousy that Therese cannot suppress whenever Eradice speaks of her father confessor. Therese refuses to believe the stories of Dirrag's particular attentions to her friend, the frequent meetings at his home, his promise that under his ministrations Eradice will soon be capable of great miracles. It is only natural therefore that Therese should require some proof of this very special relationship . . .

Eradice must have noticed that I was envious, begrudged her her happiness and, worst of all, did not seem to believe her! I must admit that I was very surprised about her tales of his confidential talks with her at his home, especially since the good father had always carefully avoided talking to me, one of his most ardent penitents, about anything else but mortification of the flesh. And I knew another penitent, also a good friend of mine, who, like Eradice, also carried the stigmata of our Lord. He had never been as confidential to her as he had been to Eradice, and this girl friend, too, had all the requirements of becoming a saint. No doubt, my sad face, my yellowish complexion, my utter lack of any sign of stigmata were enough reasons for the venerable Father Dirrag not to have any confidential talks with me at his home. The possibility existed that he saw no reason to take on the extra burden of spiritual works in my behalf. But to me it was a bone of contention. I became very sad and I pretended not to believe any of Eradice's stories.

This irritated Eradice no end. She offered to let me become an eyewitness to her happiness that next morning. 'You will see for yourself,' she contended heatedly, 'how strong my spiritual exercises are, how the good father guides me from one degree of mortification to the next with the purpose of making a saint out of me. You will be a witness to the delight and ecstasy which are a direct result of these exercises and you will never doubt again how marvelous these exercises are. Oh, how I wish, my dearest Therese, that my example would work its first miracle upon you. That you might be spiritually strengthened to totally deny the flesh and follow the only path which will lead you to God!'

We agreed that I would visit her the next morning at five o'clock. I found her in prayer, a book in her hand. She said to me, 'The holy man will arrive soon, and God shall be with him. Hide yourself in that little alcove, and from there you can see and hear for yourself the miracles of Divine Love wrought upon me by the venerable father confessor. Even to such a lowly creature as I.'

Somebody knocked quietly on the door. I fled into the alcove; Eradice turned the key and put it in her skirt pocket. There was, fortunately, a hole in the alcove door, covered with a piece of tapestry. This made it possible for me to see the entire room, without, however, running the risk of being seen myself.

The good father entered the room and said to Eradice, 'Good morning, my dearest sister in the Lord, may the Holy Spirit of Saint Francis protect you forever.'

She wanted to throw herself at his feet, but he lifted her off the floor and ordered her to sit down next to him upon the sofa. Then the holy man said, 'I cannot repeat too often the principles which are going to become the guidelines for your future way of life, my dear child. But, before I start my instructions, tell me, dear child, are the stigmata, those miraculous signs of God's everlasting favour, still with you? Have they changed any? Show them to me.'

Eradice immediately bared her left breast, under which she bore the stigma.

'Oh, oh, please dear sister! Cover your bosom with this handkerchief! (He handed her one). These things were not created for a member of our society; it is enough for me to view the wound with which the holy Saint Francis has made you, with God's infinite mercy, His favourite. Ah! it is still there. Thank the Lord, I am satisfied. Saint Francis still loves you; the wound is rosy and clean. This time I have with me a part of our dear Saint's sacred rope; we shall need it for our mortification exercises. I have told you already, my dear sister, that I love you above all my other penitents, your girl friends, because God has so clearly marked you as one of the beloved sheep in His flock. You stand out like the sun and the moon among the other planets and stars. Therefore I have not spared any trouble to instruct you in the deepest secrets of our Holy Mother Church. I have repeatedly told you, dearest sister, "Forget yourself, and let it happen." God desires from Mankind only spirit and heart. Only if you can succeed in forgetting the existence of your body will you be able to experience Him and achieve sainthood. And only as a saint will you ever be able to work miracles. I cannot help, my little angel, but to scold you, since I noticed during our last exercises that your spirit is still enslaved by your body. How can that be? Couldn't you at least be a little bit like our saintly martyrs? They were pinched with red-hot irons, their nails were torn off their feet and fingers, they were roasted over slow fires and yet ... they did not experience pain. And why not? Because their mind was filled with pure thoughts of God's infinite glory! The most minute particle of their spirit and mind was occupied with thoughts of His immense glory. Our senses, my dear daughter, are mere tools. But, they are tools that do not lie. Only through them can we feel, only through them can we understand the evil and the good. They influence our bodies as well as our souls. They enable us to perceive what is morally right and what is morally wrong. As soon as we touch something, or feel, or hear, minute particles of our spirit flow through the tiny holes in our nerves. They report the sensations back to our soul. However, when they are filled completely with the love they owe their God and Creator, when YOU are so full of love and devotion that none of these minute particles can do anything else but concentrate on the Divine Providence, when the entire spirit is given to the contemplation of our Lord, then, and only then is it impossible for any particle to tell our spirit that the body is being punished. You will no longer feel it. Look at the hunter. His entire being is filled with only one thought: his prey! He does not feel the thorns that rip at him when he stalks through the forest, nor does he notice cold or heat. True, these elements are considerably weaker than the mighty hunter, but . . . the object of his thoughts! Ah, that is a thousand times stronger than all his other feelings put together. Would you feel the feeble blows of the whip when your soul is full of the thoughts of happiness that is about to be yours? You must be able to pass this all-important test. We must know for sure, if we want to be able to work miracles, whether we can reach this degree of perfection, whether we can wholly immerse ourselves in God!

'And we shall win, dear daughter. Do your duty, and be assured that thanks to the rope of the holy Saint Francis, and thanks to your pious contemplations, this holy exercise will end for you with a shower of unspeakable delight. Down on your knees child! Reveal that part of your body which raises the fury of our Lord; the pain you will feel shall bring your soul in close contact with God. I must repeat again: "Forget yourself, and let it happen!" '

Eradice obeyed immediately without uttering a single word. Holding a book in her hands, she kneeled down in front of a little prayer stool. Then she lifted her skirts about the waist, showing her snow-white, perfectly rounded bums that tapered into two gorgeous alabaster, firm-fleshed thighs.

'Lift your skirts a little higher, my dear,' he said to her, 'it does not look proper yet. Fine, fine . . . that's a lot better. Put the prayer book down, fold your hands and lift up your soul to God. Fill your mind with thoughts about the eternal happiness which has been promised you!'

The priest pulled up his footstool and kneeled next to her, bending slightly backward. He lifted his cowl and tied it to the rope around his waist. Then he took a large birch rod and held it in front of my penitent friend who kissed it devoutly.

Piously shuddering I followed the whole procedure with full attention. I felt a sort of horror which is very difficult to describe. Eradice did not say a word. The priest gazed upon her thighs with a fixed stare, his eyes sparkling. He did not let his gaze wander for a single moment. And I heard him whisper softly, full of admiration, 'Oh, God, what a marvelous bosom. My Lord, those gorgeous tits!'

Now he bent over and then he straightened up again, murmuring biblical language. Nothing escaped his vile curiosity. After a few minutes he asked the penitent if her soul was prepared.

'Oh yes, venerable Father! I can feel my soul separate itself from my unworthy flesh. I pray you, begin your holy work!'

'It is enough. Your soul will be happy!'

He said a few prayers and the ceremony started with three fairly light blows of the rod, straight across her firm buttocks. This was followed by a recitation from

321

the Bible. Thereupon another three blows, slightly stronger than the first ones.

After he had recited five or six verses, and interrupted each of them the same way as before, I suddenly noticed to my utter surprise that the venerable Father Dirrag opened his fly. A throbbing arrow shot out of his trousers which looked exactly like that fateful snake about which my former father confessor had warned me so vehemently.

The monster was as long and as thick and as heavy as the one about which the Capuchine monk had made all those dire predictions. I shuddered with delightful horror. The red head of this snake seemed to threaten Eradice's behind which had taken on a deep pink colouration because of the blows it had received during the Bible recitation. The face of Father Dirrag perspired and was flushed a deep red.

'And now,' he said, 'you have to transport yourself into total meditation. You must separate your soul from the senses. And if my dear daughter has not disappointed my pious hopes, she shall neither feel, nor hear, nor see anything.'

And at that very moment this horrible man loosened a hail of blows, letting them whistle down upon Eradice's naked buttocks. However, she did not say a word; it seemed as if she were totally insensitive to this horrendous whipping. I noticed only an occasional twitching of her bum, a sort of spasming and relaxing at the rhythm of the priest's blows.

'I am very satisfied with you,' he told her after he had punished for for about five minutes in this manner. 'The time has come when you are going to reap the fruits of your holy labours. Don't question me, my dear daughter, but be guided by God's will which is working through me. Throw yourself, face down, upon the floor; I will now expel the last traces of impurity with a sacred relic. It is a part of the venerable rope which girded the waist of the holy Saint Francis himself.'

The good priest put Eradice in a position which was rather uncomfortable for her, but extremely fitting for what he had in mind. I had never seen my girl friend in such a beautiful position. Her buttocks were half-opened and the double path to satisfaction was wide-open.

After the old lecher had admired her for a while, he moistened his so-called rope of Saint Francis with spittle, murmured some of the priestly mumbo-jumbo which these gentlemen generally use to exorcise the devil, and proceeded to shove the rope into my friend.

I could watch the entire operation from my little hideout. The windows of the room were opposite the door of the alcove in which Eradice had locked me up. She was kneeling on the floor, her arms were crossed over the footstool and her head rested upon her folded arms. Her skirts, which had been carefully folded almost up to her shoulders, revealed her marvellous buttocks and the beautiful curve of her back. This exciting view did not escape the attention of the venerable Father Dirrag. His gaze feasted upon the view for quite some time. He had clamped the legs of his penitent between his own legs, and he dropped his trousers, and his hands held the monstrous rope. Sitting in this position he murmured some words which I could not understand.

He lingered for some time in this devotional position and inspected the altar with glowing eyes. He seemed to be undecided how to effect his sacrifice, since there were two inviting openings, His eyes devoured both and it seemed as if he were unable to make up his mind. The top one was a well-known delight for a priest, but, after all, he had also promised a taste of Heaven to his penitent. What was he to do? Several times he knocked with the tip of his tool at the gate he desired most, but finally he was smart enough to let wisdom triumph over desire. I must do him justice: I clearly saw his monstrous prick disappear the natural way, after his priestly fingers had carefully parted the rosy lips of Eradice's lovepit.

The labour started with three forceful shoves which made him enter about halfway. And suddenly the seeming calmness of the priest changed into some sort of fury. My God, what a change! Imagine a satyr. Mouth half-open, lips foam-flecked, teeth gnashing and snorting like a bull who is about to attack a cud-chewing cow. His hands were only half an inch away from Eradice's full behind. I could see that he did not dare to lean upon them. His spread fingers were spasming; they looked like the feet of a fried capon. His head was bowed and his eyes stared at the so-called relic. He measured his shoving very carefully, seeing to it that he never left her lovepit and also that his belly never touched her arse. He did not want his penitent to find out to whom the holy relic of Saint Francis was connected! What an incredible presence of mind!

I could clearly see that about an inch of the holy tool constantly remained on the outside and never took part in the festivities. I could see that with every backward movement of the priest the red lips of Eradice's love-nest opened and I remember clearly that the vivid pink colour was a most charming sight. However, whenever the good priest shoved forward, the lips closed and I could only see the finely curled hairs which covered them. They clamped around the priestly tool so firmly that it seemed as if they had devoured the holy arrow. It looked for all the world like both of them were connected to Saint Francis' relic and it was hard to guess which one of the two persons was the true possessor of this holy tool.

What a sight, especially for a young girl who knew nothing about these secrets. The most amazing thoughts ran through my head, but they all were rather vague and I could not find proper words for them. I only remember that I wanted to throw myself at least twenty times at the feet of this famous father confessor and beg him to exorcise me the same way he was blessing my dear friend. Was this piety? Or carnal desire? Even today I could not tell you for sure.

But, let's go back to our devout couple! The movements of the priest quickened; he was barely able to keep his balance. His body formed an 'S' from head to toe whose frontal bulge moved rapidly back and forth in a horizontal line.

'Is your spirit receiving any satisfaction, my dear little saint?' he asked with a deep sigh. 'I, myself, can see Heaven open up. God's infinite mercy is about to remove me from this vale of tears, I . . .'

'Oh, venerable Father,' exclaimed Eradice, 'I cannot describe the delights that are flowing through me! Oh, yes, yes, I experience Heavenly bliss. I can feel how my spirit is being liberated from all earthly desires. Please, please, dearest Father, exorcise every last impurity remaining upon my tainted soul. I can see . . . the angels of God . . . push stronger . . . ooh . . . shove the holy relic deeper . . . deeper. Please, dearest Father, shove it as hard as you can . . . Ooooh! . . . ooh!!! dearest holy Saint Francis . . . Ooh, good saint . . . please, don't leave me in the hour of my greatest need . . . I feel your relic . . . it is sooo good . . . your . . . holy . . . relic . . . I can't hold it any longer . . . I am . . . dying!'

The priest also felt his climax approach. He shoved, slammed, snorted and groaned. Eradice's last remark was for him the signal to stop and pull out. I saw the proud snake. It had become very meek and small. It crawled out of its hole, foam-covered, with hanging head.

Everything disappeared back into the trousers; the priest dropped his cowl over it all and wavered back to his prayer stool. he kneeled down, pretended to be in deep communication with his Lord, and ordered his penitent to stand up, cover herself and sit down next to him to thank God for His infinite mercy which she had just received from Him.

What else shall I tell you? Dirrag left, Eradice opened the door to the alcove and embraced me, crying out, 'Oh, my dearest Therese. Partake of my joy and delight. Yes, yes, today I have seen paradise. I have shared the delights of the angels. The incredible joy, my dearest friend, the incomparable price for but one moment of pain! Thanks to the holy rope of Saint Francis my soul almost left its earthly vessel. You have seen how my good father confessor introduced the relic into me. I swear that I could feel it touch my heart. Just a little bit deeper and I would have joined the saints in paradise!'

Eradice told me a thousand other things, and her tone of voice, her enthusiasm about the incredible delights she had enjoyed left no doubt in my mind about their reality. I was so excited that I was barely able to answer her. I did not congratulate her, because I was unable to talk. My heart pounded in wild excitement. I embraced her, and left.

So many thought are racing through my mind right now that I hardly know where to begin. It is terrifying to realise how the most honourable convictions of our society are being misused. How positively fiendish was the way in which this cowl-bearer perverted the piety of his penitent to his own lecherous desires. He needled her imagination, artfully using her desire to become a saint; he convinced her that she would be able to succeed, if she separated her mind from her body. This, however, could only be achieved by means of flagellation. Most likely it was the hypocrite himself who needed this stimulation to repair the weakened elasticity of his flagging member. And then he tells her, 'If your devotion is perfect, you shall not be able to feel, hear, or see anything!'

That way he made sure that she would not turn around and see his shameless desire. The blows of the rod upon her buttocks not only increased the feeling in that part which he intended to attack, but they also served to make him more horny than he already was. And the relic of Saint Francis which he shoved into the body of his innocent penitent to chase away impurities which were still clinging to her soul, enabled him to enjoy his desires without any danger to himself. His newly-initiated penitent mistook her most voluptuous outburst of carnal climax for a divinely inspired, purely spiritual ecstasy.

Roman Orgy

The scene is Imperial Rome and a banquet is taking place at the house of the ambitious senator Lucius Crispus. Crispus is a social climber, a vulgarian who uses his wife's money to buy himself into a the good graces of the aristocracy. His wife, Clodia, is a cool and elegant beauty who watched the antics of Lucius and his slaves with disgust. To please his guests Lucius has squandered a fortune on two erotic dancers from Spain — slim, supple girls with large breasts and no shame. Intoxicated by their sensuous skills, inspired by the plaudits of his guests and egged on by those he wishes to impress, Lucius turns his lascivious attention to his shy new Egyptian slave girl ...

Like its companion piece The Loins of Amon, Roman Orgy *is a rumbustious sex novel set against the backdrop of history. A creation of the pseudonymous Marcus Van Heller, a stalwart of the Olympia Press stable of erotic writers, it paints a picture of the slaves' revolt in Imperial Rome that is not to be found in any school textbook!*

Among the many pairs of eyes which had witnessed the using of the Egyptian slave girl by Lucius Crispus, was a pair of cool grey. At the moment they were hard eyes, very hard eyes.

They belonged in a face which any Emperor would have been proud of: a broad, strong face with a square jutting chin, a straight fine mouth and a broad forehead from which the eyes looked deeply out, hard and unafraid. A face which could have made a kingdom into an Empire, a face which was going to lead ten thousand men to their doom. The face of a slave.

It was during the lecherous performance of Lucius Crispus that the slave became aware of Clodia's eyes upon him – as they had so often been upon him of late. As Crispus was urged to greater efforts by the licentious crew of Rome's aristocracy, she finally called his name.

'Spartacus!'

He turned his grey eyes toward her and walked over to her side.

As he walked, the muscles in his calves below the tunic bulged; long lengths of muscle stirred in his arms. In spite of his height – he was slightly taller than any other man present – his body radiated a potential dynamism. It seemed unlikely that he could be taken off his guard.

He bent towards his mistress and the cloth of his tunic stretched in wrinkles across his shoulders.

Clodia's eyes held his with a look he could not understand as she said quietly:

'I'm tired of this. I'm going to bathe. I shall need you to stand guard over the door.'

She bade goodnight to her women guests who watched her sympathetically as she left. It was very hard on her, her husband acting like this in public, and Clodia such a beautiful woman and not one man noticing her leave. It was a wonder she didn't divorce him – or get herself a lover.

Spartacus strode silently after her, leaving the noise of the banquet behind, through the portico flanking the huge quadrilateral, which in turn enclosed the gardens with their walks and abours and the baths which Crispus had had specially built to the pattern and proportions of the huge public thermae.

It was not unusual for Spartacus to be asked to accompany his mistress. He was the head of the several hundred slaves which Crispus boasted as his entourage and he occupied a comparatively privileged position. Descended from the Thracian princes, he could boast at least as much culture as his master – which he had to admit was not saying an awful lot – and he knew himself to be more of a man.

But lately, it seemed, Clodia had been singling him out to be with her in nearly everything she did, everywhere she went. He had become virtually her personal bodyguard.

Watching her walk before him through the torchlit porticos, Spartacus wondered why she stayed in Crispus' house. It was well known – even among the slaves – the he treated her badly. There was nothing to stop her leaving.

Spartacus' lips tightened as his mind dwelt on Crispus. His master treated nobody well, in fact, except those he considered of superior rank and birth on whom he fawned his attentions or whom he tried desperately to impress – not without success.

Spartacus was aware that Crispus regarded him with a certain reluctant respect, which he felt sometimes bordered on hatred. For a long time he had been at a loss to understand this, but eventually it had dawned on him that, to his master, he represented the threat of enslaved but superior classes who in different circumstances would have thought him nothing but an ignorant upstart. There were many such slaves; cultured Greeks and Egyptians, many of them.

He wondered why Crispus did not put him in the slave market at times, to be rid of him, but then again it had dawned on him that he represented a challenge. If Crispus got rid of him, he would have admitted his inability to dominate, admitted defeat.

Following Clodia into the bath buildings, Spartacus wondered why she should require him to accompany her. Was she afraid one of her guests might wander away from the banquet and try to take liberties with her? – nobody would dare. Was she afraid of her slaves? They wouldn't dare – besides he was a slave. Spartacus became suddenly aware of the intimacy of leaving the bright, noisy company and disappearing through the grounds with his mistress to guard her while she bathed.

'Wait here.'

Clodia left him with this command and disappeared into one of the dressing rooms just inside the building.

Spartacus stared around him in the flickering torchlight. Beyond was a large vaulted hall, its walls of blue and white stone mosaic. The centre of the roof was taken up by a large space in the vaulting through which the sun poured at noon and the stars glittered at night. In the middle of the floor was the great bronze basin of water, water which steamed now from the heat of the hypocausta beneath.

The slaves were never allowed to use these baths, which had separate hours – like the public baths – for men and women. It was still permissible in the public baths for mixed bathing, but it was never seen. No woman cared to sully her reputation. There had been so many scandals in the past.

In the past . . . How many years had Spartacus been here in Rome, in the great town house of Lucius Crispus? How many years had he listened to the suffering and indignities of the slaves? How many years since he had seen this Thracian hills, those beautiful, free, Thracian hills? How long would it go on? . . .

His thoughts were suddenly stopped dead by the appearance of his mistress. Without a glance at him she ran across the marble floor and disappeared down the stone steps into the warm water of the sunken bronze basin. Spartacus was dumbstruck, a hundred times more so than when he had seen the Spanish maidens dance in the banquet room. Clodia had been quite naked!

He gazed incredulously through the ill-lit gloom of the bathing room. It was so. Through the gloom and the rising vapours he could see her white body floating lazily on the surface of the greenish water. Even now he could make out – how anguishingly vague – the lines of her pale breasts breaking the surface.

Spartacus' mind wouldn't function for some seconds. This had never been known. A Roman patrician woman undressing before a male slave! He turned and peered back through the gloom of the grounds, half afraid that he might be struck down for the sacrilege of having seen what had been paraded before him.

In the fleeting glimpse he had seen the body of one of the most beautiful women of Rome; a body which he knew many noble Romans would have given a fortune to see. Cold virtue in a beautiful woman always increased desire for her.

How could she have been so indiscreet? Why? She could have slipped on her stola and then bathed in one of the smaller baths out of sight. It was as if she had paraded herself intentionally.

Spartacus stood, undecided, at the entrance to the building. He felt he should withdraw to the grounds just outside, but hesitated to disobey his mistress' explicit command. It seemed further sacrilege to remain where he was, particularly as Clodia was making no effort to escape his view, seemed, in fact, to be parading herself quite unconcernedly.

As he watched her misty outline, she turned on her stomach and floated, face down in the water, her long, unloosened hair streaming over her wet shoulders, rounded tips of buttocks showing like some ghostly half-submerged fish.

Spartacus folded his arms. Under his hands he felt the smooth, tight bulging of his biceps and the feeling reassured him. This was Clodia's fault. He would stay where he was.

From time to time, he watched her leisurely lolling in the warm water, he saw her raise her head, or simply turn it, towards where he stood in the shadow of the entrance. Perhaps she was afraid he would go and leave her unprotected. Although why he would was unthinkable. To disobey an order!

Reflecting, with the image of her nudity in his head, Spartacus began to remember little incidents of the past few weeks: the way her eyes were so often upon him, the fact she had asked his advice upon some Thracian vase she had considered buying, that once her hand had rested on his arm, as if absently, when she gave him an order. Spartacus reflected on these things and gazed with his cool, grey eyes through the steam at the bronze basin.

Time passed. To Spartacus it seemed an eternity, at any moment of which he expected some guest to stray away from the noise of the banquet which he could no longer hear, and find him standing his lonely guard over the senator's naked wife.

But when at last the silent worry of his thoughts was interrupted, it was such an interruption as to fill his head with an even darker cloud of anxiety.

From the bronze basin, Clodia's cultured voice reached him. There was a trace of nervousness in the usually firm, imperious tones.

'Spartacus. A cloth and my robe are in the dressing room.'

He hesitated a second or two for her to add something, but she lay back in the water, waiting.

His heart was beating a little faster than normal as he went into the dressing room. There on a wooden seat were strewn her clothes. His face flushed as his eyes passed, in the gloom, from her stola to the under tunic, the brassiere which clasped those proud breasts, the loincloth which contained those virtuous hips.

He picked up the woollen napkin and the blue robe made of the still rare silk from the mysterious Orient.

As he strode toward the pool, muscles flexing and unflexing in his powerful legs, he was filled with the foreboding of strange things. This was no ordinary night. This was no ordinary duty he was performing.

He reached the pool's edge and stood looking down into the opaque green waters where Clodia, still unconcernedly, floated. She seemed to ignore him as he gazed down at the parts of her body which showed through the steam.

Spartacus waited, while Clodia paddled. He could

see the smooth slope of her white shoulders, the deep cleft of the upper part of her breast. Half lying in the water, she turned her eyes towards him.

Her face was radiant with the pale beauty, the clear-cut lines of a Roman aristocrat. Her hazel eyes were bright with a peculiar fire.

'You dislike your master, Spartacus,' she said. Her voice had regained its old, firm tones.

Spartacus said nothing.

Clodia laughed. One of the few times he'd ever heard her laugh.

'Your silence condemns you. He dislikes you too.'

She hesitated and still Spartacus said nothing.

'Today he finally admitted defeat. He decided to get rid of you, sell you in the slave market.'

Spartacus stared at her. So at last it had happened. But her next words astonished him.

'He wanted to sell you, but I put my foot down. Because I want to keep you.'

'My lady is kind,' Spartacus said softly.

'No, not kind,' she said, 'just self-indulgent.'

Giving Spartacus no time to ponder her words, she began to raise herself to the marble floor of the baths.

He stared at her, unable to avert his eyes as she came, like a nymph, out of the water. First her breasts stunned his eyes, large, firm and white with the red smudge of nipples a startling contrast to the colour of the skin. And then her belly, flat, smooth, white; and then her abdomen, with the two pink creases in the soft flesh and the black down of hair reaching to a point between her legs; and the long thighs, themselves like marble, supple, cold and beautiful.

She stood dripping in front if him. Her eyes were those of the sphinx. His lips opened slightly.

'Rub me down,' she said quietly. 'Have you forgotten yourself?'

The whole of Spartacus' skin all over his body seemed to be pulsating as he bent to his task. Clodia stood quietly watching the bunching of his powerful arm muscles as he wiped the moisture from her arms, her breasts, her belly, her back, her buttocks. Spartacus hesitated. Her buttocks were full, contained firmly in long sweeping lines. His hands trembled as he felt their shape and texture through the woollen napkin.

'Go on,' Clodia's voice commanded from above as he knelt. Her voice sounded firm but there was a hollow undertone as if she were steeling herself. He realised suddenly that she was trembling.

His big hands moved down the backs of her thighs, shaping the almost imperceptible down into a slim arrow. His hand contained the rounded calves in the napkin and he swivelled round and rubbed up her legs in the front.

He was more aware of the trembling. Clodia shifted her legs apart, moving on the balls of her small, bare feet. Spartacus looked up at her. Her lips were parted as she looked down on him. Her eyes pierced his with a look which was command and desire and not without a tremulous undercurrent of fear.

'Go on,' she said softly. There was a tremble in her voice as well as her limbs.

Spartacus hollowed his hands around the napkin and moved them up her leg. Astonishment had now given place to a masculine certainty and strength. There was no doubt in his mind, only a deep, luxurious wonder.

His hands moved up over the knee, soaking the moisture from the skin into the napkin. Through it he could feel the solidity of the thigh. He wanted to touch the thigh without the napkin, but he continued pulling the napkin, like a broken glove, up the leg to where it broadened into its fullness and his eyes were on a level with the crease of flesh between her thighs.

Once more he hesitated.

'Go on.' The voice above him was a controlled Vesuvius.

Spartacus held the napkin in the flat of his right hand. With the other he boldly grasped Clodia's thigh, his finger denting the buttery flesh and with a long, slow movement, he wiped the napkin between her legs, dabbing in into the intimate places of her crotch.

As he felt the soft yielding flesh under the napkin flatten out against the inside of the thighs, Clodia's hand moved uncontrollably down to his head and her fingers grasped his long, fair hair and pressed his face to her lower belly.

Spartacus rose slowly up her body, his lips tracing a path up over her navel, the taut flesh of her ribs, resting on the beautiful pearl hills of her breasts, brushing the rich, hard protrusion of nipples, sucking in the hollow of her shoulder, on up the white slender neck, until they found her lips and fastened there, his lips on those of Clodia, famed in Rome for her beauty, Clodia whose slim, smooth tongue now forced its way between his lips, between his teeth and snaked in his mouth, the mouth of her slave.

After a moment she drew away from him, trembling violently.

'Give me my robe,' she said. 'We must not be seen here.'

Spartacus put her robe over her trembling shoulders, she pulled it tightly around her and, bidding him follow her, walked quickly away from the baths.

Walking behind her once again, Spartacus was filled with the joy of incredible discovery, an emotional power which was overwhelming. Here he was following her as he had so often followed her before – but now what a difference! Now he knew those breasts which had vaguely excited him before as they pressed through her stola. Breasts which had excited so many men in Rome; breasts so inaccessible and far away. Now he knew that slender back which shaped into the girdle of the robe as she hurried before him, knew those buttocks which were outlined by the clinging silk, those thighs over which the sulk hung loosely from its swelling over the rump. Now he understood the looks which Clodia had cast toward him. Now he understood the touch on his arm. Soon she would be his, unbelievably his.

Hurrying before Spartacus, Clodia was aware that his eyes were on the tension of her buttocks under the robe. She pulled the robe tightly around her to give him a more exciting spectacle.

Now they were going to her room and she would seduce him. It was no sudden decision Clodia had made. It had been developing in her mind for months.

She was well aware of Lucius' lack of interest in her. She was no longer terribly interested in him. She had in fact made up her mind at one time to divorce him.

But then she had become suddenly aware of the slave, Spartacus. There was some magnetism in him, some superior strength of character which made her, even now, half afraid of her fascination for him.

She had seen Lucius' recognition of the same quality, had watched the battle Lucius, who could not bear to find himself in competition with a stronger man, had fought with himself. She had watched the indifference of the slave to the attempts of an inferior being to degrade him.

It was a fascination, a very physical fascination, which had kept her in Lucius' house. She would sit and watch Spartacus, his big muscles tensing in his big body as he performed his tasks; she would watch the calm, handsome face and if the cool, grey eyes alighted on her she would look quickly away lest he should notice her interest.

The desire had grown in her to touch that athletic muscular body. A desire which had finally found its outlet a few days before when she had allowed her fingers to rest lightly on his arm while directing him in some duty.

And then she had wanted that touch, that physical communion returned. Had wanted to give, to yield under the superior power which she sensed in the man.

Even now it was a desire completely physical which drove her on. The unheard of, forbidden liaison with a slave. That taboo which gave such an emotional desperation and glory to the act.

Although, it was true, a slave could eventually become a freed man – and perhaps rise to office – there was no denying the fact that a slave, as a slave, was the scum of the Empire. Such a liaison would have the whole of Rome howling for the blood of both parties; such a liaison would resound beyond the boundaries of the peninsula to the very outposts of the Empire.

It was partly the knowledge of this that had driven Clodia on in her desire rather than deterred her. She had a will the equal of most in the city and Spartacus, all unwittingly, had driven her towards the inevitable with every movement of his body, every look in his eyes, every one of the few words he ever uttered.

The noise of the banquet, still in progress, reached them as they walked in the shadow of the portico and mounted the steps to the upper story. Without a word, Clodia led the way through Crispus' room to her own. Starlight shone in through the window which looked out onto the quadrilateral. Spartacus moved uncertainly in the poor light and stood silent and still, while Clodia pulled a heavy shutter into place across the window. She lit torches in their brackets on the walls, and while she moved quietly to the door to close it, Spartacus looked with quick curiosity around her room, which he was seeing for the first time.

The room was dominated by Clodia's bed, the bed in which she must have spent so many lonely nights, listening perhaps to the breathing of her husband in the next room. It was a huge bed of oak. The woodwork

341

was inlaid with tortoise-shell, the feet were made of ivory. All three materials shone with a lustre which bespoke much labour from Clodia's female slaves. There were two divans also, strewn with exotically coloured cushions, and in a corner near the window space was a tripod table on which lay Clodia's mirrors of silver and few adornments.

The furniture, as was customary in the grand houses, was sparse but superb.

After Clodia had shut the door she and Spartacus stood looking at each other for a few moments. Her beautiful face was slightly flushed; there was a tint of fear in her eyes which she tried vainly to conceal.

The interval of walking had made Spartacus wary. He was well aware of the penalty for this sort of thing and, although his length of rigidity had itched against his loincloth from the moment he'd seen Clodia run from her dressing room, he now remained where he was, making no move towards her.

Looking at him, Clodia too, felt the slight embarrassment that the interval had built. She had a sudden, fleeting fear that she might be scorned.

She brushed past Spartacus and stretched out on the counterpane and cushions of the bed.

'My bones ache with all that sitting in the banquet room,' she said, holding his eyes again with her own. 'I want to be massaged.'

Spartacus moved towards her, his sandaled feet rustling lightly on the floor. She saw in his eyes the deep unwavering purposefulness that so many were to see and it filled her with a shuddering anticipation.

'Have you seen the women wrestlers being massaged in the palaestrae?' she asked softly. And as he nodded, she added, slipping from her robe: 'Well I am just one of them waiting for the masseur. Clodia does not exist.'

As his fingers began to move over her body and her breath fluttered in her throat, she thought, 'Perhaps this is the *only* time that Clodia exists.'

342

Once again her full, beautiful body was exposed to her slave. But Spartacus, running his hands over the beautiful tapering arms, the slim shoulders, the glossy swelling of her breasts, knew that he was no longer the slave but the master.

His strong fingers kneaded the firm flesh of her belly, drawing it in little ridges, flattening it with his palms. He stroked the sinuous lengths of her thighs, his chest palpitating, an aching pressure under his loincloth.

His hands rifled her body, knowing the virtuous flesh, all the more sensual for its virtuousness. As his fingers moved between her legs she gave a muffled squeal and jerked over onto her stomach, burying her face in the cushion. Her back heaved as his hands caressed her bare bottom. The white skin of the firm mounds was so smooth it seemed glazed. The hips flowed out from her slim waist, full and receptive; her feet twitched and her thighs rubbed convulsively together has his hands made bold love to her.

Spartacus gazed down, from his ascendant and intimate proximity, on the beautiful rounded lines of her body and choked with a desire to flop his hips down on that filled-out cushion of a bottom and nuzzle his loaded cudgel between the warm, downy pressure of her thighs where they joined her buttocks.

He worked in fingers up between the tight challenge of her thighs, with the flesh giving before his hand, running in ripples up to the arch in which the moist lips nestled.

His hand trembled as he reached his goal, trembled as he was about to touch the intimate secret of Clodia, cold, unfathamable Clodia whose beauty was the talk of Rome. And then his hand, unrestricted now by any napkin, ran along the soft flanges of flesh, savouring their warmth, their heat, their moistness of gentle perspiration.

Clodia gave a sharp intake of breath as his fingers explored, and she slid up the bed overcome with desire.

His hand followed and this time she lay still, breathing wildly as his fingers parted the lips.

As he caressed the little clitoris she gave a squeal into the cushion and the squeal became a gasp as his fingers plunged up through the elastic brim of flesh into the warm depths of her passage.

'Spartacus . . . Spartacus!'

She uttered his name as if in delirium and rolled onto her back. Her hands seized his arms, digging fiercely into their strands of muscle and pulled him down on her. Her lips pressed onto his, working on them as if she was trying to eat them; her tongue jerked into his mouth, gliding like quicksilver.

Spartacus dropped onto her body, her body taking his weight as if she were some complementary part of him, giving in places, resisting in others.

'Spartacus, Spartacus,' her mouth breathed incessantly, as if she had been saying the name to herself for months and it was a relief to say it aloud at last.

He shifted on her, hips grinding on hers, feeling, even through his tunic, the flesh of her belly billowing and swelling under him. The rigidity of his penis hurt him in its confinement.

Her hands moved round his back, arms locking him to her, legs twining with his. Her eyes were closed, mouth open. She seemed more beautiful in her passion than he had ever thought her before.

'Spartacus,' she breathed. 'Don't torment me. You are the master.'

Feverishly, yet with the same sure glint in his eyes, Spartacus raised his hips off her and slithered out of his loincloth. He didn't bother to remove his tunic; it pulled up to his waist. From the foot of the bed his sandals dropped with a thud to the floor.

Her long fingers came down between his thighs and grasped him, making it throb. Then she was stroking his small tight buttocks, urging them at her and her thighs had opened wide.

Spartacus slithered down her. He wrapped his strong arms around her body – and with a swift, full stroke, he shot into her like a Roman legion cutting through the tangled brushwood of a forest in Gaul.

Clodia gave a strangled gasp as she felt the dull pain of his entry. He seemed to split her in all directions. He was bigger by far than Crispus.

He thrust into, splitting her farther and farther as his thickening organ coursed up into the core of her body. She wanted him to fill her; she wanted him to make her ache, make her sore, make her cry with the sweet tears of exquisite pain. At last this man, this silent, magnetic man, was hers, was alone with her in the world, his mind focused only on her and the superb satisfaction of her body.

Spartacus, soaring into her with an unleashed ferocity, felt a tingling in every pore of his body where it touched her. His chest against her sleek, bolstering breasts, his belly against hers, his hairy thighs brushing her columns of marble-smoothness – above all his great, uncovered tool, hot and bursting with sensation, moving tightly, excruciatingly into her lower mouth.

He gasped out his breath, crushing his lips over her face, over all those beautiful features.

Writhing under him, moaning her ecstasy, the cold, virtuous Clodia was in a bitch-heat of passion, pulling her thighs back to her breasts, almost to her shoulders even, wriggling her buttocks so that the counterpane crinkled and dampened under the sweating movement. Spartacus exulted in his raging lust.

His hand roamed over her skin, holding the flesh which belonged to him, doing what he liked with the beautiful body which all Rome would have given its eyes to see.

Gripping her shoulders, squeezing until the white skin turned red, grasping the breasts as they overflowed from under him, holding the waist, cradling the buttocks in his big palms, feeling them overflow from

345

his fingers, so that his fingers dug into them as if they were soft, silken cushions.

Clodia groaned and panted as his hands reached under her buttocks, carressing the soft, sensitive skin, moving down to the source of their liaison.

She spread her thighs to the limit, forcing herself to endure the pain which accompanied the ecstasy, moaning with a masochisitic pleasure under his rough impalement of her. His crushing, aggressive weight seemed to be forcing her through the bed, which creaked under the furious rhythm of their intercourse. She felt inside her belly, as in her throat, a sort of growing restriction of breath, a bubble of sensation which seemed to grow and grow until she knew she could contain it little longer.

The heavy staff which surged in the wetness of Clodia's channel was the only part of himself that Spartacus could now feel. His knees slipped on the silken counterpane as he moved up to try to shove more of its length into the passage.

Her chin was on his shoulder. He could feel the heat of her normally cold cheek on his own hot flesh. Her mouth was fluttering over his face. His own name Spartacus, seemed to mix with the animal noises of her moans. She strained toward him as he felt a heat in his belly move down to his loins. She panted and the gasps became a continuous low-pitched moan which suddenly choked off into a staccato spluttering and screaming as she pushed her belly up at him.

She was still groaning as the tide of life-giving fluid swept through Spartacus making him cry out with the unbelievable ecstasy of it, making him want to destroy this beautiful creature whose body he was wildly ravaging, whose hips still squirmed slightly under his, whose cheek was still against his, whose arms clasped his shoulders tightly, whose buttocks still tensed in his hands.

He wanted to destroy, to make this woman completely his. Passion made his head swim, his eyes glaze. But to his astonishment, Clodia suddenly began to struggle under him, scratching at him with her nails so that thin weals of pain stung his arms.

'Beast, beast!' she cried. Tears were suddenly in her eyes. Spartacus fought down her arms, held them at her sides as her body writhed to escape. Bewildered he recoiled.

It was as he stumbled from the bed, confused and distracted that he heard a gasp from behind him. He whirled around in horror.

In the doorway, a look of shocked disbelief on his face, stood Lucius Crispus.

Jacqueline

The relationship between teacher and pupil sometimes spills over into life outside the class room and extra-curricular links are forged to the satisfaction of both parties. So it is in the case of the young student Jacqueline, an orphan of noble parentage, now living with her aunt in the family castle. For her niece's teacher, the lady has engaged a young philosopher who is himself an aristocrat, though estranged from his family. It will come as no surprise to the reader to learn that Countess Jacqueline and Baron Francois are soon forsaking the rigours of the intellect for the pleasures of the flesh. A fast learner, Jacqueline is as much a giver as a taker in this interchange of knowledge; and Francois's labours are so appreciated that Jacqueline invents a nickname for his main study aid — she christens his male member 'Francinet'. Thus the two of them (or should it be three?) are happily engaged when Jacqueline's cousin joins the class . . .

As usual, we took our daily afternoon stroll in the park.

After we had said hello to the statue of Leda, who, also as usual, was dying under the caresses of her swan, we wandered into the lane with the nymphs. We always like to look at those marble nymphs who laughingly and playfully surrender themselves to the lustful fauns.

Looking at them gives us a thousand voluptuous ideas, and soon we leave them to their eternal games and go into the bushes to play a few games ourselves, always trying to outdo those marble statues.

This particular day, Francois began his game by putting me down upon the grass without giving me time to take off my panties. His feverish hands groped under my dress and his nimble fingers loosened my garters and began to take off my silken stockings. He loved to hide his head under my petticoat, kissing my thighs impatiently, working his way slowly toward my curly fleece, where his tongue would be lapping the juices and his teeth put tiny marks in the rosy lips. This game usually drives me wild. I put my legs over his shoulders to make it easier for him to get his mouth deeper into my love nest and my feet tap the rhythm upon his back. Francois gets wilder and wilder and finally I reach a climax, giving a loud scream and collapsing into a delicious numbness.

Just as I fainted away I thought I heard something rustle in the bushes. I pushed Francois' head away, and though I thought it might have been a bird or a squirrel, I did not want to take any chances. I pulled up my stockings, smoothed my dress and left the bushes, motioning Francois to follow me.

I was utterly surprised. A charming young girl stood before me. Her blue eyes were wide open and expressed confusion, and the wind had disarranged her hair, which was as golden blond as mine.

When she saw us, she began to blush. But I opened my arms with a wide smile. She embraced me, kissing me upon the forehead. I kissed her ardently, meanwhile looking around if there was someone else present. As soon as I was satisfied that she was alone, I introduced her to Francois.

It was my cousin Amaranthe.

After we had strolled through the park some more we went back to the castle together. Amaranthe told us that she had just arrived, and after she had taken her second breakfast with my aunt, the latter had told her that she would find us somewhere in the park.

My cousin was very vivacious and on occasion her remarks sounded like a pun about what I was afraid she might have witnessed in the bushes. The way she looked at us, I was almost sure that she knew what we had been doing.

Francois did not say a word; he just looked at my lovely cousin who had taken my arm. We must have been a charming couple. Amaranthe was a stunningly beautiful girl, about a year younger than I, vivacious, witty and with a little bit of devil in her.

Despite what had happened, I was very glad to see her again, and I liked the idea that she was going to stay with us for a month. The idea that she would be a stumbling block to our love games did not occur to me. On the contrary! And, since she had not yet indicated what, if anything, she had seen us do in the bushes, I decided to question her about it that evening and make her my confidante.

. . . Yes! I could even give her a couple of lessons myself! This silly idea flitted across my mind when I felt her warm hand and smooth arm pressed against mine.

This idea made me so happy that I began to laugh, kissing Amaranthe on both cheeks, brushing her lips as if by mistake, but in reality I had planned it that way.

When I turned around to look at Francois, I saw that a curious smile played around his lips.

Amaranthe's room is next to mine. After dinner I decided to pay my cousin a visit. We have a lot to talk about since the last time we saw each other.

Amaranthe told me about her voyage. She vivaciously described the changes of coaches and horses, her staying at the various inns, and all the thousands of little things that happen during a long trip. She told me that she was happy as a child having escaped from her home for a while, and she also mentioned that I had changed so much, that I had become so much of a woman . . .

The one question I want to ask her burns upon my lips, but I recognise from Amaranthe's slight innuendos, her behaviour, and especially from the tone of her voice when she tells me that she went out in the park to look for us, that she is fully familiar with our secret and that she has watched us in the bushes from beginning to end.

There is no longer any doubt left in my mind when she begins to ask impish questions about my tutor.

It is no longer necessary to pretend that there is a secret. Smiling, while trying not to blush, I admit the truth to my dear cousin.

Amaranthe laughs, and says, 'Oh, yes, my dear. I have seen the two of you playing around in the bushes. And I must admit thatI have seen a lot of things which were very interesting and also ... a little bit shocking.'

'Tell me, my dearest Amaranthe, what did you see?'

'But, darling, why should I tell you! You know much better what you have been doing in those bushes than I. After all, you were a participant, and I was only an onlooker.'

'Please! Tell me ...'

'All right! As you know, I was looking for the two of you somewhere in the park. It seemed to me that those marble nymphs were pointing at the bushes, so I went in to look for you there. When I came closer I heard someone groan and moan; obviously I came even closer so that I could see what was going on. Can you imagine my surprise, darling cousin, when I saw you down on the grass, your legs sticking up in the air, and your dear tutor using his head for a purpose which I had always heard was the task of another part of a man's anatomy. It sure looked funny to see his slobbering face between your thighs ...

'But I also realised that you were enjoying it tremendously because your sighing and groaning became stronger, expressing the greatest joy. Your fists were balled, your feet drummed upon his back, and spasms seemed to jolt your body and jerk your hips.

'I stood there, not moving, frankly shocked, but against my will. My eyes were forced to stare upon the

354

spectacle in the grass. Suddenly you uttered a loud scream.

'I suddenly came to my senses and ran away, very scared. But then, you came out of the bushes, smiling and happy, and I understood immediately ... I must admit that I am a little bit jealous of you for having such a fabulous teacher ...'

During those last words my cousin's eyes were filled with lust and desire, betraying far more clearly than words her true thoughts. I knew that she was burning up inside, and could not wait to be initiated into the joys and pleasures of the game of love.

The memory of that afternoon, plus Amaranthe's vivid description of it, had made me very excited, and I embraced my cousin passionately kissing her upon the lips. At first Amaranthe was a little taken aback, but I kissed her so passionately, and held my lips so firmly upon her mouth, that her lips parted and allowed my tongue to explore her mouth. She was soon panting under my feverish kisses and let herself fall back limply upon the couch.

She began to kiss me in return, which gave me another idea! I suddenly wanted to give her the same caresses with which Francois always brought me to a climax. I pulled her legs slowly apart, pulled down her panties and lifted her skirts. For the sake of appearances, Amaranthe put up a very mild struggle which was not too convincing. Her struggle stopped the instant my lips approached her blonde fleece and my tongue went into her little rosy slit.

She shuddered under my caresses and began to moan slightly when I went on to explore her little secret spot which was so much like my own. I did my best to imitate Francois with hands, tongue and lips, and I must admit that I was doing it rather well, because Amaranthe began to groan and buck. I recognised her pleasure, because of the little cries of joy were similar to the ones I had so often uttered when Francois was sucking and licking my love spot.

I was very pleased to be able to give my cousin so much pleasure with my caresses. My tongue was very busy in that little triangle, the warm moist flower which I sprinkled with my spittle, mixing it with the warm juices exuding from her love nest.

Suddenly Amaranthe, who had been trembling like an aspen leaf, cried out loudly. She lifted her buttocks high off the couch, her legs and arms spasmed, her entire body shuddered, and I realised that she had tasted a true climax for the first time in her life. She remained motionless upon the couch, and I pulled my head slowly back, covering her marble-white thighs with ardent kisses.

I was suddenly very tired. It had greatly pleased me to initiate my dear cousin in the pleasures of love. I had passionately made love to her with my tongue and lips. It made me happy, though a curious pain was mixed with my joy; I had not had any real satisfaction. I was about to dampen my glowing desire with my own fingers when I suddenly uttered a sharp cry of surprise which awakened Amaranthe from her slumber.

Francois came from behind the Chinese screen.

I did not even have the chance to ask him how he got into the room, and whether he had seen what Amaranthe and I had been doing. He suddenly jumped towards me and mounted me as if I were a dog.

Looking at the throbbing Francinet, I realised that Francois had seen everything and that it had brought him to an extreme state of excitement. He did not waste time on preliminaries, but shoved Francinet deep inside me and began to push with such vehemence that I could feel his balls slam against my buttocks.

Ooh! It was marvelous. I was roughly taken before

the very eyes of my dear Amaranthe. Soon the passionate glow inside me was extinguished.

I was no longer able to take it, and I pushed Francois away from me. My sweet Francinet left its moist sheath; but it seemed that his excitement was too great because he immediately stretched out and became erect again, as thick and stiff as he had been before entering me.

He went directly toward my cousin; Francois mounted her and Francinet found the way to his satisfaction without any trouble at all. Amaranthe was more than prepared. First, I had whetted her appetite with my moist caresses, and secondly, she was practically under me when I was mounted and taken by Francois. The scene she had watched had more than excited her and her desire was at its peak.

At first I did not enjoy the idea at all. I was aware that my cousin was about to enjoy what I considered the ultimate climax of the game of love, and that she did not have to suffer the long months of preparation which I have had to endure. In short, I felt a tinge of jealousy.

But then I realised that it was, after all, my own fault, and that I had no right to object because of a silly little jealousy. It did not take me long to push those unpleasant ideas out of my mind, because the scene I was about to witness was extremely interesting and I became fully absorbed in it.

I looked at my dear Francois from behind and could see the muscles of his firm buttocks harden, when he pushed Francinet deep into my dear cousin and began to work her over with tremendous jolts. Amaranthe's charming legs were trampling, sticking high up in the air.

And I heard her moan and groan her little screams of joy, her Oohs! and Aahs! and finally, 'Ooh, darling . . . I'm dying . . . oooh, darling, darling . . . it . . . is . . . too much!'

A scream, louder than all the other ones, announced that the thunderstorm of love was over. I got up from my seat and walked over to the couple, who were now relaxing upon the large couch.

Francinet looked just plain terrible after this double attack. And my dear Amaranthe was in about the same condition I had been in only a month earlier. She silently looked down upon the large spot of blood which announced louder than words what she had just irreparably lost.

For a long time the three of us rested in silence upon the huge couch, and then we began to laugh. Our tiredness had passed. The curious situation which had developed was truly amusing!

My dear teacher complimented me upon the effectiveness with which I had demonstrated that his lessons had not fallen upon deaf ears, and he thought it magnanimous of me that I had wanted my cousin to share my happiness. Then he began a long lecture about love between women, pointing out the things that were missing, though he had to admit grudgingly that their mutual caresses could be infinitely more tender.

To round out his lesson for the day, Francois showed us that three people can act out more love fantasies than two.

The day after this memorable evening Amaranthe insisted upon reciprocating my little service of love and showing her gratitude for having been initiated into those precious caresses which had culminated in her receiving the ultimate delight of making love.

Francois had taken his horse and was riding in the fields to get lots of fresh air and to recuperate from his exhausting labours. He wanted to restore his powers quickly.

Amaranthe and I were alone in my room.

As a matter of fact, I was still in bed when my

charming cousin knocked on my door. She was wearing a charming night gown of lace and silk, and her clear blue eyes still showed the strain from the previous night. But they looked happy and content nevertheless, and a certain glint betrayed that she was already in a certain state of excitement.

She slipped under the covers next to me, cuddled up, and began with the youthful impatience of a beginner to caress me copiously. She imitated as well as she could everything I had done to her that previous night; instinctively she invented the most refined caresses and I quickly reached a point where I felt an intensive lust.

Even though her rather inexperienced caresses and kisses did not have the expertness of my dear Francois, who was a connoisseur in that area, I did reach a very intensified climax.

As soon as I had come to my senses again, I patiently explained to Amaranthe how much her quick approach had spoiled part of the intimacy of my excitement.

And since, by now, we were both naked in the large bed, I could demonstrate my teachings upon her own charming body. I proceeded very carefully and slowly, thereby intensifying her voluptuous yearnings and putting off the climax which she so greatly desired. I carefully went over every part of her exposed body.

I covered every corner with my kisses, the little breasts with the rosy tips, her narrow waist, her flaring hips, the insides of her slender thighs, her flat belly, the blonde curls of her armpits and the delicious fleece which was hiding her moist warm flower.

I stroked with my hands the soft skin of her belly and legs. I turned her over on her stomach and kneaded and squeezed her firm buttocks. Then I let my tongue slowly penetrate her love nest till it had found the little tickler. I rolled it around till it was quite erect, my nimble hands twitching the hardened rosy nipples of her breasts.

Amaranthe was surprised at the effects. She arched her back, her legs trampled in the air, and her fists drummed upon the mattress. I turned her around again, falling upon her and we rubbed our fleeces together. Amaranthe groaned and moaned, went into a jolting spasm and experienced a satisfying climax. When she had rested a while she noticed that the nipples of my breasts were standing proudly erect and that a hot flush covered my body. The dear girl understood immediately. She kissed them and nibbled on them, her hands searched for my fleece, caressing my thighs; in short, she did to me what I had done to her, and I, too, went into a tremendous climax. Our games went on and on till late in the afternoon and finally we fell asleep in each other's arms, completely exhausted, but happy.

The dinner bell woke us up with a start and we were rather late when we appeared for dinner. Francois stared at us with a knowing smirk, and he even used the absence of my aunt for making a few unseemly remarks which were designed to make us feel silly, also indicating that our teacher knew exactly how we had spent our day.

Poor Amaranthe blushed and was red as a peony, but I quickly changed the subject by kidding Francois about his sudden urge to be alone with his horse all day, asking him a thousand questions about his ride into the country.

Fortunately my aunt returned quickly and we sat down to dinner. Needless to say we honoured our sumptuous meal with great appetite, repairing our strength with delicious bits of meat, fowl and fish, not to speak of a reasonable quantity of burgundy wine.

The time during which my dear cousin Amaranthe stayed at the castle was one uninterrupted series of delicious joys. She participated in every respect in my lectures and became an equal partner in our daily strolls through the park.

The botanical excursions in the neighbourhood of the castle were continued and expanded, and Amaranthe was surely not the last who gave herself in full abandon to the wild caresses, kisses and other games of our beloved teacher.

My cousin showed, on the contrary, an ardent desire to learn during those games. But her stay here will soon come to an end, and it seems to me as if she is squirrelling away a great store of experiences before she has to go back to her dull parental home. I cannot blame her that she is trying to cram as much experience as she can into the few remaining days. It is understandable that she desires to know as much as she can about the game of love, because after her departure she will be on her own without the superb guidance of our teacher. She will have to pluck gallant flowers that will bloom upon her life's path without supervision, and taste the joys of lasciviousness guided by her own instincts. It is our holy task to prepare her for the future as well as it is in our power . . .

These are our last outings. The weather is beautiful. The sun's rays are burning the fields golden and bathing Nature in full splendour.

We are searching for the loneliest, most hidden spots to enable us to give ourselves completely and unhindered by curious onlookers to the most voluptuous games our combined fantasies can think of. We wander throughout the entire area; sure of the fact that friendly Nature somewhere has a place for us with a soft bed of grass, with walls and ceiling of thicket and tree leaves. And . . . we find it! The loneliness and the silence of the place are so great that it seems to us as if we are the only three people left on earth. We have no objections to Amaranthe's suggestion to undress completely. In no time Francois, my cousin and I are as naked as the day we were born. It seems as if we were transported back in time to Paradise!

Suddenly the feeling overpowers us and we play the wildest, most delicious games. Amaranthe and I embrace each other passionately, our lips firmly pressed against one another, our fleeces rubbing and our tongues playing a marvellous game.

Francois uses the opportunity to his own advantage. He climbs on top of me and sends Francinet on its natural way. Meanwhile his lips have reached the thighs and his tongue the fleece of Amaranthe; he reaches around till his tongue has discovered her most sensitive spot and Francois begins to buck and slurp at the same time, using both our bodies.

It is marvellous! Excited by the moist caresses, Amaranthe kisses me more devotedly and passionately than ever, and a double joy floods my entire being. I can feel Francinet penetrate me with doubled force. And Francois, too, is enjoying double passion; and glowing passion with which his lips explore the inner secrets of my dear Amaranthe makes itself felt by the double size of the throbbing Francinet who is pushing deep inside me.

We groan and pant, and tumble around and around in the soft grass. Arms, legs and bodies are wildly intertwined. Lips, tongues and hands caress every available part of soft flesh; our fleecy triangles are moist and twitching, Francinet grows harder and stiffer, throbbing wildly with every shove given by Francois. We stay in this passionate embrace, forming a perfect triangle, and each angle is the ultimate passion for the other. Amaranthe and I shudder in this delightful embrace while Francinet keeps pounding unmercifully into me, and Francois' tongue drives deeper and deeper into the fleece of Amaranthe.

Suddenly my cousin and I are in the grip of a long and shaking spasm. Our lips let go of one another to cry out our joy. Our happiness is complete because I realise that the tongue of Francois has given Amaranthe the same climax which I have just been given by Francinet.

The three of us continue our lessons and excursions till the very day that my dearest Amaranthe has to take her leave from us. My cousin's parents have completed their move to Bordeaux, and she must leave now to return into the fold of her own family.

Before she went to the coach she kissed both of us so intimately and passionately that it caused my dear aunt to raise her eyebrows in wonder. Her farewell kisses were obviously far more than convention demanded!

Hunger!

The blonde is dining alone in the hot smoky room. Around her the tables are busy, packed with families and tourists and, of course, sailors — for this is a sailors' town. There are six of them at the table just across the room from Julia. They stare greedily at her as she eases bright green stalks of asparagus into her mouth and licks the buttery juice from her fingers. She pays them no attention when they laugh too loudly though she knows the show is for her benefit.

Outside the crowded restaurant the light is fading. People pack the narrow street in search of a Saturday night goodtime, a swing in every step. Many sailors pass by. One looks through the window and hails the table opposite Julia. A loud conversation takes place. Julia cannot follow it all, the patois is so thick and fast, but she is not surprised when the men inside agree to join their friends. A trip to a brothel lies ahead she thinks, or an evening in a cheap cafe on the hunt for some willing skirt.

Four of the matelots rise and leave. The noise of their violent chatter fades as they walk up the street. Two of the boys remain. One has his back to the woman but she can tell from the awkward way he sits and the glimpse of down on the half profile of his jaw that he is very young. Facing her is an older youth, broad and dark, the skin of his face and arms a gleaming teak brown against the starched white of his *blouson*. He has high cheekbones and black liquid eyes which do not waver for a second in their cool appraisal of Julia as she stands to leave.

She is fifty yards from the restaurant before they catch up with her.

'Mademoiselle,' it's the dark one, of course. 'Hey, mademoiselle.'

'Yes.' She keeps on walking and they fall in step beside her, one on either side.

'You want to go dancing?'

No reply.

'You are American?'

She keeps walking.

'English?'

She nods.

'You are very pretty.'

It's still the same boy. He's getting bolder.

'You are the most beautiful woman in this town.'

Julia walks on.

'I think you have marvellous tits.'

Julia can't help smiling. The boy smiles too. He can say anything he likes now.

'I want to put my head up your skirt and suck your pussy.'

Julia holds back her laughter. She wants to know what he will say next.

'I would adore to see your arse shake while you dance on my cock all night . . .'

'And what,' says Julia, 'will your friend be doing all this time?'

Now they are in the bar of the Hotel Racine drinking cognac. The night is still hot. The sailors' white suits are crumpled. Beads of sweat are trickling down Julia's back. Her sky-blue silk blouse clings to her breasts. The boys' eyes glisten like wet pennies and their tongues are loose. The young one cannot speak English but it does not matter to Julia. Victor, the dark one, translates his urgent whispers.

'Luc says you are a famous actress.'

'That's not so.'

'He knows he is not mistaken because he has seen your photographs in some magazines.'

'He is wrong.'

'He is prepared to bet that you are the one. He says he can prove it.'

'How?'

'Because in the photograph he has seen the woman is not wearing any clothes and she has a very special mark on her body. If you have the same mark then you must be the same one.'

'What mark is he talking about?'

'He says this woman has a little butterfly tattooed on her leg.'

'Oh yes.'

'It is very high up on the left leg. On the outside. Just on the *fesse*.'

'Your friend has a lurid imagination.'

'Maybe, but can you prove to us that you do not have a little butterfly tattooed on your bottom?'

Julia does not speak. The two boys are gazing at her intently. Luc is so close to her that she can see the pulse beating in his throat. She drains the thimbleful of brown liquid left in her glass and says, 'Follow me up the stairs.'

The boys are happy now. The woman is naked — they all are. There are no words, only the sound of flesh upon flesh, of whispers and grunts and the slither of bodies on sheets.

She is sandwiched between them. She leans back against Victor, cushioned on his broad chest, his arms around her, hands busy palming the softness of her breasts while the young one kneels over and arranges her legs to his liking. There are no tattoos to be found on her smooth white flesh, but that does not matter to Luc as he buries his face in the thick brown bush between her thighs. His tongue is precociously skilful and she cries out as he finds her most sensitive spot. He looks up in alarm, scared he has hurt her. Such a kind boy. She smiles at him.

'Please fuck me,' she says.

These are words he understands. He kneels up and leans back to display his standing cock. It is an incongruous sight against such a pale and slender frame. The big bulb glows an obscene and meaty red and the instrument thrusts out from his body like another limb. Behind her Victor says something coarse as the boy spits on his hand and oils his big penis.

'Hurry up,' she hears herself saying and Luc laughs.

Then all laughter is forgotten as he slips the head of his organ between the waiting lips of her pussy and slides it sweetly home.

It is thrilling while it lasts. The boy tries to control himself to begin with, slowly working his tool in and out, savouring every tantalising second. But his excitement has been building for a long time, the seemingly unattainable woman beneath him is his to enjoy as he pleases and his mate is lying naked at his side, urging him on. The circumstances are not those in which many lusty youths could contain themselves. For a frenetic twenty seconds he drills into the woman's loins, grunting with animal delight as she wraps her satin smooth legs around him. His balls smack against the underside of her bum cheeks as his hard member roots furiously in and out. Then it's all over as, one, two, three, he squirts his juices deep inside Julia and collapses on top of her.

But there is to be no rest. Victor wants his turn, he has been patient long enough. Julia, too, has yet to be satisfied.

Luc is pushed to one side and Julia turns to Victor. They kiss eagerly, her tongue slyly flicking into his hungry mouth. He pulls her to him, his hands on the curve of her hips, his cock pressed flat against her belly. They explore each other urgently. Her slim fingers on his fat cock, peeling the foreskin down over the glans and swooping down the stubby shaft to cup his balls. He has slipped a hand between her legs to fondle the slippery folds of her pussy, now oiled by the boy's ejaculation and her own excitement.

They connect easily, she rolling beneath his broad brown frame and spreading her legs wide to accommodate his swollen organ. He sets a steady rhythm. This time she is taking no chances and unashamedly slides a finger into the groove of her cunt. As the sailor fucks her she strokes her clitoris, building the fire between her legs, tweaking and teasing her flesh to the brink of the orgasm she has been aching for ever since Victor's liquid gaze alighted on her in the restaurant.

'Oh yes,' she says, 'fuck, fuck, fuck me, you brute.'

Her obscenities spur him on. He slides his hands under her buttocks and lifts her up. He spreads her cheeks and pulls her down on his cock by the flesh of her bum.

The change of angle and the rough power of his lovemaking suddenly overwhelm her. She comes in a rush and cries out as the wave hits her, the shock singing through her body like a jolt of electricity.

Then he too is on the down-slope. The wanton behaviour of this beautiful stranger has intoxicated him. He buries his head between her opulent white breasts, squeezes her arse cheeks in his fists and shoots his semen far into the hot depths of her body.

Now they are in the shower. Julia drinks red wine from a tooth glass while the two boys wash her body with a rough flannel and a cake of soap. They lather every nook and crevice of her, paying special attention to her tits, weighing them in their hands, slapping them playfully so they swing from side to side, rolling the brown pegs of her nipples between their fingers.

'You are mother-fixated,' she tells them.

They don't understand her but who cares about that?

She passes the glass and seizes the soap. Now it is her turn to play with them. She cleans their cocks carefully, stroking and fondling them to stiffness as she does so. They stand up proudly under the foam and she laughs out loud, delighted with their youth and enthusiasm. They echo her laughter, thrilled to be allowed such liberties with this magnificent, whorish woman. Their teeth gleam white in their brown faces and in their eyes she recognises the glint of pressing need.

She drops to her knees, her face on a level with their genitals. She inspects them closely, idly wondering why the smaller man should have the bigger implement. When she is sure all the suds have been rinsed from their flesh, she takes a cock in each hand and begins to suck them in turn. First Luc, then Victor, then Luc again, swallowing the swollen helmet of each organ, rubbing the sensitive flesh against the roof of her mouth, jerking her hands on their shafts with the time-honoured skill of the experienced masturbator.

It would be nice, she thinks, to take both of them in her mouth at once. She presses the two shafts together, wanking them in a double-handed grip, but the two-headed monster won't fit. Never mind, to lick and suck and hold them like this is fun. She's never done this before. Not exactly, that is.

her tits, weighing them in their hands, slapping them playfully so they swing from side to side, rolling the brown pegs of her nipples between their fingers.

'You are mother-fixated,' she tells them.

They don't understand her but who cares about that?

She passes the glass and seizes the soap. Now it is her turn to play with them. She cleans their cocks carefully, stroking and fondling them to stiffness as she does so. They stand up proudly under the foam and she laughs out loud, delighted with their youth and enthusiasm. They echo her laughter, thrilled to be allowed such liberties with this magnificent, whorish woman. Their teeth gleam white in their brown faces and in their eyes she recognises the glint of pressing need.

She drops to her knees, her face on a level with their genitals. She inspects them closely, idly wondering why the smaller man should have the bigger implement. When she is sure all the suds have been rinsed from their flesh, she takes a cock in each hand and begins to suck them in turn. First Luc, then Victor, then Luc again, swallowing the swollen helmet of each organ, rubbing the sensitive flesh against the roof of her mouth, jerking her hands on their shafts with the time-honoured skill of the experienced masturbator.

It would be nice, she thinks, to take both of them in her mouth at once. She presses the two shafts together, wanking them in a double-handed grip, but the two-headed monster won't fit. Never mind, to lick and suck and hold them like this is fun. She's never done this before. Not exactly, that is.

An empty wine bottle stands on the dressing table. Clothes litter the floor. The wastepaper basket has rolled on its side beneath the desk in the far corner, a trail of orange peel and stained tissues in its wake.

The blonde woman fumbles on her bedside table for her watch. It is an expensive make. A Cartier. As her fingers close on its silver she thinks she is damned lucky that she still has it. The two boys last night must have been more honest than they looked.

She holds the watch close to the face to read the time. Aperitif time. If she can make it.

Now she is perched on a stool in the bar across the street from the hotel. It is an uncomfortable position because she still aches a little from last night. The sailors were so eager. The energy of youth! She has been a bit excessive of late she knows. And lucky too. Not just with the watch and things like that but in not attracting too much attention. She has learnt to be discreet but sometimes it's not easy. Somehow adventures just lie in wait for her.

Like now. That man at the table on the street is staring at her legs. She's not surprised, of course. Most men do.

Pleasure-Boat
Afloat

The days slipped quickly by. Aided by perfect weather the *New Decameron* put the knots behind her at an astonishing rate. The weather became very hot and the very lightest of costumes prevailed. The Sisters Lovett initiated the custom of appearing on deck in open-work chemises and nothing else, and the pirates all worked stripped to the waist. Of the lady pirates, Maudie invariably came on deck naked in the mornings to be douched with the hose, an example soon followed by Hony and Carrie.

The pirates showed themselves splendid seamen, and if debauchery was allowed a free hand in the evening, it was hard work during the day. The *New Decameron* was as spick and span as the hand of man could make her, and necessary fire and boat drills were never omitted.

The love affairs of the pirates and their guests soon settled down into recognized grooves. The Sisters Lovett frankly professed themselves harlots and were openly raffled for every night. Carrie developed a sentimental affection for several of the young men, and let them share her. Little Hony stuck religiously to the 'young man.' It had gone much further than mere lust with her now, and she was genuinely in love.

Miss Jepps, too, considered the matter from a purely financial point, but she threw herself heart and soul into the game, and the various pirates got full value for their money. Her one sorrow — that she had left nearly all her frocks behind on the *Mesopotamia* — was solaced by loans from the lady pirates, who had some exquisite toilettes on board.

A word as to these lady pirates: though none so exquisite as Maudie, the 'divinely tall and most divinely fair,' yet in their various styles they were very, very tempting. Connie was a brunette, apparently quite young, petite, with a perfectly moulded, supple little figure. She had laughing, hazel eyes, and a most delicious foot and ankle, which she took every opportunity of showing; in fact, when she sat down and crossed her legs she generally showed well above the knee, so that the pretty tan-coloured flesh showed a tempting bare streak between her stockings and drawers. She fell to the lot of Mr Silverwood. Mamie was American, widow of an English nobleman, who had done something really shady on the Stock Exchange and shot himself. She had been implicated but had escaped in time. She was very svelte and *Gibson girlie*, and she suited Mr Moss Hell down to the ground. Lucy, the last, was an older woman, probably thirty, very dark and Spanish, with a figure almost corpulent. Hannibal McGregor devoted his rough and ready Scotch method of love-making to her.

And what of the remaining two male captives? Herr Kunst was far too busy concocting novel schemes of piracy, with which he bored the 'young man' to extinction, to think of bodily pleasures, and as for Lord Reggie, he 'let go the painter,' frankly dated himself back, and stuck to Cyril.

Lady Tittle was rapidly assuming command of the ship. The 'young man,' infatuated with Hony, allowed her mother to do pretty well what she liked, and she *was* enjoying herself. She more than suspected her little daughter's liaison, but she winked. Her own *flagrants delits* with the bosun were so obvious that she hardly dared comment on her daughter's. She felt practically certain now that the young man *was* the Duke of St Eden, but still pried for proof. Lord Reggie, of course, knew, but his lips were sealed. Two days after the putting-in-irons episode the young man sent for him.

'You know who I am, of course,' he said.

'Of course, I do, Archie.'

'Now — now — not even here. Well, no one else does, though the old woman has her doubts, and has set the kid on to pump me. Now, I want your word that you won't give me away. One of these days you'll know the whole story.'

Lord Reggie promised, and the two shook hands and split a pint on it.

On about the seventh day out, the young man was sitting in his cabin, reading. Little Hony was curled up between his legs, her head resting on — well, where it shouldn't have been, and there was a something pressing against the girl's ear which she knew wasn't his hand. One arm was round her head, and her hand gently caressed it. As she felt the throbbing of the young man's member she gently stroked it with her soft head, and his thoughts came down to earth with a crash. He had been thinking out a wireless telegraphy problem, but now all the wireless telegraphy had descended from his brain into the top part of his trousers. He bent down and kissed her.

Hony twisted herself round between his legs, and let her fingers slide gently over the palpitating member in his trousers. Slowly her little fingers undid his fly buttons, till his cock sprang out and slapped her on the cheek. Her fingers played with it, tickling it gently with rosy, deftly manicured nails. She breathed her warm, sweet breath softly and sweetly on the delicate membrane of his penis, and then her tongue just touched the orifice of that 'root of all evil.'

Her hair — Hony could sit on her hair easily — fell forward over her face as she bent quickly down. Her soft tresses swam over the young man's penis, and he twisted a lock round it. 'By Jove,' he murmured *sotto voce*, 'this is Danaë's shower the other way round; gold, gold, gold, but she shall be paid for it in *white* — the *whitest* diamonds that ever left the Rand. "*Corpo di Baccho* — what Elysian drink have the gods sent me!"'

'*What* a shower of gold from the mount of the gods,' he said aloud.

Hony hadn't the slightest idea of what he was talking about, but she thought it sounded nice and she made no objection at all when the young man collected all her hair he could lay his hands on round that which he sometimes regretted he had ever had.

The young man knew music above a bit, and he remembered the 'Habanera' from *Carmen*.

'Listen, little darling,' he said, 'while I sing this, and keep the movements of your head in time.'

He sang, in his rich, baritone voice, that fatal song – patting little Hony's head to keep her to the right beats. He gave himself absolutely away to music and lust, and the lust won by a short head. At the last:

'And if I *love* thee, then beware'

the young man forgot *all* about the song of Bizet, and would have blinded little Hony, but she – *knowing* before her time – knew from the kiss on her head what was coming.

It came, *not* on her hair, but in her mouth: she was just in time to twist her little lips round his penis, and to drink – well – what ought to have made another pirate.

Hony wiped her lips on her delicate little lace-bordered handkerchief. The young man raised the little figure kneeling in front of him, and pulled her gently onto his knees.

He poured her out a glass of champagne, and she drank it. He took a glass himself, and sank back into the luxurious armchair with the delightful exhaustion of satisfied desire.

Hony lay in his arms, her head resting on his shoulder. With one hand he clasped her tightly to him, with the other he softly caressed her luxuriant, silky tresses.

Dreamily he closed his eyes: pictured to himself the beautiful girl as he had seen her on that first evening in the embraces of her dark-skinned lover, divested of everything, the perfect white flesh, the delicately moulded, miniature figure, the silky curls only just beginning to show between the dainty thighs.

As he recalled the vision, all his vigour returned to him, and Hony felt something between those little thighs that Leighton would have loved to paint (the thighs — not the something — though that something might have appealed to a famous Cornish artist). She was glad, for she had not been satisfied herself, and her first taste of a male organ in her mouth had made her long to feel it again in the spot which nature had designed for it.

She was consumed with desire, and her thighs twitched together as she sat on his lap — but she was not to be so easily satisfied.

The young man's hand stole over her legs, and under her light skirts. He softly smoothed the velvety skin and played with her firm little bottom, while his fingers wandered and gently tickled the tiny orifice.

It was too much for Hony. Raising her head, she slipped her arms round the young man's neck, gripping him tightly, and pressing her lips to his. Her tongue shot out, right down his throat. She writhed with lascivious passion.

The young man's fingers still further wandered and entered the cleft valley, which he had but so recently opened. It was already moist from the overflowing of her lust.

Hony withdrew her lips from his, and the young man whispered, 'Hony, darling, you remember our *first* evening when I came in and saw you with Carrie?'

Hony did not reply. She blushed and hid her face on his shoulder, and he continued. 'Hony, I want to see you like that again.' She raised her head and gazed at him.

'When?'

'Now,' he said, and Hony slipped off his knees. She commenced unfastening her dress, but he stopped her. 'No, darling, let me do that.' And bit by bit he himself gradually removed her clothes.

He stopped every now and then to kiss and admire her; he raised her arms to kiss the down beneath them, and inhale the perfume.

At last Hony was reduced to silken chemise, almost transparent. He stepped away, and watched her with intense admiration as she stood half ashamed and half pleased.

Then he said, 'Hony, let it fall to your feet and step out of it.'

Timidly, she complied. It was not mock modesty, but her nervousness was because she really loved him.

He posed her in nearly every way he could think of, watching for the effect. Each time he came back and kissed her.

At last he lifted her up, as he would a child, naked as she was, and laid her gently on his bed.

He kissed each little breast, toying with them with his tongue, and sometimes savagely sucking them as if he would bite off the rose-coloured nipples. His kisses went lower and lower; his tongue travelled over her honey-sweet skin; he came to the soft downy mount, and kissed it, opened her legs, and buried his face between them, his tongue working furiously — he almost hurt her. He felt at that moment he would like to devour her, then his kisses went still further down each exquisitely formed leg to the tiny foot. He loved the delicate feet, so perfect of shape, and so pink and white. He kissed them long and fervently.

Gently he turned her over, kissing her neck, her back, and the two beautiful rounded curves of her bottom, and one long fervent kiss between them.

He could stand it no longer, and roughly he turned her over.

Hony had almost fainted with the ecstasy of her sensual passions, such as she had never felt before, but as she felt him turn her over, instinctively she opened her thighs.

Without hesitation, the young man was on top of her, and in a few, all too brief, seconds, it was over. Hony fell asleep in his arms.

As the weather gradually grew warmer, the deck again became the favourite haunt, and the voyage perfectly enjoyable.

Hony had got accustomed to go into the young man's cabin whenever she liked, though of course she usually knocked, but one morning, rising earlier than usual, she stole out, and cautiously made her way there. She was feeling hot and excited, she felt she wanted to be cuddled and kissed, she meant to wake him gently with a kiss, then creep into his bed beside him, and she felt sure he would be pleased to see her, and *it* would happen again.

When she got to the door she quietly tried the handle, and it turned; she stepped in quickly and closed it before looking at the bed. As she did so she gave a little gasp of surprise.

The young man lay there quite naked, and on him sat Maudie with a leg on each side of his body. They had stopped all movement as the door opened.

Also on the bed was Jim; he had an arm round Maudie, and was kissing and sucking one of her breasts, his other hand was between the young man's legs under Maudie's buttocks; she could see he was playing with the young man's balls.

At first she was seized with the pangs of jealousy.

The young man noticed it, and said, 'Come here, Hony, and kiss me, you must not be jealous *here*, you know; we are all good friends, darling.'

She came over with a shade of reluctance, and kissed him, but the kiss he gave her in return drove all else from her head. He kept her mouth glued to his as she bent over him, and to her it felt as if he was sucking out her life's blood; his hand wandered under her delicately shaded, simple dressing gown, and under the soft, light fabric of her night dress it came in contact with the cool, firm flesh of her legs. An intense thrill passed over them both, and he pressed her lips even more tightly to his. His body quivered, and his buttocks rose and fell with a quick spasmodic motion. Maudie helped him, first relieving him of her weight, then letting it press down on him as much as she could, engulfing his rigid member to the uttermost fraction. Jim's hand slipped down from the young man's testicles, and he gently thrust a finger, moistened by the juice of life that had already escaped from Maudie, into that aperture which was not designed by nature to receive.

The young man's thrusts grew faster and more fierce; he roughly thrust his hand between Hony's legs, and two fingers up her now quite humid sheath. With one final convulsion he spent, and for a few seconds his body became quite rigid — then the intoxicating spasm was over.

He lay quite still, keeping Hony's lips pressed to his, and not letting Maudie get off, as she had tried to.

Notwithstanding the intensity of his feelings, and the profuseness of his discharge, he continued to feel unsatisfied.

No mere physical relief could drown the craving of lust which then possessed him.

After a slight pause he at last released Hony's lips, and drew her onto the bed.

He asked her to kiss Maudie, which she did passionately, their tongues darting in and out between each other's lips. As she turned her back to him the young man took advantage, and raising her, placed her astride his face, her beautifully rounded little bottom just above it. When her position dawned on her she softly sank back on him, almost smothering him, but he loved it, and the movements of his body recommenced.

One hand gently caressed Hony, the other he laid on the youth's stiff prick; Hony's hand also stole to it, while she still continued to kiss Maudie, and the sensation of their two hands meeting and touching on it was exquisite to those two. One of Maudie's hands crept round and toyed with the girl's dainty bottom and pink opening just above the young man's eyes.

The movements grew fast and furious, sighs escaping them all, and this time all four of them simultaneously paid their tribute to the deity of love and passion.

Hony scrambled off the young man, and lay down, exhausted and satisfied by his side. Maudie and Jim crept softly from the room.

The young man told Hony about his island, of his palace, of the natives, *and* of the perfect climate.

He told her also of the sports and amusements by which they whiled away their time, and kept themselves in good condition. He was lord and master there, his word was law, as much as on his ship. They had no *socialists* or *suffragettes* among *his* community.

Hony could not resist the temptation to ask him if he did not at times long for the Old Country, and regret that, now a pirate, he would never be able to return. He only smiled, and then he told her, what even those nearest to him of his subordinates had not dreamt of — his plan to reinstate himself and all those under his command. He was positive of his success when the proper time came, and under the most solemn pledge of secrecy, he gave her a glimpse of what it was.

It bewildered her.

These confidences led to more endearments, and this time it was Hony's turn. They did not hurry — the delightful contact of their naked flesh, and Hony's rapture that the vacuum she had been sensible of was now filled and stretched to its utmost capacity, was too heavenly to be put an end to before Nature compelled it, but at last Nature triumphed — and the commingling of their *bodies* seemed to be but part of the commingling of their *souls*.

The Cousins

Not long after Dorothy had surprised her mistress and Madame Vaudrez in the latter's bedroom where she had screwed her mistress with a dildo, Madame Lucy gave one of her famous, intimate soirees. Julia and Florentine were lucky enough to be invited; they both went under assumed names: Pomegranate Flower and Miss Evergreen. Although it was against the rules of Madame Lucy's establishment, Dorothy had explained to her former employer that both ladies had plans for the future where these names might become very important. They would only visit Madame Lucy's establishment once, because in matters of sex both ladies were very inexperienced. Madame Lucy was flattered, and allowed the house rules to be broken, just this once.

Her small, select parties to which only a lucky few — mainly the very rich, the very important and the titled — are admitted, enjoyed among the highest circles a remarkable, or rather extremely curious, reputation. The secrecy which surrounded these gatherings had made them notorious throughout Paris, and everyone who was anyone desperately tried to get an invitation.

Dorothy, of course, belonged to the small groups of friends of this hospitable lady, and she had really kept her word to wrangle an invitation out of Madame Lucy. She did not hide the fact from her mistress and Madame Vaudrez that getting the invitation had been exceedingly difficult. She also had some misgivings.

'My dearest ladies,' the devoted maid said, 'you may have to count on the possibility that as newcomers you may become highly involved, and I am almost afraid . . . what I mean is, once you are in Madame Lucy's salon, anything goes, and it is impossible to refuse anything. Won't you reconsider while there is still time?'

'Ah, rubbish, my dear Dorothy,' Julia said. 'I am not such a prude when I happen to be in the proper company, and neither is my sister. And besides, now you have really aroused our curiosity!'

Julia was not just curious but truly eager for an introduction to the home of Madame Lucy. When she was still the mistress of Count Saski she had picked up enough allusions to this famous establishment, and under no circumstances did she want to pass up the chance to see for herself what was going on. She knew full well that the happenings in Madame Lucy's house were incredibly licentious, and ladies from the finest families in Paris fought for the honor to be admitted to the odd entertainment of the intimate little groups that gathered there.

Two very important rules had to be followed strictly, exactly as laid down by the Madam of the house. In the first place, utter discretion was a must, and in the second place, everyone — without exception — had to accept the rules of whatever games were played at the particular party. If one could agree to these two stipulations, an evening of incredible delights was held out as a proper reward.

And Dorothy had told the sisters what Julia already had guessed, that whatever happened at the home of Madame Lucy was not exactly commonplace.

Madame Lucy was a widow of about forty years old, although she looked no more than thirty. She had a sister, Laura, who lived with her, and who appeared to be a few years younger. Laura was about to divorce her husband and, as far as the sisters could gather, this man lived in the colonies and made only very infrequent, short visits to Paris. Rumour had it that he lived with a negress in Africa. Anyhow, he was very rich, and his charming wife had a considerable income.

When the two sisters, together with Dorothy, entered the salon of the beautiful Madame Lucy, they met a small gathering of about ten persons.

There was the old Count de Paliseul, a very interesting gentleman 'in between the two ages,' with graying temples and a tendency to become corpulent; an officer of the General Staff, Baron Maxim de Berny, tall, blond and muscular and — as one could expect — the spoiled lover of all the courtesans and respectable women in Paris. Then there was Dorothy, well dressed and very ladylike, blonde and stately, with an enormous bosom and wide hips. Miss Elinor D. MacPherson was from the United States. She was a redhead, a real Irish devil with sea-green eyes, a wicked mouth with an incredible amount of lipstick and very beautiful pointed breasts. It was impossible to overlook this detail, if detail is the correct word. These huge things were truly remarkable, especially since the gown of this lady had the lowest plunging neckline Paris had ever seen. There was a banker, Monsieur de Lyncent, and a very pale, fragile-looking woman from Andalusia. She was Senora Padilla, who was at the party with her husband, a small, lean gentleman with pitch-black hair that seemed to be pasted down on his skull. He was the Consul from Spain. Finally there were John and Molly Teeler, brother and sister, abrim with youthful innocence, so much so that the sisters were beginning to doubt whether the soiree would take the course they had expected.

But then they were told that the latter two were performers; he an accomplished musician and she a so-called 'plastic dancer' – one of those girls who sprinkle themselves with bronze powder and then portray all the females inhabiting Mount Olympus. They were then satisfied that the evening would fulfil their expectations.

Besides, a small speech of the gracious hostess enlightened everyone completely, and there was no doubt left in anyone's mind as to what was about to take place during the course of the coming evening.

'Ladies and gentlemen,' Madame Lucy said in a low tone of voice – shortly before her little speech all the lights in the house had been doused, except for a few hidden ones which spread a discreet glow – 'you want, as far as I understand from your own words or those of your friends who were kind enough to introduce you to me, to taste with me the delights which are so frequently denied to us. You and I have now gathered in this small group. All have the same thoughts about this particular subject, and it is therefore that we shall be able to enjoy our desires without undesirable results and, above all, without restraint. I have seen to it that my servants, as usual, have the night off. There will be absolutely no unwanted witnesses to the proceedings. I fervently hope they will soon start, and I beg you to use your unbridled imaginations, and to throw off all your inhibitions. After all, we have gathered here with a delightful idea in mind and I beg you not to forget this, no matter in what situation you might find yourself.'

A softly murmured 'Bravo' interrupted the smiling Madame Lucy.

'Now, please allow me to repeat the few most important rules of our little get together. There are actually only three. Number one: shame is a plebian attitude. Number two: everyone is for everyone. Number three: the ratio is three to one which means that the ladies are allowed to reach a certain delight three times. I presume that I do not have to go into detail. The gentleman can enjoy the same ecstasy only once. For further proceedings the ratio may become six to two, and so on . . . let your imaginations work, give them free rein. It is a ratio at which I arrived after many delicious experiences, and I hope that the gentlemen can be trusted upon their word of honor.'

The last reminder, obviously, was only meant for

the men present. It seemed that the official part of the little soiree was over, and Dorothy whispered a few little explanations, telling Julia and Florentine that everyone was expected to follow the instructions of the hostess, and moreover that the rules of the game were of the greatest benefit to the ladies.

They were gathered in a rather large living room. There was no lack of a place to sit – or rather, to lie down. The rug in the middle of the room was free of any furniture, though grouped around it were four large, oversized couches. There were several sofas in the corners of the room, and many love seats and over-stuffed easy chairs. Several small tables throughout the room were loaded with bottles and plates, filled with all sorts of delicious snacks. Various exits led into smaller rooms which were discreetly lit and tastefully decorated.

The guests walked around, inspecting the various rooms, getting acquainted with one another, and slowly pairing off in small groups. If it had not been for the words of the hostess, no one would ever have thought they were amidst a rather special gathering of people.

But then came the voice of Madame Lucy again. 'Gentlemen, would you care to dance? Mr Teeler, please start the music.'

And the next moment, soft music filled the room and soon several couples danced to the exotic music. Maxim de Berny walked over to Florentine and invited her to dance with him. She accepted, and his strong arms embraced her passionately. He was a very good dancer.

Julia was asked by Senator Junoy. After a few dances they remained standing together and then sank down upon one of the couches.

'Did you get a little bit warm, my dears?' Again it was the voice of Lucy, clear but husky. 'I believe the gentlemen should be allowed to take off their coats. And I also think that the ladies should be permitted to unbutton their partner's flies . . .'

The two sisters were speechless. That is what one might call speeding up the proceedings! Hastily, the gentlemen, led by the Senator, that wicked creature, took off their coats.

'Well, Monsieur de Berny? And what about your tunic. That uniform must be extremely uncomfortable. And please, Madame,' Lucy said to Florentine, 'you will have to struggle with that hermetically sealed uniform fly!'

Florentine noticed that her partner's face reddened. 'How funny,' she thought, 'and this is only the beginning!' But at the same time she looked around for Julia. There was her sister, sitting on the next couch, together with the little Spaniard. Madame Lucy was standing next to them, obviously repeating her invitation. It seemed that the couple needed some urging, but finally her sister stretched her hand toward the pants of Senor Padilla.

Florentine had already put her hands between the legs of her escort, and what she found there exceeded her greatest expectations.

One great sigh seemed to drift through the room. All the couples were now standing, or sitting, in a big circle. The gentlemen's behaviour was still correct, though all of them were now dressed in their shirt sleeves. The ladies had their right hands extended and encircling the hardening members of their partners of that moment.

But Madame Lucy was watching carefully, and she was in full control of the entire affair.

'Well, my darlings,' she said pleasantly but firmly, 'I believe that the first introductions are over and done with, and I assume that you don't need my instructions any longer. I am very sure that all the gentlemen are now more than ready to pay slight compliments to their ladies. Please, gentlemen, don't hesitate. We women would love to get thoroughly acquainted with that which interests us most. Come to think of it, I would assume it to be very entertaining if the gentlemen would now take a firm hold of whatever is of greatest interest to them. Now, please, let's do it all at the same time. Grab firmly whatever charm it was that attracted you first to your female partner.'

What followed was positively hilarious.

Madame Lucy's suggestions were followed to the letter. Though the women had obeyed Madame Lucy's instructions rather hesitantly and shyly, the gentlemen were rather more direct and firm.

Florentine looked over at Julia and Senor Padilla. And, indeed, the little Spaniard had already taken a firm hold of those charms of her sister which had undoubtedly intrigued him most, namely her perfect, delicious breasts. His brown, strong hands fingered around in Julia's low-cut gown, and he quickly succeeded in freeing one of Julia's full, well-formed breasts.

Somewhat further on were the banker, de Lyncent, and the wife of the Spanish consul. Florentine could not exactly see where he had his hands, but it was easy to see that he was kissing the languishing Andalusian upon the mouth, trying to wriggle his tongue between her teeth.

'Our friend de Lyncent is a saint,' a gentleman remarked. He looked like one of Ruben's fauns, with his little, twinkling eyes, his reddish face, and his full white beard. 'A chaste little kiss satisfies him completely.'

This remark surely did not describe the gentleman's own desires, because he had just taken a firm hold of the charms of the silver-blonde Molly Teeler who looked, with her tousled hair and big blue eyes, like an appetizing little doll. One hand was energetically kept busy with her well-formed, obviously firm and hard bosom, and the other hand had crawled under the pretty young girl's dress. The gentleman did not even take the trouble, once he had reached his goal, to rearrange his partner's skirt, so that her marble-white upper thighs were completely uncovered. He had put his faun-like head slightly down, and was nuzzling under her armpits. It seemed to tickle her, and she burst out in a loud giggle.

'Ooh, I can't stand that . . . please . . . please . . . Oh, sir, you're tickling me too much . . . no, please, no . . . aaaah.'

The slightly tortured-sounding giggle had stopped,

because Count de Paliseul had let go of his partner's armpit and had begun to nibble upon her strawberry nipples which were smiling at him from her half-opened gown.

Without a doubt, one of the gentlemen, Monsieur de Laigle, knew his manners, because he was entertaining both ladies of the house. Each one was sitting on one side of him. Laura, who had opened his fly, was softly playing with his stiffening scepter, and he was tenderly stroking her full behind. At the same time his legs encircled the thighs of Madame Lucy, and it was obvious that his hand had already reached that spot which is covered with a tuft of hair.

The talented young Johnny Teeler — he could not have been more than nineteen or twenty years old — did not interrupt his soft musical playing. Nevertheless his hands no longer played waltzes, but they magically performed known and unknown singing melodies which increased the enchanted mood that now permeated the room.

And when Julia looked carefully at the dimly lit corner where he was playing, she noticed that he executed his paraphrases and melodies with only one hand. True, it was done with such virtuosity that nobody seemed to notice this. The only one who knew for sure was the American Miss Elinor because his left hand had taken a firm hold of one of her incredibly pointed breasts. She had taken it out of her dress and offered it to the piano player, holding it in both hands which made this pointed pear appear even larger. It was enchanting to behold this fascinating woman. Her well-filled yet slim figure rested upon a pair of firm, long-stemmed, gorgeous legs for which the American women are so justly famous. She had an unusual piquant face which was framed by fire red — one could almost call it indecent red — hair which contrasted strangely with her nymph-green, incredibly large eyes. It was not surprising at all that the young musician, whose fly was open like those of all the other gentlemen, displayed an enormous hard-on.

Maxim de Berny, too, had taken the charming cue of the hostess without any hesitation. He had become an entirely different person ever since Florentine had liberated his enormous manhood out of its uncomfortable position. Florentine loved to caress this gigantic, swollen, stiff prick. She was dreaming about how it would fit into a certain pink-coloured sheath.

His military reserve had made way for a zealous kindness. And, when the gentlemen had been asked to take possession of the charms that attracted them to their ladies, he had come more than just zealous and kind. He immediately grabbed a very firm hold of Florentine's legs.

'My dear and precious lady,' his hot breath whispered into her ears, 'I . . . I . . . have only seen you tonight for the first time. Oh, I am sure that you did not even notice me . . . there were so many other interesting people present . . . but ever since I saw you tonight, I have been haunted by a wild desire . . . I have dreamed passionate dreams . . . and I hope fervently that they will come true. My thoughts have been possessed by only one desire . . . to touch your

403

legs . . . those beautiful, gorgeous, long legs. They seem to be sculptured out of marble . . .'

His strong hands firmly underscored his words, confirming that he meant what he said. But he seemed not only interested in Florentine's legs, since his hands were also very busy with her thighs and the tuft of hair in between. He paid homage to her fleece that left no doubt as to his intentions. However, it did not disturb Florentine in the least. After all, that was what she was here for, and she fully intended to make up for her years of widowhood and her years with an impotent husband. She felt terribly passionate and could not have cared less if the blond giant had taken immediate possession of her. In fact, she would have welcomed it. But he was still playing with her legs, her thighs, her breasts and her slowly moistening hole. When enjoyed in the proper manner, erotic delights can be continued endlessly. The passion, after all, is always there. It is only a matter of the right place and plenty of time and a willing partner. Of course, Florentine knew that a brutal, quick embrace can have its own particular charm. One can even do it standing on a front porch, while the husband is occupied with opening the door, or in a men's room of a station when one's lover is about to depart for a prolonged time and hastily requires a last parting favour. It can even be done, she knew, in a public park, where one is protected by the impenetrable branches of the bushes.

.The large room in which the thirteen people were gathered was now filled with the most unusual sounds. One could hear a peculiar soft smacking, the rustling of the silken gowns of the ladies and the starched shirts of the gentlemen. There were the loving grunts and groans of the men, and the giggling and soft moans of the women. Breathless moaning, and the panting and gasping which left no doubt as to what was going on. Added to this was the typical, very exciting creaking of the furniture caused by the movements of the bodies that occupied them.

But the soft, enchanting music of John Teeler had stopped. In its place an occasional note was heard whenever Miss Elinor's elbows hit a key of the piano against which she was leaning while she straddled with widespread legs the lap of the young, blond piano player. In this strange position she went with him through all the motions that people usually perform when they are firmly pinned down on a mattress.

And they were not the only couple busily engaged in this particular delight. The skinny Spaniard had succeeded in inducing Dorothy to stretch out on the couch, and he was kneeling between her powerful legs. He was working a little bit too fast for Dorothy's taste, pushing his lance with such enervating speed against the girl's belly that she finally took his prick in her hands, forcing him to slow down. Her full breasts served as supports for the nervous Spaniard's outstretched arms and his skinny brown fingers voluptuously kneaded these enormous snow-white balls.

Monsieur de Laigle had put Lucy's sister in front of him. She offered her full, white buttocks up to his throbbing spear and he took possession of her behind with a certain nonchalance. Even while he penetrated her from behind, dog fashion, he refused to take his cigar out of his mouth. It was a curious sight. He fucked her, puffing his cigar, giving her enormous jolts. Laura kept very still, but breathed passionately and deeply every time the huge shaft of her partner disappeared up to the hilt into her wide-open cleft.

The hostess had not yet actively joined one of the many couples. She wandered from one little group to another, now cheering them on with a witty remark, then removing a piece of clothing which might be in the way, occasionally fondling a buttock, a breast or a pair of balls, whenever such a part was uncovered.

'Well, Monsieur de Berny, I am sure that Miss Evergreen is ready for you. Don't you want to honour the lady with your, as I can observe, more-than-ready sword?'

At that particular moment the couple did not need these doubtlessly well-meant encouragements, because without any further ado the strong, muscular officer had pushed Florentine down upon the couch and . . .

The girl did not think that she had ever experienced such powerful thrusts ever before in her life. The blond officer had mounted her as if he were a wild stallion, and he worked her over with tremendous force while he raised her legs high. He raved madly against Florentine's belly, his balls slamming hard against her buttocks. In a very short time she felt pains as she had never before endured. But strangely enough, the pain became pleasant, and her hips started wildly gyrating, her cleft wide open, as if she was about to swallow the whole man.

His breathing was rattling, but strangely enough, though it seemed that he could hardly get enough air, he kept exclaiming exciting words. Their monotony was, at first, strange and frightening, but ultimately Florentine became as hot and passionate as she had ever been.

'Aaaaah . . . finally, finally . . . now can I fuck between those legs . . . between those legs . . . I am fucking between those beautiful legs . . . between the legs of a most beautiful woman . . . aah . . . and what have you got between those sweet, beautiful legs? A cunt . . . a cunt . . . aah . . . how I have longed for that little hairy honey-pot of yours . . . right between your legs . . . ooh! Your legs, your legs . . . and I am fucking your right between those gorgeous legs! Ooh . . . aah . . . let me die fucking between those legs . . . the legs of an angel . . . I will never take my prick out of this cunt again . . . I want to stay between your legs . . . my hard prick in your hairy cunt . . . aah . . . how delicious to fuck that cunt between your legs . . .'

It was by now quite obvious to Florentine that her partner was particularly fascinated by her legs. It was also possible that their perfect line and form exceeded his wildest secret dreams. Anyhow, the muscular lover became wilder and wilder.

'Sweet . . . oh, how sweet . . . the way you raise those legs and spread your thighs . . . those legs . . . so that I can fuck between them . . . can you feel my balls slam against your ass? Ooh, I am fucking between the most divine legs . . . legs that seem to be praying for a harder and wilder fuck . . . I will give it to you, my love . . . I fuck that cunt . . . between your marvellous legs . . . and now you are spreading them so wide that I can put my prick in all the way . . . Ooh, don't you like it, this big dong between your divine legs? Ooh, feel how it rubs . . . ooh, my prick is at home at last . . . I am fucking you between your legs . . . I never want to stop . . . I want to fuck between your legs forever and ever . . . ooh, divine one, I am fucking you . . . between your legs . . . ooh, please, allow me to die between your legs . . .'

Florentine had to admit that it was a rather novel experience to have her legs honoured in such a peculiar way, while she, as a person, did not seem particularly attracted to the officer. But, she told herself, she did not come to find eternal love; sex was enough. And as far as that was concerned, their coupling was extremely satisfactory, and they rammed their bellies voluptuously together.

The behaviour of her partner reminded Florentine of a famous composer, a friend of her late husband, who had enticed his mistress − a divinely talented singer − to submit to him while she was singing a well-known, very difficult aria. And ever since that day he was unable to listen to her singing without being overpowered by the wild desire to possess her while the beautiful tones ran from her lips. To make this technically possible, the couple had agreed that he would rest on his back and have his mistress with the golden throat settle down upon him so that she would be able to sing her beautiful aria while he was pushing wildly under her, listening to her enchanting voice. Occasionally he would reach a certain height which would cause in her a sour note. But, on the whole, the arrangement worked perfectly for both people.

Julia, too, was literally drowning in passion. She had come twice already, though she had masterfully succeeded in hiding this. She wanted to enjoy the precisely measured, powerful jolts of Senor Padilla to the utmost. He worked without letting up, and his powerfully swollen muscle of love penetrated deeper and deeper into her longing body with every ramrod jolt.

Dorothy kept her partner working on her incessantly while she was crying out, 'Oh God, I am coming . . . I am . . . coming . . . oh, my God . . . how I . . . am coming . . . again . . . again . . . oh, God . . . I am . . . coming . . . you screw so marvelously . . . I . . . am . . . coming . . . again . . . ooh, it's fantastic . . . I am so . . . horny . . . you fuck like . . . a bull . . . aah . . . I am . . . coming all over . . . again . . . aah . . . aaaah!'

It was really very enjoyable to watch all these happy people. The big, blonde woman had turned slightly sideways. One of her extremely strong and powerful long legs, covered with a blue silk stocking, was held high up in the air by her partner, who held on to it as if it were a main mast of a sailboat, tossing in the wild seas. His lower body pushed rapidly with speedy thrusts against the widely opened cleft of his partner. He almost squatted between her full thighs, straddling

409

the one under him with his skinny legs as if he were riding a wild pony.

Dorothy was resting upon her mighty hips, showing a full view of her large and imposing behind. The gigantic cheeks shimmered milk white in the subdued light of the room. They jerked and palpitated continuously, pushing violently backwards against the belly of her partner, who kept pushing against her with short, very rapid little strokes. His peter must have sealed off her twat almost hermetically, and Julia decided to try out this obviously very satisfying position as soon as she had the opportunity.

The wife of the thus busily engaged Spaniard was about to enjoy special delights herself. She had been selected by the hot-blooded Count de Paliseul. It appeared that he was more attracted to her than to the silver-blonde Molly, and maybe he had reached his goal quicker than expected. He was now about to experience new delights.

He was zealously bearing down upon the tender, completely disappearing wife of the fiery Senor Padilla. The speed of the good gentleman was surely much slower than she was used to, but the force of his thrusts must have been incredibly more powerful than those of the skinny Spaniard. The Senora was whimpering quietly, but it could have been because of incredible delight which was forcing this soft meowing out of her throat.

'Aah, Monsieur, aah, so good you are doing it to me . . . ' she almost sobbed. 'It is so good . . . aah . . . aah . . . more, more . . . please . . . please . . .

aah . . . ooh . . . you satisfy me much . . . you are so much better than my husband . . . oh, how delicious . . . no, please, don't stop . . . it feels so good . . . more, more . . . aah . . .'

Her partner was as red as a boiled lobster. It was obvious that he was driving his shaft into her with his last remaining force, but it was equally as obvious that this task was not an unpleasant one for him. In fact, he was enjoying himself tremendously. This pale Andalusian woman, with her exotic beauty, had beautiful, graceful, finely chiseled legs and incredibly gorgeous, slender thighs. The panting, gasping fawn had put both legs across his shoulders and his heavy, fleshy hands gripped her small but muscular buttocks firmly, pressing them with a slow but regular rhythm against his own belly. This small woman was incredibly voluptuous, because every muscle in her small body shook and vibrated. She pushed herself against the huge man on top of her with such fervor and passion that it seemed as if her frail body consisted of one heavily tensed muscle.

The blonde beauty, the sister of the pianist, was now possessed by the horny banker. But it was not the normal position in which all the other couples were engaged. Either because of weakness, or because of perversity, the banker was busily engaged in an entirely different way. His gray-haired head disappeared almost completely between the widely opened white thighs of Molly, who languidly stretched out on one of the sofas.

One could almost say that the young girl was an

extraordinary beauty. Most interesting was the radiance of her appearance. Everything on her contributed to making her look like an angel. Her hair had the color of finely spun gold. The skin of her body and face was almost translucent. It was impossible to make out whether the snow of her bosom or the lilies of her thighs were whiter.

The form-fitting black silken gown, which did not hide anything on her perfect figure, was pushed up high above her waist by the horny old goat who was about to shove his facial duster into her small mother-of-pearl boudoir. It gave everyone present a peculiar feeling of tension to watch the balding gray head of the banker mix with the shimmering pubic hairs of this beautiful, innocent young girl. The zealous money lender had also pushed the gown of his willing beauty down her shoulders, thus exposing both of her full, pointed, yet very innocent-looking breasts. He took this opportunity to grab them both with lustful hands, playing around with them as if they were rubber balls. From time to time he rubbed both divinely red strawberries between thumb and forefinger – the same way a lieutenant of the guards twirls his moustache – eliciting excited groans from his beautiful partner.

The beautifully formed legs of this gorgeous creature rested upon the shoulders of the old man who was kneeling before her. It was incredibly obscene and shameless. Her legs were held up high and bent backwards. The high heels of her black lacquered shoes pierced deeply into the back of the totally absorbed man, slowly pushing him closer toward her. There was actually no need for her to do so, because the head of the insatiable banker had almost completely disappeared into her widely opened cleft, and he looked for all the world like an animal trainer, sticking his head into the hungry jaws of a lion.

Truly, the night afforded so much variety, and it was so exciting, that the sisters could not, with the best will in the world, recall every single detail. They also had no recollection how, after a certain time, the four enormous couches that formed a circle around the rug in the middle of the room were suddenly transformed into a gigantic resting place. Upon this enormous area, the couples sought and found one another. The watchful hostess saw to it that her guests' activities did not degenerate into selfish single acts, which would have robbed the people present of their sense of belonging, and which would have prevented the mutual orgy which now followed.

The bodies of the participants at this sensational soiree soon formed an incredible whole. They all formed one huge body with an enormous amount of arms, thighs, legs; a great, living thing — breathing, panting, moaning, groaning and sighing out of its many lungs. It offered breasts in all shapes — huge ones, pendulous ones, pear-shaped and melon-shaped, dark-skinned and milk-white globes, with an equal variety of nipples — from tiny strawberry-red ones to big, jutting firm ones, begging to be sucked and bitten. Buttocks, cunts, mouths, pricks, and balls in delightful opulence invited the many groping hands and eager mouths. The people who had become this huge thing moving on the enormous bed seemed to consist entirely of semen-filled cunts and mouths, throbbing pricks and slamming bellies. Now rule number two achieved its end. 'Everyone for everyone' took on its true meaning.

It would have been impossible not to follow this rule, once caught up in this indescribably wonderful mass of naked and almost naked bodies. It was impossible for any of the participants to avoid the embrace of the nearest neighbor, or to escape from a throbbing prick, a yawning cunt, or the voluptuously grabbing hands of another.

But then, nobody had the slightest intention of doing such a thing. They did everything in their power to pull as much flesh as they possibly could, to hold as many hands as was bearable and to kiss eagerly the many hungry mouths and tongues. The smell of sweat and semen worked like a powerful aphrodisiac. The groans and cries of the others seemed to spur flagging powers to even greater deeds. The two sisters found themselves now on top and then under many bodies. Sometimes they were pressed against one another and, then again, against another partner. They were in one continual hot embrace, completely entangled. It was a mystery how the various couples, or rather groups, always succeeded in getting loose from each other only to form new connections, new couplings with new partners, trying new and different techniques. They did things, and enjoyed them, which they had hitherto never thought possible.

The most incredible combinations were formed by all these steaming hot bodies! The permeating smells of come, perfume, body odors from armpits, cunts and pricks were unbearably exciting.

Everything was mixed, from the most primitive wild grabs to the most refined techniques. And each deed caused ripples of delight, running the complete gamut from voluptuous desire to gasping climax . . . over and over again. The hot spark would fly from body to body, jumping through the entire group, using the nerves of these people as if they were one single medium.

Whenever on one end of the enormous bed a female body jerked in the spasms of an incredible climax, shuddering as if tortured with unbearable pains, the next moment a body on the other side would groan and jerk, coming equally as ecstatically, as if an electric jolt had passed through the entire mass of bodies in the short span of a single second.

Florentine was no longer pinned down and fucked by the massive, muscular body of Maxim de Berny, and Julia had long since lost Senor Padilla who had had his delights both with her and Dorothy. It seemed that all the male participants of this peculiar soiree at one time or another had deposited their seed in the more than willing laps of Florentine and Julia. The two sisters, who had so far lived a chaste life, were reluctant to ever get off their backs.

In the wild group which the guests of Madame Lucy now formed, it was next to impossible to recognize even the most intimate partner of the moment, though the girls tried to identify some of them. But how should they know whose mighty member was pushing and jolting from the back against their sopping cunts? They were thrown across the heaving belly of another, like helpless booty slung across the back of a wild stallion, while at the same time they were trying to swallow someone's throbbing manhood that was trying to impale their open mouths. Julia thought that it must have been young Teeler who was stretched out next to the officer, but her hands were caught, left and right, between their wildly banging bodies, so she could hardly be sure.

And who was working her over with such vehemence? Judging by the technique, and the words he muttered, it must have been Maxim de Berny, who had spent the earlier part of that evening ripping her sister Florentine apart. On the other hand, she suspected that it could be Dorothy who had strapped on her dildo.

There . . . oooh . . . just now . . . Julia had just started to climax and already the jolting prick had squirted into her and was about to pull out of her hot and hungry quim. She was just beginning to feel sorry for herself when suddenly two powerful arms pulled her thighs even wider apart and another throbbing prick penetrated her hospitably moistened grotto . . . how delicious! Her new lover, with renewed vigor, continued the task of replacement, jolting and jarring her shivering insides. She was drowning, floating in voluptuous delights she had never known before. Her wild desire temporarily quieted down with the regular thrusts. Suddenly she felt a pair of hot lips take possession of her tickler, and the head below her formed an exciting buffer for another partner who was giving it to her from behind.

Florentine, on the other side of the bed, stretched out one hand which was just released by one of her partners. There! Wasn't that the heavy club of our insatiable faun? Yes, indeed! And before she fully realized what was happening, it had already pushed itself halfway between her lips. Then, suddenly, Florentine began to bob her head, trying to swallow it all, wanting to have this gorgeous throbbing member deep in her throat. She sucked some precious drops from it and then someone else pushed her greedy mouth aside.

The heavy cylinder, which for a short moment lay there like an orphan upon his belly, disappeared into a very moist opening, barely needing the help of someone's guiding hand. And now, in the place of the soft mouth of Florentine, another, even softer pair of lips encircled the throbbing flesh pole of the elderly gentleman, speeding up and down without stopping.

Florentine was fascinated to be allowed to witness this variation of coupling, and she tried to give both the heavy prick as well as the encircling lips as much pleasure as she could.

It is impossible to describe the heady atmosphere that ruled the orgy room. The air seemed to boil satanically. Continuous, almost frightening gasps, shrill screams, and tortured sighs filled the air. The silence which now and then fell was even more sinister.

And then, suddenly, a thumping rhythm would set in whenever several couples started to hump and fuck each other again. Accompanied by the creaking of the furniture, one could hear fanatical hands slap naked flesh, the rubbing of nude bodies slamming together, and the slurping of voluptuous lips. Now and then could be heard the characteristic sound of a softening penis slipping out of a vagina, or someone's hardened nipples slipping out of puckering lips.

Most characteristic, and also most exciting, were the spontaneous exclamations. Sometimes they were involuntary, while others were said with the specific purpose of giving vent to the wild urge of having everybody take part in the enjoyment of a particular act. Even the rather reticent wife of the Spaniard called out her feelings without shame. While she was busily engaged upon this jolting and shuddering altar of lust and passion, she chanced to come upon her husband. He was just about to attack Laura, the sister of the hostess who herself was engaged in a battle to take on the enormous prick of the blond officer.

The Senora called out in wild ecstasy, 'Miguel . . . he screws me delightfully . . . I tell you, his prick is as heavy as the spear of Saint Isidore . . . aah . . . aah, darling Miguel, I love it soo much . . . aaaah . . . aaaah . . . you, Miguel . . . Miguel . . . I have to . . . please, quick . . . quick! Tell me, darling, are you getting fucked as heavenly as I? Quick . . . quick . . . it . . . is . . . so . . .' Since she started to come at that moment the rest of her confessions stuck in her gurgling throat.

Some of them were less lyrical with their expressions. The redheaded Elinor was positively obscene. Her true character showed itself when she tried to spur her partner, or rather partners, to even greater efforts.

'Why don't you fuck me harder? Come on, let me feel that you have a Goddam hard-on in my cunt! I said harder, you dirty son-of-a-bitch! Come on, I want to be screwed . . . put it in deeper, harder . . . ball me as if your worthless life depends on it . . . stick it in deeper . . . is it in? Jesus, I can't even feel your balls slam against my ass . . . faster . . . deeper and quicker/ Come on, who can give me a real good fuck? I want to be raped as if you were a bunch of horny Cossacks who haven't seen a cunt in years! I don't want you to shove it in like a gentleman . . . ram it up my cunt like a cowboy . . .'

She veritably screamed, foaming at the mouth, 'I am horny, so Goddamned horny! Isn't there a prick among this damned bunch that knows how to fuck well? Come here with it . . . I'll stick it into my cunt myself. . . quick . . . quicker! Can't you hurry it, come on, fuck me . . . my cunt is burning up . . . Give me that hot dong . . . screw me to pieces . . . shove it up my cunt harder . . . deeper!'

And the raving redhead snatched furiously at the dripping prick of the Spaniard who had just pulled it out of Laura.

'Ha . . . here's one that just came . . . boy, did that one come! That's how I want to be screwed . . . come on, you bastards . . . I'm horny and I want to get fucked . . . by all of you! One prick after the other

. . . stick in your dong . . . dammit . . . yeah, that's it . . . one after the other . . . I want to be laid by every Goddamned prick in the house . . . deep . . . hard . . . and quick! Hurry, hurry . . . that's it . . . work it in deeper . . . a little bit faster . . . deeper . . . aah, that feels good. Finally I'm beginning to feel good . . . this one fucks me even better . . . come on . . . I . . . want . . . to . . . harder, dammit, deeper . . . a little more . . . aah . . . aah . . . ooh! Eeeeek!'

Her voice suddenly gave out, but not because this horny creature had reached a climax, or even found some satisfaction. One of the gentlemen had suddenly put his swollen penis into her opened mouth, penetrating deeply into her throat. The cork effectively stopped this wellspring of Anglo-Saxon lechery.

There was one more special climax to this evening worth mentioning. It was not that the mood of excitement had abated, but the participants were becoming slightly tired. Yet, it was obvious that all had a desire for stronger excitement. In short, the following proposition was eagerly applauded by all, even before it had been completely uttered. Young Johnny Teeler was going to fuck his own sister! Strangely enough, this had not yet happened, and it must have been by pure chance. It could never have been because brother and sister avoided each other on purpose. This would have been simply impossible in the ingenious mixing machine upon which everybody had been romping around. But now they had to make up for their omission.

'Oh, Johnny,' Molly suddenly blushed, 'should we really do . . . this?'

Like all the others, Julia and Florentine were very curious to see how the handsome Englishman would react to the proposition.

'Come on, you simply have to do it. It really makes no difference. Everyone here has fucked everyone else. Even the married couples have seen their partners screwed by others. And that does not happen too often, either!' This argument was brought forth by Miss MacPherson, who had finally caught her breath. She was still busy gagging the juices of her last partner, which dribbled out of the corners of her mouth.

'Molly, don't forget our cardinal rule, "Everyone for everyone!" After all, we can't help that you two happen to be brother and sister. After all, Laura and I are sisters. That never prevented us from showing affection for one another. And, as I understand, the ladies Pomegranate Flower and Miss Evergreen, who are sisters, have a nice thing going together, too! Think of all the famous lovers in history and mythology who were brother and sister. Why, even the Pharaohs of Egypt and the Incas in Peru couldn't get married *unless* they were brother and sister. Now, come on . . . don't be so ridiculously bashful! And don't tell me that the two of you have never slept in one bed together when you were kids. Even without touching each other!'

'Yes . . . that is true. We also used to play around a little . . . I mean, with our . . . with our . . . But what you order us to do, we have never done,' Molly stuttered excitedly.

'Well then,' Madame Lucy resumed, 'you two will just have to catch up and rectify that mistake. Oh, come on, Johnny, don't be a party pooper. Here is Molly . . . she is gorgeous . . . who cares that she is your sister. Throw her on her back and get it over with!'

The resolute Madame Lucy, with Laura's help, had already pressed the blonde girl down upon the huge bed, holding her nude body firmly upon the pillows.

'Here, Laura, help me. Take a hold of her legs and pull them a little apart. No, not roughly, just hold her lightly. It will only take a few seconds of good banging and she will lap it up.'

'Oh, please, dear Madame Lucy! Don't you know that it is a deadly sin? We have never done a thing like that! Johnny . . . don't . . . no . . . don't! You are my own brother! No . . . don't . . . no, no, no . . . how can you dare to force me . . . no . . . don't . . . no . . . no . . . ooh . . . I . . . aah . . . Johnny . . . no . . . ooh, Johnny, Johnny!'

During her last exclamation, her brother pierced his heavily swollen prick deeply into her belly. It was a beautiful performance. Her brother, one could easily see, had no difficulties whatsoever. It could have been possible that he had been waiting for a long time for an opportunity like this one. He possibly had lusted after his own sister for years, eagerly wanting to enjoy her charms. Anyhow, his zeal and his powerful thrusts were proof enough that as far as he was concerned, passion was more powerful than prudish conventions.

The guests formed a circle around the balling

couple. Everybody was curious and wanted to see everything. It was no longer necessary to hold the girl down. She was panting wildly with every thrust and her thighs opened wider and wider. The two formed a nice, charming couple. It gave everyone great satisfaction to know that Molly, who was getting the hang of it, would from now on allow her brother to screw her more often.

'Ooh, Johnny, how good . . . how good . . . how beautiful it feels to do it with you . . . Please, please, go deeper my sweet, sweet Johnny! Do you remember . . . how we . . . used to . . . play . . . husband and wife? But this is really much better . . . it is . . . really good . . . only . . . this . . . way . . . please, Johnny . . . go on, deeper . . . push deeper . . . only . . . a few more . . . I have to . . . come! Aah . . . aah! Oh, Johnny . . . lover . . . I am . . . coming . . . ooh, Johnny . . . don't stop now . . . go deeper, quicker . . . please, please . . . Johnny, screw me some more . . . fuck me, dear . . . I want to come again . . . fuck . . . fuck me . . . aaah . . . you . . . have . . . to . . . fuck me . . . often . . . and hard! Always, always . . . I want you . . . to fuck me . . . always . . . tell me, Johnny dear . . . promise that you will . . . always screw me like this . . . aah . . . aaaaah . . . you . . . you . . . you!'

And the charming little sister of Johnny Teeler reached her climax.

With Open Mouth

They lay together for some time with her stroking his neck gently. He noticed that the sun had withdrawn farther to sea and he felt a slight return of his previous embarrassment. He was not sure how to move off her, although he felt he must be heavy upon her. Inside him, apart from the embarrassment was a feeling of wonder and achievement at what had happened. But he could not bring himself to look at her.

'Look at me.'

It was as if she had read his thoughts.

'How does it feel to be no longer a virgin?'

Avelino stared at her searchingly for a moment. There was a warmth in her eyes which melted his embarrassment and in answer he kissed her gently on the cheek.

She laughed quietly, clasped him fiercely against her and then whispered:

'We'd better have a quick swim before we go.'

They swam naked out to the sun and afterwards he collected his clothes and they climbed the wall of hills which enclosed the town, to the little café with its open-air terrace overlooking the bay.

Later Avelino went home, having arranged to meet

the woman, whose name, she told him, was Janice Harvey, at the isthmus on the following day.

Once out of her presence, Avelino was beset by all sorts of mixed emotions. He felt, now, much more a man and yet still contained within himself a sense of shame. He was not sure how he felt about the woman, Janice. Fascinated by her, he was nonetheless annoyed at the ease with which she had been able to have intercourse with him. He was also very aware of her maturity in face of his own boyishness. He wondered how many men had enjoyed her and he felt, even now, a twinge of regret that there had been others.

All the Spanish girls he knew clung, by reputation, tenaciously to their virtue. It was only married women who, according to report, occasionally fell from grace. Of course, she might be married. The thought struck him like a wave but he cast it immediately out of his mind. She didn't seem married. He refused to think of it.

Avelino lived with his mother, father and two younger brothers in an old, white-washed house with blue shutters whose front door opened straight into one of the cobbled narrow streets of the town. The streets were not streets in the modern sense but narrow pavementless spaces ribboning between the houses, sandcovered, their uneven cobbles jutting at all angles.

It was to this house that he went, feeling that his secret of new life was written on his face. He felt it would be difficult for them not to see that he had changed during the afternoon.

Avelino ate his evening meal separately from the rest

of the family as he had to play and sing with the band early in the evenings. Tonight he was very thankful for the absence of his brothers and the interminable chatter of conversation that went with their presence. His father had not yet come in from the fishing and his mother was preoccupied with the neighbours' laundry which she did to supplement the family income.

The sun was still shining in a yellow half-circle above the hilltops when Avelino took his place on the orchestra dais at one side of the open-air dance floor.

The western hills were a dark, dusty green with the sun behind them and their summits were clothed in a fiery aura of red and yellow which cast a rose glow over the town. The white houses were tinted rose, and the white hulls of yachts swaying gently at anchor in the bay. The colour of faces was heightened and there was an atmosphere of the soft evening waiting for her lover, night, to come.

Avelino took his clarinet and the orchestra plunged into the well-known tunes of the sardanas. The brassy notes swept out in the still air, travelling up the narrow winding streets, pervading the houses and the little shops hidden amongst them. The tune soared out to sea, its warmth surrounding the little boats of the fishermen coming into the bay. And suddenly, it seemed, both inside and outside the dance enclosure, people were joining hands, forming circles to dance.

Letting his eyes stray from his music which he knew so well, anyway, Avelino wondered if the woman, Janice, knew how to dance the sardanas. There had been a time, which all seemed misty and lost to him when the sardanas had been forbidden in Catalonia. That had been just after the days of the civil war which had wracked this part of the country and left scars which still remained.

But gradually, the ban on the sardanas, which were typically and peculiarly Catalonian, had been lifted and now, wherever the music started, immediately little circles of people sprang up to perform the daily shuffling dance which reminded them always that Catalonia was Catalonia.

As the sunlight faded into a streak of lighter blue and rose on the hills and the lights of the town popped on merrily around the coastal path, the people were still dancing. By the time the sardanas had come to an end it was dark, the sea was calm and the sea-shore bars were ablaze with light and humming with the noise of tourists.

The concrete dance floor was thronged, now, with people of many nationalities. The light from the orchestra dais and the lamps on the tables which surrounded the floor, lit up the animated faces and movement as the rhythm of a rhumba danced on the air.

It seemed to Avelino, eagerly watching the entrance gate, that the whole of the town had taken on a new glow of interest. For months he had played the same tunes, sung the same tunes without inspiration. Since the afternoon the world seemed to have changed.

When, at last, she arrived at the gate, his heart beat a little faster, his playing almost wavered. Watching her cross the floor to the table which was always reserved for her, Avelino was suddenly overcome with a feeling of disbelief in the reality of the afternoon's events. Janice — and it almost seemed an over-familiarity to use her first name — seemed quite out of his world. In the touristic sophistication of the dance, in the glamour of the string of coloured lights which stretched like a vine around the enclosure, she appeared more beautiful and poised than ever.

As she passed the orchestra, she glanced up at Avelino with a quick smile and the exciting reality flooded back in him. At the same time however, he felt a twinge of embarrassment. He knew all about the sort of gossip that swept from door to door through the town. It was a gossip which would certainly not approve of his relationship with a woman so much older than himself — although there might be certain sections of the community who might be rather proud of it in their old age and others envious in their young. However, he had been sufficiently imbued with the spirit of the small town to feel some awe at its mass opinion.

Nonetheless she had smiled at him. It had happened. He glanced from the corner of his eyes at the rest of the orchestra. Nobody seemed to have noticed. Why should they? Any beautiful tourist might smile at the band.

By the time Avelino rose to sing into the microphone, Janice was dancing with someone who looked like a Frenchman. Her eyes, over his shoulder sparked, sometimes, in Avelino's direction, and he felt a surge of excitement and power from the secret intimacy he had with this woman.

The song he was singing was a soulful one of his being all alone, and his dark brown eyes as he sang swept the jostling throng of dancers, resting finally in a glimpse of fierce recognition on Janice. Each time she responded to his look, half-closing her eyes at him, or smiling slightly.

At the end of the dance she followed her usual habit of refusing to join the Frenchman's table. Nor did she, throughout the evening, in spite of repeated requests, which Avelino, his neck hot from the sight, witnessed, accept any of a number of similar requests.

She was still being asked to dance, however, when the night came to a close with the final quick waltz, from which couples retired continuously to their table in a flood of laughter at the mad whirl.

Unable to keep his eyes from her, and uncertain yet of the power of their relationship, Avelino watched with a growing feeling of jealousy against her partner who was a handsome young Spanish tourist he had seen strolling around the town.

But, once again, at the end of the dance, there was a little clinging to the hand by the Spaniard, a polite and smiling shaking of the head from the woman, and once more she had brushed her way back to her table to finish the drink she had poured for herself from the miniature bottle of benedictine she had ordered.

Many people sat quietly chatting, recovering from the dance, after the orchestra had stopped for the last time that evening.

The coloured lights around the enclosing trellis lit up the animation of the faces. Far out over the sea, a crescent moon shone amongst the stars, lighting up, in turn, the calm sea. It shone in great puddles of light on the water, silver against the surrounding black.

From a nearby bar, packed with people in its turn, the music of a radio floated faintly to the dance-floor and one or two couples got up to dance to the ghost music while the orchestra packed away its instruments and the dismantling of the microphone wire to the amplifiers was begun.

Janice sat, cross-legged and lovely, watching the orchestra as it disbanded.

Avelino took his time about packing his clarinet into its case. He tried to appear casual, but eventually was unable to avoid raising his eyes towards the spot where Janice was sitting.

Immediately he looked in her direction, she made a little motion towards him with her hand and her eyes invited him to join her.

He waved back, almost surreptitiously, and hesitated, a hesitation due in part to his youthful embarrassment in being seen associating with this rich, sophisticated-looking woman and in part to his knowledge of the explosion of curiosity and speculation it would give rise to in the village. But against these arose a feeling of sheer pride that he should be the only man she had any desire to ask to her table — and that all those sitting in the enclosure would see it.

Pride triumphed and with a casual farewell to his

colleagues, he strolled with studied unconcern towards her table.

He was aware of the eyes which turned and followed him as he reached her table, aware of the murmuring voices which accompanied them. He looked only at the table and at her.

Janice's eyes were laughing as she invited him to order himself a drink.

'You sang beautifully,' she said. 'I can't understand why everyone in Spain thinks Frank Sinatra's so wonderful.'

'They're used to voices like mine, but everything about the faraway world of North America seems wonderful,' he explained.

'Then you should go where you'd be more appreciated — back to Barcelona with me, for example,' she retorted.

Avelino glanced at her, startled, and she laughed merrily and he laughed and the drinks arrived.

Around them seated parties were still speculating on the event of the past few minutes and the old fishermen and young yokels, who formed a permanent leaning border on the townside rail of the enclosure, stared openly and avidly. Soon the news would have spread throughout the town in spite of the late hour. And in the morning the many who knew would be delighted to pass on this titbit of gossip to the few who didn't.

'Do you go straight home after the dances?' Janice asked, after they had been talking for some time.

'Generally I do, but it doesn't matter if I'm late,' Avelino replied.

'Good. If you'd care to walk home with me, I'll make coffee and we can have another drink.'

Avelino had agreed from the sheer unexpectedness of her blunt invitation, before, once again, doubts assailed him in a tempest. What would they think when they saw him leaving the dance with her? Where did she live? Did she live alone? What would they think if they saw him going into her house at this time of night? What excuse could he give to his parents when, as was inevitable, they heard about it?

He had answered none of these questions before he found himself, feeling completely unequal to what was taking place, strolling out of the enclosure with Janice, bidding casual goodnights to the townsfolk clustered around the entrance.

They wandered away from the still crowded enclosure and were soon beyond the streams of light flung out from its centre.

On the dusty coast road, cut off from the sea in places by a low wall against which the surf dashed, in others by sudden, expansive beaches specked with still, shadowy fishing boats, they walked.

Here and there a young couple were sitting on the sea-side parapet, or the quiet animation of old men's voices and the smell of strong tobacco would drift from a patch of shadow. The moon was a thin crescent.

As if Avelino's doubts had been spoken aloud, Janice made no motion to move in close to him or to hold his hand as he had thought she might. He was relieved, but, at the same time, the fact that she made no move in that direction, filled him with an overwhelming longing to do so.

He could see her charming, clear-cut profile as they strolled and the black stole she wore gave a pale, moonlit beauty to her skin.

As the sound and the glitter of the bars in the main plaza began to dwindle and appear only occasionally – and each time more distant as the road curved out around promontories which jutted deeply into the sea – Janice dispelled one of his unspoken doubts.

'I've rented a house here,' she explained. 'It's about the last one we come to before the wilds.'

He knew the house now. It had one Moorish turret at the eastern end, was set back from the coast road and surrounded by a small, sparse plantation of olive trees. It was doubtful whether anyone would see them go in. Already the road was deserted, although there was the cliff restaurant further on which sent a late-night wave of tourists along the road, singing and buffooning.

Beyond the house, the coast road began to cut through the hills as the coast itself became high, rocky cliffs. It wended a lonely way through scrub-covered hills to the next town some miles distant. During the day little bands of people wandered along it looking for a comfortable place to picnic. At night its only occupants were the carabinieros, patrolling in couples in the green uniforms which looked so like the scrub, in their interminable watch for smuggling.

'Here we are,' Janice said quietly, as they reached

436

the iron gate which opened from the road onto the dusty barren grounds of the house.

Away from the possibility of spectators, Avelino felt the dawning of nervous excitement. His worries concerning the outer world disappeared and he became doubly aware of the woman walking gracefully beside him, and their solitariness. When their hands brushed in walking, his heart pounded and suddenly they were hand in hand and she was close to him, her shoulder pressed against her chest, her hip brushing his, bodies inturned as they walked.

He inclined his head and kissed her gently on the forehead. Her fingers squeezed his and he felt suddenly overcome with a gush of feeling for her. He drew her round to him and she raised her head, pressing her body tightly against him. Their lips brushed gently and then locked in a fierce devouring.

They drew apart and then together again and then she whispered:

'Quickly, it is so comfortable inside.'

They walked on, slowly and entwined towards the great, brooding shadow of the house. It was a still phantom, solitary and eerie as they moved into the stone patio with its shadowy entrance arches. Around them in the grounds were the thin shadows of the olive trees, above them the dark blankness of the hills, behind them the moon glittering on the sea.

'Aren't you afraid to live here alone?' Avelino whispered.

'No. I like it,' she whispered back, gently mocking his awe. 'I get so tired of the city with interminable people, cars, complications all around me. I love the simplicity of all this — the sea, the hills, all the elemental things and sweet uncomplicated people.'

Avelino was silent for a moment, considering what she had said, while she unlocked the heavy, wooden, blue-painted door.

'Have you had a *very* unhappy life?' he asked eventually.

He followed her into the dark vestibule, listened to her fumbling for the switch.

'It's been all my own doing,' she replied, answering several questions ahead. 'A question of reading, studying, idealising, searching, reforming, trying to find a solution for the happiness of society and making oneself miserable into the bargain.'

She shut up suddenly as if aware of the fact that he would not be understanding her. But Avelino had read a few books, mainly about fallen men and women and he felt some inkling of her problem.

'Are you happy now — at this moment?' he asked.

He felt her move away from the switch in the darkness. He felt her hands on his chest, her lips against his with the soft, warm touch of the sun.

'Yes, at the moment I am happy,' she breathed.

She whisked away before he had time to hold her and the light went on, that soft, inadequate light of the low-wattage bulbs which were necessary when the influx of tourists made the demand on the power too great.

Avelino followed her from the vestibule into a long, blue room with modern furniture of varnished olive and a high ceiling with dark beams. She pulled back the heavy blue curtains which covered the French windows, opened the windows and then the heavy shutters which led out onto the verandah. Moonlight streamed into the room as she turned off the light.

She came close to him again and he felt stifled with emotion as she laid her blonde head gently on his shoulder in a gesture which seemed to demand his protection.

'It's quite romantic,' she said softly in a tone which hinted that she was trying to laugh at herself, but couldn't.

'It's very beautiful,' Avelino whispered, looking out over the glistening sea as if he were seeing it for the first time.

'How long can you stay?' she asked.

'An hour or two.'

'Let's go to bed.'

Avelino's heart began to pummel in him at her words. He tried to hide a fresh fit of quivering.

As if, with some incredible thought, she were afraid he was going to refuse, she caught his hand and drew him gaily towards the door.

'The bedroom is pink,' she laughed. 'I'm very traditional really.'

Avelino allowed himself to be pulled after her, passion and longing fighting with images of his mother looking at the clock in their strict austere home.

'I mustn't stay too long,' he said.

She looked round at him with a happy smile of triumph.

'Go now if you're afraid,' she mocked.

In answer he pulled her to him with a swift jerk and they seemed to sweep fluidly into each other in a fury of desperate passion. Avelino felt lost – completely lost. He was no longer master of himself. He was in a great deep pit whose bottom he could not see. All the longing of his adolescence had turned against him, weakening his mind so that in this first, sympathetic, beautiful contact he found a reason for living.

'I love you,' he whispered as if he were in agony. 'I love you.'

She drew her head away from him so that he could see her hazel eyes vaguely glinting in the moonlight, the shadows hollowing her face, tracing the clear lines of the bones. Her eyes were searching him as if she, now, was afraid, and then her lips had closed with his in an engulfing pressure.

The bedroom led from a short white corridor and was furnished in similar style to the first room they had entered. Janice turned on shaded wall-lights on each side of the bed and the room was suffused with the pink of the walls, carpets and draperies. The bed was enormous and low. It might have passed for a divan but for its size. Avelino was still trembling with anticipation as he looked at it, shadowy and inviting in the dim light.

It seemed too wonderful, too incredible to be true that in a short time he would again be holding this woman, naked, in his arms, this time in the warmth and comfort of a bed.

'Do you like the room?' she asked him gaily. He

had the impression that she, too, was trembling.

'It's delightful,' he said, contrasting it mentally with his own adequate but bleak bedroom which he shared with his brothers at home.

He wandered across the room to look at a set of red, leather bound books in a varnished bookcase and when he turned back Janice had already removed her dress.

She stood looking at him, almost coyly, a vague and graceful sylph. Her breasts were hardly covered in the provocative bulging by the small black brassiere — and the flimsy black briefs with their frilly edge creased tightly in the triangle of her abdomen. He could see the brown tautness of the flesh of her ribs, taut enough to accentuate enormously the proud thrust of her breasts.

She moved towards him and the flesh of her thighs rippled in sinuous hollows.

Avelino stood rooted to the spot, gazing at her. He was unable to move, could only wait for her to come. Forming a great jut under his thin trousers, his penis was hot and pulsing. He felt helpless against its pulsing and its jutting. He was aware only of her, a movement of firm, beautiful flesh towards him and the enormous, scorching tingle at the lower tip of his loins.

She reached him and as she clasped him the tenderness and love he now felt for her made his longing even stronger.

Her hands clasped his neck and pulled his face down against hers so that their cheeks caressed. At the other intimate end of her she pressed and jiggled against him, rubbing up and down against the hard protuberance of his erection.

With a feeling of despair that they were two people rather than one, Avelino buried his lips in her neck and moved his hands quiveringly down the smooth, flawless skin of her back. As his exploring fingers reached the start of the outward bulge of her hips, he strained her against him. And then his hands moved on down her body until they were cupping her buttocks in a sensual ecstasy of their own. He forced her hips in at his, crushing her against his penis until it hurt him, torturing himself.

Her buttocks were smooth and hard as she strained into him and then she relaxed and her buttocks relaxed and expanded fully into his hands.

She kissed his throat and began, at the same time, to unbutton his shirt. His whole body was trembling slightly now as his shirt came open all the way down and she eased it gently out from his trousers and helped him to pull it off his arms.

She kissed his chest tenderly and her own hands seemed to indulge in a tremoring delirium as she stroked his back, his sides and then moved down to his fly buttons.

Avelino was panting. He found it impossible to keep still as she jerked the top button open. His stomach hollowed and expanded, his hips writhed gently as if a great outside force were making them do it.

Her hands had nearly completed their work. He waited tensely for the first touch of her deftly moving fingers on the thin tissue of his pants. As he felt it he jerked his hips away and she ripped undone the last few buttons.

His trousers fell to the floor, a ridiculous pile around his ankles and he stepped out of them, revelling in the sensual freedom of the cool air on his limbs.

Janice slipped away from him and went towards the bed, stripping off her brassiere and her briefs. He watched her buttocks swaying as she walked.

At the bed she turned towards him and there once again, but more charged with sex than during the afternoon, were the heavy breasts and the naked slimness with the broad roundness of the hips. She was lovely. She looked fragile, but a fragility which he longed to take and massage in his hands, to all but break.

'Take your pants off,' she said softly.

Avelino reached down and untied his espadrilles. Where the tapes had been around his bare ankles they had left shallow red weals and he massaged the flesh for a moment, feeling slightly embarrassed, hoping she might get into bed. But she stayed where she was, looking at his strong, graceful body appraisingly.

After a moment's hesitation he slipped his pants from his hips, his strong penis flipping into view as he bent pushing the garment down his legs. His penis felt hot and clammy. he had a blind, helpless feeling like a bat brought suddenly into light.

When he had kicked his pants away and looked up, Janice's eyes were fastened on his organ and her mouth was slightly open. She moved her gaze up his body until their eyes met. Her breasts were heaving and there was a shade of anguish in her eyes.

For a moment they gazed at each other. Avelino

gulped. He had no control over the tremoring of his body. Janice moved her hands up to her breasts as if she would try to still their rise and fall and she breathed, almost as if to herself the one word: 'Come.'

Avelino stepped swiftly towards her, crushing the rug under his bare feet. He felt his testicles sway and brush against his thighs as he moved.

She waited for him to reach her hand as the impact came, her mouth opened wide and her arms swept around him . . . Their naked flesh seemed to fuse, their bodies to suck at each other, flesh against flesh in gentle pressure and oozing.

She bit at his lips as he kissed her and then her tongue was worming silkily into his mouth and she was drawing him back to the bed. The covers were drawn back and she allowed herself to fall backwards onto the soft sheets, pulling Avelino down with her.

His organ was pressing hotly against the soft, cool flesh of her thighs and the weight of a great animal instinct raged in his loins.

Janice moved one arm away from his shoulders and whipped the covers over them so that he felt the soft caress of a sheet on his back. The feeling of the covers gave him a sensation of comfort and exclusiveness as if they were in a little home of their own from which they need never go out.

For a while they lay together, he warm on top of the soft, flesh cushion of her breasts and hips. There seemed no hurry. Avelino suddenly didn't care. The whole night was ahead of them.

They kissed over and over again and from the

pink warmth of the bed, he heard her voice whisper:

'Why don't you come back to Barcelona with me?'

'To Barcelona!'

'Yes. It would be wonderful.'

Her fingers caressed his hair and his ears.

'Oh, it would be impossible. I am too poor and my mother would think I was mad.'

Her lips brushed against his cheek and came to rest close to his ear.

'You would live with me and I would give you money. I have far too much.'

'I could not take money from you in that way.' Avelino's pride was piqued. The thought of living on a woman was too much for him.

'Why not?'

'It would not be fair to you. It is the man's job to earn the money.'

She laughed softly and kissed him passionately on the lips.

'It would be more than fair to me,' she said. 'My money has done nothing but make me miserable up to now. If I choose to give you some to make myself happy, you should be pleased at the way it shows I love you.'

The words came as a shock to Avelino. Greater than the shock he had experienced when he had been chosen to sing with the local orchestra. *I love you.* They filled him with a warm, wonderful feeling which brought tears to his eyes. They made everything sure and the world evolved from a half phantom to reality.

'You love me?' he whispered.

Her arms moved around his neck in reply and the pressure was so great that when she kissed him his lips were crushed back on his teeth and he could hardly breathe.

'I love you,' she answered softly.

Under him her thighs wriggled apart and caught his penis between them, squeezing it gently between the walls of now warm flesh. His genitals seemed to break out in a sweat.

Gently Janice levered him off her and he allowed himself to fall away to her side, willing to be instructed, obedient to her greater knowledge. He subsided on his back with her warmth pressing along his side as she rolled over towards him.

With a quick movement she threw back the covers and his rampant penis, thick and veined, its broad, sensitive tip almost purple from the sensual friction with her thighs, shot into view.

He lay quiet, stroking her breasts with one hand while her eyes wandered down the length of his organ. She reached over and brushed the thick mop of hair away from its protruding rigidity and at her touch his penis gave an involuntary jolt, moving sharply towards his belly and then receding again to the perpendicular. Her eyes moved away over his testicles and her fingers moved away too to stroke them.

Avelino tensed his buttocks, giving himself over to the incredible continuation of the unbelievable set of events which had brought him to this particular place at this time. He closed his eyes and, as he tensed, his penis seemed to elongate a little more and offer itself to Janice like a rigidly rearing snake.

As if the slight movement of tension had been an offering to her lips, she suddenly flopped her head down to his loins and sucked the knob of his organ into her mouth.

At the soft, painful, startling pressure, Avelino opened his eyes. With his entrails contorted in the pain of a new sensation, he saw her, blonde head bent, eyes narrowed in passion, concentration on the gentle sucking. He watched her cheeks hollowing, her lips moving as she sucked and the urgency of his passion seemed to become unbearable.

His hips began to writhe, his sweating buttocks clamping together with each upthrust. He felt her tongue licking at his point of passion as she sucked voraciously. As he began to grunt and his lips breathed her name, she suddenly pulled her head away from his loins, drew her lips from the labour of love.

Sharply she turned on her side, extending her smooth, rounded buttocks toward him. She reached behind her, caught his hips and pulled him over so that he was lying along her back. She pulled one of his hands across the soft flesh of her hip, round to the front of her, across the softly protruding flesh of her abdomen, through the silky hair of her muff and left it at the portals of her moist vagina.

As Avelino began the gentle insertion of his finger, she gasped and undulated her buttocks against his loins so that the firm smoothness of them imprinted itself against him.

Exploring, Avelino found the hard little clitoris

which he had read about in sex books and he massaged it gently while Janice groaned and writhed her buttocks furiously at his loins.

'That's wonderful,' she breathed, almost indistinctly, and she pressed his hand hard against her orifice.

With her writhings, Avelino's penis had ridden up so that it lay along the lips of her vagina, its base lying in the groove of her buttocks. Her thighs were extended in front of her and she drew them up even higher as her hand reached behind her, searching for his penis. She found it, grasped it, squeezed it for a moment and then guided it at her welcoming aperture.

Still caressing her clitoris with his hand, Avelino drove into her vagina from behind. He entered her forcefully with a sensation of hot relief mingled with a passion which drew his lips apart in a gasp.

As he thrust he felt the tautness of her buttocks against his loins. He pushed his other hand under her body and caressed the globes of her breasts.

Already excited from the caress of her lips, Avelino felt his loins to be a tangle of tortured nerve ends. Janice, too, was already gasping and moaning with a great gush of feeling.

Brokenly, between her gasps, she whispered words to him and Avelino moved his face against hers to hear as his penis slipped in and in with a soft slippery facility.

'I'll kneel,' she was trying to say. 'That way you go deeper. It is better for both of us.'

'All right.'

She knelt up, moving onto her hands and her knees and he got to his knees with her, leaving his penis vibrating inside her as they moved.

She lay her head on the pillow and her back sloped up towards him, broadening into the buttocks between which his penis seemed to disappear. She spread her legs, moving her knees wide apart, and, ranged in a kneeling position behind her, Avelino shuffled his knees towards her between her opened thighs.

Now he could see his penis and the pink folds of flesh into which it was searing. He could also see the little ruffle of flesh, pink and hairless which was the slit between her stretched buttocks. It was the first time he had had this view of a woman and it filled him with a lust which was quite apart from his feeling of tender passion for Janice.

Moving his hands over her buttocks, he rammed into her with growing ferocity. He could see the thick stub of his flesh withdrawing in wet rapidity and then plunging into her intimate passage again until his hips cannoned into the soft buffer of her rump.

Clasping her hips tightly so that his fingers dug red marks into her brown flesh, he surged into her, swivelling his hips for greater pressure. Her passage contracted around him, sucking him in in a tight embrace. She moved her hands helplessly on the sheets and then lifted her arms behind her, reaching back to clasp his hips and pull him at her with greater force.

Feeling her fingers on his hips, virtually asking for even more, Avelino pushed her knees wider apart with his own and leaned heavily with his hands on her back, forcing her bottom up towards him. He thrust in and then left his penis in her to its full extent while he moved his abdomen against the soft flesh of her behind, from side to side so that he felt fresh stabs of exquisite agony from their flesh brushing lightly together — and then he began the punishing piston movement again, slowly, powerfully.

Gasping, groaning in a complement to her gasping, groaning, he felt her hands release his hips and brush down under her own thighs to gently grasp and caress his testicles. She fondled each separately, writhing her bottom on the end of his raging penis and he felt a fresh injection of passion from the cool touch of her fingers on the heat of his hairy lobes.

Janice began to cough out sounds from her throat until he was not sure whether he was hurting her or whether it was some choking passion. With a great effort he slowed his stabs of penetration, but immediately she forced her widespread crotch against him.

'No, no! Don't stop!' she pleaded. And her hands moved back to his hips, trying to reach right round to his buttocks to pull him more forcefully at her offered opening.

With that encouragement, Avelino bored into her again with such strong strokes that his abdomen felt bruised against her buttocks. Each thrust flattened the light brown globes of flesh as he gave a last upward flick of his organ.

'Now, now! It's coming, it's coming,' she breathed in broken, staccato tones.

With the sweat glistening lightly on his upper lip and his forehead, Avelino slowed his strokes to thickening, grinding penetrations behind which his whole body flexed and surged. His lips curled away from his teeth in the sheer barbarous sight of the woman prostrate at the mercy of his loins. He swooped his head swiftly and kissed her back and inside him there was the hot, burning sensation of hot liquid simmering.

It grew and grew into a great crushing at his penis, a sucking as if his inside was being siphoned through the tube towards the open channel. He felt powerless. Nothing could have interfered with the movement now. Had it meant he was to die if he shot into her, he couldn't have stopped himself.

She was pleading with him to hurry, seeming to hold herself back, waiting for him to reach his climax.

He felt the overwhelming weight of an undefinable sensation gathering from the root of his being, seeking for an outlet. He was panting furiously, his belly heaving. He began to breathe her name with every thrust and as he felt the weight too much to bear, sensed with gritted teeth the inevitable breaking, he in turn shouted: 'Now, now!'

Another thrust and another and Janice uttered a sudden long, low whine and her channel seemed to open to three times its size and at the same moment, the hot liquid rushed, seeming to whirl inside him and then burst, in an agony of contorting buffets and cries, from him. Each release, like a spurt from a machine gun, gave him a gorgeous relief. Throughout his emptying into her he uttered one long, low moan and her flushed face, swung in agony from side to side on the pillow.

With the last weakening thrust, he flopped forward around her, kissing her neck and after a moment she collapsed on her face so that he lay along her back, his penis deflating and slipping out of her to nestle in its shrivelled state against the join of her buttocks.

They lay there for some seconds, breathing heavily, and then he rolled from her and buried his face in her breasts, overcome with emotion.

'I love you. I love you,' he almost sobbed into the tight, brown flesh of her soothing mounds. Gently she stroked his head. There was a glint of happiness in her eyes.

Bare Necessities

It was a beautiful morning, the sun burning down out of a brilliant blue sky. Carol was alone in the house. Alone, bored and, she hated to admit it, horny. What was wrong with her these days? She'd been getting more than she'd ever had, with a whole slew of people, and here she was still not satisfied.

She stood at the kitchen sink, one hand up beneath her T-shirt toying with her bra-less breasts, rolling her nipples between her fingers. She could feel the skin puckering into hard points as she plucked and squeezed. She imagined Bart – no – some other man, suckling at her bosom, sliding a hand up her short skirt to play with her pussy. Gently slipping a finger between the crisp blonde curls to tickle her clit. Like she was doing now.

Thrilled with her own wantonness, she pulled up her skirt and shucked off her panties. Then, standing on tiptoe, the muscles in her long brown legs straining, she leaned her pelvis against the kitchen cabinet. There, just at the right height to snuggle into her crotch, was a small, rounded drawer-knob. She'd done this before, occasionally – well, quite a lot recently, since they'd started going to that damned club – and she knew just the right height to stand and the way to rub herself on the smooth wooden knob so that it built the pleasure and scratched the itch that was already raging in her loins.

She tried to settle her thoughts on a man she desired, a man untainted by recent events, a fantasy man. She'd like a really big guy, broad-shouldered, barrel-chested, all muscle but with a neat, tight ass. *How about a football player?* One of those hunks running around in skin-tight tunics, all strength and power allied to speed and skill . . . *And blond maybe, a big blond quarterback with a little blond moustache which matches the hairs on my pussy as he pushes his tongue between my cunt lips and licks up my juices. A guy who'll pick me up like a doll and sit me on a cock that fills me so full I won't be able to walk for days after. A guy I've never seen before and who I'll never see again. A guy who'll just fuck me silly.*

Maybe a guy who looks a bit like the driver of the truck parked just over the way. Yeah, just like him. Look at those tight jeans and long legs and broad shoulders. Hope he can't see me through the net curtains. It's okay, buster, there's broads all over California this morning so horny they'll fuck the kitchen cabinets . . .

The sound of the doorbell was so unexpected she took no notice. Then it came again, puncturing her excitement and deflating her instantly.

'Oh shit,' she said to herself, now frozen rigid. The bell sounded again and she knew she couldn't ignore it.

456

She was still flustered when she opened the door. Even more so as she looked up at the blond truckdriver standing on the doorstep. She could feel a pearl of juice rolling very slowly down the inside of her left thigh.

Up close he was huge, nearly a foot taller than her and twice as broad. He had an open, honest face — *but no moustache, dammit* — which was currently shrouded in gloom. At the sight of her his depression seemed to deepen. This was not a happy man.

'Is Bart Kimberley at home?' he asked.

'Oh no. He's at work. At the garage.'

'No, ma'am. I've been up there and they sent me here.'

Carol suddenly remembered, Bart had said he had to meet up with Link Arthur.

'Well, if it's a job he'll be back at the garage later.'

'Are you Mrs Kimberley?'

'Yes.'

'Well, it ain't a job. It's something personal. Something *Goddamn* personal and you an' me are both in it.'

His face creased further with pain and he looked as though he were about to burst into tears. It occurred to Carol he was probably younger than that college kid, Stan.

'In that case you'd better come in, Mr — '

He looked relieved and followed her down the hall into the living room. 'Call me Charlie, please.'

'I'm Carol. Please sit down.' She suddenly felt much better. She was in charge and somehow the man of her recent sex fantasy was sitting right across from her staring at her legs. How weird!

'The thing is, er, Rita, my wife, her car broke down on the freeway and . . . she knows your husband.'

'Yes?'

'Well, she was with my sister and I believe they invited him and a friend to a party . . .'

'So?' Carol sounded nonchalant but she had a funny feeling that she knew where this was leading.

'And then . . . what I mean is — oh shit! I'm sorry, ma'am — Carol — but you'd better take a look at these.'

As he leaned forward and pushed an envelope into her hand, Carol's stomach turned over.

She looked at the photos as coolly as she could. Appraising each one carefully, taking her time.

'I presume,' she said in the awkward silence, 'that this lady is Rita?'

'Yeah, that little slut is my fucking wife.'

An apt description, thought Carol as she took in the details of a brunette with big tits sprawling half out of her clothes across the lap of her husband. This doubtless was the nature of one of darling Bart's 'out of town' deals. She couldn't understand it — didn't he get enough at home and at the club? And there was Bob Adams, his tongue buried in the tramp's snatch — what would Shirley say? The thought occurred that Shirley would simply induct Rita and Charlie into the club . . .

'Oh God,' she said. 'I'm sorry but I've got to have a drink.' And she stumbled into the kitchen and grabbed the vodka bottle.

Charlie sat like stone, his boyish face crumpled in pain. He accepted a glass without a murmur and sank an inch of spirit in one hit.

'So, Charlie, what was the purpose of your visit? Simply to make a lonely housewife unhappy?'

'I was going to kill Bart — Mr Kimberley, that is. But first I was going to make him tell me where I could find that other guy. Then I was going to kill him too.'

Unbidden, he held out his glass for a refill.

'Well, I've got to say your idea has some merits. What about your wife?'

'Oh yeah. Rita. I put her over my knee and gave her a real good whipping.'

'If you don't mind me saying so, she looks like she might enjoy it.'

'Ah well.' His expression changed, for a moment agony was replaced by the recall of ecstasy. 'She took it like a real good gal. Afterwards she was very sweet to me. It wasn't really her fault at all.'

'So you've forgiven her?'

'Well, yeah. She swore to me she would never see those guys again.'

'Suppose I forgive Bart, too? I'll make him swear never to see Rita either — then we'll be quits, right?'

'Huh?'

'I mean why go to all the trouble of killing Bart now you and Rita have made up? You'll spend the next ten, fifteen years of your life in jail just thinking about what Rita may be doing on her own. Is she the kind of woman who could stay faithful for that long?'

Confusion now ruled Charlie's features. Carol took

the opportunity to top up his glass. She noticed that his eyes had drifted once more to focus on the expanse of thigh revealed beneath the abbreviated hem of her skirt. Then she remembered that her panties were scrunched up in a ball on the kitchen floor.

The alcohol was racing through her veins. Right now she couldn't care less if this big dummy broke Bart into matchsticks. But there *were* other, pleasanter ways for a girl to take revenge. She crossed her legs.

'Look here, Carol.' Charlie had reshuffled his emotions — now he was aggrieved. 'I bin done wrong,' he said with emphasis. 'Your husband took something that was *mine* and he ain't gonna get away with it!'

'That makes sense. I agree with you.'

'You do?'

'Sure. He took something of yours, now you've got to even the score. Take something of his.'

There was silence. Carol imagined she could hear the gears change in Charlie's head. She realized she was still sopping wet between the legs.

'Like what?'

Oh God, he was forcing her to spell it out —

'Like me, you big dufus. He took your wife, you take his . . . it's obvious.'

'But — '

'What's the matter, Charlie? Don't you like blondes with long legs? Or do you only go for short dark girls with melons on their chests?'

Carol could have bitten her tongue off after that last crack. Vodka and frustration were getting to her.

Fortunately Charlie was still digesting the significance of her earlier remarks.

It was time for action. She rose from her seat and stood over him, her feet between the angle of his great sprawling legs, her crotch two feet in front of his face.

'Come on, Charlie, be a man and even the score. At least — do it for my sake.'

And she took hold of her skirt at the sides and began to pull the material upward. His astonished eyes were glued to the hem as it rose, centimeter by centimeter, up the length of her smooth golden thighs.

'I suppose I ought to tell you,' she said as she reached the point of no return, 'that I'm not wearing any panties.'

'I know,' he replied, sliding two spade-like hands up the back of her thighs to cup the bare cheeks beneath the flimsy cotton of her skirt, 'I bin looking up your twat ever since you sat down. Boy, was I embarrassed. And, boy, have I got a hard-on now.'

'Oh Charlie.' The skirt was up around her waist and she held his curly blond locks in her fist as she pressed his great boyish face into the wet folds of her pussy.

For a dummy he ate her out pretty good, she thought. But then doubtless Rita had him well trained in that department. She ground her crotch into his face, shamelessly rubbing herself to the relief she had been cheated of by his unexpected arrival.

'Oh God, Charlie,' she wailed as the first shockwave hit her, rippling through her belly and buckling her knees. Then she tore herself from his grasp and pulled him to his feet.

Part of her was amazed at her own manic behaviour as she began to rip at his shirt and claw at the belt of his jeans. She wanted him nude. She wanted this great blond hunk stripped naked for her pleasure and she wanted it *now*!

'Hey, honey, go easy. Hey, Carol!' he cried as his shirt buttons flew across the room and her long nails tore into his belly. But he stood there placidly as, on her knees now, she yanked down his jeans and shorts in one violent tug. Then she stopped.

'Oh Christ,' said Carol.

He looked down at her smugly. Charlie knew that girls found this part of his anatomy − impressive.

'It's beautiful,' said Carol as she placed both hands on the stiff distended limb. It was almost hairless, the skin of the trunk-like shaft a snowy white in contrast to the brilliant puce of the ruby red helmet. A golden fuzz of hair shaded the pink plums that dangled beneath. Carol gripped the base of the root with one hand, then measured upward, hand over hand three times. 'Like a horse,' she said to herself, 'three hands high.'

'Satisfied?' he asked.

'That depends on where you put this thing. It sure as hell won't go in my mouth.' It was true, she was gagging on the glans now, trying without success to fit it inside.

Charlie laughed. He felt good. Especially to have this classy blonde so hot for him. Sometimes girls changed their minds when they saw the size of him. This chick wasn't running anywhere.

'Lick it,' he commanded. 'Make it nice and wet. You know how.'

She did, of course. Knew how to make herself wet, too, slipping a hand between her legs to make herself ready to take the biggest cock she'd ever seen.

He slipped his hands beneath her armpits and lifted her upwards.

'Hang on to my neck,' he said and slid his hands beneath her ass, cupping a buttock in each palm as she twined herself round him, hooking her legs over his hips and linking her ankles behind the small of his back.

'I call this the Five Easy Pieces,' he whispered into her ear as the little fingers of his hands delved into her split and delicately spread open the flaps of her cunt. Carol could feel the air between her splayed lips. She felt incredibly helpless. And incredibly excited.

'What do you mean?' Where was it, that great thing. She knew he was going to stick it in her at any moment.

'Five Easy Pieces. The new Jack Nicholson movie about this guy and all these broads and he has a big row with a waitress in a diner.'

What was he on about? And where was his great cock? She wanted it, needed it right now, up her to the hilt.

'Oh, Charlie, put it in me please. Please, Charlie. Please fuck me!'

'Well, in one scene, old Jack is dorking this girl — '

There it was! She could feel the head of it wedged between her thighs, right at the junction of her legs, solid and broad and, oh God, big, searching for the keyhole like a midnight drunk on the doorstep.

'She's daffy little babe with blonde curly hair and these really cute tits — '

Carol jinked her ass, trying to position the hungry mouth between her legs, he, too, cleverly jockeying her as he bent his knees and then — thrust up . . .

It was in her now, a column of solid flesh invading her insides. A living rod pushing higher and deeper and 'Oh, oh, oh!' — she was sitting full on it as it still pushed in, threatening to split her in two, to fill her up with pain but miraculously spreading a sweet golden glow through her veins like honey . . .

' — and Jack is walking up and down while he fucks her!'

He was still talking as she came the first time, sinking her teeth into his neck, clinging to his torso like a gibbering monkey up a tree.

Then he began to walk her around the room, jogging her up and down on the solid arm of his dick as she did so. 'Oh God, oh God,' she cried, 'don't drop me please!' But there was no chance of that, not before he had finished his party piece. Now he began to walk into the hall.

'No, Charlie! Don't go by the window!'

But he had turned and begun to walk upstairs, still holding her firmly beneath the ass, his great dick spearing in and out of her as they mounted the stairs. By the time they had reached the top landing and he had pushed the bedroom door open with her back, she had run out of protests.

He stopped in front of the full-length mirror which hung on the open door of the wardrobe.

'Aha,' he said in triumph, 'now we can see what we're doing!'

And so they could. Looking over her shoulder Carol took in the bizarre sight of her body wound round the giant's torso and the obscene out-thrust of her ass bulging over his huge sausage-like fingers. The pink eye of her anus winked out at her above the rear view of her slick pussy-mouth gorging on the thick rod of his cock. He jiggled her up and down, making the creamy ovals of her ass shiver, the hairy sack of his balls joggling oddly beneath her spread cheeks.

Then things got just little hectic. Either the erotic vision in the mirror was too much for Charlie, or else his strength finally gave out, for he suddenly pitched forward onto the bed, Carol pinned beneath him helplessly, and began to shaft in and out of her like an unleashed jack rabbit.

'Oh Charlie, of Charlie, oh Charlie − ' she found herself crying, either in pleasure, or pain, as he crashed into her with all his strength.

When it was all over, and it didn't last long, she was amazed to discover that she felt great. Satisfied, sexy and − amply revenged. What's more, she could now think straight again.

'Charlie,' she said, 'will you be up to any more vengeance today?'

'Uh?'

'I mean, the other guy in the pictures, you ought to straighten yourself out with him.'

'Right.'

Carol reached for the phone by the bed and began to dial.

Shirley answered after one ring.

'What are you doing right now?' said Carol.

'Is this an invitation?'

'You bet. I want you over here to meet a friend of mine. He's a film buff. And he's got a surprise for you.'

'What kind?'

'The kind you like best, Shirley. A very big one.'

The Three Chums

I

Charles Warner, the son of a wealthy squire who owned a large estate in the Midlands, had just arrived in town, and taken up his apartments in Gower Street, for the purpose of becoming a medical student, as of course being only a younger son, and the freehold property all entailed, his jolly parent could think of nothing better in which his sharpest boy, as he called Charlie, would be so likely to make his way in the world.

'Be a good lad, Charlie; stick to your profession, and I'll set you up with ten thousand when you marry a girl with some tin; that's the only thing a younger son can do. Should I die before that it's left you in my will. Your allowance is three hundred pounds a year, to be five hundred years when you come of age; but mind, if you disgrace me or get into debt, I will turn you adrift without a penny, or pay your passage to Australia to get rid of you. My boy,' he finally added, a tear in his eye and a slight quiver of the lip, as he said tremulously, 'you have always been a favourite; your old dad reckons on you to keep away from the girls and bad companions.'

He was thinking over these last parting words of his father as he sat by the fireside after tea awaiting the call of his two cousins, Harry and Frank Mortimer, who had written to say they would call to take him out, and see how he liked the rooms they had found for him.

He presently rang the bell to have the table cleared, and a remarkably pretty maidservant answered his summons.

'And what is your name? As I am going to live in the house and should like to know how to call you. I'm so glad Mrs Letsam has a pretty girl to attend on the lodgers.'

'Fanny, sir,' replied the girl, blushing up to her eyes. 'I have to wait on all the gentlemen, and a hard time I have of it running up and down stairs all day long.'

'Well,' said Charlie, 'I shan't ring for you more than I can help, although it is not at all strange if some of them trouble you so often, if only for the pleasure of seeing a pretty face. I suppose it isn't proper here in London to kiss the servants, although I often did at home; the girls were older than me, and had been used to it for a long time.'

'La, no sir, you mustn't, indeed you mustn't, if Mrs Letsam knew it she would turn me out of the house in a moment,' exclaimed Fanny, in a subdued tone, as if afraid of being heard, as she turned her face away from his unexpected salute.

'You mean to say you mind a kiss from a boy like me? What harm is there?'

'I — I don't know; I can't say,' stammered Fanny. 'But it's so different from those old fellows downstairs, who always give me half a crown after, not to tell.' Here she blushed tremendously. 'I — I didn't mean, sir, that I want to be paid, but that you are so different than them; they're old and ugly, and you — '

She could not say any more, for Charlie pressed his lips to her rosy mouth, saying, 'Well then, give me a kiss for forgiveness. If you only keep good friends, and look after my small wants, I shall buy you ribbons and little things of that sort, so that you can think of me when you wear them.'

His only answer was a very curious look as she returned his kiss; then slipping away took up her tray and was gone.

'I'm in luck,' soliloquised Charlie. 'Dad may lecture me to keep away from the girls. Polly and Sukey at home didn't kiss me for nothing; the sight of this pretty Fanny and the thoughts of last night when they had me between them for the last time, makes me feel quite so-so. In fact that girl has given me the Irish toothache; it was all very well for dear old dad to caution me, but they say like breeds like, and I know he got a girl with twins before he was eighteen, and had to be sent away from home to get out of the scrape.'

Here there was a tap at the door of his room.

'Come in, my boys; I know who it must be,' shouted Charlie, expecting his cousins, but to his surprise Mlle. Fanny re-enters.

'If you please, sir, there's two young gentlemen for Mr Warner, they have sent up their card.'

471

'Where is it, Fanny?' asked Charlie, holding out his hand for the bit of pasteboard.

'Well, I am pleased they've come early,' he said, catching her by the wrist, 'and especially as it gives me the chance of another kiss!'

'For shame, sir; you'll keep them waiting in the hall,' as she struggled to get away from his encircling arm.

'Just a moment, Fanny, I want to say to you they are my cousins, who will often come here, and are much better looking than me, so don't you make me jealous by taking any notice of either of them. Now, ask them up, quick, please; then run for a bottle of fizz, and keep the change for yourself,' he said, handing her a sovereign. 'We must wet the apartments the first time they call.'

It is not necessary to refer to all the greetings and enquiries of the cousins when they first met; but presently, when the champagne was opened, Harry and Frank asked if Charlie was too tired to go out for the evening, saying, 'You need not come back here to sleep, but turn in with us, as you know the governor will be so pleased to see you at breakfast in the morning. We know three jolly sisters — little milliners — who work in Oxford Street, such spooney girls, and as three to two is sometimes awkward you will just make the party complete; they live in Store Street, close by, and if we call about nine o'clock they will be expecting us, and glad to see you; it is awfully jolly, and not too expensive, we only have to stand supper. The girls think too much of themselves to take money, although nothing else comes amiss from jewellery to dresses. Nothing coarse, no bad language, and they only permit liberties when the gas is turned out.'

'I'm with you,' replied their cousin, 'and what do you think of the little servant here?'

'Charlie, you ought to be in luck there,' answered Harry, 'it's so convenient to have a nice little servant to sleep with sometimes, or now and then to let off the steam with her on the sofa, it keeps you from going out too much. My advice, Charlie, is not to live too fast, save your money for a good spree — say every ten days or so. Your racketty ones don't get on half so well with their governors, who are always grumbling. Now our dad thinks us quite good, never out after half-past eleven or so; but we make up for it with the servants at home, and keep the housekeeper square, by taking turns to poke her on the sly. She once caught us both in the girls' bedroom, but we went into hers to beg her not to tell, and what with kissing and telling her what a fine figure she was (she was half undressed when she came to see after the servants) that we took first one liberty then another, till seeing she was on the job I ran out and left Frank to roll her on the bed, which he must have done to some purpose, for she kept him all the night.'

'Ah, Charlie, I never thought a woman of fifty could be so good at the game; how she threw her legs over my buttocks, and heaved up to meet every push of John Thomas; she was a perfect sea of lubricity, and drained me dry enough by morning,' added Frank, in corroboration of his brother's assertion. 'You must

473

try her for yourself, a fair lad will be a treat to her after us two dark fellows, and there's no fear of having to pay for kids with her, as she is past the time of life, but I believe all really warm-constitutioned women get hotter the older they are. We use French letters for safety with the slaveys, or we should soon do their business, they want so much of it when we get in their room, or they slip into ours for a drop of brandy and a "bit of that", as they call it; there's nothing like good brandy to put you up to the work, but never drink gin, my boy, or your affair won't stand for some hours, it has such a lowering effect.'

A couple of hours of similar conversation soon slipped away, and then going round to Store Street Charlie was introduced to the sirens his cousins had spoken of.

II

'My cousin, Charlie Warner, just from the country to become a medical student. Miss Bessie, Annie, and Rosa Robinson, three as pretty and lovely little milliners as you ever saw or will see again,' said Harry, making the introduction as they entered.

The brothers kissed all three girls, and as it seemed the correct thing Charlie was not slow to follow their example, beginning with Rosa, the youngest, a fair, golden-haired, little beauty of seventeen; then Annie, with her light brown hair and hazel eyes, and finishing with Miss Bessie, a twenty-year-old darling, with dark auburn hair, and such a pair of glancing eyes as would almost ravish the soul of any soft-hearted youth who had not a stronger mind than our young hero, who looked on all girls as playthings rather than as being worthy of serious love.

'What a pretty supper the confectioners have sent in for you — fowls, tongue, and champagne — it made us rather expect something unusual, and we are so pleased to see Mr Warner; besides you know there is no jealousy here, and his fair face is a delightful contrast to you two rather dark gentlemen,' said Annie, adding, 'and you, Frank, are my partner for the evening, as Harry was my cavalier last time; and I'm glad there's Mr Warner for Rosa, although Bessie and I shall feel rather jealous about it, we can wait for our turns another day.'

'This is the jolliest place I know of,' said Harry, handing Bessie to her seat at the table; 'everything ready to hand, and nothing cleared away till we are gone; no flunkeys or parlourmaids to wait on us or listen to every word, and we can do as we like.'

'Not exactly, sir,' put in Annie, 'even when the light is out you must behave yourselves.'

'We have a little longer this evening for our dark séance,' said Frank; 'we are taking Charlie to the theatre, and to Scott's for supper, so they don't expect us till half past twelve or so, and the housekeeper will sit up for her reward, won't she, Harry?'

'What's that,' pouted Rosa, giving a sly look; 'oh, those two boys are dreadful, just as if they would want any more of "that" when they get home.'

'Oh, she never tells tales, so we kiss her,' answered Frank.

'Tell that to your grandmother. As if you could kiss without taking other liberties, sir,' said Annie.

This kind of badinage lasted all supper time, but Charlie pledged the sisters one after the other so as not to show any marked preference, still at the same time in a quiet sort of way he tried all he could to make himself particularly agreeable to Rosa, who evidently was rather taken with him.

'It's so nice to have you to myself,' she said archly, as the supper had come to an end, 'but mind you are not too naughty when they turn out the gas.'

Something in her deep blue eyes and look so fired his feelings that taking her unresisting hand under the table he placed it on his thigh, just over the most sensitive member of the male organisation, and was at once rewarded by the gentle pressures of her fingers, which assured him she quite understood the delicate attention. The others were too absorbed in some similar manipulation to notice Charlie and Rosa, as he adroitly unfastened about three buttons of his trousers, and directing her hand to the place, and presently felt she had quite grasped the naked truth, which fluttered under the delicious fingering in such a way that very few motions of her delicate hand brought on such an ecstatic flood of bliss as quite to astonish Miss Rosa, and necessitate the sly application of a mouchoir to her slimy fingers, as at the same time she crimsoned to the roots of her hair, and looked quite confused, whilst he could feel that a perceptible tremor shot through her whole frame. Fortunately just at that moment Bessie turned off the gas, and instinctively the lips of Charlie and Rosa met in a long impassioned kiss. Tongue to tongue they revelled in a blissful osculation.

He could hear a slight shuffling, and one or two deep-drawn sighs, as if the ladies felt rather agitated.

There was a convenient sofa in a recess just behind Charlie's chair, and Rosa seemed to understand him so well that he effected a strategic movement to the more commodious seat under cover of darkness. There he had the delightful girl close to his side, with his right arm round her waist, whilst his left hand found no resistance in its voyage of discovery under her clothes. What mossy treasures his fingers searched out, whilst for her part one arm was round his neck, and the warm touches of her right hand amply repaid his Cytherian investigations in the regions of bliss. His fiery kisses roved from her lips all over her face and neck, till by a little manoeuvring he managed to take possession of the heaving globes of her bosom. How she shuddered with ecstasy as his lips drew in one of her nipples, and gently sucked the delicious morsel; a very few moments of this exciting dalliance was too much for her. She sank back on the couch, so that he naturally took his proper position, and in almost less time than it takes to write it, the last act of love was an accomplished fact.

Then followed delicious kissings and toyings; no part of her person was neglected, and when, as a finale, she surrendered the moist, dewy lips of the grotto of love itself to his warm tonguings, the excess of voluptuous emotion so overcame her that she almost screamed with delight, when the crisis came again and again in that rapid succession only possible with girls of that age.

They had been too well occupied to hear or notice anything about Bessie and Annie with their partners, but now an almost perfect silence prevailed in the apartment, till presently Harry spoke out, saying, 'I think the spirits have had long enough to amuse themselves; what do you say to a light?'

This was agreed to, and they spent another half hour with the ladies before taking leave of them for the night. It was as curious a feast of love as Charlie could possibly have imagined, and he was quite puzzled to make out what manner of girls these three sisters could be who bashfully objected to a light on their actions, and yet were as free with their partners as any of the mercenary members of the demi-monde could have been.

'What a darling you are!' whispered Rosa to Charlie as he took a parting kiss, 'but I shan't have you next time unless there is an undress romp in the dark.'

Bessie pressed them to come to an early tea on Sunday, and have a long evening, when they would arrange some pretty game to amuse them. This was agreed to with many sweet kisses and *au revoir*, &c.

III

It was nearly one a.m. when the boys got home to the Mortimer mansion in Bloomsbury Square.

'How late you are,' said Mrs Lovejoy, the housekeeper, opening the door to them, 'and you have brought Master Charlie with you. I'm so glad to see him; your father has gone to bed hours ago, and I thought you would like a second course after your oyster supper at Scott's, so there's a little spread in my own room upstairs, only we mustn't keep it up too late.'

'You're a brick,' said Harry, 'we'll go upstairs so quietly past dad's door, and kiss you when we see what you have got for us.'

Mr Mortimer père being a rather stout gentleman, who objected to many stairs, had his bedroom on the first floor; Harry and Frank's room was on the next flight, where their sisters also had their rooms when at home from school; the two servants and Mrs Lovejoy located above them.

'There's my kiss,' said Frank, as on entering Mrs Lovejoy's cosy room he saw a game pie and bottle of Burgundy set out for their refreshment.

Harry and Charlie also in turn embraced the amorous housekeeper, who fairly shivered with emotion as she met the luscious kiss of the latter.

'He's only going to stay this one night, so it's no good taking a fancy to my cousin; besides, can't you be content with Frank and myself?' whispered Harry to her.

'But you are such unfaithful boys, and prefer Mary Anne or Maria to me at any time,' she replied, pettishly.

'Yes, and Charlie is no better; he hasn't been in London one whole day yet without making up to the pretty Fanny at his lodgings; oh, she's a regular little fizzer, Mrs Lovejoy.'

The second supper was soon discussed, and Mrs Lovejoy had placed hot water and spirits on the table just for them to take a night-cap as she called it, when there was a gentle tap at the room door, and a suppressed titter outside.

Harry, guessing who it was, called out 'come in', when the two servant girls with broad grins on their faces walked into the room, only half dressed — in petticoats, stockings, and slippers, with necks and bosoms bare.

On perceiving Charlie they blushed scarlet, but Mary Anne, a regular bouncing brunette, immediately recovered her presence of mind, and said, 'We beg your pardon, Mrs Lovejoy, but we thought only Master Harry and his brother were here, and felt so thirsty we couldn't sleep, so ventured to beg a little something to cool our throats.'

'We'll make a party of it now,' said Frank; 'this is only our cousin Charlie, so don't be bashful but come in and shut the door.'

'Gentlemen don't generally admit ladies, especially when only half dressed, as we are,' said Maria, a very pretty and finely developed young woman, with light brown hair, rosy cheeks, and such a pair of deep blue eyes, full of mischief, as they looked one through.

'No, but ladies admit gentlemen,' put in Charlie, 'don't mind me,' getting up from his chair and drawing the last speaker onto his lap. 'I guess we're in for some fun now.'

The housekeeper looked awfully annoyed at this intrusion, but Harry laughingly kissed her, and whispered something which seemed to have a soothing effect, as she at once offered the two girls some lemonade and brandy. Hers was a very comfortable apartment, being furnished the same as a bachelor's bed and sitting room combined; the bed was in a recess, and there were two easy chairs besides a sofa, table, &c., in the room.

Harry secured the sofa, where he sat with Mrs Lovejoy on his lap, and one of his hands inside the bosom of her dressing gown, whilst her hands, at least one of them, were God knows where, and very evidently gave him considerable pleasure, to judge by the sparkle of his eyes, and the way he caressed her, as well as the frequent kisses they inter-changed.

Charlie was admiring and playing with the bosom of Maria, who kissed him warmly every now and then, giving the most unequivocal signs of her rising desires for closer acquaintance.

'We shall never be fit to get up in the morning if you keep us out of bed; let the girls go now,' said Mrs Lovejoy.

Each said 'good night', and Harry, having something to say to the housekeeper, stayed behind. Frank and Mary Anne quickly vanished in the gloom of the outside corridor, and Charlie, at a loss where he was to sleep, asked Maria to show him to his room.

'You'll sleep with me, dear, if you can, and I won't keep you awake,' she whispered, giving him a most luscious kiss; then taking his hand she led him into a very clean but plainly furnished bedroom.

'Mary Anne won't be back tonight, so you shall be my bedfellow. I guess by this time Master Frank is being let into all her secrets,' saying which she extinguished the candle, which had been left burning, and jumped into bed, Charlie following as quickly as he could get his things off.

'I've got a syringe, so I'm not afraid, although Harry and Frank will always put on those French letters. Do you think they're nice?' asked Maria, as she threw her arms around him, and drew him close to her palpitating bosom.

'Never used such a thing in my life,' replied Charlie, 'for my part anything of that sort spoils all the fun.'

'Do you know,' continued Maria, 'Mary Anne and I lay thinking, talking, and cuddling one another, in fact we were so excited she proposed a game of what girls call flat c——, when we heard Mrs Lovejoy take you to her room, and we made up our minds she should not have both Harry and Frank to herself, never thinking there was anyone else; and to think I've got such a darling as you!'

The girl fairly quivered with emotion as she lay on her side kissing and cuddling close to his body, but his previous encounters during the preceding twenty-four hours rendered him rather less impulsive, in fact he liked to enjoy the situation, which was such as none but those who have lain by the side of a loving expectant young wanton can thoroughly appreciate. Her hands roved everywhere, and she conducted one of his to that most sacred spot of all, which he found glowing like a furnace, and so sensitive to his touch, that she sighed, 'Oh! Oh!' and almost jumped when she felt his tickling fingers, as they revelled in the luxuriant growth of silky hair, which almost barred the approach to the entrance of her bower of love. Charlie never had such a sleepless night in his life for, impatient of his long delay in making a commencement, she threw a leg over his hip as a challenge, and, having his wand in her hand as fit as busy fingers could make it, she directed Mr Warner so straight that he found not the least difficulty in exploring the very inmost recesses of her humid furbelow, which to judge from its overflowing state was a veritable fountain of butterine. How he rode the lively steed, till, exhausted by the rapidity of the pace, he fell off, only to find Maria had reversed positions, and there was no rest for him till seven o'clock in the morning, and at breakfast his looks only too plainly told the tale of the night's orgy, as Mr Mortimer railed at all three fellows of having had a rakish time of it, remarking that he hoped they would be more moderate in future, but it might be excusable for a first night in town.

IV

Our hero was glad to stay in his own rooms and rest the next evening, and felt rather too used up to indulge in much more than a mild joke and a kiss with the pretty Fanny, who had a rather pouting expression on her face as she bid him goodnight after what she considered to be a decidedly languid kind of kiss.

'He isn't so fresh as when he arrived, but perhaps he will be more lively at breakfast time,' she mused, going downstairs to the lower regions of the house. 'I hope Mrs Letsam won't get at him, that's all!'

Charlie was so done up that he went to bed by ten o'clock, and slept so soundly that he awoke quite early, feeling as frisky as a lark, and with the peculiar elevation of spirits which most healthy young fellows are subject to when they first open their eyes in the morning.

'J.T. is quite himself again,' exclaimed Charlie, as he threw off the bedclothes to survey the grand proportions of that part of his anatomy sacred to the service of the fair sex. Then looking at his watch by the aid of the lamp which he had left burning, 'By jove, how early; only half-past four. I'll look outside in the corridor in search of adventure, there is just a chance I might find Fanny's room, as this is the top storey; she can't go higher up, and isn't likely to be lower down.'

Quick as the idea flashed across his mind he stepped out of bed, and taking the little lamp in his hand opened his door very gently and stepped into the corridor, which was a long passage with three or four doors of rooms besides those of his own apartments. He listened at the first one, but hearing nothing passed on to the next, which was slightly ajar; hesitating for a moment he heard the loud stentorian breathing of a heavy sleeper, so shading the lamp with his hand he pushed the door gently open, when what should he see but his fat landlady, Mrs Letsam, lying on her back in bed with her knees up and mouth open. Although so bulky Mrs L was what some would term a truly splendid woman, not more than forty, very pleasing of face, and rich brown hair; whilst her open night dress displayed all the splendours of her mature bosom's magnificent orbs, as white as snow and ornamented by the most seductive strawberry nipples. In reality it was only a chemise, not a proper nightdress, she was sleeping in, so that, as well as the bosom, a large but finely moulded arm was exposed to his searching gaze, and gave him such curious ideas as to the development of other unseen charms, that he resolved to satisfy his curiosity by a manual exploration under the bedclothes. Turning down his lamp he put it outside the door in the corridor, then in the darkness knelt down by the bedside, and slowly insinuating his hand till he touched her thigh, rested till it got warm, then trembling all over with emotion he continued his investigations. His touches seemed marvellously to agitate the sleeper, for after one or two slight involuntary kind of starts, she stiffened her body out quite straight as she turned on her side with something very much like a deep sigh, and Charlie withdrew his impudent fingers, just as he felt the flow of bliss consequent on his exciting touches.

'She'll think it was a dream; most likely the old girl doesn't often feel like that,' laughed Charlie to himself as he sneaked out of the room, little guessing that Mrs Letsam had been thoroughly awakened, and stepped out of bed the moment he was gone, peeping out into the corridor to see who it was.

'Ha, Mr Warner, it's you, is it? It won't take me long to be even with you for this lark!' she said to herself as she got into bed again. 'I wish the dear boy had got into bed though; his touches gave me the most exquisite pleasure.'

Meanwhile Charlie had got to a door at the furthest end of the corridor, which opened at once as he turned the handle, and sure enough it was Fanny's room, for there lay the object of his desires in a broken restless sleep, with nearly all the bedclothes tossed off. What a sight for an impressionable youth! There she lay almost uncovered as it were, her right hand on the spot which so many men who scandalise the fair sex say they always protect instinctively with their hand whilst asleep for fear of being ravished unawares.

However that may be, Fanny's hand was there, and Charlie conjectured that it was not so much for protection as digitation, judging from the girl's agitated restless dreams; for she was softly murmuring,

'Don't! Pray, don't. You tease me so. Oh! Oh!'

He could see everything as he shaded his little lamp so as not to let the light fall on her eyes — her lovely thighs and heaving mount of love, shaded by the softest golden-coloured down, whilst one finger was fairly hidden within the fair lips of the pinkest possible slit below the dewy moisture which glistened in the light.

'By heavens! What a chance!' said Charlie to himself. 'Perhaps I can give her an agreeable surprise.'

Quick as thought he extinguished his lamp, which he placed on a table, then in the dark groped towards the bed where the pretty Fanny lay quite unconscious of his presence.

The sleeper having tossed off most of the bedcovering, it was quite easy for him to lay himself by her side. He kissed the inviting globes of her firm plump bosom but without awakening her. She simply moaned soft, endearing words as if she felt herself caressed by someone she loved so much. His right hand pushed hers aside and took possession of the tender cleft it had been guarding and pressing at the same time; then he gently placed one leg over hers, pressing his naked person close to her body. What thrills of delighted expectation shot through his whole frame! He quivered from head to foot. The temptation and the intensity of his feelings would stand no further delay. So, he glued his lips to hers in a long luscious kiss, whilst one arm held her firmly embraced, and the other was deliciously occupied in manual preliminaries for the attack on her virgin fortress below.

'Fanny,' he whispered, as she unconsciously responded to his kissing. 'It's me, darling, let me love you now?'

At first he thought she was going to scream, but he sealed her lips by the renewal of his fiery kisses, which seemed fairly to stop her breath. She did not speak but appeared awfully discomposed; deep, long drawn sighs came from her as her bosom heaved with excitement, and her hands feebly tried to push away his intrusive fingers. But desire evidently overcame modesty; her return of his willing kisses became more ardent, and her legs gradually gave way to his efforts to get between them, and instead of repulsing his advances her arms were entwined round his body.

'By Jove!' thought Charlie. 'I'm not the first; she's too easy!' but to his delight he did not find the citadel of her chastity had been stormed before; the battering ram of love had to be vigorously applied before a breach was made sufficient to effect a lodgement. What sighs! What murmurs of love and endearment were mixed with her moans of pain.

'My pet, you are a woman now,' he whispered, lovingly, at the conclusion of the first act, kissing her again and again.

'Oh, Charlie, what a darling; you have been so gentle with me. How I love you now; you will always love me, won't you, dearest? But you can't, you can't marry me, I know.' Here she sobbed hysterically as that thought broke upon her mind. Our hero did all he could to comfort her, but found nothing so conducive to that end as drawing up the curtain for a second scene in the drama of love.

'I don't know what upset me so in my sleep but, dear, I went off thinking of you, and suppose I must have wanted you. Your kissing has made me feel so uneasy and all-overish since you came to the house. No one ever upset me like that before,' she confessed to him in her simplicity, as they lay toying and kissing till daylight. She advised Charlie to take leave of his new love, and retreat to his own room for fear of discovery.

Charlie was so enamoured of Fanny that when she brought up his breakfast he urged upon her a repetition of the pleasures of the night.

'How dare you, sir, talk to me like that by daylight?' she answered, repulsing his bold advances. 'What I may do in the dark is no excuse for this. Mrs Letsam is always watching me like a cat, to see I don't stop in the lodgers' rooms a moment too long.'

It was very reluctantly he let her go. After breakfast having nothing particular to do, and feeling rather sleepy, he tried to take a nap on the sofa, when just as he was dozing off there was a light tap at the door, and in answer to his 'Come in,' who should it be but the landlady with his night lamp in her hand.

There was quite a grin upon her full, round, good-looking face, showing a beautiful set of pearly teeth.

'Mr Warner,' she said, seating herself quite familiarly by his side on the sofa. 'I didn't think you were such a young rake as to ravish my maidservant only a couple of days after coming here. Don't say a word; I know all about it, and have seen the stains in the girl's bed, as well as found your lamp in her room; a pretty scrape you'll be in if the girl falls in the family way!'

Her eyes sparkled, and she looked so curiously towards a certain part of his person, that Charlie saw at once he would have to square the fat, fair, and forty lady to prevent unpleasantness.

'My dear Mrs Letsam, how can you accuse me of such things? Now if it had been you—' he said, laughing.

'That's exactly it, Mr Warner, you despised my more mature charms for a chit like Fanny. Pray what were you doing in my room last night? As if I could sleep and not be woken up by the rude hand you pushed under my bedclothes. I ought to call a policeman and give you in charge for an indecent assault.'

Her soft hand had been placed on his thigh, right over Adam's needle, which fairly throbbed under the pressure.

'And this is the thing to run away from a lady? I shall now take as great liberties with you, young sir,' she said, proceeding to take possession of his manly jewel as it now sprang forth in all its grandeur when she opened the front of his dressing gown.

'The love! Now it's mine! What a beauty!' she exclaimed, leaning over him, and imprinting hot, wanton kisses on the head of the rampant prisoner. Charlie fairly sighed and heaved with excitement under such osculation, he had never felt such an ecstatic thrill before, it was almost a new sensation to him; a simple kiss or two by an enraptured girl, who had just experienced the delights such a darling could give, he understood as a token of extraordinary desire, but the

490

tonguing and pressures of the sucking lips of this wanton woman opened up such a new source of delight, that he almost fainted under her caresses.

'There,' she said, 'you darling, that is my style of love, and beats all the vulgar, straightforward ways of enjoyment. You may have Fanny as much as you like, but let me suck a little of your honey now and then or I will get rid of her; I don't care for a many any other way; besides, I'm not so old but I ought to be careful.'

Charlie kissed her pretty mouth, and told her how delighted he was to have got into such a nice house, adding, 'I never felt such pleasure before, so you may be sure the least touch or kiss will put me in a state to meet and rise to your requirements in a moment,' as he stood kissing her when she rose to go. 'No one ever excited me as you have done. Were you ever struck by lightning? I have heard that such people have an electric touch.'

'No, dear,' she replied, smiling, and showing her lovely teeth, which fascinated him so. 'Although I'm stout, I'm only three-and-thirty and have the misfortune to come of a particularly warm family. Goodbye, now.'

V

The reader can easily guess that Charlie felt considerably enervated after the departure of the lecherous Mrs Letsam. He spent the day reading, and also wrote a letter to his father, telling him how kind the Mortimers had been, and how he liked his rooms, which they had taken for him. Retiring early he was awakened from a sound slumber by warm moist impassioned kisses on his lips, and felt a soft lithe form nestling close to his body, as he heard the whispered words — 'Mr Warner, Charlie dear; I've come to return the visit you paid me last night. It was so nice, I couldn't sleep by myself knowing you were all alone.'

It was impossible not to respond to such a loving invitation.

'It's jolly of you, Fanny, coming into my bed like this, as it proves you do care for me a little but; I feel rather tired after our fun of last night, so I mean to make you be the gentleman this time; straddle over me and help yourself to the tit-bit I know all the girls always long for; then I can lay on my back and take it easy.'

'I rather like your saying I made you tired,' she laughed in reply; 'but you didn't know I saw her knock at your door this morning, and listened and heard all your game together. But I am not jealous, especially as I heard her say you might have me as much as you liked, if you only pleased her in a certain way. What was it, dear, I couldn't quite make out what you did with her; do tell me, there's a very nice darling?'

'It's a very curious taste, but nice to me; she doesn't care for a man to have her in the ordinary way, she prefers to suck his affair, and swallow every drop of the love juice when it comes. How would you like that, Fan? It felt awfully nice to me.'

'Ugh! That must be nasty! What do you think? I once had a girl sleep with me who would kiss and lick

492

my crack, and it made me feel so funny, but I wouldn't do it to her.'

After this they got to business in earnest, Fanny, mounting as directed, soon rode Charlie's rampant steed till she had drawn the essence of life three times from his palpitating loins, their mingled juices making quite a little flood round the root of King Priapus. At length falling asleep in each other's arms, they slept till daylight, and Fanny had to go away about her domestic duties.

Having heard from his cousins what larks went on in the parks at night, Charlie made up his mind to see it for himself, and, having no particular engagement on Friday evening, took a stroll as far as the Marble Arch, and turned into the park, taking the path across towards Knightsbridge, arriving at the drive which leads to the Serpentine, he walked along the path observing the couples sitting on the seats kissing and groping each other.

Presently near the gate he met a couple of young, good-looking girls, who as coolly as possible took him by the arm on each side. 'Come along with us, dear, and feel our soft little fannys,' said one.

Charlie made very little objection, and was soon sitting on a rustic seat under the dark shadow of a big elm tree.

'How much are you going to give us, dear? My little sister is too bashful to speak for herself; you know it's always money first in the park, we are so often bilked by mean fellows, who can't afford a proper bit of kyfer.'

Charlie gave each girl a shilling, with the promise of another if they pleased him.

They were really young and pretty girls, such as the park lecher seldom is lucky enough to pick up, the dark paths and seats being mostly haunted by worn-out hags who cannot stand the illuminating ordeal of the gaslight of the streets.

It scarcely required the groping of a soft little hand inside his unbuttoned trousers to raise all his usual fiery ardour. Each girl (they were not more than eighteen and seventeen respectively) put their arms round his neck and kissed him, the eldest whispering – 'You are a darling young fellow, so different from the dirty old men we generally pick up here, I should so like you to have me properly; my little sister doesn't know what it is yet; she is only up to the tossing off business, but I like the real thing you know, when I can get a proper young bit like you. We can only get out Tuesdays and Fridays. Will you meet us on Tuesday, and go into the Green Park; there you will see lots of fun, and can get out at any time; in Hyde Park we get shut in, and have to climb over the gate.'

He could feel her give a shudder of desire as she said this, whilst one of her hands began to play with his appendages, at the same time as her sister was delightfully manipulating the shaft above. They had slits in their dresses, so that both of his hands found employment, exploring and groping on the one side the soft incipient moss of the elder one's grot, as well as the hairless slit of her sister. The situation was

494

altogether too piquante to last many moments. The ecstatic crisis came almost instantly, and he could also feel them both bedew his fingers with their female tribute to the touches of love, which his roving fingers made them feel so exquisitely.

Our hero was so pleased that he gave each one half-a-crown as he kissed and took leave of them, promising to keep the Tuesday's appointment at the same time.

'You are a darling,' said the youngest, Betsy. 'Won't we keep ourselves for him, Sarah; we don't want much money, do we?'

'No, that we will. I hate the nasty old men; we only do it because mother can't keep the home over us unless we bring in five or six shillings a week somehow,' was the rejoinder.

The girls left him, as they said, to go straight home, refusing his offer to treat them to a drink outside the park.

Sunday came, and with it the tea party at the pretty Misses Robinson's in Store Street. His cousins called to take him with them, and the loving greeting of the young milliners was if anything even warmer than before. Bessie, the eldest, the dark auburn beauty, seemed fairly to quiver with emotion as she kissed him rapturously, whispering as she did so – 'You are my partner this evening, Mr Warner.'

'Nothing will please me better, Bessie, dear; for luscious as I found pretty Rosa, your riper charms must be superior to those of your little sister.'

'I hear what you say, Mr Charlie; just wait till I have

a chance to pay you for your broken promises of constancy to me,' laughed Rosa.

It is needless to say much about the conversation, etc, during tea time, except that Charlie induced Bessie to feel his manly instrument under the table as they sat side by side over their orange pekoe.

After a little time spent in music and singing, the usual turning down of the gas took place, and our hero soon found himself and partner seated very cosily on a sofa in one of the alcoves.

'How I have longed to caress you, Mr Warner,' sighed Bessie, 'for Rosa has done nothing but talk of her darling Charlie ever since the last evening you were here, how delightfully you pleased her, and what a splendid affair you were favoured with; she seems to think of nothing but you, as if you really belonged exclusively to her; but indeed, Charlie, it has made me long to feel in person those thrilling love strokes she must have enjoyed so much, what did you do to please her so?'

'I can't remember just now what we did,' Charlie replied, 'but no doubt as your mind is made up for a little love sport we shall play very much the same game.'

His lips met hers in a long luscious kiss, so exciting that his Aaron's rod was as stiff as possible, whilst her bosom rose and fell in palpitating heaves, and her arms pressed him to her bosom.

Presently he slipped down on his knees, and his hands were exploring the mysteries of her underclothing; her thighs opened readily at the slight pressure of his hand, and he was soon in full possession of the centre of attraction, which he found all glowing and humid from the effects of suppressed desire.

'I must kiss this jewel of love,' exclaimed Charlie, in a quick sort of suppressed whisper; 'my tongue will soon make you feel all that Rosa much enjoyed the other evening.'

She inclined her body backwards, and gave up her person entirely to his tonguing caresses, both her hands lovingly pressing the top of his head, as he ravenously sucked the very essence of her life, which she constantly distilled in thick ambrosial drops under the voluptuous evolutions of his busy tongue.

Deep-drawn sighs, too, well told of the intensity of her feelings; she threw her legs over his shoulders, and squeezed his dear face between her quivering thighs, till at length, giving one long-drawn respiration of delight, he heard her say softly – 'Now, now, Charlie, love, let me have him now; you have excited me so I can't wait another moment for the supreme joys of the strokes of rapture I know you are so well qualified to give.'

No charger ever responded to the trumpet call quicker than did our hero, his trenchant weapon was brought to the present in less time than it takes to say so, and the head, slowly entering between the well-lubricated quivering lips of her pouting love grot, was soon revelling in all the sweets she so plentifully spent from her womb. What heaves and sighs of excessive rapture followed this conjunction; each seemed to dissolve in ecstasy over and over again, till exhausted nature at last compelled them to call a halt.

They sat kissing and caressing each other in mutual satisfied delight for some little time, till Frank was heard to call out — 'Don't you think it is time for a romp without clothes?'

Harry and Charlie assenting at once, each youth slipped off his garments, and assisted his partner to do the same, till presently there was an indiscriminate groping and slapping of bottoms, as an incentive to renewed exertions by the young gentlemen, who were a little limp after their first exertions of love. Rosa somehow instinctively found Charlie.

'Now, sir,' she whispered in his ear, 'you have to do penance for saying the more mature charms of my sister must be superior to mine.'

She was holding his throbbing priapus, which she had caught him by, and the touch of her hand seemed at once to renew all its usual *élan*, he was ready for the charge in a moment, and would have pushed her down upon a convenient sofa.

'No, no, not that way; I want to suck the last drop of its fragrant essence, whilst you treat me to the same pleasure. I don't care to enjoy you the same way you have just had my sister.'

Side by side on the sofa, with heads reversed, they sucked each other's parts like two bees, till the last drop of the honey of love had been extracted.

'Now you can go and try Annie, if you can find her in the dark,' said Rosa, 'but I don't think you've much left for her.'

'Let's go together to find her,' whispered our hero, as he took her round the waist, and they searched about till in another recess they found all four of their companions, almost equally exhausted (not the ladies, for they were handling and laughing at the futile endeavours of their champions to respond to their amorous challenge). At length it was time to dress, but some mischievous one had so mixed all the apparel, they were compelled to invoke the aid of the gas before any of them could resume their attire.

This luscious tableaux of nude figures completed the evening's amusements, and the young gentlemen took their leave with promises of a renewed love feast in a day or two.

VI

Tuesday at the appointed time, Charlie went alone to meet the two sirens of Hyde Park, and found Betsy and Sarah true to their appointment.

After sitting down on a quiet sofa for a few minutes, where they enjoyed some kissing and groping, the two girls suggested a remove across into the other park, and the trio were soon seated on a bench by the walk close to the railings which divided the park from Constitution Hill.

'Now,' said Betsy, 'I want a proper one, my dear. Sarah will look out, so no one can surprise us, and if anyone sees us through the railings it doesn't matter.'

This was a matter sooner said than achieved, for Charlie found the amorous Betsy so difficult to enter on account of the narrowness of the passage, that she had to bite her lips in suppressed agony from the pain of his attempt. But courage effects everything, she was so determined to have it that at last he found himself most deliciously fixed in the tightest sheath he had ever before entered. It was simply most voluptuous, the pressures of the girl's sheath on his delighted instrument made him come in a moment or two. Then, the lubricant being applied, things went easier and a most luscious combat ensued. Betsy was perfectly beside herself with erotic passion, whilst the elder Sarah, instead of standing on guard as she ought to have done, handled his shaft and appendages in her soft hand till the excitement was more than he could bear, making him actually scream with pleasure without interruption, and Sarah would have him place the head of Mr Peaslin just between the lips of her pussy, but would not allow more at present. After spending an hour or two in this delicious al fresco amusement, they took him round the park to see the unblushing games that were going on. Soldiers rogering servant girls, old fellows fumbling young girls, and no end of the most unblushing indecency on every side; the fact being that if people, or couples rather got into the Green Park before the gates closed at ten p.m. they might stop there all night, or could at any time go out by the turnstile at the end of Constitution Hill into Grosvenor Place. The one or two bobbies who patrolled the park seemed to take no notice, or were easily squared by the girls who used the place for business.

In fact, Charlie, saw one stalwart guardian of the

peace doing a glorious grind on the grass till a Lifeguardsman came up and, slapping his naked rump as hard as he could, told him he ought to set a better example. This caused great fun to several who were looking on, especially when the soldier challenged the policeman for half-a-crown to exhibit his prick against his for that amount, the girl he was poking to be the judge.

At this moment a regular old swell came upon the scene, and offered half a sov as a prize, in addition to the wager.

'I won't show for less than a quid,' said the policeman, going on leisurely with his grinding, as he had evidently passed the crisis at the moment his arse was slapped by the soldier.

'Lend me your bull's-eye then, and I will give the quid just for a spree; but I'm damned if I don't have a good sight. I'd give five hundred pounds for a genuine cock-stand for once, it's so long since I had one. A fine prick just drawn from a swimming cunt is the most glorious sight in the world.'

The bobby handed up his lantern to the old swell, who at once turned its glare full on the policeman's arse, standing rather behind as he did so, and even stooping a little, to throw it well underneath, and enjoy the luscious sight, as they still went on with their fucking.

'Here, my boy, lend me your cane, and I'll make him feel nice,' said the old swell, tipping the guardsman a bit of gold.

'Right, your honour!' replied the soldier, taking out

a penknife and splitting the end of the cane up so as to divide it into a lot of thin ends.

Quite seven or eight persons were now round the fucking pair, as the gent commenced to lay on the bobby's brawny rump.

We could hear the stinging cuts and see big weals rise at each impact, which made the plucky fellow bound, and almost groan in pain but, in two or three minutes, it might have been less, he grew intensely excited, ramming into his girl (who evidently enjoyed it) with long, lunging strokes, as she clasped him convulsively, returning a heave of her buttocks for every home thrust.

The red weals looked as fiery as possible, for a network of lines had sprung up all over the blushing surface, when they both seemed to again come together in a perfect frenzy of excitement.

'Now, bobby, show up, before you lose that fine stiffness, see, the guardsman has got himself ready!' exclaimed the old swell, suddenly turning the bull's-eye on the soldier, who had been masturbating himself as he enjoyed the sight, but he was nowhere in the show by the side of the tremendous truncheon which the policeman exposed as he withdrew it with a plop, all glistening with luscious moisture from the girl's yet clinging and longing crack.

The bobby had his quid, and the old fellow walked off, as we supposed, to grope the soldier, who went with him.

Betsy and Sarah drew our hero to a quiet seat, where all three spent quite another hour in fucking, groping, and kissing, till at last Charlie was milked as dry as a stick, and reluctantly bade them good night, with promises of another rendezvous in a day or two.

VII

It would be too tedious to relate all the luscious little incidents that occurred to Charlie with Fanny or Mrs Letsam, or even to describe more of his frequent visits with his cousins to the three pretty milliners of Store Street.

Things went quietly for a time, as the three chums were agreed to save their coin for one grand spree, when père Mortimer would be out of town, and never know if they stayed out all night. This was to be a grand winding-up orgy, preparatory to serious study, when their term began, as all three really wished to prepare themselves to get on in after life in some good profession.

When the day arrived Charlie was to meet his cousins, or rather call for them in Bloomsbury Square, at about ten p.m.

'There's some mischief on tonight, I guess,' said Fanny, who had helped him to put on his overcoat. 'Mind where you go to, Charlie, dear; those cousins will take you to see girls, and God only knows what you may catch!' as she threw her arms round his neck, and almost sobbed with vexation. 'Why can't you come back and have the poor little pussy you pretend to be so fond of, instead of sleeping out as you say you are going to do?'

But he released himself as kindly as possible from the loving embrace, for fear his rising prick should lead him to give way to her endearments, and spoil him for the spree on hand.

'You'll get tipsy, and perhaps be locked up,' she said with a pout, as he skipped downstairs.

He found Harry and Frank quite ready to start, and all three walked off in the highest possible animal spirits. They walked along Oxford Street just as the theatres and music halls had dispersed their audiences to swell the usually crowded thoroughfare. A bevy of students were creating a disturbance, and hustling everyone off the pavement, bonneting the policeman, and behaving very roughly, even to delicate girls who might get in their way.

'Oh, do protect me, and see me safe through the crowd!' said a sweet, pretty well but modestly dressed girl of about seventeen, 'those students always frighten me so!'

'There's three of us, and we'll see you safe. Where do you want to go?'

'My brougham is waiting by Swan and Edgar's, in Regent Street; if you will see me so far, I shall be so obliged.'

'And no further?' enquired Charlie.

'Well I didn't like to be so forward; besides, you would not like to leave your friends,' she said, quietly.

'Take us, too,' said Harry; 'have you no lady friends you could ask to join the party? You must know a couple of pretty girls, for we want to make a night of it.'

'Quick, then; or we may lose them. If not engaged I promised to call before twelve at Blanchard's for two young friends and drive them home; you will be delighted if we find them; and I am pleased enough with my partner,' she said, pressing Charlie's arm, and looking archly in his face, with an expression which spoke a whole volume of voluptuousness.

The brougham was quickly found and ordered to pick them up at Blanchard's. As they walked the short distance to the corner of New Burlington Street, Charlie inquired of his charming companion if she was prepared with supper at home, and finding her resources at that late hour not quite adequate to a party of six, they secured a large game pie, bottle of champagne, brandy, &c., at the restaurant, as soon as they had made sure the young ladies were there; then calling for two bottles of fizz, they wetted the acquaintance before starting off in the brougham for Circus Road, St John's Wood.

Three more exquisitely charming girls could not have fallen to their lot than Clara Seymour, and her companions, Alice Morris and Lena Horwright, the latter an especially voluptuous creature, as will be seen in the sequel.

At length it was closing time for the restaurant, and they embarked on the voyage to the north-west, it being as much as they could all do to squeeze into a brougham only intended for four.

Jehu was in a hurry to get home, so that the clock striking one saw them at their destination, but short as the journey had been the girls managed to rack off a spend from their gentlemen, who enjoyed a delicious grope in the dark, as they jolted along.

Miss Seymour lived by herself in a neat little cottage residence, which had a coach-house and stable attached, Lord Cursitor, her chief patron, allowing her £150 a year to keep a man, horse, and carriage. A rather demure-looking middle-aged servant ushered the party into the house, and showed them into a good-sized elegantly furnished front parlour, which opened by folding doors into Clara's own bedroom, to which the ladies at once retired, leaving the three young gentlemen to themselves for a minute or two.

They were evidently high-spirited girls, to guess from the laughing and joking which seemed going on between them in the bedroom, and presently a succession of gurgling rills could be distinctly heard when they used the *pot-de-chambre* to relieve their bladders.

Charlie rapped at the folding doors, saying, 'I wish you ladies would lend us your spare chamber, we're simply bursting for relief.'

'Are you, my dears?' said Lena, opening the door, pot in hand. 'It's something thicker than water you want to get rid of, I expect.'

Charlie produced such an erection that he rushed to place his prick in Clara's hand, asking her to ease him at once. Nothing loth she drew him to the side of her bed, and raising her clothes exposed the lovely cleft to his amorous gaze.

'My fanny always expects a little kiss first,' she whispered to him, as her face slightly flushed, which added very considerably to her beauty.

Charlie was on his knees in a moment, paying his devotions to that divinely delicate-looking, pink slit, just shaded as it was by reddish golden hair, as soft as the finest silk. His tongue divided its juicy lips, searching out her pretty clitoris, which at once stiffened under the lascivious osculation. It was more like a rabbit's prick than anything, and his fingers could just uncover its rosy head as he gently frigged it, sucking at the same time.

A perfect shudder of emotion thrilled through her body.

'Oh, oh! Fuck me, quick; your kisses have set me on fire!'

Suiting the action to the words, she threw herself backwards across the bed, and Charlie rose to the charge in a moment, throwing himself over her, gluing his lips to hers, as his distended weapon forced its way between the moist but yielding lips of her tight little quim.

A quiver of delight thrilled through her frame as he gained complete insertion, her lovely legs encased in delicate knickerbocker drawers, fringed with lace, and set off by rose-coloured silk stockings and high-heeled Parisian boots were thrown amorously over his fine manly buttocks, whilst his hands were clasped round her lovely rump as it rose in agitated heaves in response to his vigorous thrusts.

Harry took Alice, as Frank was Lena's cavalier, and the three couples came to a crisis in a chorus of amorous ejaculations, as the floodgates of love gave down copious streams of mingled spunk.

Presently, when the first bout was over, they sat down to supper, the gentlemen in their shirt sleeves, and the three young ladies, who had dispensed with their dresses, were in the most charming dishabille.

As soon as the game pie was demolished, each took a girl on his lap, alternately pledging each other, glass in hand, or groping and playing all sorts of larks with each other's pricks and cunts.

Charles was anxious to elicit from each fair one the story of her first seduction, but was met with the usual reticence in such cases, till presently Lena, standing up, said she could recite them some poetry, which exactly tallied with her first experience of the forbidden fruit.

'Bravo, Lena! Go on,' they all exclaimed.

'Yes, but only on one condition, and that these three gentlemen shall have me all together, while you girls give their bums a touch of the twigs. Do you agree?'

'Yes, yes. Bravo, Lena! Go on.'

'Well then, here goes, The Maiden's Dream. But I must recline upon the sofa, with nothing on but my chemise.'

Then, suiting the action to the word, threw off her dressing gown, laid down in a luxurious position, with her eyes closed, feigning a tumultuously excited dream, one leg bent up, the other hanging over the sofa, her chemise turned up, exposing all the thighs and quim, one hand frigging gently, she lay squirming in ecstasy, as she recited:

One night, extended on my downy bed,
Melting in am'rous dreams, although a maid,

My active thoughts presented to my view,
A youth, undrest, whose charming face I knew.
His wishful eyes express'd his eager love,
And twinkl'd like the brightest stars above.
'Bless me,' said I, 'Philander, what d'ye mean?
'How come you hither? – Pray, who let you in?
'Undrest! – 'Tis rudeness to approach my bed:
'Consider, dearest youth, that I'm a maid.'
With that between the sheets one leg he thrust,
Mix'd it with mine, and sighing said, 'I must!'
Then clasp'd me in his arms: I strove to squeak,
But found I had no power to stir or speak;
My blood confus'dly in its channels ran,
My body was all pulse, my breath near gone;
My cheeks inflam'd, distorted were mine eyes,
My breast swell'd out with passion and surprise.
And still in vain I strove to make a noise,
Something, methought, I felt that stopp'd my voice,
And did at last such tides of joy impart,
That glided through each vein, and fill'd my heart,
Recall'd my dying senses back again,
And with a flood of pleasure drown'd my pain.
Thus, for a time, I lay dissolved in bliss,
As if translated into Paradise;

Alas! one prick's a farce, 'tis not enough for me.
Come on, my boys, I'm game to take all three!

All now stripped to the buff, except the slippers and
the silk stockings, which added to the natural beauty
of the ladies' legs and feet.

'Ah! I had a delicious spend!' exclaimed Lena, springing on the bed, 'but not to be compared with what I expect now, for I shall ride a St George on Charlie, take Harry in my bottom, and Frank in my mouth.'

She was raging with voluptuous desire, and straddling over our hero, as he lay on his back, impaled herself on his pego, which previous efforts to please the ladies had now brought to a chronic state of enormously stiff erection, it seemed to fill her luscious quim to its utmost capacity, to judge from the stretched appearance of the vermilion lips, as they amorously clung around the staff of life, they so delighted to suck in and out.

Harry was at, or rather in his post of duty as quickly as it can be written; then Frank, kneeling over Charlie's face, presented his prick as a bonne bouche for Lena to gamahuche, her bottom and head now moved in slow and graceful undulations, as she commenced this three-fold bout of enjoyment.

Alice and Clara, each provided with light birches, of about three long sprigs, gently touched up the exposed bottoms, till they fairly reddened under the smarting cuts, and quickened the love canter into an impetuous gallop, so that, when the emitting crisis came, the three young fellows fairly howled and shouted with excess of delighted emotion, whilst Lena, going into a fit of hysteria, laughed, cried, and stiffened herself over Charlie, almost throwing Harry out of her bottom, whilst her teeth closed so convulsively on Frank's prick that his delight was considerably mixed with pain.

510

When they had a little recovered themselves, 'After all,' said Clara, 'if you have ever read the "Education of Laura," there is a scene there that beats you, Lena, for Rose finishes off five young fellows at once, by frigging one in each hand, as well as three, like you just had our friends.'

'I could very soon do that,' retorted Lena, 'But I don't want to be selfish. Now, which of you girls will volunteer to let me birch you, to excite their three cocks to another grand fuck.'

Alice was agreeable, if someone would horse her on his back and hold her firmly by the wrists. 'I'm such a coward, the first cut will make me wince, yet I know how nice and delightful the finish is,' she exclaimed.

Frank engaged to be the horse, as he felt rather spiteful and wished someone to feel real pain, saying he should much prefer to hold Lena on his back, and know her bottom was being well skinned for biting his poor John Thomas.

'I am very much obliged to you for your kind wishes, but Alice's tender rump will give you just as much satisfaction, poor boy, when I once begin to apply some of Mrs Martinet's scientific touches to it.'

'This is a serious business,' she continued, 'so I shall just take a double-sized switch of twigs, from the cupboard. Those thin ticklers are only useful just to touch up a man in the act of fucking. Alice's whipping must be much more severe in order to stimulate the now languid tools of our friends, and rouse them again to a state of lustful fury by the sight of the red flesh and dripping drops of the ruby, as it is distilled from the abraded skin.'

'Oh, pray don't be so bad as that, Lena,' said Alice, apprehensively, as she slightly resisted Harry and Charlie trying to mount her on Frank's back.

'No, Miss Pert, no nonsense, no drawing back, or I really will make it worse for your bum!' exclaimed Lena, standing up and looking fiercely at her helpless victim, now firmly held over Frank's manly back, whilst Harry and Charlie knelt down on either side to hold her legs, whilst the pretty Clara promised to play with each of the gentlemen's cocks in turn, so as gradually to work them up to a state of glorious stiffness.

'Oh, it stings so! Ah, not quite so hard, Lena, dear,' sighed Alice, as the first two or three light touches made her buttocks tingle under the smart.

'Is that better, you rude girl? Didn't I catch you frigging yourself in bed this morning?' asked Lena, with a spiteful smile on her face.

'Ah, ah, oh, no! My God, how you cut me! I shall die. I never frigged myself. I should be ashamed to do such a thing,' she sobbed, the tears trickling down her blushing face.

'Just listen to the hardened thing. It's as bad as saying I'm a liar!' retorted Lena, with two vicious cuts, which made poor Alice scream in agony, and drew the blood up under the skin of her rump.

'Ah, you bad girl, I'll whip the frigging fancy out of you. Wouldn't it be nice to be frigged just now your fanny is rubbing against Frank's back?'

'Oh! Oh!! Oh!!! I didn't!' screamed Alice.

The cuts fell in rapid succession on the devoted bum. The victim still struggled and writhed under Lena's scathing cuts, but her head fell forward on Frank's shoulder, her face suffused with crimson flushes, and eyes closed in a kind of voluptuous languor.

Charlie had acted on the frigging suggestion, and, by his light touches on her excited clitoris, had made her almost faint under the combination of excitements, as she spent so profusely that her thick, creamy emission trickled over his busy fingers and down Frank's back.

'Lay her on the bed and fuck her,' exclaimed Lena, flinging down the rod. 'Who'll have me on the horse-hair sofa? Will you, Harry?'

'I'm randy enough for anything, my love!' exclaimed Harry, flashing his pego. 'Charles and Clara are not thinking of us; see, he is into her on the hearthrug; look, how she heaves her arse! It's just how Adam and Eve must have shagged on the grass in Eden.'

'Oh, it does prick the flesh so,' exclaimed Lena, as she plumped her bottom on the horse-hair, 'but it's the finest thing to stimulate a woman you can think of, the little prickly ends of the stiff hair are like pins, and make your arse bound under every single stroke, it's simply delicious; no one but those who try it can appreciate the delights of a horse-hair sofa fuck.'

How she bounded and writhed as Harry fairly and furiously pounded his prick into her swimming cunt, which seemed to be perfectly insatiable; she was spending again and again every two or three minutes, till at last, with a perfect howl of delight, she drew down his pent-up emission, which shot up into her vitals like a stream of liquid fire.

Kissing and billing they lay entranced in each other's arms for a few minutes, till someone remarked that it would be soon time for breakfast, if they didn't have a little rest.

Thus ended an ever-to-be-remembered night of Charlie Warner's student life, and after breakfast a few hours later they left the three ladies with many expressions of gratification, and promises to renew the pleasures of the past night at an early opportunity.

VIII

Four o'clock, a.m., of a glorious sunny morning, as Charlie Warner opened his eyes to find himself lying in Fanny's arms, almost naked on his bed, the covering having evidently slipped off onto the floor during the amorous play of the preceding night; they were fast embraced, or rather locked together, his prick as stiff as possible, throbbing against the soft ivory skin of his companion's person, the curly hair of their organs of love mingling together in the close conjunction of their bodies.

Fanny's lips were slightly open, displaying a lovely set of small pearly teeth whilst her arms ever and anon clasped his form with a light nervous tremor, as if she was still dreaming of the delights of the past night.

'She fucked me as dry as a stick, last night,'

soliloquised Charlie, 'yet I feel brimming over with spunk again, and ready to spend over her naval.'

'Wake up, Fanny, my love!' he softly whispered, putting two of his fingers into her still damp slit, and rubbing gently on her excited clitoris. 'Wake up, sleeping beauty, I must have one quick. See how stiff he is. Look at your darling. Don't you know that is the Queen's birthday, 24th May, 18 − and, in honour of her Majesty, I mean to fuck as many girls as I can today, at least between now and tomorrow morning, and I mean to begin with you.'

'You randy fellow, do you think I will oblige you after such a speech as that?' laughed Fanny, as she woke with a start. 'I can't help myself this minute, because I've been dreaming of you all night. You seemed always in me, spending and spending till I seemed actually dissolving in love, and then you wake me up with a reference to having other girls during the day. Still I can't refuse this delicious morsel just now, but it will be different when you come home tonight, after your day's whoring. I shall look at you with disgust then.

'Oh, put it into me quick!' she ejaculated with a sigh, opening her legs, to receive the object of her desire.

It was a short hot affair, as most first fucks in the morning are, when the blood is heated from wine, champagne, &c., imbibed over night.

He stroked her twice, to Fanny's infinite satisfaction, before he withdrew from the tight folds of her deliciously warm cunt.

Then they slept till nearly six o'clock, when Fanny had to get up for her daily work.

Our friend Charlie indulged in another two hours' snooze, till he was awakened by the sensation of feeling his prick sucked by a delightfully warm mouth, and found Mrs Letsam, his landlady, indulging in one of her erotic suckings, which usually gave him so much pleasure and, on this occasion, the thought that she was cleaning his pego of all the dried-up spendings that Fanny had left on it so excited his fancy that he came in a perfect frenzy of emission, till the spunk fairly frothed in her mouth and oozed from its corners as she ravenously tried to swallow every drop.

After breakfast, Charlie again racked off Fanny's juice on the sofa, and then started to call upon Clara, in her little house at St John's Wood.

Only Lena was at home with Clara, but they were overjoyed to see him so brimful of spirits, and his prick, as soon as he got into their company, was as rampant as ever.

The two girls were having a light breakfast as they sat in their dressing gowns, fresh from the matutinal cold bath, their cheeks rosy with youthful health, stimulated by the cold douche which, with the hard rubbing they had given each other, had roused all the warmth of their blood, till they were in that state of voluptuous readiness, so fit for the reception of a fine young fellow like Charlie.

Each pretty girl tipped him the velvet end of her tongue, as he kissed their cherry lips, Lena saying: 'How nice of you to call so early, Mr Warner; it is just in time to give each of us "one of them", before we go out for a drive round Regent's Park. Don't you know a fuck is truly delicious to a girl in the morning, just after she has had her cold bath, when she is all aglow, and the blood tingles through her veins from head to foot?'

'A cup of coffee, and then — ' said Clara, pouring out one for their visitor.

'Without milk or sugar, if you please,' replied Charlie. 'I shall get all that as I gamahuche you both, and suck up your spendings.'

Impatient for another go in, he soon led them into the bedroom, where there was a delicious and soft cool air from the open window of a small conservatory, which communicated with Clara's *chambre à coucher*.

They were soon as naked as Cupids, and Charlie, making them lean back on the bed, sucked each cunt in turn, till they writhed and spent on his active tongue, as its ravishing touches then rolled round their lascivious clitorises.

'This is Clara's house, so she is entitled to have the first put-in,' said Lena, 'and you shall suck as much honey as you can from my little buttercup fanny, whilst you fuck her.'

'We'll show you a new position, Charlie dear,' added Clara, as she extended herself on the bed. 'Get between my legs and as soon as you are in — yes, that's it; now throw your left leg up over my loins, and put your right under my right leg, and then lay your body away from me, fork fashion, and gamahuche Lena, as she sits up and presents her fanny to your lips; isn't it awfully nice? Your cock goes into the exact corner of my quim, and touches the very entrance to my womb! Ah, ah! Oh, oh! You do make me spend. I can't help it. Go on quicker, dear boy! Ah, Lena, it drives me mad. He seems to make me melt all over.'

Charlie, on his part, was in ecstasies, and his delighted prick was so sensitive to the clinging grip of Clara's lascivious fanny, that he was compelled to cry out he could not bear it any longer, as his hot spunk spurted into her cunt.

Lena was so randy that she took possession of Charlie's prick the instant he withdrew, and, doubling her knees up towards her face, threw her legs over his shoulder, as he rammed it into her longing gap, whilst Clara lovingly kissed, sucked, and tongued his balls, bottom, and buttocks from behind, her busy fingers doing their best by handling his impetuous shaft, as it worked in and out of that foaming cunt, which was literally overflowing with their thick creamy emissions.

He kept himself back for a final spend, and so drew out the length of that glorious fuck that Lena fixed her teeth in his shoulders, till her lips were crimsoned in his blood.

Clara, the while, frigged herself with one hand, and at the finish, they rolled over together in a perfect fury of amorous frenzy.

After this, Charlie dressed himself, placed two sovereigns on the dressing table, although the dear girls protested they would not take his money as he had pleased them so, then, taking leave of them as they still lay on the bed, rang the bell for the servant to show him out.

Emma, the servant, was a pretty little brunette, about eighteen and, as the saying is, 'fresh cunt, fresh courage', Charlie put half-a-crown in her hand, and he kissed her behind the door, and whispered, 'My dear, I should just like to fuck you. You shall have a half-a-sov if you run down and let me in at the area door, as I pretend to go out down the front steps.'

Without speaking she returned the kiss and shut the door sharply behind him, so, running down to the area, he was presently in the arms of another sweet randy girl.

His prick stood in a moment as he lifted her on to the kitchen table and put his hands up her clothes, their lips meeting in luscious kisses and tongueings.

Emma was quite as hot as her mistress, and fuck'd with all the abandon of a true little whore, till he gave her cunt a warm douche of the elixir of life.

Her eyes were shut, and her head rested on his shoulder, as she whispered, 'Oh, give me another before you go; it was such a beautiful fuck. I don't often get a treat like that. Oh, do, do! There's a dear!'

Luckily for him, just then the upstairs bell rang, and he was able to effect a hasty retreat up the area steps.

Taking a cab, he called on his cousins to arrange for the evening, after which he returned to his own rooms, and rested the remainder of the day.

About ten p.m. found our three chums, arm in arm, elbowing their way down Regent Street, where the crowd became denser every moment, and at places was quite impassable, where the illuminations were more splendid than ordinary.

The groping for cocks and cunts seemed the proper thing to do, everyone in the crowd seemed to understand that, and the three friends had immense fun with a modest old lady and her daughter who, although awfully indignant, were perfectly helpless, and were so teased and handled that they sighed and spent with desire, in spite of the shame that they felt.

Next a large closed furniture removal van which they were jammed against attracted their attention. It had portholes, like a ship, along the sides, and was lighted up inside.

Charlie mounted on one of the wheels, till he could peep inside, and found two old swells and several girls, nearly as naked as they could be, sporting their quims to amuse the old fellows, who had each got one of the nymphs of the pavement to frig him.

'Hullo!' shouted Charlie, forcing in the round glass, which acted as a pivot. 'Don't you want some real fucking in there? We've got three good stiff pricks out here, if you'll let us in.'

'Eh! Egad! It wouldn't be amiss,' said one of the old gents. 'Let's have them in for a lark.'

It was a matter of the greatest difficulty to effect an entrance by getting round to the rear of the van, and squeezing through the partially opened door.

'You look proper sharks,' said one of their entertainers, opening a bottle of fizz. 'Just a wet, by way of introduction, then the girls will soon take the stand out of you. Have you had some good gropes among the crowd?'

'Just what we wanted! They're three beauties,' exclaimed the girls, as they brought out the stiff pricks of Charlie, Harry, and Frank.

There were six girls in all, and the three chums had all their work to do to give a fuck to each girl in turn. This, however, they did, much to the delight of the two jolly old cockolorums, who handled their fine firm pegos with unbounded delight, postillioning their bottoms, and licking their fingers with the greatest of gusto, after they had thrust them into the reeking quims of the girls, to see how the fucking was going on.

One of their hosts in particular was ravenous to gamahuche and lick up all the spending from the swimming cunts after each go in.

Little notice was taken of the illuminations as the lumbering van slowly forged it way through the surging crowd, which little suspected the lascivious orgy being enacted inside the sober-looking van.

For three hours the game was kept up with spirit, till the three friends were so tired out and overcome by champagne they had taken that, when at length the van was driven into the grounds of a private house and stopped before the hall door, they were too stupid even to put on their clothes, and along with the girls were carried into the house by two or three flunkeys, who deposited the dissipated crew on some ottomans and sofas in a large and brilliantly lighted saloon.

Charlie was not quite so drunk but he had a dim

recollection of curious liberties which the old gents took with his naked person, and for a day or two afterwards Frank and Harry as well as himself confessed to feeling rather stretched and sore, as if their rear virginity had been ravished when they were helpless to prevent what they afterwards felt quite disgusted at.

But it is anticipating the course of events. At about five in the morning our hero quite recovered himself and, waking from the short deep drunken sleep, found the sun streaming in through a window so, drawing aside the light lace curtains he found it looked onto a beautiful croquet ground surrounded by parterres of splendid flowers and screened on every side by dense foliage of shrubs and trees.

Turning to the apartment, the two old gentlemen were fast asleep in armchairs, each with his trousers down and a naked girl resting her head on his thigh, side by side with the languid prick which she had been in the act of gamahuching when they were all overcome by sleep.

Frank and Harry were lying mixed up with the other four girls on a very large and splendid catskin rug, all naked, forming a charming tableau, as the golden rays of the sun glanced on the warm flesh tints.

Just then a lovely young lady wrapped in a dressing gown peeped into the room and Charlie, all naked as he was, bounded across from the window to meet her, but she, putting her finger to her lips, signalled him to follow her as she withdrew from the room. He crossed the vestibule close behind her into a magnificent boudoir, the door was locked, and she threw herself into his arms, exclaiming 'At least I am sure you are not one of the filthy unnatural fellows my uncles usually bring here, I have not the least doubt you three have been tricked, made tipsy and outraged by them! Oh pity me, for I am a prisoner in this house – they have cheated me out of my father's immense fortune – and made me their lady housekeeper. Just because I can't help myself and have the hope of some day succeeding to what they have cheated me out of, I have to shut my eyes and pretend not to see their horrible goings on, and even sometimes myself submit to their unnatural whims in my own person, without ever getting from them the satisfaction which a warm female nature requires. My case is like that of the lady you read of in the Arabian Nights who, although the jealous Genie kept her locked in a glass box, yet managed now and then to get a fresh lover, but very few suitable youths come to this house, they are mostly those debased men-women who prostitute themselves for money. Only four times in three years have I had the delight to welcome to my boudoir such a one as I could surrender myself to. Do you know why you awoke first? It is because, when I looked over the lustful group asleep after their beastly orgy, you charmed my eye. So, scattering some drops of a very somniferous essence over all the others, I applied reviving salts, &c., to your nostrils, and here you are my prize. We're safe for several hours!' she concluded, opening her dressing gown and throwing her lovely naked form upon his equally nude figure.

Receiving her in his arms, his prick as rampant as ever (how could it be otherwise when thus challenged by such a lovely creature), taking her in his embrace, he carried her a few steps till she fell back upon a soft, wide couch.

Her delicate hand had already taken possession of his throbbing staff and now at once applied its head to her burning notch, which was literally brimming over from a luscious anticipatory emission.

Drawing him upon her, her legs enlaced over his buttocks, she heaved up her bottom in enraptured delight as the shaft slowly entered the well-lubricated sheath.

Then they paused for a moment or two, billing and kissing, tongue to tongue, as both evidently thoroughly enjoyed the sense of possession that they imparted to each other by mutual throbs and contractions, till, giving a long-drawn deep sigh of desire, she challenged him by her motions to ride on and complete her happiness.

Charlie literally trembled from excess of emotion, and the rapidity with which this bewildering and luscious adventure had fallen upon him. Her first few moves made him spend before he wished to, and in spite of his unsatisfied desires, his pego at once lost its stiffness, to the great chagrin of the lovers.

'Ah, I understand,' she exclaimed; 'it is over-excitement, after the enervating debauch of last night. Wait a moment, my dear, and we will soon be happy enough!'

Saying which, she ran to a cabinet for some Eau de

Cologne, sprinkling a few drops over his excited face then, pouring the rest of the bottle in to a small china bowl with water, she sponged his limp prick with it. Then she dried it on a soft handkerchief and kissed, sucked, and caressed the manly jewel with such marvellous endearment that she soon had him standing again in all his glory of ruby head and ivory shaft. The sight seemed quite to ravish her senses, for she threw herself on the sofa and begged he would at once let her have the only thing that could possibly assuage her raging lasciviousness.

'Ah, I'm afraid you'll think me awfully lewd!' she sighed, blushing more crimson than ever.

This charming appeal was irresistible. He now charged her foaming fanny with such effect that she raved in ecstasies of delight, biting and kissing him by turns in her voluptuous frenzy, twisting and squirming her body, and then stiffening out straight in the dying ecstasies of spending. All the while his prick revelled in the warmth and extraordinary lubricity of the tight grasping sheath which held it so passionately that it stiffened more and more from excessive lust, so that when he came it was quite a painful acme of delight. The tip of his pego was so tender that he positively could not bear the loving, sucking contractions of her womb, as it drank up every drop.

After a while they renewed these delights, and kept it up till prudence dictated his return to the salon, where the sleepers were still unawakened; so Charlie, dressing himself, aroused Frank and Harry and assisted them to dress. Then, slipping away for a moment to his unknown inamorata, took a loving leave and by her advice they left the house.

It was almost five o'clock in the afternoon when our hero took leave of his cousins in Gower Street, sending them home to sleep off the effects of the long debauch. He also resolved to let this be the very last orgy for a long while to come, and content himself with the love of his little slavey and the occasional erotic osculations of Mrs Letsam, soliloquising to himself as, after a cup of tea, he lay on his own sofa; I mean to study and rise in my profession, so this of my sprees shall be . . . the end.

The Yellow Room

It was a beautiful summer's night. The air was heavily laden with the sweet perfume of the flowers in the garden below the windows, which were thrown wide open. There were besides several china vases, or rather bowls, standing about the room, full of roses, of shades varying from the deepest crimson to the softest blush scarcely more than suggested upon the delicate petal. The only sounds were the gentle rustle of the summer zephyr amongst the trees and the weird hoot of the owls. The deeply shaded lamps gave animation to the rosy tints of the boudoir. They were emphasised by the yellow flame of the fire which, notwithstanding the season, crackled merrily in the grate. (A fire upon a summer's night is an agreeable thing.) Between it and Alice there at once appeared to be something in common. She and the fire were the only two black and gold things in the rosy apartment. The fierce flame struck Alice as being a very adequate expression of the love she felt seething in her veins. She felt intoxicated with passion and desire, and capable of the most immoral deeds, the more shocking the better.

This naughty lust was soon to have at least some

gratification. Maud had seated herself at the piano — an exquisite instrument in a Louis Seize case — and had played softly some snatches of Schubert's airs, and Alice had been reclining some minutes on a rose-coloured couch — a beautiful spot of black and yellow, kept in countenance by the fire — showing two long yellow legs, when Sir Edward noticed that every time she altered her position she endeavoured, with a slightly tinged cheek, to pull her frock down. Of course he had been gazing at the shapely limbs and trying to avail himself of every motion, which could not fail to disclose more — the frock being very short — to see above her knee. He thought once that he had succeeded in catching a glimpse of the pink flesh above the yellow stocking.

Alice, sensible of her uncle's steadfast observation, was more and more overwhelmed with the most bewitching confusion; her coy and timid glances, her fruitless efforts to hide herself, only serving to make her the more attractive.

Maud looked on with amusement from the music stool, where she sat pouring liquid melody from her pretty fingers, and mutely wondering whatever had come over Alice, and whatever had become of the healthy delight in displaying her charms of which she had boasted before dinner. Maud felt very curious to know how it would end.

'Alice,' at length said her uncle, with a movement of impatience, 'have you begun to write out that sentence I told you to write out fifty times?'

'Oh no, uncle! I have not.'

have anything to say to her — she would have to fly to the mountains and the caves. She had not realized until it came to actually writing it out how difficult, how terrible, how impossible it was for her to do it. If her uncle knew, surely he would not insist. He could not wish her to humiliate herself to such an extent; to ruin and destroy herself with her own handwriting; neither could he have realized what it would be for her to write such a thing. While these thoughts were passing through her mind, she kept unconsciously pulling and dragging at her frock. If only she could cover herself up. So much of her legs showed; and the long yellow stockings made them so conspicuous under her black frock. Although they were above her knee, unless she kept her legs close together she could not help showing her black garters. And her arms and her neck and her breast were all bare. She began to feel almost sulky.

'Well, Alice,' at length said her uncle, 'when are you going to begin?'

'Oh, uncle! it is dreadful to have to say such a thing in my own handwriting — I am sure you have never thought how dreadful.'

'You must chronicle in your own handwriting what you did, miss. Writing what you did is not so bad as doing it. And you will not only write it, but you shall sign it with your name, so that everyone may know what a naughty girl you were.'

'Oh, uncle! Oh, uncle! I can't. You will burn it when it is done; won't you?'

have anything to say to her — she would have to fly to the mountains and the caves. She had not realized until it came to actually writing it out how difficult, how terrible, how impossible it was for her to do it. If her uncle knew, surely he would not insist. He could not wish her to humiliate herself to such an extent; to ruin and destroy herself with her own handwriting; neither could he have realized what it would be for her to write such a thing. While these thoughts were passing through her mind, she kept unconsciously pulling and dragging at her frock. If only she could cover herself up. So much of her legs showed; and the long yellow stockings made them so conspicuous under her black frock. Although they were above her knee, unless she kept her legs close together she could not help showing her black garters. And her arms and her neck and her breast were all bare. She began to feel almost sulky.

'Well, Alice,' at length said her uncle, 'when are you going to begin?'

'Oh, uncle! it is dreadful to have to say such a thing in my own handwriting — I am sure you have never thought how dreadful.'

'You must chronicle in your own handwriting what you did, miss. Writing what you did is not so bad as doing it. And you will not only write it, but you shall sign it with your name, so that everyone may know what a naughty girl you were.'

'Oh, uncle! Oh, uncle! I can't. You will burn it when it is done; won't you?'

'No; certainly not. It shall be kept as a proof of how naughty you can be.'

And as she kept tugging at her frock and not writing, her uncle said:—

'Maud, will you fetch the dress-suspender? It will keep her dress out of her way.'

Maud discharged her errand with alacrity. In less than three minutes she had returned with a band of black silk, from which hung four long, black silk ribbons. Making Alice stand up, Maud slipped her arms under her petticoats and put the band round Alice's waist next her skin, buckling it behind, and edged it up as high as the corset, which Janet had not left loose, would allow. The four ribbons hung down far below the frock, two at the right and two at the left hip − one ribbon in front, the other at the back.

Maud then walked Alice over into the full blaze of the fire. Putting her arms round her and bending down, she took the ribbons at Alice's left side one in each hand, and then pulled them up and joined them on Alice's petticoats and dress up about her waist, disclosing her left leg from the end of the stocking naked. Maud, with little ceremony, then turned her round, and, taking the ribbons at her right side, tied them across her left shoulder, thus removing the other half of Alice's covering and displaying the right leg. She then carefully arranged the frock and petticoats, smoothing them out, tightening the ribbons, and settling the bows. And by the time she had finished, from the black band round her waist nearly to her garters, Alice was in front and behind perfectly naked

– her breast and arms and thighs and navel and buttocks. The lower petticoat was, it will be remembered, lined with yellow, and the inside was turned out. It and the stockings and the two black bands intensified her nakedness. She would sooner have been, she felt, stripped entirely of every shred of clothing than have had on those garments huddled about her waist, and those stockings, which, she instinctively knew, only heightened the exhibition of her form and directed the gaze to all she most wished to conceal.

'Now, miss,' said her uncle, 'this will save you the trouble of vain and silly efforts to conceal yourself.'

'Oh, uncle! Uncle! How can you disgrace me so?'

'Disgrace you, my dear? What nonsense! You are not deformed. You are perfectly exquisite. With,' he continued, passing his hand over her, 'a skin like satin'.

Feeling his hand, Alice experienced a delicious thrill, which her uncle noticing, recommended her to sit down and write out her imposition – a task which was now a hundred times more difficult. However could she, seated in a garb which only displayed her nakedness in the most glaring manner, write such words?

'Alice,' said he, 'you are again becoming refractory.'

Putting his arm round her, he sat down and put her face downwards across his left knee. 'You must have your bottom smacked. That will bring you to your senses.' (Smack – smack – smack – smack – snack – smack.)

'Oh, uncle! Don't! Oh!' – struggling – 'I will write anything!' – smack – 'Oh! How you sting!' – smack – smack – 'Oh! Oh! Oh! Your hand is so hard.'

Then, slipping his hand between her legs, he tickled her clitoris until she cooed and declared she would take a delight in saying and writing and doing the 'most shocking things'.

'Very well, miss! Then go and write out what I told you; sign it; and bring it to me when it is finished.'

So Alice seated herself – the straw seat of the chair pricking her bottom – resolved, however, to brazen out her nakedness, and wrote with a trembling hand. Before she had half completed her task, she was so excited and to such an extent under the influence of sensual and voluptuous feelings that she could not remain still; and she felt the delicate hair in front about her cunt grow moist. Before she had completed the fiftieth line she was almost beside herself.

At last, for the fiftieth time, she wrote the dreaded words and, with a shudder, signed it, 'Alice Darvell.'

During her task Maud had looked at what she was writing over her shoulder, and Alice glowed with shame. So had her uncle; but Alice was surprised to find she rather liked his seeing her disgrace, and felt inclined to nestle close up to him.

Now Maud had gone to bed, and she was to take her task to her uncle.

He was seated in a great chair near the fire, looking very wide awake indeed. He might have been expected to have been dozing. But there was too lovely a girl in the room for that. He looked wide awake, and there was a fierce sparkle in his eye as his beautiful ward, in her long yellow stockings and low dress, her petticoats turned up to her shoulders, and blushing deeply, approached him with her accomplished penance.

She handed it to him.

'So, Alice,' said he sitting bolt upright, 'here is, I see,' turning over a page or two, 'your own signature to the confession.'

'Oh, uncle, it is true; but do not let anyone know. I know I disgraced myself and behaved like a beast; but I am so sorry.'

'But you deserved your punishment.'

'Yes; I know I did. Only too well.'

He drew her down upon his knee, and placed his right arm round her waist, while he tickled her legs and her groin and her abdomen, and lastly her clitoris, with his hand and fingers.

He let her, when she was almost overcome by the violence of her sensations, slip down between his knees, and as she was seeking how most effectually to caress him, he directed her hands to his penis and his testicles. In a moment of frenzy she tore open his trousers, lifted his shirt, and saw the excited organ, the goal and Ultima Thule of feminine delight. He pressed down her head and, despite the resistance she at first made, the inflamed and distended virility was very quickly placed between the burning lips of her mouth. Its taste and the transport she was in induced her to suck it violently. On her knees before her uncle, tickling, sucking, licking his penis, then looking in his face and recommencing, the sweet girl's hands again very quickly found their way to his balls.

At last, excited beyond his self-control, gazing through his half-closed lids at the splendid form of his niece at his feet — her bare back and shoulders — the breast which, sloping downwards from her position, he yet could see — her bare arms — the hands twiddling and manipulating and kneading with affection and appreciation his balls; his legs far apart, himself thrown back gasping in his arm chair; his own most sensitive and highly excited organ in the dear girl's hot mouth, tickled with the tip of her dear tongue, and pinched with her dear, pretty, cruel ivory teeth — Sir Edward could contain himself no longer and, grasping Alice's head with both his hands, he pushed his weapon well into her mouth and spent down her throat. He lay back in a swoon of delight, and the girl, as wet as she could be, leant her head against his knee, almost choked by the violence of the delightful emission, and stunned by the mystery revealed to her. How she loved him! How she dandled that sweet fellow! How she fondled him! What surreptitious licks she gave him! She could have eaten her uncle.

In about twenty minutes he had recovered sufficiently to speak, and she sat with her head resting against the inside of his right leg, looking up into his face; her own legs stretched out underneath his left one — she was sitting on the floor.

'Alice, you bold, bad girl. I hope you feel punished now.'

'Oh no, uncle, it was delightful. Does it give you pleasure? I will suck you again,' taking his penis, to his great excitement, again in her warm little palm, 'if you wish.'

'My dear run along and go to bed.'

'Oh, I would rather stay with you.'

'Although I have whipped you and birched you and smacked you and made you disgrace yourself?'

'Yes, dear uncle. It has done me good. Don't send me away.'

'Go, Alice, to bed. I will come to you there.'

'Oh, you dear uncle, how nice. Oh, do let down my things for me before I go. Some of the servants may see me.'

'And,' she continued, after an instant's pause, with a blush, and looking down, 'I want to be for you alone.'

Touched by her devotion, her uncle loosed the ribbons; let fall, as far as they would, her frock and petticoats; and giving her a kiss, and not forgetting to use his hand under her clothes in a manner which caused her again to cry out with delight, allowed her to trip off to her bedroom. But not without the remark that she had induced him to do that which did not add to her appearance; for the rich, full, and well-developed girlish form had been simply resplendent with loveliness in the garments huddled about her waist; the petticoat lining of yellow silk relieved by the black bands from her waist to her shoulder crossing each other, and bits of her black frock, with its large yellow spots, appearing here and there. And as the eye travelled downwards from the pink flesh of the swelling breasts to the smooth pink thighs, it noted with rapture that the clothes concealed only what needed not concealment, and revealed with the greatest effect what did; and, still descending, dwelt entranced upon the well-turned limbs, whose outlines and curves the tight stockings so clearly defined.

Sir Edward, who had made her stand facing him, and also with her back to him, was much puzzled, although so warm a devotee of the Venus Callipyge, whether he preferred the back view of her lovely legs, thighs, bottom, back, nuque, and queenly little head, with its suggestion of fierce and cruel delight; or the front, showing the mount and grotto of Venus, the tender breasts, the dimpled chin and sparkling eyes, with the imaginations of soft pleasures and melting trances which the sloping and divided thighs suggested and invited.

The first thing which Alice noticed upon reaching her room was the little supper-table laid for two; and the next that there were black silk sheets on her bed. The sight of the supper — the chocolate, the tempting cakes and biscuits, the rich wines in gold mounted jugs, the Nuremburg glasses, the bonbons, the crystallised fruit, the delicate omelette — delighted her; but the black sheets had a somewhat funereal and depressing effect.

'What can Maud have been thinking of, my dear, to put *black* sheets on the bed; and tonight of all nights in the year?' asked Sir Edward, angrily, the instant he entered the apartment, and hastily returning to the sitting-room, he rang and ordered Janet up. She was directed to send Miss Maud to 'my niece's room, and in a quarter of an hour to put *pink* silk sheets on the bed there.'

Then Sir Edward returned, and giving Alice some sparkling white wine, which with sweet biscuits she said she would like better than anything else, he helped himself to a bumper of red — standing — expecting Maud's appearance. Alice was seated in a cosy chair, toasting her toes.

Presently Maud arrived in a lovely déshabille, her rich dark hair tumbling about her shoulders, the dressing-gown not at all concealing the richly embroidered *robe de nuit* beneath it, and the two garments clinging closely to her form, setting off her lovely svelte figure to perfection. Her little feet were encased in low scarlet slippers embroidered with gold, so low cut as to show the whole of the white instep.

Her manner was hurried and startled, but this pretty dismay increased her attractions.

'Maud,' asked her uncle, 'what do you mean by having had black sheets put on this bed, when I distinctly said they were to be pink?'

'Indeed, indeed, uncle, you said black.'

'How dare you contradict me, miss, and so add to your offence? You have been of late very careless indeed. You shall be soundly punished. Go straight to the yellow room,' he went on to the trembling girl. 'I will follow you in a few moments and flog you in a way that you will recollect. Eighteen stripes with my riding-whip.'

540

'Oh, uncle,' she gasped.

'Go along, miss.'

Alice, to her surprise, although she had some little feeling of distress for Maud, felt quite naughty at the idea of her punishment; and, noticing her uncle's excitement, concluded instinctively that he also felt similar sensations. She was, consequently, bold enough, without rising, to stretch out her hand and to press outside his clothes the gentleman underneath with whom she had already formed so intimate an acquaintance, asking as she did so whether he was going to be very severe.

'Yes,' he replied, moving to and fro (notwithstanding which she kept her hand well pressed on him). 'I shall lash her bottom until she yells for mercy.'

'Oh, uncle!' said Alice, quivering with a strange thrill.

'Go to the room, Alice. I shall follow in a moment.'

Poor Maud was in tears, and Alice, much affected at this sight, attempting to condole with her.

'The riding-whip is terribly severe, however I shall bear it I can't tell.'

'Oh, Maud, I am so sorry.'

'And I made *no* mistake. He *said* black sheets. The fact is, your beauty has infuriated him, and he wants to tear me to pieces.'

Sir Edward returned without trousers, wearing a kilt.

'Now come over here, you careless hussy,' and indicating two rings in the floor quite three feet apart, he made her stretch her legs wide, so as to place her feet near the rings, to which Alice was made to strap them by the ankles. 'I will cure you of your carelessness and inattention to orders. Your delicate flesh will feel this rod's cuts for days. Off with your dressing-gown; off with your nightdress.' Alice was dazzled by her nakedness, the ripeness of her charms, the whiteness of her skin, the plump, soft, round bottom, across which Sir Edward laid a few playful cuts, making the girl call out, for, fixed as she was, she could not struggle.

Alice then, by her uncle's direction, placed before Maud a trestle, the top of which was stuffed and covered with leather, and which reached just to her middle. Across this she was made to lie, and two rings on the other side were drawn down and fixed her elbows, so that her head was almost on the floor, and her bottom, with its skin tight, well up in the air. Her legs, of course, were well apart. The cruelty of the attitude inflamed Alice.

'Give me the whip,' said her uncle. As she handed the heavy weapon to him, he added, 'stand close to me while I flog her, and,' slipping his hand up her petticoats on to her inflamed and moist organ, 'keep your hand upon me while I do so.'

Alice gave a little spring as he touched her. her own animal feelings told her what was required of her.

Maud was crying softly.

'Now, miss,' as the whip cut through the air, 'it is your turn' – swish – a great red wale across the bottom and a writhe of agony – 'you careless' – swish – 'wicked' – swish – 'disobedient' – swish – 'obstinate girl.'

'Oh, uncle! Oh! Oh! Oh! Oh! I am sorry, oh, forgive – ' – swish – 'no, miss' – swish – 'no forgiveness. Black sheets, indeed' – swish – swish – swish – 'I will cure you, my beauty.'

Maud did her best to stifle her groans, but it was clear that she was almost demented with the exquisite torture the whip caused her every time it cut with relentless vigour into her flesh. Sir Edward did not spare her. The rod fell each time with unmitigated energy.

'Spare the rod and spoil you, miss. Better spoil your bold, big bottom than that,' he observed, as he pursued the punishment. The more cruel it became the greater Alice found grew her uncle's and her own excitement, until at last she scarcely knew how to contain herself. At the ninth stripe, Sir Edward crossed over to Maud's right to give the remaining nine the other way across.

'A girl must have her bare bottom whipped' – swish – 'occasionally; there is nothing' – swish – 'so excellent for her' – swish – 'it teaches her to mind what is told her' – swish – 'it knocks all false shame' – swish – 'out of her; there is no mock modesty left about a young – lady after' – swish – 'she has had her bottom under the lash.'

Alice trembled but, when her uncle began to lecture Maud, Alice began to revive and she noticed that, while Sir Edward again approached boiling point, Maud gave as much lascivious movement as her tight bonds permitted.

'You will not forget again, I know,' said Sir

Edward, as he wielded the terrible instrument. 'You careless, naughty girl, how grateful you should be to me for taking the trouble to chastise you thus.'

The last three were given and Maud's roars and yells were redoubled; but in an ecstasy of delight she lost her senses at the last blow.

Alice, too, was mad with excitement. Rushing off, as directed, to her room, she, as her uncle had also bid her do, tore off all her clothing and dived into the pink sheets, rolling about with the passion the sight of the whipping had stimulated to an uncontrollable degree.

Sir Edward, having summoned Janet to attend Maud, hastened to follow Alice.

Divesting himself of all his clothing, he tore the bedclothes off the naked girl who lay on her back, inviting him to her arms, and to the embrace of which she was still ignorant, by the posture nature dictated to her, and looking against the pink sheet a perfect rose of loveliness. Sir Edward sprang upon her in a rush and surge of passion which bore him onwards with the irresistible force of a flowing sea. In a moment he, notwithstanding her cries, was between her already separated legs, clasping her to him, while he directed, with his one free hand, his inflamed and enormous penis to her virgin cunt. Already it had passed the lips and was forcing its way onwards, impelled, by the reiterated plunges of Sir Edward, before Alice could realize what was happening. At last she turns a little pale, and her eyes open wide and stare slightly in alarm, while, finding that her motion increases the assault and the slight stretching of her cunt, she remains still. But the next moment, remembering what had occurred when *it* was in her mouth, it struck her that the same throbbing and shooting and deliciously warm and wet emission might be repeated in the lower and more secret part of her body, and that if, as she hoped and prayed it might be, it was, she would expire of joy. These ideas caused a delightful tremor and a few movements of the buttocks, which increased Sir Edward's pleasure and enabled him to make some progress. But at length the swelling of his organ and his march into the interior began to hurt, and she became almost anxious to withdraw from the amorous encounter. His arms, however, held her tight. She could not get him from between her legs, and she was being pierced in the tenderest portion of her body by a man's great thing, like a horse's. Oh, how naughty she felt! And yet how it hurt! How dreadful it was that he should be able to probe her with it and detect all her sensations by means of it, while on the other hand, she was made sensible *there*, and by means of *it*, of all he felt.

'Oh! Uncle! Oh! Dear, dear uncle! Oh! Oh! Oh! Oh! Wait one minute! Oh! Not so hard! Oh, dear, don't push any further – oh, it is so nice; but it hurts! Oh, do stop! Don't press so hard! Oh! Oh! Oh! Oh! please don't! Oh! It hurts! Oh! I shall die! You are tearing me open! you are indeed! Oh! Oh! Oh!'

'If you don't' – push – push – 'hold me tight and push against me, Alice, I will – yes, that's better – flog your bottom until it bleeds, you bold girl. No, you shan't get away. I will get right into you. Don't,' said he, clawing her bottom with his hands and pinching its cheeks severely, 'slip back. Push forward.'

'Oh! I shall die! Oh! Oh! Oh!' as she felt she pinches, and jerked forward, enabling Sir Edward to make considerable advance, 'Oh! I shall faint; I shall die! Oh, stop! Oh!' as she continued her involuntary motion upwards and downwards, 'you hurt excruciatingly.'

He folded her more closely to him, and altogether disregarding her loud cries, proceeded to divest her of her maidenhead, telling her that if she did not fight bravely he would punish her and he slipped a hand down behind her, and got the middle finger well into her arse.

After this, victory was assured. A few more shrieks and spasms of mingled pleasure and pain, when Sir Edward, who had forced himself up to the hymen and had made two or three shrewd thrusts at it, evoking loud gasps and cries from his lovely ward, drew a long sigh, and with a final determined push sunk down on her bosom, while she, emitting one sharp cry, found her suffering changed into a transport of delight. She clasped her uncle with frenzy to her breast, and throbbed and shook in perfect unison with him, while giving little cries of rapture and panting — with half-closed lids, from under which rolled a diamond tear or two — for the breath of which her ecstasy had robbed her.

Several moments passed, the silence interrupted only inarticulate sounds of gratification. Sir Edward's mouth was glued to hers, and his tongue found its way between its ruby lips and sought hers. Overcoming her coyness, the lovely girl allowed him to find it, and no sooner had they touched than an electric thrill shot through her; Sir Edward's penis, which had never been removed, again began to swell; he recommenced his (and she her) upward and downward movements and again the delightful crisis occurred — this time without the intense pain Alice had at first experienced, and with very much greater appreciation of the shock, which thrilled her from head to foot and seemed to penetrate and permeate the innermost recesses of her being.

Never had she experienced, or even in her fondest moments conceived, the possibility of such transports. She had longed for the possession of her uncle; she had longed to eat him, to become absorbed in him; and she now found the appetite gratified to the fullest extent, in a manner incredibly sweet. To feel his weight upon the front of her thighs — to feel him between her legs, her legs making each of his a captive; the most secret and sensitive and essentially masculine organ of his body inside that part of hers of which she could not think without a blush; and the mutual excitement, the knowledge and consciousness each had of the other's most intimate sensations, threw her into an ecstasy. How delicious it was to be a girl; how she enjoyed the contemplation of her charms; how supremely, overpoweringly delightful it was to have a lover in her embrace to appreciate and enjoy them! How delicious was love!

Sir Edward, gratified at length, rose and

congratulated Alice upon her newborn womanhood; kissed her, and thanked her for the intense pleasure she had given him.

After some refreshment, as he bade her goodnight, the love-sick girl once more twined her arms about him, while slipping her legs on to the edge of the bed, she lay across it and managed to get him between them; then, drawing him down to her bosom, cried, 'Once more, dear uncle; once more before you go.'

'You naughty girl,' he answered, slightly excited; 'well, I will if you ask me.'

'Oh, please, do, uncle. Please do it again.'

'Do what again?'

'Oh! It. You know, What – what – what,' hiding her face sweetly, 'you have done to me twice already.'

'Don't you know what it is called?'

'No. I haven't the slightest idea.'

'It is called "fucking". Now, if you want it done again, you must ask to be fucked,' said he, his instrument assuming giant proportions.

'Oh, dear, I do want it ever so; but however can I ask for it? Please, uncle – will – will you, please – please – f – f – fu – fuck me once more before you go?' and she lay back and extended her legs before him in the divinest fashion.

In a moment he was between them; his prick inserted; his lips again upon hers; and in a few moments more they were again simultaneously overcome by that ecstasy of supernatural exquisiteness of which unbridled passion has alone attempted to fathom the depths, and that without reaching them.

Exhausted mentally and physically by her experiences and the exercises of the evening, Alice, as she felt the lessening throbs of her uncle's engine, found she was losing herself and consciousness in drowsiness. Her uncle placed her in a comfortable posture upon the great pillow, and throwing the sheet over her, heard her murmured words of thanks and love as she fell asleep with a smile upon her face. Janet came and tucked her up comfortably. And she slept profoundly.

French Skirt

The lorry was black and the number plate had been altered. Nonetheless, Hartnell felt distinctly uneasy as he drove it east from London towards the coast.

It had been three days since he'd last seen Gracie and only a week since he'd first met her and taken her out to dinner. During that time Francie, it appeared, had spent quite a lot of time somewhere in the country and Gracie had not been bothered with him. But still she was not prepared to clear out. Hartnell had done his utmost to persuade her, but she was somehow numbed to the hope of success. And now she was afraid that he would cross Francie and that something terrible would happen to him.

So here they were hanging on, aimlessly, and here he was, with Johnny once more beside him, driving out on some unspecified job which he didn't want to do. It was as if some force outside himself had taken a hold on his life and was running it for him.

In front of them the Riley with Francie, Bill, Jake and Jim was nosing its way through the traffic, racing a long way ahead and then slowing down to wait for the lorry like an impatient terrier.

'What's the mystery about this one?' he asked

Johnny when they were out in open country, heading southeast.

'Didn't Francie tell you?'

'No.'

'I guess 'e doesn't trust you yet. Well, we're going to pick up some skirt!'

'Pick up some skirt?'

'That's right. Fresh from Gay Paree. 'Igh-class French skirt.'

'Don't talk in riddles, Johnny. What the hell do you mean?'

'Well, these girls are interested in the money what they can make in London, but they're all tabbed by the French authorities and they wouldn't be let out. So — trust Francie — we're going to pick them up from a fishing boat and they're going to join Francie's little business.'

'Francie's little business?'

'Yeah. I guess you an' Francie ain't bosom pals yet. 'E doesn't tell you very much.'

'What's Francie's little business?'

'Well, I don't suppose I'm breakin' any confidences. You'd know later on today anyway. 'E runs a call-girl outfit.'

Hartnell pursed his lips. Next, he'd be hearing that Francie ran an assassins agency. Whiskey and cigarettes! What a load of bull that had been.

'Course it hasn't been doing too well 'cos it needs fresh blood,' Johnny was continuing. 'But these Frenchies should revive interest in it quite a bit.'

The sooner I get out of this, Hartnell was thinking,

the better. Sooner or later there's going to be a crash somewhere and then it's going to be just too bad for everyone.

It was growing dusk when they drove through the little east coast village to the big house back from the beach which Francie had rented a month before for this special purpose. The Channel was calm, dotted with lights from boats way out on its sleek surface. A white foam rolled gently up the narrow stretch of beach.

'Not much around here,' Johnny said, as they drove over the dusty ground to the roughly fenced off grounds of the house. 'Trust the boss to find the best spot for the job.'

The Riley was already parked and lights flashed on in the house as they climbed down and walked towards the main door.

Inside, the other four were sitting smoking in the main ground-floor room. Francie was staring out to sea through the big windows which overlooked the beach. The house was sparsely furnished with enormous, old-fashioned furniture. There were heavy brocade curtains at the windows and covering the doors.

'Well, we've got quite a little while to wait,' Francie said. 'But, we'd better not show ourselves in the village just in case. We brought some food in the Riley.' He looked around the room. 'Hye, Jake,' he said. 'Go out and bring in the grub and the bottles — in the boot.'

Jake ambled out of the room and Francie stared back through the window. Still staring he said:—

'Well, Roger old chap, here we are and it's just as well you should know what we're up to.' He nodded out across the dim expanse of the Channel. 'Somewhere out there,' he went on 'is a little boat with half a dozen beauties on board. Not French racehorses, I mean, but French pros — high class mind you. They'll be pulling in here just down to our right about two in the morning. They're coming to make a bit of money for yours truly — and for the rest of us here.'

'Another nice little racket, Francie?'

'Not bad is it? Make us a mint of money they will. Nothing like a bit of ooh — la — la to make an Englishman's eyes light up.'

'How'd you get hold of them?'

'Oh, I got friends everywhere. 'Igh class friends. I'm going to make it worth somebody's while over there to bring 'em over here. Suppose you might speak French?'

'Yes, I do.'

'Thought you would. Well it's only the fishermen'll bringing them so you might have to talk some English to 'em. Les girls are supposed to speak English, but you can never count on that — and it's not very important from our point of view.

Jake came in with sandwiches and the whiskey and they all began to eat and drink.

'Bring the cards, Bill?' Francie asked. 'There, there boy. Don't look so bored, always worth the wait until they come, isn't it? Then you can 'ave one to yourself.' He chuckled and turned to Hartnell.

'We always try the goods out just to make sure we 'aven't been cheated,' he explained.

The lights in the house were put out at one o'clock and they sat for a while in darkness, smoking and looking out over the water. There was a crescent moon and no sound apart from the gentle breakers.

'A good night,' Francie commented. 'We'd better go down in a few minutes in case they come ashore further down.'

They left the house and walked over the rough ground past the vehicles. They jumped from the higher ground a few feet down to the sloping beach, their feet sinking deep into the silvery grains.

'You stay here, Jake,' Francie said, when they'd reached firmer sand quite near the water's edge. 'If they come in here and we don't see 'em, give a whistle.'

As he walked beside Francie along the shore, Hartnell wondered vaguely about coast guards and people like that. But, as was usual with Francie, he felt the man would have left nothing to chance, that everything would be known beforehand and taken care of. He felt like a child in comparison.

One by one at distances of a few hundred yards the others stopped and waited until only he and Francis were left striding along the beach with the salt breeze in their nostrils.

'We'll go along as far as those rocks,' Francie said, indicating a clump of boulders ahead. 'If they come up any further away than that they'll have to find their own way to the house.'

They sat in the shelter of the rock peering out to

sea. Lights were still winking far out. There were no lights coming from the village about a mile away.

'Hope they don't keep us waiting,' Francie said. 'Some of the boys haven't had a bit of skirt for a long time. It'd be a shame to have them getting frustrated.'

Hartnell was thinking of Gracie. He didn't dare look at Francie because every time he did he had to resist the temptation to sock him. How he wished he and Gracie could be out there now in the Channel, maybe heading for the French coast, or perhaps for Spain, anywhere away from this mess. He allowed his mind to dwell upon himself and he could hardly believe the reality of himself sitting here on this beach with this other man waiting for this strange, criminal arrival in this fantastic set-up.

For a long time he sat there, not saying a word, thinking — of Gracie, of Dora who'd been upset when he'd moved out, but had let him go without too much fuss, of Gracie again, always coming back to Gracie, the charm of her lovely face and voice and the beauty of her breasts, her slim woman's body, the desire with which the thought of her choking breath when he loved her, always filled him.

Francie was silent too, lost in his thoughts which were also of Gracie and that inner core which she had, which he couldn't get at, that something which she kept unattainable, the only woman he'd ever really wanted.

There was a low whistle from up the beach and they both scrambled to their feet and began to run along the surf's edge.

The dim shape of a large rowing boat met them, growing out of the dimness into phantom near-reality and then substance. Bill and Jim were already there, helping to pull it in.

'Ask them if everything went okay,' Francie said.

Hartnell addressed the nearest of the two French fishermen, asking what sort of trip they'd had.

The fisherman grinned and said it had been fine but the 'young ladies' had suffered a little from sea sickness.

Hartnell told Francie and then he noticed the women, huddled in the boat.

'That's all right,' Francie said. 'They'll be suffering more than a little from prick-sickness soon.'

Shivering slightly, in spite of the thick coats they were wearing, the girls began to climb from the boat, walking from seat to seat in their dainty high heels, helped by the fishermen as the boat swayed, and then jumping ashore.

'Well, well. Hello girls,' Francie said. '*Parlez vous anglais*?' It was one of his few expressions in the language.

'A leetle,' said the first girl. 'We all speak a leetle. We were seek, but it is better now.'

'I trust you all know how to *faire l'amour* a leetle,' Francie said with a coarse chuckle which was echoed by Bill and Jim and the others who had now arrived on the scene.

The girl giggled and rubbed her tongue along her lips at him.

As soon as they were all on dry land the fishermen

pushed off and rowed quietly and rapidly back towards their boat, leaving a strange little crowd of people behind them on the beach. It was just two o'clock.

They walked in a body up the beach. When they came to a high step to the road, the women were helped up by the men and there were so many playful shrieks as hands held buttocks and ran up between thighs that Francie called out for quiet.

As soon as they were in the house, Francie pulled the heavy curtains across the windows. He switched on the light and leaned against the door with a smile on his face.

'Well, well,' he murmured. 'It couldn't 'ave worked out better.'

Hartnell studied the women while Jake doled them out sandwiches and whisky. The colour began to come back to their pale cheeks as they ate and drank. They were certainly very attractive, he decided. Most of them had typical dark, French good looks, with a faint olive tint to the skin and prominent but delicate bone structure. They all looked astonishingly vivacious. When they began to remove their coats, the voluptuousness of their figures brought unrepressed whistles of appreciation from the men.

'Go and have a wash, dears,' Francie said, after they'd eaten, 'and then we'll see if you know your stuff.'

None of the girls seemed the slightest perturbed by his words and they all trouped out quite happily after Jake who was to show them to the bathroom. Impatient at having to wait, Jake seized the last one to enter and mauled her big breasts as he kissed her. She bit his ear and pinched his penis through his trousers.

Half an hour later they had all returned to the main room where the men were drinking fresh whisky. Eyes moved over them avidly as they came in.

Francie stood up and walked over to them. His sensual mouth was smiling, his eyes as hard as granite chips.

'I'm Francie,' he told them. 'And, I'm your boss. Tomorrow we'll all go up to London and start arranging for you to make a fortune. In the meantime, the boys here are anxious for a bit of continental screw an' I'm sure you must be a bit frustrated after that trip so tonight we're all going to get to know one another.' He paused, looked around the room and saw Hartnell. 'If there's anything you don't know how to say,' he added, 'then you can just ask the gentleman over there 'cos 'e's got class like me and he speaks your lingo like an onion boy.'

The girls looked at Hartnell with interest and several glances remained fixed on him even when Francie resumed speaking.

'Now girls,' he said. 'We'd all like to see how you look folies bergere style, you know, *nu* — so starting with you' — he pointed to a petite brunette — 'get those togs off and let's have a look at you.'

'Togs?' the girl queried.

Francie glanced at Hartnell and then grinned.

'Bit of Old Blighty,' he said. 'Clothes, my dear — skirts, brassieres, knickers — you know.'

The girl giggled, repeated the word 'togs' to herself and began to strip.

She took off her clothes with the tantalizing technique of a professional striptease and when at last she was standing naked in front of them the gang were breathing very heavily.

'Get a load of that,' Johnny muttered.

She had big breasts, almost too big for her size, with enormous, angry-looking nipples, her waist was slim and her hips were also broad for her size. They seemed to shine with an oily olive gloss and the tangle of dark hair at her thigh junction muffed out in glossy profusion.

'Yes, I think you'll do,' Francie said, with a leer. 'Let's 'ave a look at your behind.'

Unabashed the girl swivelled round like a mannequin and playfully jutted a pair of glossy, olive buttocks at him, arching her back inwards to accentuate them.

'I see you've been sunbathing without any togs,' Francie said and all the women giggled.

'All right,' Francie said, pleased with his own humour. 'Don't stop the show. Next buttocks please.'

The pantomime continued until all the girls had slowly peeled their clothes from their bodies and paraded before the watching, desire-filled eyes. They all had bodies well worth any man's money. Some, like the first, were plump in the right places to the point of being exaggerated, others were elegantly well developed with long, svelte lines.

'Anybody who can't wait for privacy?' Francie asked, hopefully.

And Jake, who still felt the pressure where the girl had pinched his organ, stood up with a deep flush. He took another swig of his whisky and then drained the glass with a grimace.

'Go on then, Jake. Give us a show,' Francie encouraged.

Jake's eyes were fixed on the girl who had first stripped — the one he had kissed outside the bathroom — while he unbuckled his belt. She came over towards him, seeing from his glance that she was the one he wanted.

'You wan' me to 'elp you?' she asked and began to unbutton his trousers.

'Go easy or he'll faint and then we'll all be sorry,' Francie said. Jake leered at them amidst the guffaws which followed.

With the help of the little brunette he got his clothes off. Towards the end she was taking them off for him alone, because he couldn't do anything with his hands except run them over every glossy portion of her body he could reach. The girl herself had begun to tremble and had jerked the last garments off him with some savagery.

'Go to it, Jake,' Francie cried.

Jake had a bit of a paunch, which wasn't too big, considering his size, and his penis jutted out from under it almost vertically. His big hands caught the girl, who squirmed up close to him and rubbed his penis between her soft, fleshy thighs. Jake uttered a couple of gasps which the laughs of the company did not affect. He kissed her and she clung to him passionately writhing, exploring his body with her fingers as he explored hers.

Suddenly, placing her arms up around his neck, she leapt up, twining her legs around his waist.

'She's a gymnast, as well,' Francie declared in a torrent of fresh guffaws, guffaws which held an edge of lewd violence.

Jake placed his hands under the girl's stretched behind, played with her anus for a moment, found his rod waving near her open vagina and wormed it in.

With a little gasp of 'Oh chéri!' the girl flopped down onto the fleshy mast and began to squirm on it, mouth open, murmuring in French and English.

With her jogging on him, Jake carried her to a rug, and flopped down on top of her. The company moved into a circle around them to watch, offering encouraging suggestions. One of the girls bent and gave Jake a couple of playful taps on his behind to a burst of fresh laughter.

The girl on the floor was squirming like a mad thing and Jake kept shuffling his knees further in between her widespread thighs, trying to stop himself from slipping on the rug. Panting, he leaned on her thighs, pushing them father apart and the spectators had a perfect view of his big, white organ ramming into the red gulf, surrounded by its forest of black hair between her legs.

'Oh chéri, oh chéri,' she kept murmuring as he split her apart.

Jake pushed her legs back now, pulling back the thighs against her big, trembling breasts, leaning forward on them so that she was bent almost double, holding out her nether portions to him as if she wanted only those parts to exist.

Jake leaned up off her and pushed forward his hips like a matador attracting the bull. His rod disappeared to the hilt with each thrust while the girl waggled her upturned bottom, whose gaping white roundness was there to further inflame those who watched.

Around the floor scene, some of the gang had caught hold of the naked girls as they watched, and, still watching, were fondling their breasts, running their hands over the svelte lines of bosom and belly, playing with buttocks. Without taking their dark eyes from the pantomime, the girls, too, were feeling for bulging organs, opening fly buttons, losing their relentless fingers inside protecting clothes.

With every stroke, now, Jake was belching forth a strangled gasp of breath, giving a final agonizing flick to his hips as his bulging, excited penis seared into the girl's moist vagina.

She had unwound her legs and wrapped them around his waist, squeezing them tight with every intrusion he made into her channel. Her grasping, clawing hands had made red weals across his back.

Jake held her buttocks, each in a cupped hand and lifted her slightly off the rug so that she rested on it only with her head and shoulders. The different position gave him even greater penetration and the girl gave a little shriek. Her eyes on the ceiling were unseeing.

'Fuck me, fuck me to death!' she pleaded.

'She certainly 'as a good grasp of the English language,' Johnny said as he sucked the ear of a slim, dark girl who, standing with her back towards him, had taken out his weapon and was rolling it between her legs.

Jake was straining into the girl whose head slid back on the rug every time he jerked into her. He had a finger in her behind and was seeing how far he could lose it, while the girl kept clamping her buttocks together tightly around it.

'Hurry, hurry cheri,' she spluttered. '*J'arrive*, I'm coming, hurry.'

Jake let her fall back onto the rug and lowered himself onto the soft ramp of her hips, still pistoning into her. He leaned onto her and bit her neck. She bit his ear in return and bit it again in passion.

'Uuuuuugh,' Jake bellowed as she bit him.

His mouth had opened, his eyes were wild, full of sweet pain, his strokes slowed, grinding in like a thick, slow screwdriver.

The girl's loins were almost turning circles, rotating furiously, her buttocks brushing the rug, screwing it up under them. They were both gasping as if their lungs would burst.

Jake's mouth moved, his hands held her shoulders as if he would pulverize them.

''Ere it comes,' he cried. 'Ere it comes, now . . . Uuuuugh!'

The girl gave a shudder. Her hips went into a paroxysm.

'Oh, oh, oh, oh, chéri, chéri, chéri — oooh!' she screamed.

As they both began to subside in dwindling activity, Francie turned to the other girls.

'She'll do,' he said. 'Now we'll see about the rest of you.'

The gang began to break up, each man leading a girl away into other rooms for a more private pleasure. Eventually Jake and his girl stood up and went off to find a bed for a fresh bout.

Only Hartnell was left, sitting on a table, his legs swinging nonchalantly to and fro. Across the room, the odd girl stood, undecided.

Hartnell, in spite of the show could not summon any great enthusiasm to make love to any of these professional women. He remembered his only-too-frequent nights with Gracie, the torment they left inside him, the feelings of love, passion and protection they left within him. All this was cheap in comparison and he could only think of her.

He looked at the girl who remained and realized she was waiting for him to do something. She was a slim, dark girl with big breasts and a rather sharp, attractive face. He noticed she was not wearing lipstick and that her lips were a gentle shade of pink, well shaped and soft-looking.

'Go to bed,' he said. 'I don't feel like it.'

She raised dark eyebrows in surprise and came across to him.

''Ow is that, darleeng?' she asked, putting her hand on his shoulder.

Hartnell grinned inwardly at the situation. He thought of earlier occasions when he would have loved to have had just such an attractive girl standing nude in front of him asking why he didn't want to make love to her. Things have come to a pretty pass, he thought.

'I guess I'm just tired,' he said.

'But I will make you wide awake again,' she insisted. 'Am I not beautiful enough?'

She made a little pirouette in front of him, displaying her curvaceous back view with the perkily protruding rounded buttocks, and giving a little laugh which brought out dimples in her smooth, brown cheeks.

Hartnell felt a sudden warmth down in his trousers.

'Oh, you're great,' he assured her. 'I just don't feel like it.'

'Perhaps you are un'appy in love?' she suggested, putting her finger unwittingly straight on the wound.

'Perhaps I am,' Hartnell agreed.

'Is true — this?' she asked.

'Is true,' he said.

She moved closer to him, throwing back her head a little so that her firm breasts stood out towards his face inviting.

'Then it is better that you make love — make you 'appier,' she assured him.

'I wish you were right,' Hartnell said.

She misunderstood his words a little and put her hand down on the bulge which had grown, without him being fully aware of it, in his trousers. She ran her fingers over it, feeling it, measuring it.

'You see — you want it really,' she said.

With her hand titivating his penis through a couple of thicknesses of material and her breasts so close under his face that he would only need to sway forward to kiss them, Hartnell felt a doubt in himself. He didn't really want her. But just for the few minutes of physical delight which would allow him to forget everything? Might it not be a good thing? But then he saw Gracie lying in the bed thinking of him, wanting him and the desire dissipated.

'Come. You come upstairs — or we stay here?' the girl asked. She was rubbing her thighs together, pressing against his legs, working herself into a state of excitement.

'No,' he said. 'No — not tonight.'

'No? Why is no?' she asked.

She began to undo his buttons and he realized his erection hadn't gone down. He couldn't make the effort to get up or push her away.

She undid them all the way down and searched for the opening in his pants, found it and worked his organ out into view. She held it gently in her hand looking at the blunt cudgel of a knob, the thick white staff.

'Is big,' she said appreciatively.

Her fingers on his penis had made a certain warmth of feeling gush into it and find an echo in his throat. He looked at her body, at the thin fingers stroking his flesh.

'You still not sure you want it?' the girl asked, but her eyes were twinkling with certainty.

She bent suddenly and took the knob in her mouth.

The movement took him by surprise, sending a sharp pain of sensation through him, making his penis swell in her mouth to even greater size.

She glanced up at him quickly.

'I eat it,' she said.

Her mouth went back to enclose him and he watched the top of her head with its short black curly hair jogging about.

She was using her tongue and he could feel it swiping around him, stimulating his rod to make little involuntary jerks in her mouth. Her lips were soft as they moved down the staff, taking all she could into her mouth, surrounding the flesh with the warmth of her breath, the moistness of her saliva.

Her tongue was like the suction end of a vacuum cleaner. As she licked his prick he felt as if this slender morsel of flesh, this tongue was drawing the very dregs of feeling out of him, electrifying his whole body.

She began to suck voraciously, rubbing her legs together all the time and he leaned back on the table, pushing his hips at her face, moving his penis farther towards her throat.

He wouldn't stop her now, he realized. It had gone too far now. He thought about Gracie and the thought quite apart from what was happening down there under her moving head. It was easier to recognize the difference when it was happening and it didn't matter so much.

She bit him gently and he squirmed. He leaned forward and ran his fingers through her hair and then reached down to stroke her breasts. She didn't look up, but continued with her sucking, continued rubbing her thighs together and breathing heavily over his rampant phallus.

His heart began to pound. He wanted to tense his legs together and strain his hips at her. His loins were growing hot. He was sweating between his legs.

Releasing her breasts, he let himself fall gently backwards until he was lying across the table. She moved back with him, keeping his penis in her mouth, burying her head in his loins.

Now he was on his back and could sense himself. He did so and felt an immediate crush of feeling at that stiff protuberance which her tongue was working on like a mad thing. His lips moved apart and his breath made the only noise in the room.

He felt her hand exploring in his trousers and then she pulled out his testicles so that his genitals were all exposed in a neat little triangle. She stroked the loose sacks of flesh while she sucked and he felt a fresh intoxication run through his body, finding its extreme point at the head of his cudgel.

His breath shot in little explosions into the still atmosphere of the big room. His hips were grinding against her face. He glanced down and saw her engrossed in her sucking, eyes closed, fluttering every so often, her breasts pressed against his knees, her legs still tight against him and rubbing. He bit his lip and tensed his hips watching her pretty, unrouged mouth eating sensually on his penis.

The stem of his penis, that part which wasn't

engulfed in her mouth, was dead white. In contrast, he knew, the knob would now be dark, flaming red.

It would be getting redder and redder, darker and darker, all the blood drawn into it just as the sperm was already tingling to move into it. He panted in a continuous stream, writhing his hips, gritting his teeth at the pinpoint of furious sensation lost in her mouth.

He wanted to grab her, twist her over and shove it in her with furious energy, but he couldn't move from his position. His passion had trapped him there, making him incapable of breaking the rhythm.

His fingers clawed at the polished tabletop, bringing out thin scratch lines on its smooth surface.

In his belly he could feel the imminence of the explosion, the boiling to great heat. He gasped, gasped loudly, so that the sound echoed in the big room and the girl renewed her tonguing with even greater energy.

Deep inside the boiling was under way. He could feel it growing and growing and the thought that he was going to flood into her mouth filled him with an overwhelming perversity of pleasure. He worked his hips, hurrying the climax for fear she would jerk away before it was reached.

He was lost now. It had to be finished. Not to finish now, for her to pull away now, was the equal of death, of torture and then death.

He gasped, uttering formless words. He looked down at her as he felt the flood start. Her face was flushed with passion, eyes still closed and fluttering, mouth working furiously. He forced his neck to stay in that position so that he could see her. His eyes screwed up with the effort. There were sharp spears running along the inside of his penis: an enormous flood of them hurtling along the tube with greater and greater velocity.

He cried out and her face didn't shift its position. She seemed to be entranced.

And as the sperm burst from his penis with agonizing gusts which were like the dragging of his entrails out into the light, he saw her swallowing gluttonously before he fell back, giving all his mind to the sensation and the effort of arching his hips at her face.

When he lay still, filled with lassitude, after it was over, she didn't let his deflated organ escape from her lips. She continued to suck it gently. She continued the gentle friction of her legs against each other. He lay back, letting her carry on, feeling momentarily exhausted, thinking that it had been one of the most acute feelings he'd experienced.

After a while his organ began to thicken again in her mouth. She licked it and bit it gently, revelling in her power to rejuvenate it after its collapse.

When it had stretched out, elongated to its full length once again, and he was starting to feel the desire rekindle in his loins, she took her lips off him for the first time.

'Are you going to make love to me now, darleeng?' she asked. 'I need it very bad.'

He slithered off the table and took off his trousers and shorts. She held his penis under his shirt and stroked his testicles.

'Let's have it here on thees table,' she said.

He caught hold of her. His prick was an enormous itch now, wanting to bury itself into soft flesh.

'I wan to be spleet in two,' she said.

She turned into his arms and stretched face-down across the table, so that its edge cut across the crease of her hips and her feet touched the floor. She spread her legs wide and reaching behind her caught his penis and dragged it at her open vagina.

With a grunt, Hartnell rammed it deep inside her. He leaned heavily on her while he shagged in and in and she clawed the table the way he had while her buttocks hollowed and filled under his eyes.

My Life and Loves

My Life and Loves

At the next table to me I had already remarked once or twice a little, middle-aged, weary looking man who often began his breakfast with a glass of boiling water and followed it up with a baked apple drowned in rich cream. Brains, too, or sweetbreads he would eat for dinner, and rice, not potatoes: when I looked surprised, he told me he had been up all night and had a weak digestion. Mayhew, he said, was his name, and explained that if I ever wanted a game of faro or euchre or indeed anything else, he'd oblige me. I smiled; I could ride and shoot, I replied, but I was no good at cards.

The day after my talk with Smith, Mayhew and I were both late for supper: I sat long over a good meal and as he rose, he asked me if I would come across the street and see his 'layout.' I went willingly enough, having nothing to do. The gambling saloon was on the first floor of a building nearly opposite the Eldridge House: the place was well kept and neat, thanks to a colored bartender and waiter and a boy for all work. The long room, too, was comfortably furnished and very brightly lit – altogether an attractive place.

As luck would have it, while he was showing me

around, a lady came in. Mayhew after a word or two introduced me to her as his wife. Mrs Mayhew was then a woman of perhaps twenty-eight or thirty, with tall, lissome, slight figure and interesting rather than a pretty face: her features were all good, her eyes even were large and blue-grey; she would have been lovely if her coloring had been more pronounced. Give her golden hair or red or black and she would have been a beauty; she was always tastefully dressed and had appealing, ingratiating manners. I soon found that she loved books and reading, and as Mayhew said he was going to be busy, I asked if I might see her home. She consented smiling and away we went. She lived in a pretty frame house standing alone in a street that ran parallel to Massachusetts Street, nearly opposite to a large and ugly church.

As she went up the steps to the door, I noticed that she had fine, neat ankles and I divined shapely limbs. While she was taking off her light cloak and hat, the lifting of her arms stretched her bodice and showed small, round breasts: already my blood was lava and my mouth parched with desire.

'You look at me strangely!' she said, swinging round from the long mirror with a challenge on her parted lips. I made some inane remark: I couldn't trust myself to speak frankly; but natural sympathy drew us together. I told her I was going to be a student, and she wanted to know whether I could dance. I told her I could not, and she promised to teach me: 'Lily Robins, a neighbor's girl, will play for us any afternoon. Do you know the steps?' She went on, and when I said, 'No,' she got up from the sofa, held up her dress and showed me the three polka steps, which she said were waltz steps, too, only taken on a glide.

'What pretty ankles you have!' I ventured, but she appeared not to hear me. We sat on and on and I learned that she was very lonely: Mr Mayhew away every night and nearly all day and nothing to do in that little dead-and-alive place. 'Will you let me come in for a talk sometimes?' I asked.

'Whenever you wish,' was her answer. As I rose to go and we were standing opposite to each other by the door, I said: 'You know, Mrs Mayhew, in Europe when a man brings a pretty woman home, she rewards him with a kiss.'

'Really?' she scoffed, smiling; 'that's not a custom here.'

'Are you less generous than they are?' I asked, and the next moment I had taken her face in my hands and kissed her on the lips.

She put her hands on my shoulders and left her eyes on mine. 'We're going to be friends,' she said; 'I felt it when I saw you: don't stay away too long!'

'Will you see me tomorrow afternoon?' I asked. 'I want that dance lesson!'

'Surely,' she replied. 'I'll tell Lily in the morning.' And once more our hands met: I tried to draw her to me for another kiss; she held back with a smiling, 'Tomorrow afternoon!'

'Tell me your name,' I begged, 'so that I may think of it.'

'Lorna,' she replied, 'you funny boy!' I went my

way with pulses hammering, blood aflame and hope in my heart.

Next morning I called again upon Smith but the pretty servant ('Rose,' she said her name was), told me that he was nearly always at Judge Stephens', 'five or six miles out,' she added. So I said I'd write and make an appointment, and I did write and asked him to let me see him next morning.

That same morning Willie recommended to me a pension kept by a Mrs Gregory, an English woman, the wife of an old Baptist clergyman, who would take good care of me for four dollars a week. Immediately I went with him to see her and was delighted to find that she lived only about a hundred yards from Mrs Mayhew, on the opposite side of the street. Mrs Gregory was a large, motherly woman, evidently a lady, who had founded this boarding house to provide for a rather reckless husband and two children, a big pretty girl, Kate, and a lad a couple of years younger. Mrs Gregory was delighted with my English accent, I believe, and showed me special favour at once by giving me a large outside room with its own entrance and steps into the garden.

In an hour I had paid my bill at the Eldridge House and had moved in. I showed a shred of prudence by making Willie promise Mrs Gregory that he would turn up each Saturday with the five dollars for my board; the dollar extra was for the big room.

In due course I shall tell how he kept his promise and discharged his debt to me. For the moment everything was easily, happily settled. I went out and ordered a decent suit of ordinary tweeds and dressed myself up in my best blue suit to call upon Mrs Mayhew after lunch. The clock crawled, but on the stroke of three I was at her door: a colored maid admitted me.

'Mrs Mayhew,' she said in her pretty singing voice, 'will be down right soon: I'll go and call Miss Lily.'

In five minutes Miss Lily appeared, a dark slip of a girl with shining black hair, wide, laughing mouth, temperamental thick, red lips, and grey eyes fringed with black lashes; she had hardly time to speak to me when Mrs Mayhew came in. 'I hope you two'll be great friends,' she said prettily. 'You're both about the same age,' she added.

In a few minutes Miss Lily was playing a waltz on the Steinway and with my arm around the slight, flexible waist of my inamorata I was trying to waltz. But alas! After a turn or two I became giddy and in spite of all my resolutions had to admit that I should never be able to dance.

'You have got very pale,' Mrs Mayhew said, 'you must sit down on the sofa a little while.' Slowly the giddiness left me; before I had entirely recovered Miss Lily with kindly words of sympathy had gone home, and Mrs Mayhew brought me in a cup of excellent coffee; I drank it down and was well at once.

'You should go in and lie down,' said Mrs Mayhew, still full of pity. 'See,' and she opened a door, 'there's the guest bedroom all ready.' I saw my chance and went over to her. 'If you'd come too,' I whispered, and then, 'The coffee has made me quite well: won't you, Lorna, give me a kiss? You don't know how often I said you name last night, you dear!' And in a moment I had again taken her face and put my lips on hers.

She gave me her lips this time and my kiss became a caress; but in a little while she drew away and said, 'Let's sit and talk; I want to know all you are doing.' So I seated myself beside her on the sofa and told her all my news. She thought I would be comfortable with the Gregorys. 'Mrs Gregory is a good woman,' she added, 'and I hear the girl's engaged to a cousin: do you think her pretty?'

'I think no one pretty but you, Lorna,' I said, and I pressed her head down on the arm of the sofa and kissed her. Her lips grew hot: I was certain. At once I put my hand down on her sex; she struggled a little at first, which I took care should bring our bodies closer, and when she ceased struggling I put my hands up her dress and began caressing her sex: it was hot and wet, as I knew it would be, and opened readily.

But in another moment she took the lead. 'Someone might find us here,' she whispered. 'I've let the maid go: come up to my bedroom,' and she took me upstairs. I begged her to undress: I wanted to see her figure; but she only said, 'I have no corsets on; I don't often wear them in the house. Are you sure you love me, dear?'

'You know I do!' was my answer. The next moment I lifted her on to the bed, drew up her clothes, opened her legs and was in her. There was no difficulty and in a moment or two I came, but went right on poking passionately; in a few minutes her breath went and came quickly and her eyes fluttered and she met my thrusts with sighs and nippings of her sex. My second orgasm took some time and all the while Lorna became more and more responsive, till suddenly she put her hands on my bottom and drew me to her forcibly while she moved her sex up and down awkwardly to meet my thrusts with a passion I had hardly imagined. Again and again I came and the longer the play lasted the wilder was her excitement and delight. She kissed me hotly, foraging and thrusting her tongue into my mouth. Finally she pulled up her chemise to get me further into her and, at length, with little sobs, she suddenly got hysterical and, panting wildly, burst into a storm of tears.

That stopped me: I withdrew my sex and took her in my arms and kissed her; at first she clung to me with choking sighs and streaming eyes, but, as soon as she had won a little control, I went to the toilette and brought her a sponge of cold water and bathed her face and gave her some water to drink – that quieted her. But she would not let me leave her even to arrange my clothes.

'Oh, you great, strong dear,' she cried, with her arms clasping me. 'Oh, who would have believed such intense pleasure possible: I never felt anything like it before; how could you keep on so long? Oh, how I love you, you wonder and delight.

'I am all yours,' she added gravely. 'You shall do what you like with me: I am your mistress, your slave, your plaything, and you are my god and my love! Oh, darling! Oh!'

There was a pause while I smiled at her extravagant praise, then suddenly she sat up and got out of bed. 'You wanted to see my figure'; she exclaimed, 'here it is, I can deny you nothing; I only hope it may please you,' and in moment or two she showed herself nude from head to stocking.

As I had guessed, her figure was slight and lissome, with narrow hips, but she had a great bush of hair on her Mount of Venus and her breasts were not so round and firm as Jessie's: still she was very pretty and well-formed with the *fines attaches* (slender wrists and ankles), which the French are so apt to overestimate. They think that small bones indicate a small sex; but I have found the exceptions are very numerous, even if there is such a rule.

After I had kissed her breasts and navel and praised her figure, she disappeared in the bathroom, but was soon with me again on the sofa which we had left an hour or so before.

'Do you know,' she began, 'my husband assured me that only the strongest young man could go twice with a woman in one day? I believed him; aren't we women fools? You must have come a dozen times!'

'Not half that number,' I replied, smiling.

'Aren't you tired?' was her next question. 'Even I have a little headache,' she added. 'I never was so wrought up; at the end it was so intense; but you must be tired out.'

'No,' I replied, 'I feel no fatigue, indeed, I feel the better for our joy ride!'

'But surely you're an exception!' she went on. 'Most men have finished in one short spasm and leave the woman utterly unsatisfied, just excited and no more.'

'Youth,' I said, 'that, I believe, makes the chief difference.'

'Is there any danger of a child?' she went on. 'I ought to say "hope,"' she added bitterly, 'for I'd love to have a child, your child,' and she kissed me.

'Do you know you kiss wonderfully?' she went on reflectingly. 'With a lingering touch of the inside of the lips and then the thrust of the tongue: that's what excited me so the first time,' and she sighed, as if delighted with the memory.

'You didn't seem excited,' I said half reproachfully, 'for when I wanted another kiss, you drew away and said "Tomorrow"! Why are women so coquettish, so perverse?' I added, remembering Lucille and Jessie.

'I think it is that we wish to be sure of being desired,' she replied, 'and a little, too, that we want to prolong the joy of it, the delight of being wanted, really wanted! It is so easy for us to give and so exquisite to feel a man's desire pursuing us! Ah, how rare it is,' she sighed passionately, 'and how quickly lost! You'll soon tire of your mistress,' she added, 'now that I am all yours and thrill only for you,' and she took my head in her hands and kissed me passionately, regretfully.

'You kiss better than I do, Lorna! Where did you acquire the art, Madame?' I asked. 'I fear that you have been a naughty, naughty girl!'

'If you only knew the truth,' she exclaimed, 'if you only knew how girls long for a lover and burn and itch in vain and wonder why men are so stupid and cold and dull as not to see our desire.

'Don't we try all sorts of tricks? Aren't we haughty and withdrawn at· one moment and affectionate, tender, loving at another? Don't we conceal the hook with every sort of bait, only to watch the fish sniff at it and turn away. Ah, if you knew − I feel a traitor to my sex even in telling you − if you guessed how we angle for you and how clever we are, how full of wiles. There's an expression I once heard my husband use which described us women exactly, or nine out of ten of us. I wanted to know how he kept the office warm all night: he said, we damp down the furnaces, and explained the process. That's it, I cried to myself, I'm a damped-down furnace: that's surely why I keep hot ever so long! Did you imagine,' she asked, turning her flower-face all pale with passion half aside, 'that I took off my hat that first day before the glass and turned slowly round with it held above my head, by chance? You dear innocent! I knew the movement would show my breasts and slim hips and did it deliberately, hoping it would excite you, and how I thrilled when I saw it did.

'Why did I show you the bed in that room,' she added, 'and leave the door ajar when I came back here to the sofa but to tempt you, and how heart-glad I was to feel your desire in your kiss. I was giving myself before you pushed my head back on the sofa-arm and disarranged all my hair!' she added, pouting and patting it with her hands to make sure it was in order.

'You were astonishingly masterful and quick,' she went on, 'how did you know that I wished you to touch me then? Most men would have gone on kissing and fooling, afraid to act decisively. You must have had a lot of experience? You naughty lad!'

'Shall I tell the truth?' I said. 'I will, just to encourage you to be frank with me. You are the first woman I have ever spent my seed in or had properly.'

'Call it improperly, for God's sake,' she cried laughing aloud with joy, 'you darling virgin, you! Oh! how I wish I was sixteen again and you were my first lover. You would have made me believe in God. Yet you are my first lover,' she added quickly. 'I have only learned the delight and ecstasy of love in your arms.'

Our love-talk lasted for hours till suddenly I guessed it was late and looked at my watch; it was nearly seven-thirty: I was late for supper, which started at half-past six!

'I must go,' I exclaimed, 'or I'll get nothing to eat.'

'I could give you supper,' she added, 'my lips, too, that long for you and — and — but you know.' She added regretfully, 'He might come in and I want to know you better first before seeing you together; a young god and a man! — and the man God's likeness, yet so poor an imitation!'

'Don't, don't,' I said, 'you'll make life harder for yourself — '

'Harder,' she repeated with a sniff of contempt. 'Kiss me, my love, and go if you must. Shall I see you tomorrow? There!' she cried as with a curse, 'I've given myself away: I can't help it; oh, how I want you always: how I shall long for you and count the dull dreary hours! Go, go or I'll never let you — ' and she kissed and clung to me to the door.

'Sweet — tomorrow!' I said, and tore off.

Of course it is manifest that my liaison with Mrs Mayhew had little or nothing to do with love. It was demoniac youthful sex-urge in me and much the same hunger in her, and as soon as the desire was satisfied my judgment of her was as impartial, cool as if she had always been indifferent to me. But with her I think there was a certain attachment and considerable tenderness. In intimate relations between the sexes it is rare indeed that the man gives as much to love as the woman.

Next day at three o'clock I knocked at Mrs Mayhew's: she opened the door herself. I cried, 'How kind of you!' and once in the room drew her to me and kissed her time and time again: she seemed cold and numb.

For some moments she didn't speak, then: 'I feel as if I had passed through fever,' she said, putting her hands through her hair, lifting it in a gesture I was to know well in the days to come. 'Never promise again if you don't come; I thought I should go mad: waiting is a horrible torture! Who kept you — some girl?' and her eyes searched mine.

I excused myself; but her intensity chilled me. At the risk of alienating my girl readers, I must confess this was the effect her passion had on me. When I kissed her, her lips were cold. But by the time we had got upstairs, she had thawed. She shut the door after us gravely and began: 'See how ready I am for you!' and in a moment she had thrown back her robe and stood before me naked. She tossed the garment on a chair; it fell on the floor. She stooped to pick it up with her bottom toward me: I kissed her soft bottom and caught her by it with my hand on her sex.

She turned her head over her shoulder: 'I've washed and scented myself for you, Sir: how do you like the perfume? and how do you like this bush of hair?' and she touched her mount with a grimace. 'I was so ashamed of it as a girl: I used to shave it off, that's what made it grow so thick, I believe. One day my mother saw it and made me stop shaving. Oh! how ashamed of it I was: it's animal, ugly, − don't you hate it? Oh, tell the truth!' she cried, 'Or rather, don't; tell me you love it.'

'I love it,' I exclaimed, 'because it's yours!'

'Oh, you dear lover,' she smiled, 'you always find the right word, the flattering salve for the sore!'

'Are you ready for me,' I asked, 'ripe-ready, or shall I kiss you first and caress pussy?'

'Whatever you do will be right,' she said. 'You know I am rotten-ripe, soft and wet for you always!'

All this while I was taking off my clothes; now I too was naked.

'I want you to draw up your knees,' I said: 'I want to see the Holy of Holies, the shrine of my idolatry.'

At once she did as I asked. Her legs and bottom were well-shaped without being statuesque: but her clitoris was much more than the average button: it stuck out

589

fully half an inch and the inner lips of her vulva hung down a little below the outer lip. I knew I should see prettier pussies. Kate's was better shaped, I felt sure, and the heavy, madder-brown lips put me off a little.

The next moment I began caressing her red clitoris with my hot, stiff organ: Lorna sighed deeply once or twice and her eyes drew it out again to the lips, then in again, and I felt her warm love-juice gush as she drew up her knees even higher to let me further in. 'Oh, it's divine,' she sighed, 'better even than the first time,' and, when my thrusts grew quick and hard as the orgasm shook me, she writhed down on my prick as I withdrew, as if she would hold it, and as my seed spirted into her, she bit my shoulder and held her legs tight as if to keep my sex in her. We lay a few moments bathed in bliss. Then, as I began to move again to sharpen the sensation, she half rose on her arm. 'Do you know,' she said, 'I dreamed yesterday of getting on you and doing it to you, do you mind if I try?'

'No, indeed!' I cried. 'Go to it, I am your prey!' She got up smiling and straddled kneeling across me, and put my cock in her pussy and sank down on me with a deep sigh. She tried to move up and down on my organ and at once came up too high and had to use her hand to put my Tommy in again; then she sank down on it as far as possible. 'I can sink down all right,' she cried, smiling at the double meaning, 'but I cannot rise so well! What fools we women are, we can't master even the act of love; we are so awkward!'

'Your awkwardness, however, excites me,' I said.

'Does it?' she cried. 'Then I'll do my best,' and for

some time she rose and sank rhythmically, but, as her excitement grew, she just let herself lie on me and wiggled her bottom till we both came. She was flushed and hot and I couldn't help asking her a question.

'Does your excitement grow to a spasm of pleasure,' I asked, 'or do you go on getting more and more excited continually?'

'I get more and more excited,' she said, 'till the other day with you, for the first time in my iife, the pleasure became unbearably intense and I was hysterical, you wonder-lover!'

Since then I have read lascivious books in half a dozen languages and they all represent women coming to an orgasm in the act, as men do, followed by a period of content; which only shows that the books are all written by men, and ignorant, insensitive men at that. The truth is: hardly one married woman in a thousand is ever brought to her highest pitch of feeling; usually, just when she begins to feel, her husband goes to sleep. If the majority of husbands satisfied their wives occasionally, the woman's revolt would soon move to another purpose: women want above all a lover who lives to excite them to the top of their bent. As a rule, men through economic conditions marry so late that they have already half-exhausted their virile power before they marry. And when they marry young, they are so ignorant and self-centred that they imagine their wives must be satisfied when they are. Mrs Mayhew told me that her husband had never excited her, really. She denied that she had ever had any real acute pleasure from his embraces.

'Shall I make you hysterical again?' I asked, out of boyish vanity. 'I can, you know!'

'You mustn't tire yourself!' she warned. 'My husband taught me long ago that when a woman tires a man, he gets a distaste for her, and I want your love, your desire, dear, a thousand times more even than the delight you give me — '

'Don't be afraid,' I broke in. 'You are sweet; you couldn't tire me; turn sideways and put your left leg up, and I'll just let my sex caress your clitoris back and forth gently; every now and then I'll let it go right in until our hairs meet.' I kept on this game perhaps half an hour until she first sighed and sighed and then made awkward movements with her pussy which I sought to divine and meet as she wished, when suddenly she cried:

'Oh! Oh! Hurt me, please! hurt me, or I'll bite you! Oh God, oh, oh,' panting, breathless till again the tears poured down!

'You darling,' she sobbed. 'How you can love! Could you go on forever?'

For answer, I put her hand on my sex. 'Just as naughty as ever,' she exclaimed, 'and I am choking, breathless, exhausted! Oh, I'm sorry,' she went on, 'but we should get up, for I don't want my help to know or guess: servants talk — '

I got up and went to the windows; one gave on the porch, but the other directly on the garden. 'What are you looking at?' she asked, coming to me.

'I was just looking for the best way to get out if ever we were surprised,' I said. 'If we leave this window open I can always drop into the garden and get away quickly.'

'You would hurt yourself,' she cried.

'Not a bit of it,' I answered. 'I could drop half as far again without injury; the only thing is, I must have boots on and trousers, or those thorns of yours would gip!'

'You boy,' she exclaimed laughing. 'I think after your strength and passion, it is your boyishness I love best' – and she kissed me again and again.

'I must work,' I warned her; 'Smith has given me a lot to do.'

'Oh, my dear,' she said, her eyes filling with tears, 'that means you won't come tomorrow or,' she added hastily, 'even the day after?'

'I can't possibly,' I declared. 'I have a good week's work in front of me; but you know I'll come the first afternoon I can make myself free and I'll let you know the day before, sweet!'

She looked at me with tearful eyes and quivering lips. 'Love is its own torment!' she sighed, while I dressed and got away quickly.

The truth was I was already satiated. Her passion held nothing new in it: she had taught me all she could and had nothing more in her, I thought; while Kate was prettier and much younger and a virgin. Why shouldn't I confess it? It was Kate's virginity that attracted me irresistibly: I pictures her legs to myself, her hips and thighs . . .

The next few days passed in reading the books Smith had lent me, especially *Das Kapital*, the second book

593

of which, with its frank exposure of the English factory system, was simply enthralling. I read some of Tacitus, too, and Xenophon with a crib, and learned a page of Greek every day by heart, and whenever I felt tired of work I laid siege to Kate. That is, I continued my plan of campaign. One day I called her brother into my room and told him true stories of buffalo hunting and of fighting with Indians; another day I talked theology with the father or drew the dear mother out to tell of her girlish days in Cornwall. 'I never thought I'd come to work like this in my old age, but then children take all and give little; I was no better as a girl, I remember,' – and I got a scene of her brief courtship!

I had won the whole household long before I said a word to Kate beyond the merest courtesies. A week or so passed like this till one day I held them all after dinner while I told the story of our raid into Mexico. I took care, of course, that Kate was out of the room. Towards the end of my tale, Kate came in: at once I hastened to end abruptly, and after excusing myself, went into the garden.

Half an hour later I saw she was in my room tidying up; I took thought and then went up the outside steps. As soon as I saw her I pretended surprise. 'I beg your pardon,' I said. 'I'll just get a book and go at once; please don't let me disturb you!' and I pretended to look for the book.

She turned sharply and looked at me fixedly. 'Why do you treat me like this!' she burst out, shaking with indignation.

'Like what?' I repeated, pretending surprise.

'You know quite well,' she went on angrily, hastily. 'At first I thought it was chance, unintentional; now I know you mean it. Whenever you are talking or telling a story, as soon as I come into the room you stop and hurry away as if you hated me. Why? Why?' she cried with quivering lips. 'What have I done to make you dislike me so?' and the tears gathered in her lovely eyes.

I felt the moment had come: I put my hands on her shoulders and looked with my whole soul into her eyes. 'Did you never guess, Kate, that it might be love, not hate?' I asked.

'No, no!' she cried, the tears falling. 'Love does not act like that!'

'Fear to miss love does, I can assure you,' I cried. 'I thought at first that you disliked me and already I had begun to care for you' (my arms went around her waist and I drew her to me), 'to love you and want you. Kiss me, dear,' and at once she gave me her lips, while my hand got busy on her breasts and then went down of itself to her sex.

Suddenly she looked at me gaily, brightly, while heaving a big sigh of relief. 'I'm glad, glad!' she said. 'If you only knew how hurt I was and how tortured myself; one moment I was angry, then I was sad. Yesterday I made up my mind to speak, but today I said to myself, I'll just be obstinate and cold as he is and now — ' and of her own accord she put her arms around my neck and kissed me — 'you are a dear, dear! Anyway, I love you.'

'You mustn't give me those bird-pecks!' I exclaimed. 'Those are not kisses: I want your lips to open and cling to mine,' and I kissed her while my tongue darted into her mouth and I stroked her sex gently. She flushed, but at first didn't understand; then suddenly she blushed rosy red as her lips grew hot and she fairly ran from the room.

I exulted: I knew I had won: I must be very quiet and reserved and the bird would come to the lure; I felt exultingly certain!

Meanwhile I spent nearly every morning with Smith: golden hours! Always, always before we parted, he showed me some new beauty or revealed some new truth: he seemed to me the most wonderful creature in this strange, sunlit world. I used to hang entranced on his eloquent lips! (Strange! I was sixty-five before I found such a hero-worshipper as I was to Smith, who was only four or five and twenty!) He made me know all the Greek dramatists: Aeschylus, Sophocles and Euripides and put them for me in a truer light than English or German scholars have set them yet. He knew that Sophocles was the greatest, and from his lips I learned every chorus in the *Oedipus Rex* and *Colonnus* before I had completely mastered the Greek grammar; indeed, it was the supreme beauty of the literature that forced me to learn the language. In teaching me the choruses, he was careful to point out that it was possible to keep the measure and yet mark the accent too: in fact, he made classic Greek a living language to me, as living as English. And he would not let me neglect Latin: in the first year with him I knew poems of Catullus by heart, almost as well as I knew Swinburne. Thanks to Professor Smith, I had no difficulty in entering the junior class at the university; in fact, after my first three or four months' work I was easily the first in the class, which included Ned Stephens, the brother of Smith's inamorata. I soon discovered that Smith was heels over head in love with Kate Stephens, shot through the heart, as Mercutio would say, with a fair girl's blue eye!

And small wonder, for Kate was lovely: a little above middle height with slight, rounded figure and most attractive face: the oval, a thought long, rather than round, with dainty, perfect features, lit up by a pair of superlative grey-blue eyes, eyes by turns delightful and reflective and appealing, that mirrored a really extraordinary intelligence. She was in the senior class and afterwards for years held the position of Professor of Greek in the university. I shall have something to say of her in a later volume of this history, for I met her again in New York nearly fifty years later. But in 1872 or '73, her brother Ned, a handsome lad of eighteen who was in my class, interested me more. The only other member of the senior class of this time was a fine fellow, Ned Bancroft, who later came to France with me to study.

At this time, curiously enough, Kate Stephens was by way of being engaged to Ned Bancroft; but already it was plain that she was in love with Smith, and my outspoken admiration of Smith helped her, I hope, as I am sure it helped him, to a better mutual understanding. Bancroft accepted the situation with extraordinary self-sacrifice, losing neither Smith's nor Kate's friendship: I have seldom seen nobler self-abnegation; indeed, his high-mindedness in this crisis was what first won my admiration and showed me his other fine qualities.

Almost in the beginning I had serious disquietude: every little while Smith was ill and had to keep to his bed for a day or two. There was no explanation of this illness, which puzzled me and caused me a certain anxiety.

One day in midwinter there was a new development. Smith was in doubt how to act and confided in me. He had found Professor Kellogg, in whose house he lived, trying to kiss the pretty help, Rose, entirely against her will. Smith was emphatic on this point: the girl was struggling angrily to free herself, when by chance he interrupted them.

I relieved Smith's solemn gravity a little by roaring with laughter. The idea of an old professor and clergyman trying to win a girl by force filled me with amusement: 'What a fool the man must be!' was my English judgment; Smith took the American high moral tone at first.

'Think of his disloyalty to his wife in the same house,' he cried, 'and then the scandal if the girl talked, and she is sure to talk!'

'Sure not to talk,' I corrected. 'Girls are afraid of the effect of such revelations; besides a word from you asking her to shield Mrs Kellogg will ensure her silence.'

'Oh, I cannot advise her,' cried Smith. 'I will not

be mixed up in it: I told Kellogg at the time, I must leave the house, yet I don't know where to go! It's too disgraceful of him! His wife is really a dear woman!'

For the first time I became conscious of a rooted difference between Smith and myself: his high moral condemnation on very insufficient data seemed to me childish, but no doubt many of my readers will think my tolerance a proof of my shameless libertinism! However, I jumped at the opportunity of talking to Rose on such a scabrous matter and at the same time solved Smith's difficulty by proposing that he should come and take room and board with the Gregorys — a great stroke of practical diplomacy on my part, or so it appeared to me, for thereby I did the Gregorys, Smith and myself an immense, an incalculable service. Smith jumped at the idea, asked me to see about it at once and let him know, and then rang for Rose.

She came half-scared, half-angry, on the defensive, I could see; so I spoke first, smiling. 'Oh Rose,' I said, 'Professor Smith has been telling me of your trouble; but you ought not to be angry: for you are so pretty that no wonder a man wants to kiss you; you must blame your lovely eyes and mouth.'

Rose laughed outright: she had come expecting reproof and found sweet flattery.

'There's only one thing, Rose,' I went on. 'The story would hurt Mrs Kellogg if it got out and she's not very strong, so you must say nothing about it, for her sake. That's what Professor Smith wanted to say to you,' I added.

'I'm not likely to tell,' cried Rose. 'I'll soon forget

all about it, but I guess I'd better get another job: he's liable to try again, though I gave him a good, hard slap,' and she laughed merrily.

'I'm so glad for Mrs Kellogg's sake,' said Smith gravely, 'and if I can help you get another place, please call upon me.'

'I guess I'll have no difficulty,' answered Rose flippantly, with a shade of dislike of the professor's solemnity. 'Mrs Kellogg will give me a good character,' and the healthy young minx grinned, 'besides I'm not sure but I'll go stay home a spell. I'm fed up with working and would like a holiday, and mother wants me . . .'

'Where do you live, Rose?' I asked with a keen eye for future opportunities.

'On the other side of the river,' she replied, 'next door to Elder Conklin's, where your brother boards,' she added smiling.

When Rose went I begged Smith to pack his boxes, for I would get him the best room at the Gregorys' and assured him it was really large and comfortable and would hold all his books, etc.; and off I went to make my promise good. On the way, I set myself to think how I could turn the kindness I was doing the Gregorys to the advantage of my love. I decided to make Kate a partner in the good deed, or at least a herald of the good news. So when I got home I rang the bell in my room, and as I had hoped Kate answered it. When I heard her footsteps I was shaking, hot with desire, and now I wish to describe a feeling I then began to notice in myself. I longed to take possession of the girl, so to speak, abruptly, ravish her in fact, or at least thrust both hands up her dress at once and feel her bottom and sex altogether; but already I knew enough to realize certainly that girls prefer gentle and courteous approaches. Why? Of the fact I am sure. So I said, 'Come in, Kate,' gravely. 'I want to ask you whether the best bedroom is still free, and if you'd like Professor Smith to have it, if I could get him to come here?'

'I'm sure Mother would be delighted,' she exclaimed.

'You see,' I went on, 'I'm trying to serve you all I can, yet you don't even kiss me of your own accord.' She smiled, and so I drew her to the bed and lifted her up on it. I saw her glance and answered it: 'The door is shut, dear,' and half lying on her, I began kissing her passionately, while my hands went up her clothes to her sex. To my delight she wore no drawers, but at first she kept her legs tight together frowning. 'Love denies nothing, Kate,' I said gravely; slowly she drew her legs apart, half-pouting, half-smiling, and let me caress her sex. When her love-juice came, I kissed her and stopped. 'It's dangerous here,' I said, 'that door you came in is open; but I must see your lovely limbs,' and I turned up her dress. I hadn't exaggerated; she had limbs like a Greek statue and her triangle of brown hair lay in little silky curls on her belly and then — the sweetest cunny in the world. I bent down and kissed it.

In a moment Kate was on her feet, smoothing her dress down. 'What a boy you are,' she exclaimed, 'but that's partly why I love you; oh, I hope you'll love me half as much. Say you will, Sir, and I'll do anything you wish!'

'I will,' I replied, 'but oh, I'm glad you want love; can you come to me tonight? I want a couple of hours with you uninterrupted.'

'This afternoon,' she said, 'I'll say I'm going for a walk and I'll come to you, dear! They are all resting then or out and I shan't be missed.'

I could only wait and think. One thing was fixed in me, I must have her, make her mine before Smith came: he was altogether too fascinating, I thought, to be trusted with such a pretty girl; but I was afraid she would bleed and I did not want to hurt her this first time, so I went out and bought a syringe and a pot of cold cream which I put beside my bed.

Oh, how that dinner lagged! Mrs Gregory thanked me warmly for my kindness to them all (which seemed to me pleasantly ironical!) and Mr Gregory followed her lead; but at length everyone had finished and I went to my room to prepare. First I locked the outside door and drew down the blinds: then I studied the bed and turned it back and arranged a towel along the edge; happily the bed was just about the right height! Then I loosened my trousers, unbuttoned the front and pulled up my shirt: a little later Kate put her lovely face in at the door and slipped inside. I shot the bolt and began kissing her; girls are strange mortals; she had taken off her corset, just as I had put a towel handy. I lifted up her clothes and touched her sex, caressing it gently while kissing her: in a moment or two her love-milk came.

I lifted her up on the bed, pushed down my trousers, anointed my prick with the cream and then, parting her legs and getting her to pull her knees up, I drew her bottom to the edge of the bed: she frowned at that, but I explained quickly: 'It may give a little pain, at first, dear: and I want to give you as little as possible,' and I slipped the head of my cock gently, slowly into her. Even greased, her pussy was tight and at the very entrance I felt the obstacle, her maidenhead, in the way; I lay on her and kissed her and let her or Mother Nature help me.

As soon as Kate found that I was leaving it to her, she pushed forward boldly and the obstacle yielded. 'O – O!' she cried, and then pushed forward again roughly and my organ went in her to the hilt and her clitoris must have felt my belly. Resolutely, I refrained from thrusting or withdrawing for a minute or two and then drew out slowly to her lips and, as I pushed Tommy gently in again, she leaned up and kissed me passionately. Slowly, with extremest care, I governed myself and pushed in and out with long slow thrusts, though I longed, longed to plunge it in hard and quicken the strokes as much as possible; but I knew from Mrs Mayhew that the long, gentle thrusts and slow withdrawals were the aptest to excite a woman's passion and I was determined to win Kate.

In two or three minutes, she had again let down a flow of love-juice, or so I believed, and I kept right on with the love-game, knowing that the first experience is never forgotten by a girl and resolved to keep on to dinner-time if necessary to make her first love-joust ever memorable to her. Kate lasted longer than Mrs Mayhew; I came ever so many times, passing ever more slowly from orgasm to orgasm before she began to move to me; but at length her breath began to get shorter and shorter and she held me to her violently, moving her pussy the while up and down harshly against my manroot. Suddenly she relaxed and fell back: there was no hysteria; but plainly I could feel the mouth of her womb fasten on my cock as if to suck it. That excited me fiercely and for the first time I indulged in quick, hard thrusts till a spasm of intensest pleasure shook me and my seed spirted or seemed to spirt for the sixth or seventh time.

When I had finished kissing and praising my lovely partner and drew away, I was horrified; the bed was a sheet of blood and some had gone on my pants: Kate's thighs and legs even were all incarnadined, making the lovely ivory white of her skin, one red. You may imagine how softly I used a towel on her legs and sex before I showed her the results of our love-passage. To my astonishment she was unaffected. 'You must take the sheet away and burn it,' she said. 'or drop it in the river: I guess it won't be the first.'

'Did it hurt much?' I asked.

'At first a good deal,' she replied, 'but soon the pleasure overpowered the smart and I would not even forget the pain. I love you so. I am not even afraid of consequences with you: I trust you absolutely and love to trust you and run whatever risks you wish.'

'You darling!' I cried, 'I don't believe there will be

any consequences; but I want you to go to the basin and use this syringe. I'll tell you why afterwards.'

At once she went over to the basin. 'I feel funny, weak,' she said, 'as if I were — I can't describe it — shaky on my legs. I'm glad now I don't wear drawers in summer, they'd get wet.' Her ablutions completed and the sheet withdrawn and done up in paper, I shot back the bolt and we began our talk. I found her intelligent and kindly but ignorant and ill-read: still she was not prejudiced and was eager to know all about babies and how they were made. I told her how my seed was composed of tens of thousands of tadpole-shaped animalculae. Already in her vagina and womb these infinitely little things had a race: they could move nearly an inch an hour and the strongest and quickest got up first to where her egg was waiting in the middle of her womb. My little tadpole, the first to arrive, thrust his head into her egg and thus having accomplished his work of impregnation, perished, love and death being twins.

The curious thing was that this indescribably small tadpole should be able to transmit all the qualities of all his progenitors in certain proportions; no such miracle was ever imagined by any religious teacher. More curious still, the living foetus in the womb passes in nine months through all the chief changes that the human race has gone through in countless aeons of time in its progress from the tadpole to the man. Till the fifth month the foetus is practically a four-legged animal.

I told her that it was accepted today that the weeks

occupied in the womb in any metamorphosis correspond exactly to the ages it occupied in reality. Thus it was upright, a two-legged animal, ape and then man in the womb for the last three months, and this corresponded nearly to one-third of man's whole existence on this earth. Kate listened, enthraled, I thought, till she asked me suddenly:

'But what makes one child a boy and another a girl?'

'The nearest we've come to a law on the matter,' I said, 'is contained in the so-called law of contraries: that is, if the man is stronger than the woman, the children will be mostly girls; if the woman is greatly younger or stronger, the progeny will be chiefly boys. This bears out the old English proverb: 'Any weakling can make a boy, but it takes a man to make a girl.'

Kate laughed and just then a knock came to the door. 'Come in!' I cried, and then the colored maid came in with a note. 'A lady's just been and left it,' said Jenny. I saw it was from Mrs Mayhew, so I crammed it into my pocket, saying regretfully: 'I must answer it soon.' Kate excused herself and after a long, long kiss went to prepare supper, while I read Mrs Mayhew's note, which was short, if not exactly sweet:

Eight days and no Frank, and no news; you cannot want to kill me: come today if possible.

Lorna

I replied at once, saying I would come on the morrow, that I was so busy I didn't know where to turn, but would be with her sure on the morrow and I signed 'Your Frank.'

Of course, I went to Mrs Mayhew that next afternoon even before three. She met me without a word, so gravely that I did not even kiss her, but began explaining what Smith was to me and how I could not do enough for him who was everything to my mind, as she was (God help me!) to my heart and body; and I kissed her cold lips, while she shook her head sadly.

'We have a sixth sense, we women, when we are in love,' she began. 'I feel a new influence in you; I scent danger in the air you bring with you: don't ask me to explain: I can't; but my heart is heavy and cold as death. If you leave me, there'll be a catastrophe: the fall from such a height of happiness must be fatal. If you can feel pleasure away from me, you no longer love me. I feel none except in having you, seeing you, thinking of you — none! Oh, why can't you love like a woman loves! No! like I love: it would be heaven; for you and you alone satisfy the insatiable; you leave me bathed in bliss, sighing with satisfaction, happy as the Queen in Heaven!'

'I have much to tell you, new things to say,' I began in haste.

'Come upstairs,' I broke in, interrupting myself. 'I want to see you as you are now, with the color in your cheeks, the light in your eyes, the vibration in your voice, come!'

And she came like a sad sybil. 'Who gave you the

tact,' she began while we were undressing, 'the tact to praise always?'

I seized her and stood naked against her, body to body. 'What new things have you to tell me?' I asked, lifting her into the bed and getting in beside her, cuddling up to her warmer body.

'There's always something new in my love,' she cried, cupping my face with her slim hands and taking my lips with hers.

'Oh, how I desired you yesternoon, for I took the letter to your house myself and heard you talking in your room, perhaps with Smith,' she added, sounding my eyes with hers. 'I'm longing to believe it; but, when I heard your voice, or imagined I did, I felt the lips of my sex open and shut and then it began to burn and itch intolerably. I was on the point of going in to you, but, instead, turned and hurried away, raging at you and at myself – '

'I will not let you even talk such treason,' I cried, separating her soft thighs, as I spoke, and sliding between them. In a moment my sex was in her and we were one body, while I drew it out slowly and then pushed it in again, her naked body straining to mine.

'Oh,' she cried, 'as you draw out, my heart follows your sex in fear of losing it and as you push in again, it opens wide in ecstasy and wants you all, all – ' and she kissed me with hot lips.

'Here is something new,' she exclaimed, 'food for your vanity from my love! Mad as you make me with your love-thrusts, for at one moment I am hot and dry with desire, the next moment wet with passion, bathed in love, I could live with you all my life without having you, if you wished it, or if it would do you good. Do you believe me?'

'Yes,' I replied, continuing the love-game, but occasionally withdrawing to rub her clitoris with my sex and then slowly burying him in her cunt again to the hilt.

'We women have no souls but love,' she said faintly, her eyes dying as she spoke.

'I torture myself to think of some new pleasure for you, and yet you'll leave me, I feel you will, for some silly girl who can't feel a tithe of what I feel or give you what I give – ' She began here to breathe quickly. 'I've been thinking how to give you more pleasure; let me try. Your seed, darling, is dear to me: I don't want it in my sex; I want to feel you thrill and so I want your sex in my mouth, I want to drink your essence and I will – ' and suiting the action to the word, she slipped down in the bed and took my sex in her mouth and began rubbing it up and down till my seed spirted in long jets, filling her mouth while she swallowed it greedily.

'Now do I love you, Sir!' she exclaimed, drawing herself upon me again and nestling against me. 'Wait till some girl does that to you and you'll know she loves you to distraction or, better still, to self-destruction.'

'Why do you talk of any other girl?' I chided her. 'I don't imagine you going with another man; why should you torment yourself just as causelessly?'

She shook her head. 'My fears are prophetic,' she sighed. 'I'm willing to believe it hasn't happened yet, though — Ah, God, the torturing thought! The mere dread of you going with another drives me crazy; I could kill her, the bitch: why doesn't she get a man of her own? How dare she even look at you?' and she clasped me tightly to her. Nothing loath, I pushed my sex into her again and began the slow movement that excited her so quickly and me so gradually for, even while using my skill to give her the utmost pleasure, I could not help comparing and I realized surely enough that Kate's pussy was smaller and firmer and gave me infinitely more pleasure; still I kept on for her delight. And now again she began to pant and choke and, as I continued ploughing her body and touching her womb with every slow thrust, she began to cry inarticulately with little short cries growing higher in intensity till suddenly she squealed like a shot rabbit and then shrieked with laughter, breaking down in a storm of sighs and sobs and floods of tears.

As usual, her intensity chilled me a little; for her paroxysm aroused no corresponding heat in me, tending even to check my pleasure by the funny, irregular movements she made.

Suddenly, I heard steps going away from the door, light, stealing steps: who could it be? The servant? or — ?

Lorna had heard them, too, and though still panting and swallowing convulsively, she listened intently, while her great eyes wandered in thought. I knew I could leave the riddle to her: it was my task to reassure and caress her.

I got up and went over to the open window for

a breath of air and suddenly I saw Lily run quickly across the grass and disappear in the next house: so she was the listener! When I recalled Lorna's gasping cries, I smiled to myself. If Lily tried to explain them to herself, she would have an uneasy hour, I guessed.

When Lorna had dressed, and she dressed quickly and went downstairs hastily to convince herself, I think, that her maid had not spied on her, I waited in the sitting room. I must warn Lorna that my 'studies' would only allow me to give one day a week to our pleasures.

'Oh,' she cried, turning pale as I explained, 'didn't I know it!'

'But Lorna,' I pleaded, 'didn't you say you could do without me altogether if 'twas for my good?'

'No, no, no! a thousand times no!' she cried. 'I said if you were with me always, I could do without passion; but this starvation fare once a week! Go, go,' she cried, 'or I'll say something I'll regret. Go!' and she pushed me out of the door, and thinking it better in view of the future, I went.

The truth is, I was glad to get away; novelty is the soul of passion. There's an old English proverb: 'Fresh cunt, fresh courage.' On my way home I thought oftener of the slim, dark figure of Lily than of the woman, every hill and valley of whose body was not familiar to me, whereas Lily with her narrow hips and straight flanks must have a tiny sex. I thought, 'D . . . n Lily,' and I hastened to Smith.

*   *   *

611

I went downstairs to the dining room, hoping to find Kate alone. I was lucky: she had persuaded her mother, who was tired, to go to bed and was just finishing her tidying up.

'I want to see you, Kate,' I said, trying to kiss her. She drew her head aside: 'That's why you've kept away all afternoon, I suppose,' and she looked at me with a side-long glance. An inspiration came to me. 'Kate,' I exclaimed, 'I had to be fitted for my new clothes!'

'Forgive me,' she cried at once, that excuse being valid. 'I thought, I feared – oh, I'm suspicious without reason, I know – am jealous without cause. There! I confess!' and the great hazel eyes turned on me full of love.

I played with her breasts, whispering, 'When am I to see you naked, Kate? I want to; when?'

'You've seen most of me!' and she laughed joyously.

'All right,' I said, turning away, 'if you are resolved to make fun of me and be mean to me – '

'Mean to you!' she cried, catching me and swinging me round. 'I could easier be mean to myself. I'm glad you want to see me, glad and proud, and tonight, if you'll leave your door open, I'll come to you: mean, oh – ' and she gave me her soul in a kiss.

'Isn't it risky?' I asked.

'I tried the stairs this afternoon,' she glowed. 'They don't creak: no one will hear, so don't sleep or I'll surprise you.' By way of sealing the compact, I put my hand up her clothes and caressed her sex: it was hot and soon opened to me.

'There now, Sir, go,' she smiled, 'or you'll make me very naughty and I have a lot to do!'

'How do you mean "naughty",' I said, 'tell me what you feel, please!'

'I feel my heart beating,' she said, 'and, and – oh! wait till tonight and I'll try to tell you, dear,' and she pushed me out of the door.

For the first time in my life I notice here that the writer's art is not only inferior to reality in keenness of sensation and emotion, but also more same, monotonous even, because of showing the tiny, yet ineffable differences of the same feeling which difference of personality brings with it. I seem to be repeating to myself in describing Kate's love after Mrs Mayhew's, making the girl's feeling a fainter replica of the woman's. In reality the two were completely different. Mrs Mayhew's feelings, long repressed, flamed with the heat of an afternoon in July or August, while in Kate's one felt the freshness and cool of a summer morning, shot through with the suggestion of heat to come. And this comparison, even, is inept, because it leaves out the account the effect of Kate's beauty, the great hazel eyes, the rosied skin, the superb figure. Besides, there was a glamour of the spirit about Kate: Lorna Mayhew would never give me a note that didn't spring from passion; in Kate I felt a spiritual personality and the thrill of undeveloped possibilities. And still, using my utmost skill, I haven't shown my reader the enormous superiority of the girl and her more unselfish love. But I haven't finished yet.

Smith had given me *The Mill on the Floss* to read; I had never tried George Eliot before and I found that this book almost deserved Smith's praise. I had read till about one o'clock when my heart heard her; or was it some thrill of expectance? The next moment my door opened and she came in with the mane of hair about her shoulders and a long dressing gown reaching to her stocking feet. I got up like a flash, but she had already closed the door and bolted it. I drew her to the bed and stopped her from throwing off the dressing gown. 'Let me take off your stockings first,' I whispered. 'I want you all imprinted on me!'

The next moment she stood there naked, the flickering flame of the candle throwing quaint arabesques of light on her ivory body. I gazed and gazed: from the navel down she was perfect; I turned her round and the back, too, the bottom, even, was faultless, though large: but alas! the breasts were far too big for beauty, too soft to excite! I must think only of the bold curve of her hips, I reflected, the splendour of the firm thighs, the flesh of which had the hard outline of marble, and her − sex. I put her on the bed and opened her thighs: her pussy was ideally perfect.

At once I wanted to get into her; but she pleaded: 'Please, dear, come into bed, I'm cold and want you.' So in I got and began kissing her.

Soon she grew warm and I pulled off my night-shirt and my middle finger was caressing her sex that opened quickly. 'Ah,' she said, drawing in her breath quickly, 'it still hurts.' I put my sex gently against hers, moving it up and down slowly till she drew up her knees to let me in; but, as soon as the head entered, her face puckered a little with pain and, as I had had a long afternoon, I was the more inclined to forbear, and accordingly I drew away and took place beside her.

'I cannot bear to hurt you,' I said. 'Love's pleasure must be natural.'

'You're sweet!' she whispered. 'I'm glad you stopped, for it shows you really care for me and not just for the pleasure,' and she kissed me lovingly.

'Kate, reward me,' I said, 'by telling me just what you felt when I first had you,' and I put her hand on my hot stiff sex to encourage her.

'It's impossible,' she said, flushing a little. 'There was such a throng of new feelings; why, this evening, waiting in bed for the time to pass and thinking of you, I felt a strange prickling sensation in the inside of my thighs that I never felt before and now' — and she hid her glowing face against my neck, 'I feel it again!

'Love is funny, isn't it?' she whispered the next moment. 'Now the pricking sensation is gone and the front part of my sex burns and itches. Oh! I must touch it!'

'Let me,' I cried, and, in a moment, I was on her, working my organ up and down on her clitoris, the porch, so to speak, of Love's temple. A little later she herself sucked the head into her hot, dry pussy and then closed her legs as if in pain to stop me going further; but I began to rub my sex up and down on her tickler, letting it slide right in every now and then, till she panted and her love-juice came and my weapon sheathed itself in her naturally. I soon began the very slow and gentle in-and-out movements which increased her excitement steadily while giving her more and more pleasure, till I came and immediately she lifted my chest up from her breasts with both hands and showed me her glowing face. 'Stop, boy,' she gasped, 'please, my heart's fluttering so! I came too, you know, just with you,' and indeed I felt her trembling all over convulsively.

I drew out and for safety's sake got her to use the syringe, having already explained its efficacy to her: she was adorably awkward and, when she had finished, I took her to bed again and held her to me, kissing her. 'So you really love me, Kate!'

'Really,' she said, 'you don't know how much! I'll try never to suspect anything or to be jealous again.' She went on, 'It's a hateful thing, isn't it? But I want to see your classroom: would you take me up once to the university?'

'Why, of course,' I cried. 'I should be only too glad; I'll take you tomorrow afternoon. Or better still,' I added, 'come up the hill at four o'clock and I'll meet you at the entrance.'

And so it was settled and Kate went back to her room as noiselessly as she had come.

The next afternoon I found her waiting in the university hall ten minutes before the hour, for our lectures beginning at the hour always stopped after forty-five minutes to give us time to be punctual at any other classroom. After showing her everything of interest, we walked home together laughing and talking, when, a hundred yards from Mrs Mayhew's, we met that lady, face to face. I don't know how I looked, for being a little short-sighted, I hadn't recognized her till she was within ten yards of me; but her glance pierced me. She bowed with a look that took us both in. I lifted my hat and we passed on.

'Who's that?' exclaimed Kate. 'What a strange look she gave us!'

'She's the wife of a gambler,' I replied as indifferently as I could. 'He gives me work now and then,' I went on, strangely forecasting the future. Kate looked at me, probing, then, 'I don't mind. I'm glad she's quite old!'

'As old as both of us put together!' I retorted traitorously, and we went in.

These love-passages with Mrs Mayhew and Kate, plus my lessons and my talks with Smith, fairly represent my life's happenings for this whole year from seventeen to eighteen, with this solitary qualification, that my afternoons with Lorna became less and less agreeable to me.

As soon as I returned from the Eldridge House to lodge with the Gregorys again, Kate showed herself just as kind to me as ever. She would come to my bedroom twice or thrice a week and was always welcome, but again and again I felt that her mother was intent on keeping us apart as much as possible, and at length she arranged that Kate should pay a visit to some English friends who were settled in Kansas City. Kate postponed the visit several times, but at length she had to yield to her mother's entreaties and

advice. By this time my boardings were bringing m
in a good deal, and so I promised to accompany Kat
and spend the whole night with her in some Kansa
City hotel.

We got to the hotel about ten and bold as brass
registered as Mr and Mrs William Wallace and wer
up to our room with Kate's luggage, my heart beatin
in my throat. Kate, too, was 'all of a quiver,' as sh
confessed to me a little later, but what a night we had
Kate resolved to show me all her love and gave hersel
to me passionately, but she never took the initiative
I noticed, as Mrs Mayhew used to do.

At first I kissed her and talked a little, but as soo
as she had arranged her things, I began to undress her
When her chemise fell, all glowing with my caressings
she asked, 'You really like that?' and she put her han
over her sex, standing there naked like a Greek Venus
'Naturally,' I exclaimed, 'and these, too,' and I kisse
and sucked her nipples until they grew rosy-red.

'Is it possible to do it − standing up?' she asked
in some confusion.

'Of course,' I replied. 'Let's try! But what put tha
into your head?'

'I saw a man and a girl behind the church near ou
house,' she whispered, 'and I wondered how − ' an
she blushed rosily. As I got into her, I felt difficulty
her pussy was really small and this time seemed ho
and dry: I felt her wince and, at once, withdrew. 'Doe
it still hurt, Kate?' I asked.

'A little at first,' she replied. 'But I don't mind,
she hastened to add, 'I like the pain!'

618

By way of answer, I slipped my arms around her, under her bottom, and carried her to the bed. 'I will not hurt you tonight,' I said, 'I'll make you give down your love-juice first and then there'll be no pain.'

A few kisses and she sighed: 'I'm wet now,' and I got into bed and put my sex against hers.

'I'm going to leave everything to you,' I said, 'but please don't hurt yourself.' She put her hand down to my sex and guided it in, sighing a little with satisfaction as bit by bit it slipped home.

After the first ecstasy, I got her to use the syringe while I watched her curiously. When she came back to bed, 'No danger now,' I cried, 'no danger; my love is queen!'

'You darling lover!' she cried, her eyes wide, as if in wonder. 'My sex throbs and itches and oh! I feel prickings on the inside of my thighs: I want you dreadfully, Frank,' and she stretched out as she spoke, drawing up her knees.

I got on top of her and softly, slowly let my sex slide into her and then began the love-play. When my second orgasm came, I indulged myself with quick, short strokes, though I knew that she preferred the long slow movement, for I was resolved to give her every sensation this golden night. When she felt me begin again the long slow movement she loved, she sighed two or three times and putting her hands on my buttocks, drew me close but otherwise made little sign of feeling for perhaps half an hour. I kept right on; the slow movement now gave me but little pleasure: It was rather a task than a joy; but I was resolved to give her a feast. I don't know how lon the bout lasted, but once I withdrew and bega rubbing her clitoris and the front of her sex, an panting she nodded her head and rubbed hersel ecstatically against my sex, and after I had begun th slow movement again, 'Please, Frank!' she gasped, ' can't stand more: I'm going crazy — choking!'

Strange to say, her words excited me more than th act: I felt my spasm coming and roughly, savagely thrust in my sex at the same time, kneeling betweer her legs so as to be able to play back and forth on he tickler as well. 'I'll ravish you!' I cried and gave mysel to the keen delight. As my seed spirted, she didn' speak, but lay there still and white; I jumped out o the bed, got a spongeful of cold water and used it or her forehead.

At once, to my joy, she opened her eyes. 'I'm sorry, she gasped, and took a drink of water, 'but I was so tired, I must have slept. You dear heart!' When I hae put down the sponge and glass, I slipped into her agair and in a little while she became hysterical: 'I can't hel crying, Frank, love,' she sighed. 'I'm so happy, dear You'll always love me? Won't you? Sweet!' Naturally I reassured her with promises of enduring affectior and many kisses. Finally, I put my left arm round her neck and so fell asleep with my head on her soft breast.

In the morning we ran another course, though, sooth to say, Kate was more curious than passionate.

'I want to study you!' she said, and took my sex in her hands and then my balls. 'What are they for?' she asked, and I had to explain that that was where my seed was secreted. She made a face, so I added, 'You have a similar manufactory, my dear, but it's inside you, the ovaries they are called, and it takes them a month to make one egg, whereas my balls make millions in an hour. I often wonder why?'

After getting Kate an excellent breakfast, I put her in a cab and she reached her friend's house just at the proper time, but the girl friend could never understand how they had missed each other at the station.

I returned to Lawrence the same day, wondering what fortune had in store for me.

One evening I almost ran into Lily. Kate was still away in Kansas City, so I stopped eagerly enough to have a talk, for Lily had always interested me. After the first greetings she told me she was going home. 'They are all out, I believe,' she added. At once I offered to accompany her and she consented. It was early summer but already warm, and when we went into the parlor and Lily took a seat on the sofa, her thin white dress defined her slim figure seductively.

'What do you do,' she asked mischievously, 'now that dear Mrs Mayhew's gone? You must miss her!' she added suggestively.

'I do,' I confessed boldly. 'I wonder if you'd have pluck enough to tell me the truth,' I went on.

'Pluck?' She wrinkled her forehead and pursed her large mouth.

'Courage, I mean,' I said.

'Oh, I have courage,' she rejoined.

'Did you ever come upstairs to Mrs Mayhew's

bedroom,' I asked, 'when I had gone up for a book?'
The black eyes danced and she laughed knowingly.

'Mrs Mayhew said that she had taken you upstairs
to bathe your poor head after dancing,' she retorted
disdainfully, 'but I don't care: it's nothing to do with
me what you do!'

'It has too,' I went on, carrying the war into her
country.

'How?' she asked.

'Why the first day you went away and left me,
though I was really ill,' I said, 'so I naturally believed
that you disliked me, though I thought you were
lovely!'

'I'm not lovely,' she said. 'My mouth's too big and
I'm too slight.'

'Don't malign yourself,' I replied earnestly; 'that's
just why you are seductive and excite a man.'

'Really?' she cried, and so the talk went on, while
I cudgelled my brains for an opportunity but found
none, and all the while was in fear lest her father and
mother should return. At length, angry with myself,
I got up to go on some pretext and she accompanied
me to the stoop. I said goodbye on the top step and
then jumped down by the side with a prayer in my
heart that she'd come a step or two down, and she
did. There she stood, her hips on a level with my
mouth; in a moment my hands went up her dress,
the right to her sex, the left to her bottom behind
to hold her. The thrill as I touched her half-fledged
sex was almost painful in intensity. Her first
movement brought her sitting down on the step above

622

me and at once my finger was busy in her slit.

'How dare you!' she cried, but not angrily. 'Take your hand away!'

'Oh, how lovely your sex is!' I exclaimed, as if astounded. 'Oh, I must see it and have you, you miracle of beauty,' and my left hand drew down her head for a long kiss while my middle finger still continued its caress. Of a sudden her lips grew hot and at once I whispered, 'Won't you love me, dear? I want you so: I'm burning and itching with desire. (I knew she was!) Please; I won't hurt you and I'll take care. Please, love, no one will know,' and the end of it was that right there on the porch I drew her to me and put my sex against hers and began the rubbing of her tickler and front part of her sex that I knew would excite her. In a moment she came and her love-dew wet my sex and excited me terribly; but I kept on frigging her with my man-root while restraining myself from coming by thinking of other things, till she kissed me of her own accord and suddenly moving forward pushed my prick right into her pussy.

To my astonishment, there was no obstacle, no maidenhead to break through, though her sex itself was astonishingly small and tight. I didn't scruple then to let my seed come, only withdrawing to the lips and rubbing her clitoris the while, and, as soon as my spirting ceased, my root glided again into her and continued the slow in-and-out movement till she panted with her head on my shoulder and asked me to stop. I did as she wished, for I knew I had won another wonderful mistress.

We went into the house again, for she insisted I should meet her father and mother, and, while we were waiting, she showed me her lovely tiny breasts, scarcely larger than small apples, and I became aware of something childish in her mind which matched the childish outlines of her lovely, half-formed hips and pussy.

'I thought that you were in love with Mrs Mayhew,' she confessed, 'and I couldn't make out why she made such funny noises. But now I know,' she added, 'you naughty dear, for I felt my heart fluttering just now and I was nearly choking.'

I don't know why, but that ravishing of Lily made her dear to me. I resolved to see her naked and to make her thrill to ecstasy as soon as possible, and then and there we made a meeting place on the far side of the church, whence I knew I could bring her to my room at the Gregorys in a minute; and then I went home, for it was late and I didn't particularly want to meet her folks.

The next night I met Lily by the church and took her to my room. She laughed aloud with delight as we entered, for indeed she was almost like a boy of bold, adventurous spirit. She confessed to me that my challenge of her pluck had pleased her intimately.

'I never took a "dare"!' she cried in her American slang, tossing her head.

'I'll give you two,' I whispered, 'right now: the first is, I dare you to strip naked as I'm going to do, and I'll tell you the other when we're in bed.'

Again she tossed her little blue-black head. 'Pooh,'

she cried, 'I'll be undressed first,' and she was. Her beauty made my pulses hammer and parched my mouth. No one could help admiring her: she was very slight, with tiny breasts, as I have said, flat belly and straight flanks and hips: her triangle was only brushed in, so to speak, with fluffy soft hairs, and, as I held her naked body against mine, the look and feel of her exasperated my desire. I still admired Kate's riper, richer, more luscious outlines: her figure was nearer my boyish ideal; but Lily represented a type of adolescence destined to grow on me mightily. In fact, as my youthful virility decreased, my love of opulent feminine charms diminished and grew more and more to love slender, youthful outlines with the signs of sex rather indicated than pronounced. What an all-devouring appetite Rubens confesses with the great, hanging breasts and uncouth fat pink bottoms of his Venuses!

I lifted Lily on the bed and separated her legs to study her pussy. She made a face at me; but, as I rubbed my hot sex against her little button that I could hardly see, she smiled and lay back contentedly. In a minute or two, her love-juice came and I got into bed on her and slipped my root into her small cunt; even when the lips were wide open, it was closed to the eye and this and her slim nakedness excited me uncontrollably. I continued the slow movements for a few minutes; but once she moved her sex quickly down on mine as I drew out to the lips, and gave me an intense thrill. I felt my seed coming and I let myself go in short, quick thrusts that soon brought on my spasm of pleasure and I lifted her little body against mine and crushed my lips on hers: she was strangely tantalizing, exciting like strong drink.

I took her out of bed and used the syringe in her, explaining its purpose, and then went to bed again and gave her the time of her life! Lying between her legs but side by side an hour later, I dared her to tell me how she had lost her maidenhead. I had to tell her first what it was. She maintained stoutly that 'no feller' had ever touched her except me and I believed her, for she admitted having caressed herself ever since she was ten; at first she could not even get her forefinger into her pussy she told me.

About eleven o'clock she dressed and went home, after making another appointment with me.

The haste of this narrative has many unforeseen drawbacks: it makes it appear as if I had had conquest after conquest and little or no difficulty in my efforts to win love. In reality, my half-dozen victories were spread out over nearly as many years, and time and again I met rebuffs and refusals quite sufficient to keep even my conceit in decent bounds. But I want to emphasize the fact that success in love, like success in every department of life, falls usually to the tough man unwearied in pursuit. Chaucer was right when he makes his Old Wyfe of Bath confess,

And by a close attendance and attention
Are we caught, more or less the truth to mention.

It is not the handsomest man or the most virile who

626

has the most success with women, though both qualities smooth the way, but that man who pursues the most assiduously, flatters them most constantly, and always insists on taking the girl's 'no' for consent, her reproofs for endearments, and even a little crossness for a new charm.

Above all, it is necessary to push forward after every refusal, for as soon as a girl refused, she is apt to regret and may grant then what she expressly denied the moment before. Yet I could give dozens of instances where assiduity and flattery, love-books and words were all ineffective, so much so that I should never say with Shakespeare, 'He's not a man who cannot win a woman.' I have generally found, too, that the easiest to win were the best worth winning for me, for women have finer senses for suitability in love than any man.

Now for an example of one of my many failures, which took place when I was still a student and had a fair opportunity to succeed.

It was a custom in the university for every professor to lecture for forty-five minutes, thus leaving each student fifteen minutes at least free to go back to his private classroom to prepare for the next lecture. All the students took turns to use these classrooms for their private pleasure. For example, from eleven forty-five to noon each day I was supposed to be working in the junior classroom, and no student would interfere with me or molest me in any way.

One day, a girl Fresher, Grace Weldon by name, the daughter of the owner of the biggest department store in Lawrence, came to Smith when Miss Stephens and I were with him, about the translation of a phrase or two in Xenophon.

'Explain it to Miss Weldon, Frank!' said Smith, and in a few moments I had made the passage clear to her. She thanked me prettily, and I said, 'If you ever want anything I can do, I'll be happy to make it clear to you, Miss Weldon; I'm in the junior classroom from eleven forty-five to noon, always.'

She thanked me and a day or two later came to me in the classroom with another puzzle, and so our acquaintance ripened. Almost at once she let me kiss her, but as soon as I tried to put my hand up her clothes, she stopped me. We were friends for nearly a year, close friends, and I remember trying all I knew one Saturday, when I spent the whole day with her in our classroom till dusk came, and I could not get her to yield.

The curious thing was, I could not even soothe the smart to my vanity with the belief that she was physically cold. On the contrary, she was very passionate, but she had simply made up her mind and would not change.

That Saturday in the classroom she told me if she yielded she would hate me: I could see no sense in this, even though I was to find out later what a terrible weapon the confessional is as used by Irish Catholic priests. To commit a sin is easy; to confess it to your priest is for many women an absolute deterrent.

About this time, Kate wrote that she would not be back for some weeks: she declared she was feeling another woman. I felt tempted to write, 'So am I, stay as long as you please,' but instead I wrote an affectionate, tempting letter, for I had a real affection for her, I discovered.

When she returned a few weeks later, I felt as if she were new and unknown and I had to win her again; but as soon as my hand touched her sex, the strangeness disappeared and she gave herself to me with renewed zest.

I teased her to tell me just what she felt and at length she consented. 'Begin with the first time,' I begged, 'and then tell what you felt in Kansas City.'

'It will be very hard,' she said. 'I'd rather write it for you.'

'That'll do just as well,' I replied, and here is the story she sent me the next day.

'I think the first time you had me,' she began, 'I felt more curiosity than desire: I had so often tried to picture it all to myself. When I saw your sex I was astonished, for it looked very big to me and I wondered whether you could really get it into my sex, which I knew was just big enough for my finger to go in. Still I did want to feel your sex pushing into me, and your kisses and the touch of your hand on my sex made me even more eager. When you slipped the head of your sex into mine, it hurt dreadfully; it was almost like a knife cutting into me, but the pain for some reason seemed to excite me and I pushed forward so as to get you further in me; I think that's what broke my maidenhead. At first I was disappointed because I felt no thrill, only the pain; but, when my sex became all wet and open and yours could slip in and out easily, I began to feel real pleasure. I liked the slow movement best; it excited me to feel the head of your sex just touching the lips of mine and, when you pushed in slowly all the way, it gave me a gasp of breathless delight: when you drew your sex out, I wanted to hold it in me. And the longer you kept on, the more pleasure you gave me. For hours afterwards, my sex was sensitive; if I rubbed it every so gently, it would begin to itch and burn.

'But that night in the hotel at Kansas City I really wanted you and the pleasure you gave me then was much keener than the first time. You kissed and caressed me for a few minutes and I soon felt my love-dew coming and the button of my sex began to throb. As you thrust your shaft in and out of me, I felt a strange sort of pleasure: every little nerve on the inside of my thighs and belly seemed to thrill and quiver; it was almost a feeling of pain. At first the sensation was not so intense, but, when you stopped and made me wash, I was shaken by quick, short spasms in my thighs, and my sex was burning and throbbing; I wanted you more than ever.

'When you began the slow movement again, I felt the sensations in my thighs and belly, only more keenly, and, as you kept on, the pleasure became so intense that I could scarcely bear it. Suddenly you rubbed your sex against mine and my button began to throb; I could almost feel it move. Then you began to move your sex quickly in and out of me; in a moment I was breathless with emotion and I felt so faint and exhausted that I suppose I fell asleep for a few minutes, for I knew nothing more till I felt the cold water trickling down my face. When you began again, you made me cry, perhaps because I was all dissolved in feeling and too, too happy. Ah, love is divine: isn't it?'

Kate was really of the highest woman-type, mother and mistress in one. She used to come down and spend the night with me oftener than ever and on one of these occasions she found a new word for her passion. She declared she felt her womb move in yearning for me when I talked my best or recited poetry to her in what I had christened her holy week. Kate it was who taught me first that women could be even more moved and excited by words than by deeds. Once, I remember, when I had talked sentimentally, she embraced me of her own accord and we had each other with wet eyes.

VICTORIAN EROTIC CLASSICS
AVAILABLE FROM CARROLL & GRAF

☐ Anonymous / Altar of Venus	4.50
☐ Anonymous / Autobiography of a Flea & Other Tart Tales	5.95
☐ Anonymous / Black Magic	6.95
☐ Anonymous / Careless Passion	5.95
☐ Anonymous / Confessions of an English Maid & Other Delights	5.95
☐ Anonymous / The Consummate Eveline	4.95
☐ Anonymous / Court of Venus	3.95
☐ Anonymous/ Best of Erotic Reader	6.95
☐ Anonymous / Eroticon	4.95
☐ Anonymous / Eroticon II	4.95
☐ Anonymous / Eroticon III	4.50
☐ Anonymous / Fallen Woman	4.50
☐ Anonymous / Harem Nights	4.95
☐ Anonymous / The Intimate Memoirs of an Edwardian Dandy	4.95
☐ Anonymous / The Intimate Memoirs of an Edwardian Dandy, Vol. II	4.95
☐ Anonymous / The Intimate Memoirs of an Edwardian Dandy, Vol. III	4.95
☐ Anonymous / Lay of the Land	4.50
☐ Anonymous / The Libertines	4.50
☐ Anonymous / Maid and Mistress	4.50
☐ Anonymous / A Man with a Maid	5.95
☐ Anonymous / Memoirs of Josephine	4.50
☐ Anonymous / The Merry Menage	4.50
☐ Anonymous / The Oyster	4.50
☐ Anonymous / The Oyster II	3.95
☐ Anonymous / The Oyster III	4.50
☐ Anonymous / The Oyster V	4.50
☐ Anonymous / Pagan Delights	5.95
☐ Anonymous / The Pearl	6.95
☐ Anonymous / Pleasures and Follies	3.95
☐ Anonymous / Romance of Lust	5.95

☐ Anonymous / Rosa Fielding: Victim of Lust	3.95
☐ Anonymous/ Sharing Sisters	4.95
☐ Anonymous / Secret Lives	3.95
☐ Anonymous / Sensual Secrets	4.50
☐ Anonymous / Sweet Confessions	4.50
☐ Anonymous / Sweet Tales	4.50
☐ Anonymous / Tropic of Lust	4.50
☐ Anonymous / Venus Butterfly	3.95
☐ Anonymous / Venus Delights	3.95
☐ Anonymous / Venus Disposes	3.95
☐ Anonymous / Venus in India	3.95
☐ Anonymous / Victorian Fancies	4.50
☐ Anonymous / The Wantons	4.50
☐ Anonymous / White Thighs	4.50
☐ Anonymous / Youthful Indiscretions	4.50
☐ Cleland, John / Fanny Hill	4.95
☐ van Heller, Marcus / Adam and Eve	3.95
☐ van Heller, Marcus / Lusts of the Borgias	4.95
☐ van Heller, Marcus / Seduced	5.95
☐ van Heller, Marcus / Unbound	5.95
☐ van Heller, Marcus / Venus in Lace	3.95
☐ Villefranche, Anne-Marie / Passion d'Amour	5.95
☐ Villefranche, Anne-Marie / Scandale d'Amour	5.95
☐ Villefranche, Anne-Marie / Secrets d'Amour	4.50
☐ Villefranche, Anne-Marie / Souvenir d'Amour	4.50
☐ von Falkensee, Margarete / Blue Angel Confessions	6.95
☐ "Walter"/ My Secret Life	7.95

Available from fine bookstores everywhere or use this coupon for ordering.